REGENT BOOKS BY J. LEA KORETSKY

NOVELS
Wall of Darkness
The Eternity Look
Domino
The Sweat Box
Under Dragon House
Blueprint
Snapshot, Collected Stories
Rope
Trojan Park
Border
Belvatown
Crimes and Offenses
Mandated Reporter
Sabaru
Murders at Bishop

POETRY
Cherished Memory
(Poems & A Play)
Damascas Rose
Love's Errand

PLAYS
The Voyage
The Stars

PSYCHOLOGY
Social Work From A Therapeutic Perspective

Assignment Zero

5 Mystery Novellas

by
J. Lea Koretsky

KQUEEN
Berkeley, California

copyright © 2020 by J. Lea Koretsky

ISBN 13: 978-1-58790-478-3
ISBN 10: 1-58790-478-0
Library of Congress Control Number: 2020942497

Any description of place or person
is not intended by the author to have pertinence
to reality past or present.

Manufactured in the U.S.A.
KQUEEN
Berkeley, California

For information about availability and distribution please call
510-845-1196

10 9 8 7 6 5 4 3 2 1

ASSIGNMENT ZERO / 1

SOHO / 47

MOON OVER GIZA / 117

INQUISITION / 167

DIRTY MONEY / 275

ASSIGNMENT ZERO

March 2000

"I say, George, are we having it on?"
"We won't know the least until the stars are in."
"When is a good day for fishing?"
"Depends on the damp fog and windward till."

There was nothing to say at what point the voices emanated from. The coast positioned landfall at fourteen hundred miles off a Meridian station on the coast. The probable charting placed their voices at destination for scuttling big ships in gigantic rushing fog where only diving staff was permitted. There was nothing else out there. No ships or airplanes were permitted in the area off the coast of Slave; that left the only way in by train leaving Port Alexandria, Egypt, or by small headway airplane flying into the wind at a twenty degree westward departing from Somalia.

This was the only area in the world that descended old ships. In the past year the government had sunk approximately twelve old galleons. Any ship or plane located at 0, 0 sank. Prime meridian at the equator was zero latitude by zero longitude which lay in the ocean quadrant at Ghana on western Africa off the Gulf of Guinea.

0N, 0E. It was known as a dead zone. Despite this, the sail produced a decent wind on a sparkling sea. Far inland in the brush of the savannah, large unsightly mammals, those being elephants, stalking lions, giraffe and rhinos, lost their sighting and died in the salty rushes, instantly attracting scavengers and packs of flies. Crashed ships on Gibraltar island were buttered with lazy fluid that allowed steel and plank to loosen and innards torched prior to nail enlisting it on the plunder schedule.

There was a fan sound of a helicopter above shouting voices of men on the coarse sand beach. In the dark a light that was turned off in a cabin flashed like an X-ray. A bus came at eleven at night, strong headlights picked out stucco houses, sand, and the white washed palace at the end of the craggy peninsula. Vans came in with the roar of ocean.

It took hours to drop a ship. All engines were flood throttled. The sharp profusion was like a sliding window slamming shut twice that could be heard for blocks. A drum beat rolled as a ship wrestled in the ocean down its stairway, its doors ajar; the ocean sounded mechanical like a wooden crate being dragged on a street. Overhead an aircraft flew at the sky and faded fast.

On any agonizing ship, the clock still worked; a tenth oil read on the gauge; keys were in ignition. Gales far out on the horizon raged. Two hundred photos read nine by four per sheet for 9 ships; at ivory coast ship exposure was 100%; at gold coast 15%; and at slave the read out was 3% before the final plunder; wood creaking, innards shifting, inside houses the sky cast a crimson thin yellow ice look over the walls; sound of fog horn was evident, one mass of clouds all in wind upheaval; flying tree debris stuck to land.

In port a read had come in for a previous year; in a Chicago south side two story brownstone revealed unmetered letters, flaps open, glued to the A-line attic twenty-four across starting at the height measuring six rows down; at the headquarter post office in Illinois sixty bags of mail hung from the glass canopy where they had crashed through a sky lit roof, dangling like storks in a wind off far branches. The request should have gone to Beijing, instead it was sent to Ghana Wind seaboard during the drift season. The first of sixteen tasks was routed as usual to one of three chiefs who oversaw the duties of fifty analysts. Chief Gorly Bhangan was a dark from Nairobi who had worked Port for thirty-four long years. He was a divorced, willowy man with a confident stride who rarely ate. He estimated the request would take maybe all of a few days to resolve. Chief Bhangan sent all glass roof photos to the lab for enlargements to ascertain the presence of an airplane or helicopter overhead.

The lab took all forty photos of the roof and put them on developer plate. Six came clean for proof. A glistening web of rotating blades shone in the mid afternoon at about eighty feet above the roof.

Velocity data showed a speeding twister headed from West Point headed for Chicago at two in the afternoon. By six, the Stallion helicopter which flew the mail for the Army for Erie took a sharp turn on its axle at Chicago Cook County when a fast wind kicked it sending cuffed fully stuffed postal bags to fly free crashing through the roof exploding splinters of glass everywhere snagging sixty bags and descending another thirty onto the floor.

Of course, the African savannah had its fair share of mail delivery problems including floating mail out of train windows from a speeding train and shooting mail bags like hung possum from tree branches of tall trees standing in five feet of water in long rivers in marsh.

This merely struck him as accidental. It wasn't until he took names and addresses of dispersed mail that he discovered a coincidence. They were the names of the African Flyer Army stationed in Port New Jerusalem a kilometer or so from the tempest winds of the north coast of Africa. These flyers had disbanded in 1979 after the airports opened to American flights and required a much larger army to handle security. In their day, they flew for Nairobi Interpol handling investigative inquiries across the continent for the home base located in Ontario in a grouping of offices amidst her forests and tiny lakes.

Here, the Canadian government drew its straws as to which subsidiary domain conducted international defense of worldwide trade violations. Africa, of course, mailed its agented material to Canada as opposed to Great Britain to offset hostage taking of information. Once Canada observed a complaint on its databases, the mail was forwarded through the cities of the Great Lakes before being permitted to be sent to other cities.

The shades were drawn in summer because there was no wind to offset the unrelenting sunlight which was often a stultifying 109. The darkened rooms retained quiet. From room to room the dark halls and baths conjured up a respite that calmed although they offered no real coolness. Outside the equatorial heat was oppressive with almost no scurrying winds; just a blanket of high clouds like a barrier permitting almost no descending air except occasional rain.

On the beach thirty fishermen kept to their long canoes listening for the final slate of the sinking ship heard as a sliding window slamming shut in the wake of low wind as massive amounts of ocean pressured inside and thronged the broad plank beneath the surface. A visiting group to the Cape Coast Castle had finished a tour for the National Geographic having done a walk-through of its underground rooms and tunnels. They would now go by van to the surrounding towns to examine outdoor markets and clothing outlets to determine conditions of cleanliness and of meats and shellfish. As soon as their report cleared customs, nearby hotels would receive their ratings. In this part of the world where independent unapproved industry had entered by night to tack up stalls and marketplaces and then departed an otherwise abandoned beachfront, the probability of assailing the public with dysentery was greater.

The African army unit had lost at least one man who had flown off course in ill weather. He was listed as DJ2 identity interpreted as a birth date during December, January or February having come from Canada. He was also Swahili spoken, a documents handler, and a seasoned pilot of air train bagging and flying the mail; last name Laura.

The man himself was African. That was the problem. The world port policy was Africans could never leave. Only the mail shipped. An African who had left Africa and entered any other continent was dead.

Last heard from he had flown off the coast into a squall rounding the head. Chief Gorly Bhangan from Nairobe found a man in his ranks to proceed through Rome to Quebec on a late night flight to travel to the United States to examine the opener in the Chicago attic for any relevance to the punctured glass rooftop a mile away and detain his man. Certainly if a renegade group had access to mail trade through packaging code, it would serve diplomatic relations on both sides to learn what the problems were.

September 1989

The World Airline taxied down the runway at Tambo International Airport and cruised to ceiling for a smooth take-off and in minutes was circling over the chaotic industrial transoms that comprised Johannesburg. At length the salty brine extracted coast along the ship lanes of the Suez Canal became evident with about fifty ocean liners dotted over the width. Jeremiah Torfu leaned back in his window seat with a Joburg magazine and perused the astounding interiors of gold molding and glittering floor tile of the lifestyles of the Johannesburg Five, a group of industrialists venturing in gold and diamond production whose content rested in glass high rise overlooking the once barren Randburg. Jeremiah was a post office Inspector for African Customs Division of Great Britain which hired twenty-six inspectors, each who wore the very distinguished, decorated by three medals to the left collar in Victorian Cross Winner uniform. He was half Somali and half Moroccan, age forty-four, bronze hair and tan complexioned, tall, very thin, to the point of being considered emaciated.

His target was Moroccan white. Laura was from Port Morocco. In winters he flew the Megiddo ship searching for crazy dock turns. It was hard to place him in the same cob as with a salty croak, but he nevertheless had surfaced in a bad realm. Jeremiah could only imagine that with the type of experience he had gotten a similar job. This meant the Great Lakes along the lanes, communicating to the tugs to get ships turned around, steered under bridges or docked. The theft of mail found inside an attic caused local investigators to check for USPS employees who would have processed the mail for money orders or cash, or ships on the lakes that carried mail to other towns. The suspect had to get hold of it some way; there was just too much mail to have to explain the amount of loss.

Local post office inspectors examined all camera functions for the day of the loss, verifying by drawer handlers that money certificates were paid for and issued; letters and oversized envelopes sealed and metered, code number placed and put on computer, and mail routed by zip code to internal distribution. They found the thief eventually on ninety computers for 10:45 am. A non employee entered the Detroit yard that hired five hundred people and climbed inside a delivery van and drove off through open gates. Stations came on line as the van passed them. Investigators correlated tracking codes to every stolen letter and determined all letters that were dropped from the glass roof had previously been stolen in that particular theft. This was felony armed robbery even though the amount taken was small.

At least four stations recorded the van and the driver's handprint. A quick feed gave name, place of birth and method of entry into the US, but he had no address. He lacked work history for any post office and had no criminal history.

The loss report read seventy letter filled bags missing; where did they go? By evidence of tracking code, money orders and checks totaled $19, 043.

That suggested a light bulk of purchase of a home and food.

What was going on here? Were two crimes related, was one criminal directing another by posting mail inside an attic in Chicago?

When the tracking codes were finally tracked to a final destination, the post station found a four story house in Chicago on the waterfront very similar to an actual postal station in Key West, Florida; a large red building with attic designed by William Kerr in the Richardson Romanesque structure.

Was the attic in fact utilized for reasons of secrecy? If there was a basement or garage, why store mail in an attic where it was stifling hot? Possibly because no one knew he was there; very realistically he might see all roads in the city that led to the house as well as train and small airplanes sitting on a landing strip. The first question was, how did he have access to the house, maybe he slept in attics and had attic ideas. Technically no one lived there since it was declared a potential fire trap in which the kitchen was attached to a furnace hose under the house. In all likelihood he broke inside houses which sat empty.

A raid on the house was made in the middle of the day. It was abandoned. The five detectives stormed inside, weapons drawn, searched all rooms. They came across six rows consisting of a hundred and forty-four standard size letters which all read for declassification. They took photographs, sketched drawings, labeled the tracking codes. Oddly there was not a single insect, it must have been something he consumed that repelled them, maybe citronella or lavender tea although the place collected no dust to indicate living; the attic was not new and mail was not wet and revealed no signs of having been exposed to damp through the roof.

They batch coded Laura's selection. In either direction the grouping of numbers read similarly; 1234 across read 1345 down by one row; 67 89 across read 7890 down; lots of non deletions. It meant something to him, but there were nothing for intimations anyone might think to derive. Under what circumstances might numbers correspond? It could be damn near anything that took a man to imitate such a system. It must have taken nights to collect.

24 letters across, not desks in a classroom, not cells in a jail. A collection of zip codes in a post office possibly; six rows for each area of the country likely.

Fort Wayne maybe, 24 lawyer offices in each of seven blocks of long houses with a courthouse on an open plaza which they returned to bomb. They were arraigned there originally in 1943 for a sky diving stunt on Lake Superior after getting caught for flying onto industrial houses; all were from India and hence were placed as teenage wards of Indiana. One day in 1960 after their men were released from pink city, they recast their crime to the marine lighthouse, killed all the guards, got in the guard parachute gear, sailed off the roof and landed on a ship, steered to the high falls of New York, where they fell into the falls and almost died, and were placed in nine prisons for forty years.

Who was Laura to them? Besides a brash red haired male who escorted the girls to the speak easy for a few gins and wild talk about the savannah and the high crashing waves breaking against dirty beige beaches of a state controlled prison that resembled an Arabian castle. He was a charmer, good with a grease monkey, who picked up a few jobs a year at auto van repairs. Although India was separated from the Suez and Africa by oceans, he knew everything in between for the ports, the ships and wave crashers. He was a honey girl's promise, not yet a delinquent until he delivered his first post office van to the station that requisitioned the overhaul on the fuel line.

Their culprit had left. The letters were all that remained. The inspector crew had his fingerprints, so they would eventually find him and could arrange a tow truck for the van to haul it to an impound.

They referred across the country to their Intel. Sixty-five databases on a weekend were given the responsibility for locating him. Their computers could determine by any existent access where he was within a hundred and six days turnaround. There was no way to obtain fresh information more quickly.

The day the Intel matched him to a Cook County lakeside motel and warrants were signed, a fire wiped out the local post office obliterating it. The Intel handled the photos off the post office teller cameras. The very first item the network observed was the absence of men inside that station. Time of night was eleven on the eighteenth, a Monday. Fortunately the janitor service was not due until the end of the week.

What did one have to do to be wanted by the warrant bail offices? Seize mail. Steal a postal truck. Rob a casino. There had been a big casino heist in 1963 when crooks took a love ship from 0, 0 to France where they split up with money. Perhaps it would be that this time they planned to stow aboard a severely weathered ship to 0, 0 and there, sink it, thus eliminating evidence, but it was a real mystery how they could get anywhere to dispose of a gambling ship. The Panama border was boarded by agents, the Hudson shot airplanes into the water; Miami didn't depart for months.

The Intel bureaucracy for crime detection was ringing off the line, seventy computers per floor searching off state road databases for all sorts of troubling propositions. While this was not a robbery in progress for which the street maps were essential, it nevertheless had to be reconstructed. A section correlated legal findings for older streets which had been removed, housing torn down, and highway access exits built. The burned post office occupied a corner where a pharmacy once stood when there were three back alleys, all replaced by a department store plaza and loading dock. Across town in a new part of town, a new Intel safely guarded high speed chases of traffic crime. The crime on its monitors was of a high speed chase of a red sports car conducted by four patrol cars with flashing sirens and chaser sight lens rifles.

Five supervisors per floor reviewed the requests and information and signed off on any communiqué. Their chief assigned aircraft tracking and snowmobile registration on interstate roads. The day before the fire viewed sixty vans that loaded mail bags in the yard. Indicator staff each received a bucket to track each van. Mail delivery was brought to the airport at 9:20 am, noon and four for outbound flights during which tracking codes for city were documented. Send out pallet staff read for people who walked in and out all day until closing at 7pm and tracked them to vehicles and final destinations examining for suspicious activities. U. S. Mail trucks returned three hours later, loaded up letter carrier bags designated for local house distribution, and went on their way.

A gangly tall Caucasian redhead crew cut dressed in white jeans and long sleeved green shirt who sent a letter to New York dropped it in the mail slot in the lobby at 6:50 pm. He drove away in a blue 1989 Honda. He drove along a country road to a market where he purchased groceries after which he went to a small house made of grey shingles contained by a black picket fence. His fingerprint placed him by Intel inside a red house in Michigan having stolen mail. None of the systems entered the realm of permissible jurisdiction of the others. The Intel was a private entity meant to assist 911 for speed of emergency medical response, but it could not access the post office, interstate tracking, the telephone company or police maps. It was a voice call image system.

The problem rested with deportation of illegal residents who were sent by ship to a facility at which they could be identified.

2

Like someone had let the beach go to scrap. Nothing but chunky sand piling up against fortress walls in a calling wind. The ocean raged at a mile, its mounting hurls louder than caterwauls.

Lloris listened straining to pick up evidence of severed connections when sparse shouts where far up the shoreline a truck had unloaded shacks and there they stood empty, brilliant yellow, pink and green ready to be scorched by the searing sun in less than five years; the blended voices of carols choral music to be heard all about for several instants, a choir diffusing chants as oared boats rowed by ten men apiece took into the sea. He was a transplant from Canada, having left in 1880 to join fishing sequences over the lower hemisphere. Tall, bony, blond, a New Yorker off the train docks, he went in search of windswept ocean. He knew everything.

In a semblance of crashes the sea took the ship down to its dregs heard as a lamentable burden heaving to breath and sorrow. The world views carnage as time in a bottle. Life gives and removes. Society records and relieves. Prisons hold evil in abatement until the levied sentence is reached. As much apart of any culture as markets, cost houses, homes, institutions, education, normalization and hospitals, prisons rank for a necessary military and marine. Fathoms deep slate finality for every barge shunted into a catapult of waves until the manifestations surrender hold harmless, each and all like writing on a wall, held to a locker of metal stairs opined to stone fortresses joined to the sands of advancing ocean fronts.

Within the ladder markers along the hull maybe forty snails in the seams of the wood wrenching wood from aft.

It was therefore odd that along the floor of the Erie channels three divers had set to ply a ship while on board twenty-five shipmates slept lulled to deep sleep by rocking harbor waves. The port authority relied upon videos zero to cruising to make determinations as to a man's body seen under stern with mail letters clinging to fern in floating tall standing brine. Volleying sirens shot a cacophony of punctuated alarms over the wharf. Bright lights from the Brigham Building cancelled moonlight, clamped on with actual warning. Footsteps hurried in every direction; marine boats screamed up the canal, captains stood at the stern looking for any Ahab in shackles, combing the slips for victims swimming. It was another lifetime that Erie Canal took a bomb to a ship, fish wave style, warping wood of the lower ship hull that caused it to capsize. When it was hoisted to dry dock, appraisers instantly concluded the ship had withstood two years of harrowing.

Ocean sounded like chanting at a rally in Vatican Square heard so faintly in distance it was elusive, fetching in fog.

Far from Cote d'Ivore, city of hospitals, schools; an airstrip, the average age being twenty; four hundred miles further from Abidjan, a Paris of revolving neon night life secreted in the heart of West Africa; the beige sand beaches hid tracks into water The Marine Life and Storm Ship Center which sat at the fringe of road off a wide bastion of beach, a two floor building made of white stone and narrow lengthy windows, balconies with wire chairs, coveting a boast of trees and driveway below four smallish restaurants, Daida had drawn a hacker on the broadband; after he took the first overseas note. He was lean, tall, long childish red brown hair in pigtails; speed typer 220, dictation 112, long lens for hurls.

He traveled to a European or American university to work graphics for six years for an archive, otherwise life was slowly paced.

The days were long and tiring with nothing to do. It would prove a hot and wet August after an almost indomitable season. Drapes pulled against glare of afternoon light and low sky, sandwich half eaten on counter beside a bottle of red melon soda. All living existed through mail order books.

The cranium was a huge place, endless barren landscape in which the continent generals were non abdicated, Abidjan, Acca, Acra in Soledad. The wind swept up streets tossing food wrappers into beach front. There was salt in the air, muggy, a spot of light at the horizon. No phones, installation computers, soft white, fryers on the stove; a mile walk to leche and pan with café at a dance hall where all sixty people from town came; often one stared out at the sea thinking next to nothing; fell asleep for hours.

He awoke to the Dinner half minute low siren which penetrated stillness. He stopped in at the center after a two hour long meal to see a movie on the last sinking.

Chief Bhangan decided on the outcome.

17 ships and two light ships had entered around Great Falls, Canada for dry dock repairs from nowhere. Plank off fifth deck entered at height of fourth floor where there was only one door for the foreman who was known as a peel shop because he was never there. Where was he when Armagasso sank on an ice flounder right outside six Erie ship lanes that pulled up to Brigham Bldg built in 1874, Stavern Lloris in charge of dept. This was where the Chinese 50 out of Canton were brought in dead and laid out after two ships flooded inside their lanes.

The first deck man froze lights on a man on the gazebo roof with three post office bags who had a shaved head, not Chinese or Asia, who had shipped from Fez Oman having arrived with four prison wards into Chillingworth Ford County where they would prosecute nine Iranians and fifty Slovaks.

Only in Cape Erie Chinatown did the county administrator, a man by the last name of Slorm, began his starlit career on Erie in the customs office of the shipping department on the top floor in a small room which overlooked two of six lanes. He had run The Shorenum Building in St. Louis, Missouri built the same way with customs rooms on a rotunda on a top floor. Not on Great Lakes; off a tributary.

The only post office of NY sat on a wharf overlooking 2 schools and a red mill house on Hungary Road. Man dropped into the water carrying a satchel, a Houdini in chains, dove under an icy plow ship; all 25 hands on deck at once. Everyone started work on both sides of the street, it was same resemblance of people coming and going. The lanes were shut down, all nine divers swam to floor. For half the night up to dawn underwater lights gleamed the entire channels. Dock warehouses stationed, kill forces were assigned dragnets. The mail bag ordered brought in. The subject was identified. He had traveled in the brig in ankle cuffs the entire Atlantic passage. Hair dark blue, face rigid.

In a minute the mail bag found draped on hook of pier; mail came from Huron at post office called Toronto Station for a cannon outside; man was snagged between wall lanes.

Bhangan instructed Mail released and bag refilled with new letters and hung from interior of roof. He estimated a five day weapon search, on foot, possibly across farm, late at night. This was the start of a chase without a lead.

3

The contents of the mail bag were photographed, determined for origination and destination, and matched to routing track advice. Once dried, two hundred letters were tacked to an evidence board for disposition to the international trade zone in nine rows of twenty-four across, and a tenth row of two. Nine rows signified an origination in Egypt; any in ten rows alleged Alaska. The complication of a tenth final line had to be questioned carefully by an analyst for the postal inspector to assess whether mail was added.

Prints were taken by aid of laser light and results sent to the CDC lab at Florida. Canadian mail handlers were produced along with seven unknowns. A tracer decided their identities, one a postal clerk, two wanted adult males for post office yard robberies, the others included a fashion wear display clerk and three Wisconsin home owners who retired ten years ago having worked a library, a pool house, and a county clerk.

4

They began at dawn. The insistent drone of the plane cast an awareness of the inevitable. Somewhere above in the heavens it sounded like a pipe becoming dislodged possibly about to stall and fall out of the sky. Below, miners awakened to pan the bays for chunks of gold. One could readily see that adult men cut at lakes, allowing them to flow onto dirt paths and pool up forming new ponds while in the water gold specks swam in eddies. It could be said that at most every resort there was an air of anticipation, of some unforeseen catastrophe about to catch the wind. The government had fallen to the jeopardy of harm. Even law enforcement was alert to the sense that there were bad crooks lurking about hidden in a multitude of forests.

The desk just about jumped as if startled by the jangling phone after hours of stillness.

"Duluth Police Department." The dispatch officer answered.

"Hello? Can I talk to someone in charge? I wish to report a crime."

"Certainly, just a moment. I'll transfer you."

There was a slight wait.
"Sergeant Cooper speaking."
"Hello, I want to report a crime."
"Is this an incident you observed?"
"Yes."
"May I have your name?"
"Billie Mack."
"Age?"
"38."
"Your address?"
"Silhouette Corner."

He was familiar with it. A market, café and bar, and gas station on Sunrise Lake Road.

"When did the crime occur?"
"Yesterday, Sunday, about 1pm."
"What did you see?"
"A black man thrust a knife in a tall, blond middle aged man."
"Is the victim injured?"
"Yes. He took a knife wound."
"Was there an altercation?"
"I didn't hear one. The black man had just come out of the post office and the white man was filling up his car with gas. The black man drove off in his car."
"Make and year?"
"I don't know cars all that well. It was small like a VW. It may have been white. It zoomed past me."
"Were you in a car?"
"No, I was walking."
"Were you observed yourself?" Eye witnesses usually were. It came with the turf. Horror gave a person away like a sixth sense.
"I think he followed me out of the area."
"Where are you right now?"

"I have a boat. I'm at Pine Lake."

Awfully candid. But Hopper promised he'd send a deputy to talk to her in about an hour.

Probably more like two days even if the deputy himself worked at Pine Lake Sheriff Station. All these guys were on call. Despite a population of less than two hundred, the forested island stretched out in peninsulas and inlets for over nine miles on three separate bays.

Cooper wrote up the report and e-mailed it to the Pine Lake Sheriff.

It was dusk before two patrol cars showed up. They parked on sloping grass and walked up the path to a log cabin bungalow with a sign that said, Manager. They were inside for about fifteen minutes. When they left, they returned to their vehicle and road a twisting frontage lane through a wooded area for slightly over a mile to a cluster of cabins.

They pulled alongside a stairway of four planks and knocked on the blue door.

The door was pulled open by a short white haired Caucasian female dressed casually in a white shirt having a ribbed bib and blue jeans and barefoot. She had painted her toe nails bright dark red. She had attractive high arched feet.

She observed them in a remote sort of gaze, not really seeming relieved, asked to see their badges which they showed her – Jim Herrera and John Costa – before she invited them inside a fairly decent size, all wood studio with a rotating ceiling fan and far kitchen. They were two medium height, average intelligence, reddish blondes in beige uniforms.

"You reported a crime." Jim said, referring to a summary in his hand.

"I spoke to the Duluth police, a captain Cooper."

"Yes, we verified with the ambulance. They responded to a civilian wounded at the market."

"He was stabbed."

"We will be posting an APB. John here will help with a drawing of the assailant. Can you describe his features?"

Billie did. Mild cool black, line mouth, small polite nose, brown eyes spaced evenly apart, tucked in ears, white person's brown hair crew-cut short growing out but still short. White collar beneath a black wool sweater, black trousers, grey saddle shoes neatly tied. A deceptively trusting face.

John got him on a first sketch. It was really amazing.

"Good likeness. That's him."

"Probable age?"

"Forties maybe, it's hard to tell with Blacks. They're often younger than you'd think," she said.

"Yes, ma'am," Costa replied non committal.

Jim explained the picture would go out on the broadband. Her job was done.

In the aftermath of a tense morning, she grabbed her chalk and oil briefcase set, walked to the pier, untied her boat and piloted her outboard and floated over the glassy water thinking little except that the crazy incident was in the past and she could focus on her painting. She steered to a private thicket and turned off the motor and removed her briefcase, unsnapped it and selected three chalk colors, grey, dark blue and orange. She began applying faint orange to a predawn sky on a painter's pad, smoothing in darker lines, smudging in grey like a mist, then placing vertical sharp lines for trees, a lengthy blue flowing river and hint of reflecting sky and blooming trees. She had signed up for an art class camp on a river cruise which would last a month on the lakes. The class would give her one credit toward a therapy license. It had just come at a bad time, as luck would have it, but as she chalked in the idea of damp cold on the ground in blue, she thought of the reality that it was probably a one-time endeavor she ought not to miss out on.

The lake areas had changed in demographics in twenty years. Lots of builders, bible thumpers, people living in vans or on houseboats. A vagrant tourism that attended college and then moved on. People who disappeared into the woods. Loners. Billie kept to herself so she understood an instinct for it. She had married a detective Lou while young but her inability to have a baby earned her a swift divorce leaving her bitter. Her mother-in-law shut her out; but her brother-in-law kept in touch. Over the twenty or so years she learned to make peace with them, she told herself thank god she hadn't put him through law college. Her parents were dead at early ages of stress and fatal diabetes as a result of over consumption of fatty foods, bacon, pork, fried potatoes, greasy spoon, pies, cakes, lard made cookies. She was an only child for whom the idea of gaining a family had seemed desirable but their attitude was to put her in a toll house for which nothing appeased. She would have been surprised to learn that the man who weeded the swamps of a killing plant that drank water down to the gut of soil was the post office vandal. This Laura from the craggy coral reefs off Africa at 0, 1 who served hard time at the infamous lighthouse Bay-Gaun listening to the raging ocean pound away at every surface out there. Laura was usually to be seen in a canoe chopping at the unruly weed staying his measure out on the actual lake. He was an unknown descript in woolens and cap; she could never make out hair features nor height who had appeared one year during a meticulous investigation of following a group of felons into the back woods of the eastern Minnesota lakes and its thousands of dark wilds off silent stillborn waters. Just another boater bound by destiny who enjoyed the serenity was how she read him.

The fact that ditchwater might strangle a man sobered her often. She had heard stories at the bar: grown men found frozen in less than a half foot of mud; men suppressed by the helm of their boats; children drifting oar bound in the northern confluence.

She shaded in a peculiar windy sky with tufts of grey and added a wisp of blue, a stark flash of light red, a pastel of lilac, and signed it. She motored downstream to where she could see the flank of an office of which the roof rose above the land like a factory and switched off the engine. A mild breeze turned the boat. She fished out another blank page off the painter's pad and began a stencil in dark yellow of the riverbank, willow reeds, conflagration of thistles and blades of wild grasses and dangling roots until she had a fairly extensive trough. The only color that ever impressed her was an appearance of lifeless undergrowth – this tended to repress all other memory. If she saw through a person's basic character sometimes a sense of green sprang to view, a hint at what hid in that individual's repose.

By the time she moored back to her shoreline, it was raining, coming down hard and fast in long splotches causing the lawn and back wood stairs to be drenched and slippery. She rushed inside into the kitchen and grabbed a towel to tousle dry her hair. A window stood wide open and she realized someone had trespassed inside. She didn't like the feeling it gave her; that there was a psychopath spying on her.

The High Court with Justice Marty Stan who was an extremely tall Black commissioner standing in nylon stocking feet six foot four and slight from the State of Minnesota presiding was back in session on the matter of an injunction against mail handlers stealing the mail. Wisconsin law maintained that mail theft was a felony and not civil vandalism. Mail was property as well as legal extrapolation. The case involved four hundred pieces of mail found in seven houses predominantly in Great Lakes cities most of it in attics. This was essentially a contamination lawsuit because the mail had been treated to massive amounts of warfarin, a toxic chemical utilized for killing pests and insects.

"Have you made a finding?" Judge Stan for the Court posed to counsel for the prosecution.

"We have, Your Honor. All mail succumbed to the pesticide was stolen, driven across ten states, and placed in farthing lake areas replete of pests."

"Did you determine a perception?"

"It is our belief that a certain John Smith did require to direct Mr. Laura as to water ways he thought should be bombed."

"How have you ascertained an exact intention?"

"We have correlated the arrangement of stolen mail to a consequential code as we shall demonstrate."

"Very well. Call your first witness."

Two post office commissioners testified under oath as to the significance of roll call for mail. A consultant for the prosecution linked significance to bombings of the eight canals.

A marine scientist for the defense stated he believed that mail once it got wet attracted rats to it.

The final decision took less than forty-five minutes. Mail had to be bagged securely tied by a winch and not transported in trays.

As to mail theft from a postal yard, these acts were to be regarded as treasonable felonies sentenced by prison terms in penitentiary.

A ward hold was posted for all nine people who stole US Mail.

Marty Stan frequently boasted that a good meal was all that a middle aged man needed to get to sleep at night. He told the joke at every courtroom he convened. It brought him hearty cheerful laughter and killed the black dog in the closet. Every man worth his salt had a ferocious bully to contend with. His were dumb assholes who pretended they hadn't heard a question and made a prosecutor seem like an idiot. A witness had to walk tall in his presence. They had to be forthcoming, precise. Normally the docket was split into three trials in the morning and one in the afternoon for the voir dire. Each trial lasted three days. Within that time all expert testimony had to be heard, evidence and exhibits presented, and conclusions drawn. He despised continuances as much as a poorly laid out strategy. He detested the girls who lied on the stand in hopes of getting another five years and an appointed officer to raise their toddlers. He was alright with apparent back stabbers; people who gave evidence were often perceived that way. He painstakingly examined each shred of proof. He rarely suppressed evidence. His required ten cop years taught him to always carefully advise a jury. He never had declared a mistrial. Because of his exactitudes he was least admired as a thorn in one's raw behind.

The pretenses of liaisons in and among agencies of persuasion maintained a rigorous momentum where law was concerned. Thus at the end of the day, court having adjourned, occasionally it was for a thirty day window to give counsel additional thinking time over admission of evidence, Marty walked around the corner to the Law Circuit for a straight session of martinis to air out the decisions of the day. His favorite collaborators were Judges Mathews and Stencil, both recently appointed to the Great Lakes halls of justice on penal law, all cases being felony trials. John Mathews was horribly young, a mere fifty, wavy blond grey hair, liberal shades of civil rights, a doer who advised predominantly for the post office trials, in at seven, out by nine, kept the calendar clerk late hours, but beamed as a favorite to the court reporter pool. Clem Stencil, a fiscal seventy year old Walter Cronkite conservative from Savannah where pink was on every accent wall, kept a gold bronze bowl with saltwater taffy on his desk with pecan turtles and British divinity bites; was a trim turned out Southern gent of six feet even, long bronze panel-like hair to his shoulders, a red bow tie, beige shirts and army green proper trousers and spar rust boots. The ninth hour crowd was almost entirely counsel, several lab, clerk aides to jury selection, lively chatter, some pork loins and brick oven baked beans, sauerkraut, roast chestnut yellow squash, and a dessert trifle of rum smothered angel cake, custard and boysenberry jam. They'd squeezed into a booth and were sipping Brut when a hullabaloo busted loose.

"Who here is in favor of continued intercession?" a boisterous voice called out. "How many of us have short wings to intern for the rostrum?"

Everyone knew that was where the assembly placed its priorities. Each intern was worth twelve a semester. In a dry spell it was a good way to earn money.

"Hey, Rumbag, do us all a favor, get off the saucer. It's not as though you wind up shrift." Another mock term rookie yelled.

There were a few rumbles of arguing before the drunkards quieted down.

"It is a real heckler," Marty said. "We can't deny the unscrupulous activities, although we believe there's more to it than rats in the attic."

"The governing doctrine should be ship law," Clem put in rather disagreeably. "But we're on the lakes for which train law takes precedence. The trains carry the mail; the ships merely arrive. They are viewed as ascorbic."

Matthews inhaled a Dutch weiber cigarette edged in gold trim tobacco paper and an industrious sip of Brut. "Well, the Welland Canal transport has not agreed to ship mail. Then there's the train law that oversees the mail. It says only trains or small airplanes. Then lost mail is not reimbursable if the lugs were registered in port. If mail becomes confined in houses due to bleak weather, then storm advisory has a five day hold regardless of freight."

"The incidental costs far exceeded prank," Clem said, playing now to the party.

"Over twenty thousand, I agree," Marty replied. "I got a day out of it."

"That's all you should have," Matthews commented. "You have to go after this Smith and Laura both."

"Smith was found dead floating downstream. He was from Cairo of all places. Eastern Division raided the houses," Marty explained. "They found grand theft, straight by the book 496."

"But didn't it prove on unlawful litter?" Clem inquired, taking his interest as usual in rote limits of law definition.

"Contamination. It's not conspiracy or mayhem yet." Marty was dutiful in his precision.

"What about the ward who leaped into the water?" Clem asked.

"Nothing there," Marty answered. "He says in the

hurry he just fell in. He thought he was shoved."

"Unlikely with so many similarities to Eastern Africa's train ports," Clem scoffed. "What did anyone have to say about the mail frozen beneath surface rightly resembling a shark pond?"

"Nothing there." Marty countered. "Nothing about the other ward hanging his sack from the roof of the ship dock house like a sack of bananas either. The investigators hung the other three bags identical in case something unnatural was intended."

"Someone should look up this Laura." Matthews quipped. "Why was he sent to Bay-Gaun? That's in the middle of nowhere. Western Africa on a reef, that's solitary isolation."

"He plundered a mail ship. When divers went down for the scullery, the mail had drifted onto floating weeds like shafts of light seen under the ocean at surface."

"Where do you suppose he got such a notion to begin with?" Matthews pressed.

Marty shrugged. "Stairs maybe. A building he lived in could have fallen in."

"Yeah, who knows, right?" Clem posed, always the last to have his say. "Some lawyers up north opposite Ontario think he squired a few ship bombs with fire sticks. Those produce an obnoxious arson in the hole, fumes and exploding sparks."

"Not the Girl Scout pins hammered to a hull?" Matthews was giddy, showing off in front of his more experienced learned counsel, and added to his state another few sips that left him feverish.

"Not the promised flounders," Clem confirmed. "If you must know, the query usually asked to a river island arson is, has the individual ever handled debris ash? Well, one can't appreciate his own arson fire without having that knowledge. Only one chemical keeps debris intact and that is airplane fuel. If your investigators find lots of estimable debris in the ashes, that's what puts it there."

"Must make the quality invaluable," Matthews remarked dryly.

"In this day and age, probably," a dour Marty injected. "A rich, expensive truffle." The chief prosecutor was still stationed out at Ft. Bragg, thus he expected such a case would fall to him. While he was not permitted to know a thing about the situation, he never worried. "Three ships, I heard."

"Four," Clem said neatly. "All in one afternoon out there on the Welland. Canada issued the summons for protectorate. The thirty agents are still combing through the bulwark."

"It suggests plenty of organization to have involved felons." Matthews gave a candid dry look. "Where would they have met except at family contact visits?"

"Indecent," Marty said. "Don't know why prisons don't discourage this sort of bravado. It's not as though inmates are expected to comply with an overhead of sanctions."

Clem who had counseled the judiciary on this matter said, "Eight divers went down for the screw. Imagine, eight engine capable felons dousing it on in troubled waters. Where were the ship mail quarter ensigns?"

Marty knew that would be the only question that would ever come up. The deck schedule never released even two engine felons at once.

"It becomes a tedious matter," Matthews espoused. "Who at the purchase end wanted so much trouble?"

"It might be someone in prison," Marty remarked. "Most likely it was a docking clerk who exercised irregular authority. The constitution might pose the problem for years."

"Too crazy for acquiescence," Clem said.

"If it wasn't a dock schedule that brought in eight warden releases, it must have been that the number of releases exceeded the excursion ships in a twelve month period," Marty surmised.

It was a big problem to explain how three got on each of three ships when there was just one yearly and to comprehend how sixteen staff per ship wound up dead after three ship explosions that the canal insisted on two a year every fifteen months to avoid future crisis.

The three judges were cognizant of the chaos that escaped detainees created. They had each sat for sessions involving marshal warrants and knew just how deadly wrong an obstruction could last. Although the law allowed for grievous commitments, seldom did the bench press for extenuating circumstances. Each federal law upheld to a narrow definition. Only the finite event controlled a predicament. There was no such thing as a forgiveness margin of error.

"What do you suppose this Laura wanted over the years?" Marty asked, to play advocate.

"Chaos," came Matthews stringent reply. "The mail is simply there; it's an idea to be construed."

"Could be an entirely different matter," Clem mused. "Might be lumber, stations, close in the gap, that sort of thinking."

"Could there have been a fence?"

"Now you're being autocratic," Clem told Marty.

"We should consider manipulation. The government scrambles."

"Lots of wood clucks," Matthews went for it. "Cabins, resorts, boating."

"Well, it's almost midnight," Marty said. "We should do a little research, attempt to learn what this man thought he traded in on. I think without control that port could not accept wards. "

"Corralling prison to Chicago. I wonder why," Clem mulled over the reality. "Maybe someone there wants to know who they are."

"Might be the sole explanation as to why nothing seems right; a conglomeration of scurrying, sparks and midnight suffocation of mail transport ship clerks." Clem sounded aghast but confident.

"Might be much worse. They needed to see who could identify them."

Matthews said. "Gents, it's past my bedtime."

"Amen to that." A bleary eyed Clem was ready to drop.

It was late when they departed, plans made to get together in a month to eat at the old factory on Clements in the tar district.

Marty when he poked his head in on his wife in their brick steel wall home would go downstairs to the basement, jot down some notes, pour himself a stiff bourbon, watch the news, and drift off to sleep. Matthews would snag a taxi and speed across town to his high heeled mistress in the Charles light lamp district because he and his wife were separated, and Clem would drive home to his walk-up and awaken the mother of his two sons away at law college and talk to her until morning and if he were lucky would sleep until jurisdiction and term were set. They all had happy lives; none had missed out on destiny nor lost at the wheel.

Marty called his alma mater from the grave cemetery days of cop tracking, old man Kestor. "Clem says the score reads nine to one on a prison escape off the Mississippi."

"I'll look it up," the gruff voice answered. "How's Joanie?"

"She's good. She just retired."

"Teaching is a killer."

"It's put her through her paces. Will you check the files for damp mail? "

"Yes, I'll get back to you in a day and a night." Always said with a wry amusement as if nothing of consequence ever actually mattered.

"Goodnight then."

Laura never was off dry land. No one really understood this until they tried to track him. He was adept at skillfully deploying them even though he would leave exact footprints after a first night rainfall. They would climb under fences, over climbing tatters, along creek beds, until at the last they evaded bounty in fields and wilds. What were they after all, but a handful of entrusted engineers who had bed-rocked a ship in a mercurial pond too far east to be found. A stone break in a land formation was to be had as a result of the Welland Canal problem.

He had five houses each with a separate set of rows inside an attic proven found by mail delivery for postal routes.

The man who drove the mail rack across the country to The Country Squire book nook café shop collected $340 for his efforts and another $170 after he tacked the mail to an attic of a requested address. Lead detectives wanted to know how each address was determined.

They assigned an Intel to the traveling man. After a theft of mail out of the yard, he removed a top tray of federal post, placed it in his wagon and drove across country to the café shop on the coast of Erie in Pennsylvania to its wharf where it went as a display into the window.

When he arrived he received a phone call that directed him to an address.

The analyst, a man named Cool, decided each of five clerks hired had specific jobs, one clerk had to drive mail to correspondent school John Smith to hand deliver his mail to his addresses. Two clerks worked mail bag. One worked county hall and one followed robbers to final end run.

He sent his request to Law department for actual wording tape off any pay phone, for which there were six on the Atlantic coast.

The wording whenever it returned had to match the one clerks notes submitted to the café whose addresses proved non-existent which had left them nowhere.

Law answered in a day. There were nineteen tapes accompanied by transcriptions. Imprint matched for African, white, Alexandra.

Make sure no one follows you.
Your address is Route 9 in the lakes, only yellow weed.
Place 24 letters in a cross like a phrase.

Sign in with your names.
Look for a well, pronounced A WOL.
Is the home in chains?
Is there a foot lock.
One house or two.
Is the gold lake in view?

Describe your trip.
Leave your letter in a cell block house in the attic at the edge of the lake.

Do floats transport sand?
Remove 1 book when you leave.

Who has a car at the inn?

So here it was; a realistic list for the status of mail delivered by vehicle to destination. Why was this done? To bring mail to an international shipping zone without it having traveled under its appropriate registry. Well, just suppose it had gotten on board the correct ship for various destinations? So why bother? It seemed an elaborate farce even if continuous segments were stolen. There had to be a connection to The Reading Room on 17th Street in Oakland where the four stolen bags were taken, opened, read and logs sent on to a clerk near Larchmond Canal at Ontario.

The logs were found in US houses and the actual mail in Canada after this man Laura disappeared in ankle chains from a jail bunkhouse on the Minnesota lakes. Laura was now wanted in connection for the death of John Smith of Cairo on the Mississippi who had collected stolen mail out of Oakland. What were these attic demonstrations intended to generate? Cool decided to check any person of origin having left the lakes to reside in Oakland who might know café shop clerks in and around that Oakland station. Two came up straight away, Deff and Shelly, both who waitressed in The Reading Room.

5

The waning daylight set into the trees radiating in a crimson glow sliding between slippery elm bark of bandaged white bark like a predicament of oncoming night. Between the knees of killed tense legs separated by maiden fern moss lay a bitten trouble of radiant gleaming blond worst, a juggernaut of a long married female complaint of boredom and misbegotten grumble for any logging mill. Just the grievance of sunken ambition made the muddy brown river seem all the more sinister. The morning mist arose from the wood barren roots which cut along the eddies nevertheless did not drink in any water. A supper of paradigms, the laid grass caused no further mud to slip to the bottoms although as the river became more saturated in deeper brown, it fell to a somnambulant sleeping state which coagulated and intertwined deep dark juice-like roots to the tweed of woven brush. The real issue of course was the wanted man pushed water to bays, drying up vast lakes and then sprung ponds on fertile seed land rising it in welts of stored ponds. He did this by stirring mud and transposing it probably to obscure himself or he had worked laying sand and had some sort of knowledge about weeds.

Small airplanes flew over trying to spot him but leafy trees and forage kept him hidden.

The rain came down steadily all day slowing periodic traffic and boats. Along the river café windows steamed up, at the back the doors to the parking lots and piers were left open. Soaking mud made a mess on dirt roads. A shore-pin of rash-minded criminals were hard at work laying stones with the intention of slipping ships and customs agents who were hunting them down with dogs and guns into swirling ignited waters in hopes they could evade capture after they bombed the ship in the canal. The two men who were captured were saviors to the other eight who couldn't live without them. The women most at risk were petite, white, curly orange blond redheads with an obvious thinking disorder that made them kill. They were found their supple arms tied to trees in the stream in 1963. There was a superstition that men with rifles who felled a ravenous lion or a pouncing rhino were worth following to the end of the earth.

The one man had caught up to the other on the cactus swamps, and like two hobos down on their luck they dragged row boats over the weed, and slept in any field or house they could locate for a night.

"When was your last good fuck?" The white man Laura asked the car robber Nimes.

"Oh about 22 years ago; I got a divorce."

"You get a divorce that's the end of fucking. Who brought you here?"

"I walked from the thousand lakes after a clinic I lay dead in sank in a flood."

"That must be the worst story I have ever heard. I thought maybe you fobbed the Canadian canal."

"Someone must have told you that."

"I know a man who tracks postponed envelopes and selects a list of match fields to find a person. He says sleep walking factor, not the trait, is a sign of insanity or lesser intelligence. He says all canal bombers are sleep walkers."

"Are you trying to be upsetting?"

"Why? Are you a sleep walker too?"

"It's a contradiction in terms. One is either sleeping or awake." The black man answered, thinking himself momentarily the smarter man, although it was clear to him the other man would keep them both from drowning.

"Not sleeper's awake, H.G. Wells. He believed in an utopian declaration."

"Maybe you misunderstood his meaning. Men don't live on the moon either."

They ran amuck calling out coo coo's as the sky darkened. They were cold, scared, hungry, not made for the swamps, their mistake even evident to themselves. Fearing hunger, they transplanted sorghum weed to each and every plat of soil. It was the forager grain that fed all living, that held the deadbeat waters back. The years just blurred together and the men became trabunckled like roots to the harrow. In cold chill blizzards washed into fundamental landscapes cracking soil and freezing lakes until life were a drastic causality borne of stagnant chill and leaning trees like a beaten down trodden path, lightning a bluish grey emblem. There, they fed in a barn under any worst they could find. At one point they slept in the car, heat turned on, until they regained a strict clot afar from purgatory.

"Why did prison let you go?" The white man inquired.

"I stabbed a man. I served my time. How about you?"

"Alexandra, Africa. I robbed a mail train."

"Must feel like home to you here," the car thief said.

"No, it doesn't. Too much water."

"Whole territories, nothing but ice. No way to find a soul you need."

"Who did you look for?"

"I was led to believe there were friendship houses with clean beds and heated showers along the canal where a man might pick up work for a week."

"Shovel work, you mean." The white man said.

"Anything. Haulage, can one come by it."

"The task of setting ship crates at a port for the train is skilled work, difficult for most contractors to obtain."

The boast came almost unbidden. "I was admitted to a single work shift house. I had to follow simple directions in exchange for a month's stay."

"What work was that?"

"I had to take boxes of letters, record sender and office on a log and place each in a row of twenty-five across the attic."

"Where was this?" The white man persisted.

"I couldn't tell you how to get there. 1288542 nearest Round Lake off the lace ice flow in spring of the Minnesota River or flooded in East Grand Forks town situated above the motel."

"Middle of nowhere."

"One can get there in a canoe just paddling. The lakes are connected by the river. It was a nice white house at the water up near the canal start," and then the over confidant boast that said he knew something he shouldn't, "I sat a car for the bust in Granite Falls the year Blondie's Lucky Day opened. Blondie, you know, made a tear on the vault next to the café and took 2. 4

million in bags and split downriver."

"I've never heard of Blondie."

"Oh, yeah, a notorious crook from Chicago, but not as bad as the post office robber of the Treasury."

Laura eyed him in sudden confrontation. "Any chance I can stay there?"

"Okay with me; cost you a swab. "

The white man drew out a pistol and showed the black man the head cock lever. They separated on friendly terms.

The river wound through flat brush in stands of blue thistle that towered high above cockle wild berry trees. He steered to rows of branches in the direction of the cloudy wispy purple orange setting sun. From time to time he stopped into a café for a stew. The journey took nine days.

The lone house stood on a promontory overlooking a lake. He broke in a window. The house contained a long kitchen, small living room, enclosed porch, two bedrooms up stairs, and a spacious attic accessible by a ladder.

The letters were each addressed illogically to him, Donovan Laura. They twinkled at him in shiny blue ink on white stationary, each stamp one of five cities, Cairo, Erie Falls, Ft. Wayne, Wichita, Galveston. Like magic. Suggestive. A chain letter. He hadn't been inside a house ever, only motel rooms, and it made him wary. He hoped he wasn't followed.

A posse of a hundred armed riders approached by dead of night, their horses sounded like a mean thunder on the star studded horizon. They infiltrated the lake town, rented all thirty hotel rooms, and waited out the winter over five months methodically collecting their final evidence. They were taking a big risk leaking the find to the Cody Scranton press by telephone. The newspaper ran a center page expose on Laura and every person he met in six years. Marshal deputies tracked the attic mail for an illegal job board for his two rail mail station hits for a 1961 Santé Fe GP60 through Barstow after which the rail chopped off for grand larceny of a million and a rail fanning office in Pennsylvania of 1963 monitored by nine Mumbai India horsemen.

Deputies joined him at breakfast, played pool at the bar room with him, sold him food at the mart, tinkered on cars outside the house, and chased him to the next city. They knew everything about him including the day he stepped out wearing a grey and red striped tie and blue jacket and suit.

By the day and hour Laura got caught, a dozen men surrounded the single story house standing in the dark at front and back doors, pistols cocked, and crashed the establishment as he lay sleeping, his hand cupping the breast of a dyed silver haired floozy young enough to be his child. The police team photographed the wall – nineteen on the second row for a state vault and seven on the third for a delivery by Greensboro pony express train to Kansas respectively. The working hypothesis was that men in the Treasury had arranged billet larcenies and had means to trade the stolen checks for cash. Who in the industry out of hundreds of employees would conspire to steal money? It seemed a ludicrous activity. But there it was, a bungled impulsivity, jailed and charged.

Ernesto Salcido was missing the usual at the Bellagio, his dry martini, wanton cress soup, square of squash and crushed macadamia nuts in butter, five strips rib eye, and dollop of spumoni. He had decided to stay in and give himself plenty of time to review the eight reports, four jurisdictions, along with the photos of stage coach robberies. He was a thin Italian, five foot eight, an FBI for the post office wharves, dark black hair like a band aid slapped over his egg shaped head, dark blue eyes, never without trousers and plain black tie, a meticulous analyst for the superior courts. He had heard there was a girl involved and he needed his wits about to figure out what her role was. Otherwise it was just busywork. He had awoken at four, made a cup of Turkish coffee and sipped it while reviewing the interrogatories; eaten a bite of French toast and strawberries and left over half on the Spode plate, and then gone and sat in the sitting room in front of the fire with his notes. This Laura had been at large for nearly a decade. All sorts of parole agents had gone into the territories and along the big rivers to find him. Rumor had it he left a bag of mail like a sack of bananas dangling off every glass ceiling after each train robbery. He was tied to three bad bunkers and it was assumed he had spawned copy cats. Bhangan was at the ready to return him to an ocean prison off West Africa, and just as well for all the chase he cost a hundred men. It had proven a tortuous convoluted roundabout to nail him despite frequent entries into a labyrinth of tangled warrens. Thus Salcido's first task was to confront his bailiwick, the next to cite his past crime at Alexandra and removal from society and his release by postal ship to Canada and eventual deployment of the Larchmont lock for the Cheshire bank roll to Erie for lake post offices. The similarities to the east African shoulder and countenance for change rates, not just tax, would mete out the rash of stolen deposits for twelve cities. The attic declarations had to be proof of some sort, train numbers likely, 109, 8, and 198 with zone, city and destination, careful documentation as to robber identity and original mailbag planked. The court papers included witness statements, fingerprint verifications, discarded clothing sent to evidence, innkeeper photos, treasonable acts including theft of bags, trespass into vault rooms and clerk locked doors, stolen police vans, and detaining a private citizen. If not for the entry into the country by mail bag assignment, no one could be sure of the identity of these felons nor their involvements. He would then have to file for arraignment and once he obtained disposition on the evidence move to a conviction. There would be seven counts in all including bomb to a prison ship, mail theft at two sites, armed with a dangerous weapon, fleeing the jurisdiction, hanging mail inside a ship dock, and holding up an abandoned postal stop. He doubted he could add destruction of land by replanting grain shrub as no one cared which way the Missouri flowed, or that a finding could even be construed for the amount of mud building up in any shore along the Mississippi confluence. That was about what any attorney might expect. By the time morning arrived he had completed his address to the court, prepared his witness list, tagged the evidence and finalized his descriptions on hold boxes. He had worked until he could scarcely think clearly but he believed he had cleared out the worst case in years.

Soho

1

NINTH STREET, SOHO

A night janitor who came on duty at five noticed the pile of bodies and called police to the refurbished First Street Theatre on Second where prior engagements that May included the plumed Patti La Belle, Michael Cortez, and raspy Billie Holiday. The stucco theatre was filled with sixty-three people who had collapsed in the aisles and central rows. From the Jinead County Building on Hudson that housed the city police, six officers were dispatched. They arrived in four minutes, left their blue and white patrol cars in the street, sirens blaring, and dashed inside the theatre, and minutes later carried out bodies on stretchers to ten ambulances directed to county hospital. A growing crowd of onlookers had to be held back. Among them watched the tight fisted brick layers Hoyfea and Cerfu who were blamed for killing a man inside a car trunk and sinking half a dozen Fords off the wharf in rainy weather.

Dubbed an end of the world cult crime, the dead were diagnosed with cyanosis by a drug Maloxcene administered for shortness of breath given in tabs at the door and Noxilcene that tightened the skin from ceiling spray meant to clean upholstered seats.

That same night at midnight all 24 city buses were bombed in front of the firehouse on the waterfront on First. These buses normally drove from Chinatown's neon lights to 110th to the Cotton Club, a white heroin salon where rich blacks frequented, all who were physician hospital administrators. Both heroin tar and powdered pharmaceutical IVs were proffered by girls who were something to gawk at, lanky, leggy flat-chested beauties with long coiffed hair, tight black pants and see through blouses.

It was rumored the job was bought as a mob hit by a flower parlor silent partner Toto Riina. His parlor man Jack Ruby stand-up comic had entered Springfield, Illinois nightclubs at Nick & Nino's at the stunning all gold glass Kinzie 8 off Capitol Mall plaza. The chief payouts were theatre owner of Magnet Theatre and toll bridge cashier a comic who together had four warehouses crammed full of mirrors, tables, loge chairs, costumes. Theatre acts were fast becoming a new venue to sell bred heroin. The lounge with topless waitresses sold cigarettes fixed with the drug and a bar fizz of morphine or belladonna. The success came with nightly club dance acts and famous revues.

No victims, affected businesses stacked up for two evidence labs, NY State Bridge toll, trains, markets, ninth street police precinct and all elementary schools, opens access to ocean, thereby plummeted streets into a Hudson River. Buildings built after the bus crimes were Museum of Art, NY State Zoo, and Staten Island ferry station. Westside had a high school in New Jersey that trained pharmaceutical clerks and theatre movie management. Products produced in NY since 1945, trains, fabric, paper, silverware, banking, farms of cabbage and soups made of lentils, chickpea, rhubarb, consume. In time a host of French restaurants popped up in the four block by one block Soho.

In Illinois at the state capitol the sun shone on a neatly maintained city of empty streets. Fourteen fountains shot streams of water in the park plaza in front of the six floor senate building. The Grace Lutheran church on the corner with chapel spire and the Dana Thomas house in blue aged copper continued to be the most photographed landmarks in addition to a clean quaint Sixth Street office district. Five trains were moving through the locomotive yard at nine in the morning; steps to Trinity Lutheran High School an all brick conservative church building educated sixty students, many who would work for the Pillsbury plant; Quincy news, or radio 110 FM.

Here in Washington State Park, a massive park of refined greenery surrounded by blocks of stately county buildings, a man lay dead under a hedge, underwear evident. He was a senator aide for Jack Warren from the chapter house assembly of Springfield, in his seventies, a regular on rostrum, six feet, black hair, elegant pink tie with a black stripe, decent white suit and Mocktoes, a teaser baggie of ragged coke known as cotton inside his lapel pocket.

In his thirty years in the precincts starting on 138th Avenue at Alexander in Bronx James Ganlon had seen so much train shuttle crime that he had become a hardened man. Murders came at a speedy clip such that the jails were overcrowded denizens of intolerance. He was average height, fifty, balding sideburns and eyeglasses. Dedicated combat, he rode a canine patrol with an Italian partner Lyle Oberon from the Central Park West division who was used to jumping fences to corner suspects in an alley. The OD incidence had increased to include severe drunk and disorderly, knifings, telephone cord strangulation, opiate vomit. The First Street Theatre deaths were looking to be accidental except for the bile. No victim had choked by noxious substance. Teeth gnashing resulted from cord strangulation from killers who stood over each person.

2

The poor man had a ragweed addiction at a grand per inch, preferred two inches, all smelt lasting a month. The governing question was who paid him that much money that enabled him to spend two a month.

The case was assigned to an FBI man named Bogin. Bogin was a senior roll call specialist, a Spaniard from Prado district, used to a penthouse view of Manhattan, six feet, black wiry hair, glasses, small nose, pressed lips. In the past he was the police consultant relegated to the church run clinics. Bogin considered Shore began his tawdry career handling killings and eventually graduated to bombs. Bogin had on good authority that Soho's sole problem was the mask bag hit man. Somewhere there was a snapshot of him fishing the tab out of the fried wonton bowl for the pay dough.

He had made his first of three reports to James and Lyle the day after the bus disaster. In it he stated evidence showed a body inside a bus, a probable mob hit vengeance over new bus camera filming of a petrol warehouse wharf fire of medicinal morphine conducted by a congressional cop. His report lay in pieces attached to sleazy photos of building fires. Half a dozen were in

Cook County spread across the sleepy highways like Molotov cocktail mind benders. The pics didn't say much, a leg, a shoulder, a hand; enough for a conviction.

The clear day was breezy, a salty air composure. There were two cars in the yard awaiting the Internal Affairs agents who by noon had to be uptown for the inquest. Inside the phones rang non-stop. Dispatch had two officers on since nine. The Squad room was quiet, thirty cops completing narrative summaries to beat the rush in preparation for superior court trials. James had a thirty hour window before counsel resumed disposition. The pleading had to address any new evidence for sentencing. It would be his call on handling of properties, witnesses on the body, writ of habeas, human remains.

His desk was normally immaculate, notes on a handheld spiral bound pad and a small Dictaphone, and green glass banker's lamp. On a back board his calendar was of student seminars at universities. The atmosphere was one of studied contemplation, soft typing noise, periodic rustling of papers, an occasional consultation of penal law code books. James made his way through a plethora of evidence on the buses. Gasoline bags, more of the same, combined with forensic red, a tired explosive which burst into roiling flames and lasted a few days, each bus decimated in black gaseous flames extending the wharf line. Two teams submitted laser photos taken off police cameras by ATF and US Marshall separately taking a full day. Photos showed man's body carried onto bus and laid stretched out at back of bus to Plymouth. The victim had been shot in skull gangland style by son in Jamaica outside Beaverton Bar on 139th across from Rexall Drugstore as a result of father kicking out a Sorentino Lad Brook from the west coast rainy season airport hills out of his nightclub.

Entire remains left a charred skeleton. The county lab declared hydrogen, also ribonucleic amino acids; and carbuncle, human disfigurement, showing bone fragments, typical of fires for which a dead body lay inside a burned structure which was airtight.

A bottle of Livingston's champagne sat on the stone stairs that led to the museum contained two fingerprints of Melones, a west coast bar owner operating out of Hayward on the main drag. It was believed he was wanted for a heist of treasury T-bills which he laundered in games and parlors. Of all the betting laid on Soho semi clad girlie shows he was the lone contender to a bevy of tile house fires assaulting the two coasts.

A dreary winter in February began with a fully mortared round of flying bullets to pedestrians in the storage district of Manhattan. A beat patrol cop due for night patrol of the bus line up was stupidly fired upon. Windows slammed shut everywhere at once. Wind factor raged at forty miles per hour. Sirens shrieked. Adults on the droll were in abundance. Like a population of zombies, not a hairpin in place, haphazard street crossings suggested a totality of moronic functioning. Four backup beat officers for the bus yard were stabbed, and the entry gate left wide open.

This year might bring in fifty dispositions a month to the courts. Child abuse, wayfarer homeless, civil infractions, abductions, crashes. Along with patients on opiates who lined up outside the free clinics, so did hypochondriacs, anxiety disorders, phobias, obsessions, suicide, sexual violence, pathological gambling, schizophrenics, bipolars, ADHD, kids on Ritalin and binge eating already peppered the rolls at coroner headquarters. In addition to a dozen drowning deaths, household domestics, ship dock crashes, government extortion, and drug related fatalities; a fan motor for a fix, stockyard, a way to earn more from storage docking fires along with hiked crime statistics, overworked weather stations; and lighthouse scans on the blink.

A host of education centers to train police, fire, therapists and lab were given up to the ghost.

Who had that much control over the buses?

James thought the buses were bought out by a school of ten hair dressers who worked late nights as guards, but the belief gave him no rest. In a foresight he perceived occasional dark discontent, melancholy; dispirited temperament, a reactive attachment of intensely depressed internal conflict aimed at warding off rejection. To this demeaned earnest bleakness, he isolated himself, was offish, often alone. Lyle ignored the moods, took in apparent concerns and fed off the brusqueness.

What makes the man so important. Lyle asked.

He shot the vic.

Do you have enough for arraignment.

Oh, it will never see the light of day.

What makes you say that.

Look at who these men are. Coin change operators.

Who is their boss.

Fourth street market in Dutch Manhattan. They are willing to back change.

Were the coins removed.

Yes, no money was on any bus. That's what I mean. It was a hit.

No one's going to lie down on a barbeque.

I lack a motive.

Could it be a broad.

Ruled out.

James poured two coffees and they sat thinking.

I suppose the murdered man D'Leues paid his tax. Lyle ventured.

Yes, every last cent. I think his son wanted his empire of vans for the resorts.

Worth some money.

James answered wryly, Not much, few hundred thou'.

Families kill for less.

Indeed. They destroy over feuds.

Was there a disagreement.

On how long should a fire truck ladder extend.

You must be kidding.

Kid you not.

Ridiculous.

So I got to thinking, Is this any way to prove a point.

Was the son a crazy.

A no good. Was in a mental ward as a kid.

So let's go for insanity.

Won't get a sentence.

He's not doing the crime.

Nope, not even in town. He's with Ruby that week.

Did Ruby get anything out of this.

Saved a mint on wine sales. He owes to the old man.

What say we file on Ruby.

Could, but he's in Springfield.

So they couldn't get a hoot right away, was Lyle's portent.

The photos showed four crabs, a black and three white look a likes to the back-up cops. All on the spoon. In reverse they'd hopped a subway, doused the buses, and escaped gleefully into the night; a pack of teen wolverines.

The fan had a chink in its rotation that sounded like a man eating with chopsticks. In the cool darkness he made out Andy step into the hall, her silvery knee length crepe nightgown the color of moonlight. She cast a worn out smile for which he felt as tired. Their marriage had suffered ups and downs usually over her inability to carry a child, and now childless, they had come to terms more or less with the length of time of endless nights. He made up his mind long ago he had fallen in love the moment he laid eyes on her, blond short hair, lithe, a girl of sixteen. He maintained a practice of being at her side and did not worry about his need for sitting alone. Every night for forty years he lay beside her and held her hand until she drifted to sleep and thought about work; he couldn't imagine his life without her, they were peas in a pod.

Come sit for a bit, he said, to which she came to him and settled onto his lap.

Where have the years gone, he asked her.

Is it a very serious matter.

The worst by far.

Tell me about it.

So he began, looking about the wood cabin as he spoke to claim what was their life, three couches, yellow gladiolas on red background, a green carpet on an ash pine floor, the kitchen peering in, pink Formica and pink walls and dark cabinets, a dark green marble tile lit hearth, grandfather clock, walnut dining table and matching six chairs, leaded glass windows. The three bedroom home paid for, a garden of grass, birch trees and hammock. Life was precious, one's sanctuary all the more appreciated.

He delved into the intricacies of the case. A devil's forum.

Oh, sweetheart, you have had more severe; dead police. Each case is different. Each one draws blood.

But a son.
Electra slew her father over his army.
There's few to compare. It just makes you sick.
Maybe they'll round him up and take him.
Whatever is done won't be any too soon.
Were points of position staffed.
Burned to the ground.
Film stores.
Not a one. A wipe out.
Fire trucks.
Five. The ladders took pictures of the burning buses. The subject upon arrest was determined by lab to have imbibed a full cooker of gray rag. It starts with rapid absorption in a burst of enthrallment for a few minutes, an immediate let down lasting a half hour and then feeling invincible for a week, capable of any strength. It made him walk real slow.

Where did he obtain it.

In Illinois at The Fairmount. The summaries indicate a chronological menace. Tying people up in packaging tape while setting off a bomb inside the stove all over Michigan, a block at a time. It's an awfully expensive idea of living, not at all concerned with humanism.

He lifted her and carried her into the bedroom and placed her on the bed. She had lit the fire and drawn the blue curtains and pulled the heavy purple drapes.

What are you thinking about, he asked her when she reached for him.

How nice it would be to keep you home for a week.

Can't; this situation probably will take a good half year.

Why can't they get someone else.

They won't. He lay beside her and cradled her face.

I love you, James.

Me too.
I miss you terribly.
I'd like nothing better, Andy, but you know how it is.
I know. It's a bad one. I hope I helped.
You did, honey. I always need you. This is home.
You are my life. I have nowhere else.

He knew she had fallen asleep because her clasp loosened. He covered her and kissed her mouth at which she'd come drowsily awake.

Have me, James.

He slipped beneath the coverlet and raised the gown and pushed down his pants and pressed himself between her beautiful legs.

Oh, have me, James; have me, have me, have all of me, I do so love you.

To which he joined her, saying, I am so taken, Andy.

He had intended to return to the outer room but instead surrendered to sleep, mouth open to her nipple.

He had always been a man of the sea. In their early years when they took a cabin on the coast in pouring rain he sat by the window immersed in the sharp hail as though nature itself were an instruction of quiet thinking, a way to let go of the demands of fastidious police work. Now of course the storm shook the foundation and roof, a veritable wrestling match of climates on a warm air front. The fierce rain was without let up. The whistling wind drove up shore, trees slapped wet bent and swayed, sails in the harbor flapped; a cement grey bay like a hard worn carpet. He found he suffered from anxiety of lacking enough sleep. The heater sounded like a man coughing, The rain washed the bay like in a pail, repetitive tapping metal, then retreated going back out to sea. The heavy sound of a boat motor hammered in the wake.

As a child who had been force fed on a regimen of strict Catholicism, he had had to separate between mere skepticism and the rigors of terror often which left him with a profound sense of anticipation of life. Thus when tragedy fell he was seized by a conniving belief that it had already begun unseen. He said his crib of catechisms nightly to a deceitful god who redeemed deceit. From time to time he spied out his father crying over his own bead prayers. There had been almost twenty years reposed the arsons of two stone churches on that same quadrangular park where today had Chinatown by a set of school boys of the Christian faith, Pelts, Bolo, Sturgis, a black armory night guard, and Renner, all who were rounded up and sent to upstate New York for forty years on devastation wards. One had set himself on fire trying to ignite an ounce of black. These were men who despite their ages were considered child mental deficit. They were taught life skills in parochial schools to run track, do arithmetic, cook and clean.

Life was a real mystery when it came to arson, each criminal a staunch believer. Even if they did it for money. James joined in the belief that destination was sacred; no one should not be merited. Life was ordained, and thus living had to be assured. Plumes of bright yellow charged the night sky to the horror of the original residents on Ninth Street of which James was a mere child and could be seen as far as the two Harlem's and across the bay in pastures that would become Brooklyn and Bronx.

This recent crime could only be afforded to the rising squall of the medicinal heroin dependency of trafficking drugs now commonplace to leisure in lower Manhattan. As yet, without the advent of the automobile, trains raced to oblivion under purple skies.

In the rumor mill on the new suburban highway, the intellectual candy said that spoon fed camaraderie for achievement oriented presumptions put the early seeker in the morgue. Lots of manufacturers of synthetics got upset if attacked for carrying substances such as yellow or blue, typically used in butane, chemisol, carrend, and other everyday uses.

As fitful as the rain swamped the state, the most lasting capable hour took James to an unusual conclusion that the nomenclature of historical crime was nevertheless thriving. Just how such a crime was possible without bombs stood in the incandescence of light on a rainy night, all told photos showed no more than a herd shed of dripping catheters stemming from gas tanks lit by butane.

It was shift change at 3pm and he and Lyle had just finished consuming salami sandwiches and dill ordered from the Italian Genovese corner deli across the street. James was on his first espresso. They had briefed for four hours with damned little success. All they deduced was that the Italians ordered this crime also; they thought because their markets were failing. They failed to bring in even enough to pay the cost of meat which was twelve cents on the pound for lean and brisket so the money was going somewhere illicit. These foreigners couldn't get started. Even milk had its depressants amidst caviars of roe. It fetched a higher IV dollar than spoon. The toxic nature of milk turned fifty to a hundred stiffs over to the junk yards every year. The gambling at the horse races was killing off the city's needs to raise city taxes. This over time would be the big boost to fund stage three crimes, the Nero cocaine produce that would bring a shot in the arm to small dope peddlers. The problems didn't look like problems because they had always been there, chemicals used by industries were where they had always been. The state became acclimated to their presence until there was a chemical industrial explosion. Often whoever came forward denied knowledge. No way to get around a sour tip. When evidence produced it was picked up on.

The aide to Sen. Philip Warren had had his wrists slit before he was in a fatal car crash; that's how the state police knew he had been murdered for becoming whistle blower to an inmate. He told on the famous parallax murder on Jamaica streets, told him by an anonymous phone tip, later confirmed by bus and airplane camera.

For tracking the info and keeping his office safe, James stood to make chief. He was ready. He had ideas as to how to clip the wings of stage six arson and the wave of hospital distribution onto the street. If it were up to him, he'd toss out every hospital administrator on golden handshakes and retire them to state prison.

Two teams of two had been assigned to go out and interview suspects. James and Lyle were up next on rotation. Their call came in at five to interview an eye witness. To talk to him they had to drive to the marina and board his two deck cruiser. The boat bobbed in the harbor at the back of a hundred boats. The cruiser was ninety feet long by forty feet across, its top deck beneath a white cloth awning, motor capable of eighty miles an hour in the jet stream, at idle could drift at two an hour. They positioned at its rear and climbed aboard the lower cabin deck. Classical symphony music emanated from the interior where navy drapes covered porthole windows. They walked along the white floorboard deck to the cabin door where they descended down three stairs into a sitting room and bar.

Their subject was a John Geonard, a Mediterranean

man of sixty, white hair crew cut, icy bedroom blue eyes, five foot ten, dressed in light denim shirt and dark denim pants, and tan leather boots. He held the subpoena in his left hand before a table with choice blue oysters on the half shell and glasses filled with white Chablis Blanc.

Are you here to arrest me.

Not at the moment.

You have some questions to ask me.

If you don't mind. Did you see the car crash with Senator Aide Crimm?

Yes, I was pulled up to a stoplight.

All said very matter of fact.

I wasn't worried. I had just departed the constitutional square. I was listening to the full weather report on the news and to breaking news stories when the crash occurred. It was behind me. I rushed to see if I could help.

And could you?

No, the guy was a goner. He was dripping blood on his arms.

Could you see what the trouble was?

Not at first. Another bystander called for the cops. He thought the guy had sliced his wrists.

What was the weather?

I beg your pardon?

The weather report.

Oh. Rain that day and snow by nightfall.

Did you recognize the man?

Yes. Yes I did. He was Warren's aide.

Do you know what he was lobbying for?

A surcharge on wine.

Were you in favor of it?

No, but I didn't kill him.

Had you seen him that day?

No. I have only met with Warren himself.

They didn't pull him in for further questioning. There was nothing further to go on, but they listed him as a primary suspect in the purchase of the bus fires even ahead of Ruby, whose name said never a bomb, straight torch.

They rode in silence, alarm on through the warehouse district off the train yards, passing lonely offices and chemical plants, onto the deserted high bridge back to the precinct, hitting every red light once they came off the exit.

He just didn't strike me as sincere. Lyle was concluding on the fifteen minute ride home.

No way to bust him. I'd have liked better to have found him in a brothel making pay on the hit.

James peered through the sun visor.

It was six in the late afternoon.

He had pulled up beside Lyle's green Porsche to let him out.

Any practical course suggesting a bribe, James said.

I don't like all the favors. I'd think twice on a McClarren betting angle, maybe at Potter's field terminal. Might very simply be a feud over bottling.

He's a bit of a zipper; I thought he devised the no cash on site after dark.

He's a slick one, alright. Lyle opened the door, stuck out his leg. Just for the record; the guy had bought a beer joint not even ten days before the bus shit. Maybe he laundered the bill.

For Warren?

Oh, don't know. Why would he want into action like that?

Well, he's a bartender at Cotton Club, he does solo at The River Front on Third, he dabbles in the races, he's plenty fluid. That much money, where's it coming from? It's got to be heroin or cotton.

Do you have him with a female?

Young Cajun girl named Rennie, pretty, silver blonde, spindly arms, legs, body, sort of a Blue Monday; he keeps her on tab by the month.

She have a record?

She sits for the horses last day of the month during each season.

Maybe we should stop in at the Cotton.

We could do every club that side of the bridge in a sweep.

Could. I'll sleep on it.

The clock had come on for 12:55. I have to get going, James said.

Lyle stepped out, slammed the door, waved.

The duo dressed in pin-striped suits, James in black and thin silver and Lyle in tan and moderate blue, dark blue ties both, white galvanizer shoes, crew cuts slicked back with Arrow.

Lyle took a blonde bombshell named Gina on his arm from the county health department in paternity and deeds.

It was scene after scene on a Friday night, the orchestra playing a Bessie Smith revue, followed by the renditions of Cab Calloway music, the loves of the twenties, the score of musicians tilting forward as if in prayer, and a scalp cut frizzy haired Nina Simone playing piano, low lights, red stage on 125th directly beneath the bridge, the Cotton Club a modern wharf extravaganza of glass and smooth concrete, light skin, semi-Hispanic blacks out for a stroll on the edge. Some action going down at the far back of the salon, finger blades sold for a fifty.

It was evident the Warren contingency kept the

bright lights off the dealing and back room gambling took position over the good times of drugs and hospitality. From James' point of view the chorus walk of delectable girls in vagina skimpy garments was an outrage, acts of prostitution despite the fact no skin touched skin. It was a suggestion of sex, neither wanton nor immoral but it sold barbiturates by the handful, gave license to stalk a girl for her calmer ingénue, and took in limousines scores of handsome black men to alleys of drifting dreams, a success of livelihood as far as pimps were concerned.

They hit the Savoy for Ladies Night Out at ten, a classier club in neon lights like a movie theatre for the upper status blacks, females dressed to the hilt in every pastel color backless floor-length silk and men in satin, lilac, orange, crimson, pink, pale blue, purple; featuring Art Blakey jazz; all cocktails on the bar.

By midnight they entered Sugar town where the dime was sold in packets for a bathroom blow, the jazz flair of Jesse Owens trombone backyard blues, a back parlor for card betting, winner takes all, profits going to a Chinese storekeeper who owned supermarkets, cheapie apartments, low cost boutiques and rings and gemstones, the height of spring indulgences in walk-ups overlooking the steely Hudson banks. There she sat, Rennie, at the piano on stage, practically naked slipped in see-through crepe that showed her lean body, almost a boy's in features of flat chest and thin torso, laughing it up in a sugary voice, an impresario at the musical keyboard playing Porgy, then Lonesome River, ending with Jack the Knife and Ain't You a Fancy Man, at once thin as a whisper and brassy as a vulture. She stood her stage, all five feet of her, a muscular shoulder, fingers coming down hard on the keys and treble clang of abrupt deeper tones; one could almost hear her shakedown, C'mon,

Baby, are you gonna blow me or not?

Maybe she didn't fit the senator angle, but plenty of them driving up from Chicago for a peek.

It was hard to picture her at the Savoy or Apollo burning the wick as she performed a striptease. When she was on her last act she twirled a black umbrella as she stripped down to her red heels. In the daylight she'd be asleep until two in the afternoon; it was the life of nightclubs, an underworld of darkness.

Lyle told her, Darling, we'll be back with a warrant to chat so don't run away, and stuffed a fifty in her garter which she regarded with distance as though she didn't hear him.

The wailing reminiscent twang had the same effect on James it always had since he first heard it, like he was alone waiting on a train platform for a train that was already three hours late;

Oh, baby, won't you fox me out the hole, fix me up some rock?

He had never touched a drug in his life, but he felt the sad rejection of life and prostitutes down to his bones. It lay as a nagging sorrow that caused him to wince and he instantly thrust it away.

At one they sat down to River Walk jazz at Connie's to take in the eerie trombones and trumpet horns; cutting the hour with a new jet set Frankie Spanos and Gena Harley in the star cast lights; and finished at the Owney Madden at the water's edge for champagne and red caviar on the soda biscuit where Jack Riina was the bouncer looking to shanghai a suspect wanted in a stabbing.

Shortly before closing they put in at Lucille's, BB King's bar and grill in NYC, for steak and crab, a late night feature for the retired octogenarian who awaited coach and buggy at the Georgetown plaza of show palaces. There was nothing much going on, nothing to worry over except cost of meat and taxes.

Pre-dawn was just lighting up the sky in an awareness of pink light as tinsel town was getting ready to serve breakfast to weekend commuters training to work in the six o'clock in the morning rush.

You want to chase the warrant? James asked.

Sure, will do.

You'll have to talk to her.

No problem.

He was home by three, Andy was in her silver gown, her hair swept up high on her head, rouge and mistletoe, sipping a blue frosted glass of Pinot, playing solitaire, alone, he could see in waiting.

Sweetheart, he kissed her on the forehead.

How do I compare to the felines downtown?

Honey, you shouldn't have bothered, he said, but slipped a hand down her front and ran his palm over her breast. You should know I don't look at the women.

Cut any glass? She asked. She'd done up her hair, it was swept into a do, sugary stiff.

He poured himself a cup of coffee, took spaghetti Alfredo leftovers out of the fridge, and sat down, lit up a cigarette despite the best of intentions to eat a bit of dinner first. You look stunning.

Don't lie to me, Jimmy.

He grinned. Lots of girls, Honey. The bad ones are the prettiest. Skin and bones like they haven't eaten in four years.

Got a make on the sugar candy?

Not yet, but we do know she drove the Bentley with the stiff tied up in the back seat. The suspect paid for her apartment on Tenth.

Is Owney Madden named?

Not any of the bar owners. But they each come out in profits, so who's to know.

Was this girl in trouble for the whiskey?

She was on tender hooks for the sap. She owed like a grand before she agreed. It is rumored that from her hotel flat she saw the Mack who was later the subject of singer Bobby Darin's 1959 song Mack the Knife, and his barstool decided they should track her down, so she's put down, another pigeon.

Possibly she only did business with Geonard; she wasn't his sweetheart.

Unlikely. She's a leg on a chorus line. It's how she scores.

That's fairly pessimistic.

I'm running an investigation, sweetie, not a sop mill. She's wanted for the Kinnard body. How does she get involved – it's commonplace, she's hooked.

The first crimes were the stabbings?

Six, on the lower east side, all pretty, each youthful, each on bad drugs, heroin and salt peter.

That probably killed them. She lifted her gown, unhooked her black garters, slipped off her stockings one at a time. Am I to your liking, James?

He let his cigarette burning; got up and knelt to her placing both hands beneath her gown, the cool chenille cloth seductive to his touch, and kissed her knees and thighs. Rob me of sanity, he said in a whisper, and she grabbed his hair in a sudden ecstatic clutch and then gripped him by the back of his neck.

James, make me the same as her.

To which he kissed her belly and lastly her breasts, each hung succulent, a swollen craving of sweet fulfillment.

Love me, James, I love you, don't you know.

Her husky sentiment rode out the night; he swallowed her ribcage even as he held her close against him, her supposed inaccuracies the craven lust of a fortuitous night.

They slept in until nine. He was up first and went to prepare two French Roast espressos which he brought in on a tray with buttered wheat toast. She smiled, satiated in his tenderness, and welcomed his inclination to discuss what she assumed were the depravities of the case.

I couldn't comprehend her distinction as a single girl, he said, once she was fully awake and had sipped her cup. She must be a mere forty.

Most women want to be married, Andy said; all the better if it's to a man of importance. A woman less than a man will trade in for a divorce. A few adapt to a single life, but most will remarry. How does this girl exist in such a dangerous world without a man?

Then it's a deception.

Right, exactly, there's a man somewhere; or she is greatly affected by her adversaries.

She is rumored to be the favored bedmate of this Geonard.

I think he is her pusher. He provides the ladle that keeps her crooned.

She's strung up too severely to not need access to a regular supplicant.

I think he weans her to it, Andy said.

He has his reasons if she has seen him knife girls.

It's a deadly score. She must at some point be captivated to it.

Captured by it is more like it, he remarked. One doesn't have to ask, why does she do such a deadly crime when it's readily apparent she's in debt for rinse. Any other girl would disappear, vanish off the earth than agree to this sort of a kill.

For her to have a readiness, there must be some disturbing element; or she is paranoid.

She runs the bets at the horses.

It couldn't be that, Andy interjected. She's up to her eye balls by now. Does she know who's after her.

She isn't plum to the sauce yet. I imagine someone hard core tracked her down. She's a party girl who fell prey to her own necessity of pleasure.

Andy surmised, Maybe she's after her own club act. Plenty of girls are in the invitation.

James kissed her on the lips tasting bitter coffee. Were it you, I wouldn't get past it.

If there's no one to look after her, she falls prey to a rather simplistic fashion.

I've wondered. What made her look out her window to begin with.

Could be she recognized the victim's voice, she speculated and sipped in a long sip to the dregs.

Maybe she realized who the knife was.

Or she was told at the club.

It's a problem what she must know.

But for whom? It suggests the shadow operates the clubs.

I could accommodate that, a man who is always on the scene because he resides in Soho himself. Soho is a small limited arena, less than fifty apartments, a mere dozen clubs, most featuring boudoir, ample drugs, the worst of IV anywhere.

A doctor, do you think?

Probably.

She set aside her demitasse and welcomed James back

into bed. He stretched out, feeling as he extended there was no rationale as to why he perceived himself aged, but looking at her with selfish concern as she began to mouth his member that they were knowledgeable only to each other and therefore there was no great reserve.

I love you, he said.

She tugged at him certain he could derive even moderate thrill.

He reached for her head and with two hands took her face. Do me.

She kissed him as if neither time nor awareness converted to a damn misgiving. As he felt the start of gleaming, she sipped him lightly and hard and positioned her buoyant breasts on his thighs, gathering in his habitual stirrings.

I love you, he said as he began to be aroused.

She held him firmly like a hose, readying for a send out, pressed her overripe breasts to his legs, and began whimpering, take me, sweetness.

If he became overcome by joy, he told himself it was love speaking to him warding off the spellbound nature of egocentricity, not to be altruism until he had to leave her for the work day; he brimmed unexpectedly, a luminous force charged through him. He and his Andy; they had been in love since their college days at Harvard in the same law classes, in the crook of elbow of ecstasy, virgins known only to one another, a couple promised for brilliant awakenings, he ceased to feel anything but amazement.

The precinct analyst turned in his report. In it he waxed philosophical. The cruel motivation was the victim's control of the drug marketplace.

Life must never learn the tragic misgivings of spite. Petty trivialities too suddenly turn to venomous grudging. The doers perceived him with malevolence, unkindness and malice. Their wish to do harm; or according to law, to commit an unlawful or unjustifiable act that would cause injury stood in the foreground as vindication.

Andy had invited the precinct over for drinks and noshes. They stood in proximity in the celebrated garden on the patio making small talk about the report, a dedicated group of twenty-four men and one female, each had worked the bus crime down to the soil of the sorry yard. Each surmised the market was restricted through extreme violence; like a promissory note that made good on tight controls and no one disagreed. The party which was meant to be festive maintained a dour caution. The entire group had to worry now over DJ's, bouncers, guards and warehouse spics. There was a scrutiny about that passed for repression and sharking; particularly in the hospital districts among physicians who bought the Cad; it was a whole new loan class to launder massive payoff fortunes. A felling industry the personal car aided and abetted the sale of weed and brush into dark dens in the water front clubs.

Lyle had busted the girl Rennie after she said she had the vic in her car tied up biting a rubber bar. Now he was triumphant, a solid cop on his way up the ladder.

Lyle had passed his exquisite blond date and stood close enough to her to touch her full breasts as drinks in hand they chatted and laughed about their night on the town; she decidedly a looker in a low cut emerald green dress that showed her smooth cleavage to her chest. Every so often Lyle leaned into her and courted her with a hand at her waist, and she, another long term married who had not brought her cop husband, pressed against him in obvious succor, all smiles and friendly aperture and tousled hair style, took his hand and placed it on her bare bosom. He was enjoying himself, a leisurely adulterer, sumpting up to her in the gaze of onlookers, a douse of envy by many.

Andy caught James in the kitchen between servings. Is Lyle having an affair?

Of course not.

But an hour later he came across them in the TV room, Lyle with his pants down giving Gina a thrust of ecstasy with her dress hiked up. She was breathless and eager and clinging, and James closed the door and left them to their privacy.

Are you sure, Andy asked after the last guest left.

You were right. Lyle's having an affair.

He didn't bring Joanne; or she was busy.

I wouldn't worry. I've never known Lyle to be dishonest.

The note on Lyle's desk read, I checked paternity for the two Machete brothers and found it is Cham who is negative. Bernie is positive.

The lab hasn't said diddly, Lyle explained when James asked if he could be hiding evidence.

How about I ask?

Won't matter. They don't intend to inform us.

Must be they haven't made final determinations.

How long are they going to take? It's already two months.

James said, Will your frivolities affect this investigation?

It was the first clear blue sky day in a weekend of thunder storms and they were each agitated with waiting to get out and collect information.

I'm in the throes of divorce, dear fellow. Joanne's left

me for another cop. We split up half a year ago. I thought we'd patch things up, but she's firm. She has sued me for the house. My lawyer thinks I should just bail out.

I'm sorry. Gina's quite a girl.

I've been lucky. She looks out for me, like with this case. The bones on the bus are Rh negative so right there we have his identity. I say we get a head start on the case and run down Cham.

He was an asshole.

Well, don't let anyone hear you. I have it on good authority he had cut out the wine from earnest tax.

Is the brother cited?

No, only the son.

So it's a vendetta.

Well, it might be. Word is Ruby set it up.

That's old news. What do we have on photo?

Just this bimbo, Rennie.

Who removed the body from her car?

The son. There's no one else but him on wharf street lamp.

The final photos showed the son Mathew verifying his father was dead. He rode to the mortuary to view last remains of the consumed flesh.

I am often looking for some sign I made a difference, Rennie said.

Maybe you did. Who put him in your car?

Molly. He dances at the Cotton in the jungle dance tour d'force.

Was he dead.

I'm not sure he had kicked, but he was plenty quiet, like a stone, out cold.

Where was he before Molly helped him in.

At Norma's penthouse. He liked to sing to the

flamingo birds.

They took off in their patrol car; and found Molly between stage acts.

Molly was a spic from Havana.

I should have been promoted; I was more like a son to him. He needed action was me who took care of business.

What sort of action.

Muscle, when one of the runners shook down a chase.

What did you think about the old man's IV drug policies.

I don't think he should have decided who gets and who waits, or for how long. He played God, and he had the ability to distribute fairly all over the city.

Was the slab expensive?

Who cares; he had more than to supply an entire cloud 9 to every club in New York City.

Did he make you a boss.

He didn't think much of me. He liked me as a chez la femme.

Did you tie him up in the back seat?

Me? No, why would I do that; I worked for him.

How did he wind up dead?

No idea. He had some tail. Maybe you should find her.

We have you on film rolling him into the back tied up.

He had fits. The rope kept him from banging his head. Take a better look. He often went home tied.

He was dead.

No, he couldn't have been. Ask Mathew. He met him at the house every night.

Do you deny he was dead the night of the buses?

I didn't do him. Possible he just made a mistake on

his own.

No one believed that. He had border to contend with, not just his pride. They shot out to the Long Island Sound, a modern apartment on the peninsula; to Norma's where she had relocated from First. Norma was an older black lady, soft skin, green eyed, five foot ten, French barrette style wavy hair to her shoulders. Every man wanted a younger version.

Dilantin? James asked, after introductions.

Every needle. Had to keep my boy safe from biting or the girls wouldn't hold him, he'd get volatile.

Which girl had him that night?

Nora. She's my best with the elder men. She's a physician from Rochester.

She called for her. Nora was a svelte icy blond, long straight hair to her back, sybaritic in through the torso and hips with firm voluptuous breasts, wary dark eyes, a moodiness a man might fall for.

Yes, I gave him his shot. He was sweating through and through. He'd had a biscuit earlier. He was still flying, said his wife wouldn't allow him home until he was calmer. He was flushed, but after an hour could hold a conversation. I gave him a few shakes, a few kisses and we shared a knife of heroin; and then I rode in the elevator with him and let him soak me.

She said wisely, they never make it as teens without being adults first.

Did you put him into the car? This would be the night of the bus fire.

Sure, but he was all smiles.

Who tied him up?

Never did. I raised my dress, let him touch me one last time; even wondered what his wife did when she got him home. He was probably over-sexed, couldn't not have it, you know.

Who was driving?

Rennie from the Cotton Club.

They thanked her.

We're missing a stopover, Lyle remarked in vexation. Where do you suppose he went to; and why don't we have it on tape?

That's the final hour. Rennie's driving, so she's the liar. She must know where he gets tied up.

We better study the pictures again. Someone deletes off the film; or this occurs before he arrives to the club.

Is this before or after his shot? James asked.

Must be before the Dilantin, wouldn't you say? Maybe we are missing a few takes.

I'm going to say it occurs after he's booked. Sometime before dawn. So what would that give us?

A stop after Norma.

They called it a night.

James called it a complete waste.

3

They went through their notes.

Cham Machete was in his late seventies, dependent on Dilantin for grand mal seizures, a godfather in the spoon trade, manager of the waterfront clubs, Cotton Club, Savoy, Apollo, Connie's, and another four smaller lounges that specialized in nightclub jazz. He distributed spoon and its IV equivalent for ten a folded ebony paper. The night the buses burned, he had dropped into the Cotton Club to see his newest pussy cat dance the jungle revue. He had her drive him to his son's in Soho and stop at Norma's for treatment where she administered a shot of Dilantin before she sent for Nora who permitted him wet orgasms. That night he reported he had a lack of coordination in his fingers and limbs. When Rennie drove him home to Soho, Cham was tied up. His son Mathew hauled him out of the limousine.

Lyle's first question was, where did Cham go after he left his wife earlier that day. James felt he was missing out on some truth, a narrow existence of personal enlightenment, although he had his job and had Andy, he felt he lacked some infinitesimal reality, a space in time that was a lapse, that evaded him despite his thinking his way to it. This inability to grasp its essence to see exactly what lay at the perimeter haunted him, and he felt he had mislaid a significance that he took many times between his two fingers, a sort of breakthrough in a catechism of repeated acceptance of one's own bewilderments. Why had they looked past this very basic starting place. They came in somewhere in the middle, after the ugly, uncharitable fact of death.

The detective bureau had seen the crime in a more simplified fashion. A man was killed at his own club and driven to his ultimate death. His son had done the deed; a senator's henchman in another state had arranged it. One person had decided some people could not get to the subways for a week. There were truths and falsehoods and he didn't know how they stacked up. From anyone's point of view the release of six automobiles into the market for five hundred a piece plus financing of three hundred did exactly as was predicted.

He called for every photo possible on Cham to be able to assess where information failed them.

The stack of photos lay on his desk that Monday. There were over a hundred cam releases, most from the buses themselves, several from the train yards, a few from airplanes in flight over the Sound, one taken off a ferry docking in Ellis Island. By the time he lined them up, he may as well have had the man's daytime life, as well as type text. Pieced together, Cham had left his pretty wife that morning and she had called Warren's man who sent a female to collect him at the ferry and took him to Soho to the Midnight Club to inspect the newest shipment of IV speedball chase for the black upper class girls at the clubs.

Cham had approved distribution. He had injected twelve girls himself in the Apollo salon with weep, a sugar base of tar and a small amount of coke, before he injected himself with two underage girls and spent a few hours kissing and fondling them. He was left to sleep off the first chaser for an hour before he was awakened to go to the other clubs. He was at the Savoy for five gimmicks. By nine he had collected his first two grand. At the Cotton Club to watch the bottomless jungle dance troupe he took Rennie off stage to a dressing room where they made love and he hit her with two needles to her legs. She got him off but he elicited little response saying his wife kept him on a leash. When he got in her car, he was unrestrained and talking.

So the other photo of him tied up had come later. Rennie took him to Connie's and waited in the car; then it was back to the Cotton Club where he sat through a burlesque for forty minutes. Toward eleven he complained of numbness and went in search of Molly who put him in a Cad and tied him up and paid Rennie to drive him to Norma's.

The death of the maestro was big news.

The cheese was in the trap, and the new foundation of loans was getting written for a jazz era of upholstered cars. Springfield came out smelling like a rose.

The trouble with the loaded syringe was soon to fade into the night along with a torch of yellow and green cancelled checks spent for illegal medicinal supplies.

The cops went after every fallacy they could.

They had sixty cops walking the streets at once.

The first tip was the antique gold Brentwood stopped on the Brooklyn Bridge with a quarter ton of dish in its trunk, like some grass heathen chose to walk the poor line rather than be caught for trafficking heroin to the god spell of black beauties wired to a fix.

No Machete would ever concede he sent girls to their dreams.

Nor would he fess that he had offices burned for proof they pedaled product.

I said, Mama, go back to sleep.

Oh, big boy, come git yer medicine.

I ain't tired, Sugar. Don't wait up, you hear? You got too many girls you're spooning to.

Mama, I done put you in silks; don't give me no grief. You hear me, Lucille?

My daddy's unhappy with you, Big Boss.

Don't you complain to your daddy, neither, darlin'. No man's goin' to put up with yer balling yer eyes out.

She had had him followed by an ace of deuce.

He was proven untrue in about fifty photos.

She gave it to him one last time.

Those harpies ain't your needle, husband. Least you can do is come to our bed.

'I hear you knocking but you can't come in,' was the lonely caution in all the south side clubs. Machete didn't take the warning.

His wife was his business.

If he thought her too old to please, that was his business too.

He was making time, selling more bum than anyone thought could be had; and he left most of the dough for her, usually it was a grand a week.

He was taking in a grand a night, and nothing was going to stop him.

'Oooh, pusher man, can I see your wares.'

The winter pulsed, and Machete was humping three broads a night, pumping a full catch into their veins while getting his promises shaken in ecstasy like a horn sounding on a tug as the ferry pulled firm from the wharf.

On the night in question his wife dressed in sapphire

silk and hair spun up in webs of lace came to fetch her husband and found him in the wicked arms of a jungle spirit, each drunk in a fine ardor, the band waiting for the girl's entrance onto a stage of crimson and blue, Lucille bashed her husband and his whore until they lay stone cold and bloodied and strode out saying she would shut the place down and turn it into a band and drinks, no more hustle or drug.

He had stayed home a month earlier and kept her the entire weekend to reassure her.

She had dressed in a garter and stockings and heels and nothing else, a chest of perfect breasts, thinnest rib cage on any female in her fifties, weary lines on her face due to the weep; she consoled him with purrs and tongue in his ear, rendering him buzzed hard so that he came the entire weekend. She was certain she had him under her control.

'No one but you,' he was heard to slobber in the night. 'No one like you, doll.' He was affiliated to the stupor of a bad drug, and he went where the drug might do its worst.

'Baby, kill me with your dreams,' she could be heard from their bedroom. 'Rock me to hell, Big Boss; tell me I'll always be yours.'

No one doubted she had a thing for him, or he for her.

'Isn't this what your daddy is for,' he'd coax her. 'Don't you want jus' me?'

And all night long the two would be wheedling and cajoling each other.

Lucille would pant long and hard, and Machete would sound as though he were sneering, 'C'mon, honey, your love truck is waiting. Don't make me wait too long.'

'Honey, fix your angel another.'

And they would go on and on all night long, until he awakened and had to get to the bars to pick up the wad.

She crashed on him one night and dragged him into the john for a fix.

Through the door her voice could be heard, 'Oooh, love, don't let me down,' and his husky response, 'Darlin', it's anything you want.'

A maid said he was abusive. He often stayed away for nights and when he returned, usually drunk and unmanageable, he awakened her to slap her hard on the face, uttering, 'You bitch, one day I'm going to walk through them doors and teach you a lesson for saying no to me.'

'I can't keep up with you,' she'd sob and he would soften a bit.

'I can't wait on you, Mama,' he'd say. 'It's not fair.'

'Oh, Boss, don't leave.' She'd be tears and pleas, urging him to her, saying, 'Boss, I'm the only girl who can fix you good.'

It was not to James' liking, this go round, but clear as day Lucille Machete bought her husband's death.

The question was, was it over jealousy; over his playing around. A man who couldn't keep his pants on didn't keep his truth. Of course who was going to contradict him. Who was there who could take away his trade. The casino doctors weren't up for it; they had actual private practices to run, not to mention surgery by the hour three nights a month at general hospital, abortions, mania medication, heroin induced ataxia and lethargy; methadone treatment. How many nights did she learn he was wagging his tail instead of going through the books. There was just her one telephone call to Geonnard, not really enough to prove intent or motive; The photos while suggestive did not prove. At the moment the mayor was good for accidental death and signed the insurance to the wife.

They left the precinct and headed out to talk to the son. The son Bernard resided in a penthouse in Soho in view of the bus yard. It was all glass like a restaurant with an upper loft and interior silver and tan carpeted stairwell that led to a long living room furnished with two black sofas each with a tan stripe and two chairs and a stereo. He resembled his dad in the bones, his face was gaunt, thin hair in a page boy that gave him a young fresh look despite white streaks at his temples. Dad fooled around some but it was no big deal.

Mom's a weeper. She's never been straight. I'm the parent for both of them.

You put your dad in the bus the night of the fire.

Often did. Best place for him. The safest with what he'd go through but he had to be tied up so he didn't thrash and swallow his tongue.

Why not keep him at home.

He'd get loose, or he'd break everything.

Who came up with the bus idea.

A bus driver, it was the end of the line.

Why do you think your mother asked Geonnard to arrange his funeral.

She'd have no reason to. Are you sure she actually said that.

Lyle answered. As sure as we are standing here talking to you.

James asked, Could your dad have been going broke. Maybe the weep kept the clubs going.

You are on a fishing expedition is my guess.

It wouldn't be my guess, said Lyle, with condescension.

Do you have her on the trim.

We have her and a handful of dust on the gramophone.

Which are you questioning didn't pay for itself; the meat or the booze, Bernie inquired, exhibiting all the patience in the world who presumably didn't know a thing.

Once they were back at the precinct, they found at their desks tapes of conversations of Machete.

The first tape contained a call that had an odd echo to it as though made from a distance.

The son was talking. I haven't got anyone to work the warehouse. My man reported in ill.

Okay, then I'll have to send someone down. Good bye.

It was an odd occurrence in light of the tragic event that occurred that same night.

Well, what does that mean? Lyle asked. The old man was still alive. Which is the warehouse?

It's on First and Front. It contains the coal bin for the lounges in Soho.

So maybe you wanted to ascertain the old man is on site.

I wouldn't need to. I knew where he was.

Why didn't you go back for him?

I tried. Wind had gotten the flames by then. The fire crew had just arrived. It was out of my hands.

The yard supervisor had no knowledge about the arrangement. He felt sorry for the old guy who he was certain felt his grief. The old guy was plenty busy making sure his kitchens were adequately supplied.

Did he have any ideas as to how the man died there.

No, he didn't. The doors and windows flapped open in a fire or underwater, no way for someone to get trapped.

I'll show you the photo. He's on the floor.

I can't explain it. Maybe the old man was knocked up and had a cerebral concussion.

Where were the guards?

A temporary was on duty.

Looks to me like you assisted by giving them the night off.

What bothered him was being called a liar. He was too old for this to pose a living problem, but it still got his wind up. He'd never really got past it, stupid comments; it was just more grist from the mill.

The yard man asked, Who pulled the man out?

The fire department, far as I know.

Wonder why the son didn't if he put him there?

It was a decent question. Anyone having to analyze the situation would ask it. Where did time and life leave off; did anyone see the signs in an advancing maelstrom and start questioning the probable outcome. There was a rumor floating about that the industry put a hit on the son first for taking a police bribe on the dozens; on bilking the johns for accounts for crazy girls high on the big stakes. For a while the belief was credible. Then the terrors lit like a match. Always the son was seen standing out there after two on the wharf in mist waiting for the dust boat. Once when the sheriff association went out fishing, when they returned at four, a man's body had been discovered tangled up in the rough nets bobbing in the low tide. It took the fourteen New York precincts two years to realize Bernie had become a dangerous element. Lucille tried to shut the door in their faces to which they kicked the door in, cuffed her and marched her out to the van and rode her downtown and booked her on murder in the first. In the booking office she stood five seven and looked haggard like a scare crow, a scar face in a scowl, wild hair ends dipped blond. During the mug shot she fell on her side onto the floor. She placed a call to her son who sent a white aged lawyer within the hour. In the distance the EE train had pulled onto the upper rail station howling like a shrieking meme. A flood of people got off and descended, choking the street intersections. There wouldn't be another cross town train for three hours. They had her on five arsons in prima face in Harlem, each drug spoon identified. She was going down for the fourth time in ten years for hard labor.

During her trial the deli and dress store managers across the street saw a car toss out a few wine bottles before the windows caught on fire in a blaze. Her stores in downtown corner on 165th Street in West Jamaica and two in Jamaica Queens under the El; a long distance from stylish Kew Gardens or Queen's Close, older brick and cement edifices at stations on the sound looking at the Manhattan skyline; an island escape for a pair of head jammers. From across the street no one could see a damn thing either. The hoods had masks and they didn't get out of the car. The pharmacy didn't catch the act; neither did the furniture mart, their managers sat at the back or upstairs. The fire bombed places were consumed in less than an hour. It wasn't she had her own stores burned and didn't carry insurance; That wasn't the point.

The fires were just too big to not endanger public safety.

I can't burn an entire city to the durst.

In rebuttal, the prosecutor asked,

Do you consider yourself to have a fast throwing arm.

Fairly good.

Have you ever played pitcher mound.

Yes.
How fast is your pitch.
Six miles per hour.
Is that considered a swift fly.
Very.
Are you in the backseat of this car.
She did not reply.
The camera caught your hand. Is that your tattoo, a skull and heart. He pulled her hand to expose her tattoo.
Did you fly the bottle at your building.
Again she had no answer.
What was stored in your warehouses.
Nothing.
Isn't it true you had cancelled checks for six clubs. Isn't it true the clubs were going bankrupt.
We were fine; doesn't take much to keep a bar.
Did you think your husband was an intelligent man.
Usually. Most men aren't though.
Do you think your husband thought you were neglected.
He wasn't around much. He two-timed me.
Was he addicted?
That was our life.
Was he an addict when you first met him?
He was my pusher.
Did he ever withhold drugs from you?
No. He always supplied me.
Did he ever establish an alibi for you?
He might have.
Did he threaten to bring home a permanent mistress?
Never. When he was home, he was all mine.
How often did he come home?
Five days a week.
Did he ask you to check on his warehouses?

He asked me to show the accountants the books.
How were you able to do that?
I had the keys.
Did your husband keep files?
Yes, for each business he had about fifty filing cabinets. For Cotton he had over eighty.
Why do you think he trusted you?
He was married to me.
Did you ever cheat behind his back?
No, I was only for him.
Did you at any time buy your husband Cham's death?
No, of course not.

In hours to come, during a court recess of four hours, James and Lyle left to confirm a piece of information.

Since testimony was not permitted to be investigated, all lines of inquiry having already been advanced to the judge before the disposition began and approved, they had to confine themselves to case legitimacy to meet with a secured witness. In the opening summation, counsel promised to establish before god and all its presumptive evidence as to every count to prove murder in the second degree.

At two the trial reconvened.
What do you do for a living.
I am the bartender for The Salty Lime in Soho.
Did you have occasion to wait on Lucille Machete and Ronald Harmaaz.
Once. That would be October last year.
How did you know who they were?
I carded them.
What did they order?
Two whiskeys neat.
Did you overhear their conversation?
Yes. He said he could handle the job, and she asked

what he would do. He said he would use a crippling agent as part of a blast-up. He had a man who was efficient. She laid a wad of dough on him; it was a tight pack, maybe a few hundred g's. Then she left.

How did she appear when she left?

She was tottering in spiked high heels. She could barely stand up.

Call your next witness, the judge instructed peering over his podium.

Mathew Clarkson, counsel requested.

Mathew Clarkson, the bailiff yelled.

A man was brought in by a federal special agent.

The Manhattan Fire Chief Mathew Clarkson was sworn in.

The Defense lawyer approached the witness.

Are you physician competent?

Yes, I am a coroner.

Is it possible for a person to walk with a bullet in their brain?

It is. We've seen this occurrence many times.

Would a person crippled be able to flee a blazing arson?

They should.

What if they were in restraints?

They still could. It's almost unheard of to get actual human remains.

Can you offer a deduction as to why the vic did not leave the moment the first whoosh of blaze is perceived?

He may have been given a drug that seriously impeded movement.

For what length of time would this type of fire burn before it became charcoal black?

Maybe all night. At least three hours.

Under these circumstances, would a person be likely

to try to flee?

Yes. Chances are they would flee even if it meant significant risk to their body.

They had Bobby Shore in the pen for strangulations and Lucille Machete going down for husband killing. They turned their sights on Bernard Machete for sticking his dad in the straight jacket. It was really insignificant that he worked the south side of the Hudson when he had the control over the bad drugs wheeling their way into the two Harlem towns and into poor Spanish black Jamaica. He had started in furniture; he had repossessed, sold and set up dozens of retail outlets in that part of New York that kept a watchful eye over stoned cold addicts. By the day he was fifty he knew every trick that turned a lunch. As far as the cops were concerned he swindled for a mob in another state seeking to produce a rich federacy for a handful of senators who could keep out the interference from their nightclubs. The world was full of deception. The creation of a drug life existed on trickery and dishonesty by necessity of being illegal. James wasn't the first police officer to encounter it on the rag. Cop duty to the hotels involved pulling up to the door and if there were no inebriates there driving through back to the street. The portico of the Soho grand hotel lobbies at the entrances to the elegant five story stage coach apartments that lined the avenue of leafy park side grace contained galleries of imitation art better than the masters themselves, on ensconced walls vivid paintings, abstracts of streets, reds and blacks of slab color fixed onto light green and white stills of sunlight. The famed Washington Square came alive with decorous front columns and fire escapes, iron balconies and ledges, where downstairs off three street stairs one entered embellished halls near the park beneath lamplight, thin Parisians and Dutch men feeding the mallards. This was the vogue guard of the fabric industry from the French West Indies to await two ships a year leaving Miami port bound for five countries to sell trousers, silk vests and low cut strapless dress gowns, gloves and shoes, sequined harlequin jackets, all accessories of the haberdashery. Neo-classical buildings with arched sash windows, twelve across, dark colors on light, green on yellow, grey on blue, rust on pink, black on white; five facades by a tenth block; eight floors; a gentleman's comfort, three apartments per floor, four rooms each, sixteen by forty, large kitchen, sitting room, bath and bedroom; gentrified semi-industrial offices, black frame long windows on red block or brick, taxis pulled up to the curb; two restaurants, two art studios each block, here and there a dress shop; gallery openings, cocktails of champagne in long stemmed glasses with blue oysters on the half shell, a white tablecloth on four tables with baked lasagna, rolled catalane, spiked brie and caviar, dumplings and pork bow, a scourge of desserts, cheesecakes, crumble cakes, custards, zabaglione, trifle, parfaits and demitasse espresso coffees. Men in trousers and bare chest bows and jackets and women in halter tops and long see through skirts and heels, hair swept up off the nape, gold strands of necklaces. Fashion in the extraordinary, silks and crepe and naked seduction.

 Jazz and wailing discordant chippies; ballroom floor shows under soft blue lights, Rumba, twist, dance train, fox trot, tango and salsa; horns blaring and drums rolling, and clashing cymbals; lively energetic public amidst city street sounds, cars honking, Times Square clock chimes.

J. Lea Koretsky

The 460 block was an elegance of affordability with arcade thin buildings, French deco, era Grecian Corinthian, linear tile roof and rows of arched windows, blue, brown, red; third floor being the best, better than Hollis would be, gents in long trousers and top hats, Irish shillelagh walking sticks. The bay waking waves breezing about with birds flocking to the sound, sticks of old docks churning up, boats at rest, small children playing on the sand, hava nagila in dance halls and Berundt wedding dances in churches. James favored the older bell tower in Jamaica of Little Corner. At home the pilaster bronze entry, a room that looked out to the deck; always the sand piled up and blew to sea, a glass of tea on the glass marble tan dijun with saucer and book of verse of Mathers. Andy lay on a lounge recliner asleep in the sun, a lazy wind rippling her dark blue crepe chenille and blue box pleat skirt, dinner having been at US Dept of Gold, Chinatown, shrimp peas, German bows, swordfish and a bell captain soup; they had gone with his cousins who had come in on the Pimlico train which stopped in Cincinnati having descended from western Baltimore, parasols and long gowns arriving to the station plank in daylight; colors weaving in a rush of wind; every couple Virginia born and educated, fox stole and leather carrying purse indicative of basic elegant dress boutique.

 Andy awoke to James rummaging through a box of files and setting them up in the sitting room on his table stacking the interviews on one side and the evidence on the other.

 What do the interviews show?

 Nothing as yet. I am waiting on the car victim in Springfield.

 What for, honey?

Ohio sent in an investigator on the bus fire. He was beat up in Jamaica by an alleged handler and left for dead and driven to Springfield and placed inside a car he had never driven botched to the nines.

Who wanted the bus?

Baby, I can't guess. It's just a bad crime.

Whose fingerprints were found on his clothing and body?

Only Porgy.

The money man?

For the warehouses, correct.

Where does your photo stack come from?

The bloom takes on one bus parked in Chinatown near the park. It's a gigantic fire.

A bunch of chauvinistic shits, Andy remarked. What did they want?

The ragweed, no doubt.

It's all due to drugs? That's a rumor. She came inside and sat on his lap.

We don't have motivation yet, but we suspect the manager is moving inventory.

You work too hard, James, she said and tousled his head.

He unbuttoned her blouse and slipped her brassiere down.

Oh, James, you leave me breathless. Do enthrall me.

He brought his arms around her back and bent her forward as she positioned her legs around his thighs. You are my wet dream, honey.

I adore you, James. There is no one like you at anything. She clung to him, her sole possession in life.

Help me, sweetheart, what am I overlooking? He whispered, his precious soul hard with excitement.

She replied, drunk from the sunshine, Nothing,

dearest. It's an ugly crime, the original murders at the arson den Capitol Expressway theatre. Probably all were witnesses.

Guilty witnesses make for speculative indulgences.

Don't forget, the entire state was watching. The buses had cameras under the new state protection laws.

Why does Porger butcher a man in cold blood in broad daylight?

I heard the victim made a pass at his wife.

Does that sound like a reason for murder to you?

Well, then, what's the slaying about? Not about love. The slain is male. He was a frolic.

But who was he; we still can't make that absolute recognition. We still can't obtain a photo. He kissed her on the neck in the depths of his mortal interior for all time known to his lifetime, all thermostats rising sequestered. Oh, Jesus, I can't comprehend what you put me through.

Only you, James. You possess me to my very bones. You must have the evidence by now.

It doesn't add up. It was practically around the corner on 135th and Seventh in the late afternoon.

She quickened. I love you, James. I am breathless, Jamie.

He was a man who stole a prison key that allowed him to open prison bars while on the Inside. An evil man as far as anyone is concerned.

She was breathless. But who was he, another Francois Ruby?

The photos do not allow him to be seen.

Was the victim a pope?

Oh, heavens, not the arch bishop. Who in their right mind would constellate to the worlds?

What could have been the purpose of a killing like that? What would the man have attended to?

We don't expect to know that until we have his identification, sweetheart.

Did either man work refuse or garbage?

James brought her into his embrace, holding her. Life isn't that easy. Even the man who was dispatched from Code Index was completely butchered left strangled in his new all brown and pink Chevrolet.

How did the two men know each other? Were they related?

The Captain doesn't think so. It's simply a murder in little Jamaica on 139th Street, Brooklyn.

But over what sort of situation? It's too limp to even formulate a Supreme Court case.

Nothing inside the hospital. Tropics only; cancers.

Due to a crime?

The killing of doctors.

Perhaps this was an argument between a government and the Latin church of Roman sequestered popes.

The victim was the tax collector for the warehouses,

The seagulls flew off the sound, a flurry of wings in a mad storm. Across the water Manhattan was rising amidst her flat existence in tall flanks of glass and steel, her Capricorn high rise sought to dominate over a domicile church which kept to a single hospital and several soup kitchens on the upper East First Avenue. The ledger belonging to Jack Ruby, parlance of ragweed, who was soon to bring in serpentine at $10 per bark, had been sponsoring the rich man's dope rag a buzz drug for white chintz girls dating accountants including to people who weren't guilty yet of crime. The ledger read the off-shore telephone number for the pusher man, a tallish minister capable of saving the masses who arranged for hospital admissions to receive drugs legally. Only the Dominican Republic under youthful John Franklin

Kennedy oversaw the government of Manhattan for last vows and medicines under all laws.

Lyle sipped a whiskey pint with eggs and sausage. In bed lay the camera act, a brown flamingo dancer, all arms, from Steadman who danced the clubs on alternate weekends between hollering Ella Fitzgerald and Keeper Grasshopper, stepping Sammy Davis, king of tap. Lyle lay in bed waking in summer at eleven o'clock parlor time, the savage ballet in his arms, ready to start a new day looking the beat over for the illustrious drugs getting sold at the clubs. No one paid much attention that he was two-timing the leggy Bawana Mitchee for the drug cozen, Mama Marmalade. He had been assigned the connection between them.

The bus fire took off so fast it burned off half a man's body before anyone could get the man off. Who did this sort of work? Race as in color of skin wasn't an issue. Many port officers were darks sent to the Soho to evaluate goods for museum and gain; farmers who tilled the South along the Carolinas who died were trans-disposed to New York bench across from Manhattan, numerous physicians were brown who staffed the wards; it was the senator accountant all eyes focused upon. Population was ten to one cops who staffed prisons, hospitals, and museum plazas; monitored for false IDs and substance consumption, tampering of bond notes; abandoned private property; lost property, vehicle throwing substance, and missing runaway teens.

4

Lyle and James took coffee at the Soho Café in the park on 2nd.

He knew he had the four youths but they vanished at night into the dunes on the peninsula. He figured they rode a subway out of state.

The photos were about a year coming in and then a first run was five.

James said they could have boarded a ship by then out of Miami.

Lyle replied they weren't likely to drive; there were dragnets everywhere on all main roads.

Many a band went down to find them.

On dusty roads, little one room bars where the vodka tasted like dry soap, to garden hole cabins on a bayou, all the way toward the keys to rooms with a ceiling fan and porcelain tub.

The gods who descended were richly muddy rainstorms that poured into swamps of crimson crocus, mauve dahlia and umber thistle.

They found abandoned cars to sleep in, coffee plantation houses, seedy bars gone to let, soft pastures on the road on the way to Savanah in birch forests where measuring a stand paid a dollar a day.

Lyle might often say only the everglades ever hid a man from the posses searching for him.

He finally ran a cross for each name based upon first entry into the country.

There stood an appropriations of history, no name known to another but tallied up as though it stood the grace of time, only posted by a parish of forgotten wayward presumptions.

This little known diversion presumed by adoption mills was condemned by anyone having papers who was put to a test of stolen properties.

Who writes about New York who is from Springfield, Lyle asked. Not that life is so different, but Springfield has the bishopric senators whose task it is to compile anti-cop groupings of crime in the first degree.

James nodded. Illinois sends out the aides to review the murders and to look at the mission hospital depressed who view the crimes from a sorry staircase step.

Springfield, Illinois to Indianapolis, Indiana to Columbus, Ohio to Pittsburgh, Pennsylvania to New York, a straight line of fortification through five states, what was the sorry point? Except they shared a railroad and a series of rail yards.

Iris and carnation, state flowers; for Springfield.

They moved downtown to a bistro where they sat at the back of a dim lit lounge having ordered a side of garlic bread and minestrone.

What caused the assault, Lyle asked James.

I think it was the nearness of the precinct.

Were they recent releases.

No, these were thugs.

Oh the mob.

Do we have warrants on file.

Not yet. We are still looking at the bus camera stills.

What do they reveal?

Jack Fortune assaulting a priest in Jamaica. He gutted him fish style in the gut.

Any of the same disposition on the dead theater? James asked.

None so far.

I thought we got a fire there first.

We did, man was sentenced to Stag 1 at Cape Fear. The theatre was rebuilt and Fortune supplied the chairs, typical upholstered seats.

So maybe he bagged the audience. Could he have done Front Street?

He only seems to kill. We want him on the Ohio killing of the congressional aide. He really roughed him up.

Do we know why.

There's some speculation the aide had Fortune investigated.

What brings people to dead theatre.

Free spoon. Illegal street mixture that cripples.

Heroin.

Much of it.

Do physicians inject?

No, of course not. Some are doctors who have mistreated surgeries in unnecessary treatment too great to be overlooked. Lyle said.

So what are we left with?

It's a war between illegal drug use and legal hospital-approved ventilation.

I suppose it's an odd turn of phrase.

The reality is not to be overlooked. Dead people in cellophane bags is an abomination as much as is people knifed in their homes simply on account of being cops in areas that overbill for residence.

It's a war favored by home builders, an attempt to take over in unscrupulous methods. What could have started it? James remarked.

A war on living. I don't know how to fix it.

No one does; so many willing street bombers is inconceivable the only goal were men hired by the one Jack Fortune to come ashore from warden-controlled bilious turnpikes to release hoards of water into cities to offset building crime.

A terror of narcissist irregularities from Springfield to Newark, a straight line on a map cutting through five industrial cities. Lyle lit a cigarette.

Unchain my heart, you worry me night and day, let me go, I am like a man in a trance, please set me free.

It's a tune meant only for the damned in love. It's scarcely the point.

Leave on the light, he sang quoting the Joe Cocker, you can leave your hat on; bend down and touch my love light; you don't know what love is.

Lyle and James departed at the corner under the street light; Lyle waved down a taxi and gave instructions for `142nd Street and sat back to enjoy the ride up Broadway into Spanish Harlem. The Spanish blacks were the worst to control, usually they were training for the boxing mat or a sprinter's team. Brownstones flashed by, an old stepping jazz man sat on a front porch passing the time.

The real problem for the dead theater was their main suspect was hidden in a crowd behind other people thereby making prints impossible, and when solitary he was wearing thick garden gloves. Lyle'd have to go through metro to obtain photos of the man by himself dressing which could take a month to a year, the city was so backlogged as to requests.

5

The newly awakened prison population of lesbian, gay, bisexual, transvestite in the Greenwich village of abandoned factories formerly known as Washington Square ran a perpendicular from Macy's on Thirty-Fourth down to Fourteenth and fronted five courthouses, their noble iconic columns, broad stairs and circular maidenheads of marble floors and amphitheater Doric library halls. In the midst of twelve public parks, a galleria filled with statuary of naiads and nymphs overlooking a pond and dozens of spice, thyme, rosemary, dill, sage and oregano, lay the eastern equivalency of the Hyde Park and ivy adorned outdoor theatres and its pink-orange and green mansions. Girls in sequined dresses played in the fountain of the arcade amidst a populous of NYC art students. Howl and Naked Lunch starred the new Beat generation featuring Allen Ginsberg, Herbert Huncke, a small time drug pusher addict, Lucien Carr, Gary Snyder and Jack Kerouac. The radio music city hall opened with its winter ice rink to the tunes of woeful Soul Train. Blocks away the museums showed new themes on art among them a new world class American artists, Carl Holty, Ansel Adams,

Francis Criss, Beauford Delaney, Esther Rose, Lee Gatch, Richard Lindner, Maxine Albro, mosaic; Mark Rothko, Charles Alston and Karl Zerbe, to name a few.

The day lay tired, a mild sixty-nine, somewhat chilly, sky clouded, an ambush worth of media and news reporters gathered in front of the gold glass turning doors, microphones held out to lawyers trying the case on calendar, a spook of white sedans lined up at the curb, onlookers busting to break loose past the police line and yellow tape. James waited in a Charleston Amery car reviewing his notes on summation, dressed ornately in light blue ruffles and bib and all white tier, Mock tans, his hair curled for the win. The query was simple, unavoidable actually, had the Warren aide from Ohio been seen downtown talking to bartenders on Front about the attempted murder of a warehouse accountant over the theater slayings? James tracked down forty-one interviews, most of them conducted on the premises of the Harlem Night Beat, Cotton Club, Savoy and the Capitol.

An expansionist plan pursued by a New York mafia gave opportunity to a host of properties set at bay of a handful of ocean prime rock bays, each more luxurious than the next.

Life was running lucrative in its escape from sandy shores seeking to outlast a conquest of trade crop insignias, among them oil, fish and parcel estate stone. While New York was drying up for her hidden presumptive of released prison lifestyles, and each precinct losing to its shell beaches over twenty years, nameless forests were plundered for sudden wealth to actors and middle eastern oil conglomerates yearly. Once a private unexplored beach in the islands, the benefit of embargo unofficiated princes kept to a high executive estate paid for out of secret funds by a corrupt government in the Carolinas.

In California the offshore oil rigs were Irene, Hidalgo, Harvest and Hermosa, a wake's worth from Heritage and below boom at Millhouse and Harmony, where every signal turn brought in the same harmony on the rig ladders. The world was trading on coastlines for oil which outran its spend thrift every few years, helmet on or quake side up, like any beach where the boom took to sea faster than its yield. In less than a generation the pull had climbed a shore and the sturdiest oil was running the boom to spill a sturdy harvest worth four years before it began again.

Hired as a conduct administrator for the State in its pursuit of what happened in the slaying of a youth under age 27, James was assigned for affiliated recriminations.

James would vehemently disagree on the sore subject of oil fruition saying that between Cape Wandry off the Carolinas and California's seasonal coast there was enough oil exploration to shark an old girl to her fevers. It therefore proved a bale commodity that the Asilomar tide pools came rich with microbes which lent ocean shale with a wealth of oil bearing plankton. When he stood before the New York State Supreme Court to answer the questions of the nine justices, he delivered the best of his presumptions.

How often is citrine used to pump up an oil platform on the ocean?

Twice a year, regular. A plant has to offset hard amber so that it can squeeze out impurities of rock and pebble during a nitrous cycle he explained.

What other chemicals are typically utilized?

Orange is very popular. An industrial third of any mixture combines orange to its weave.

How much is referred to as gold?

Gold restores to green and isn't used unless your plant depletes. Depletion requires a strong column so as to establish a fortified beat.

A beat being what?

There are several depending upon ocean depth. The more common in a bay is a beat block; the best for an ocean depth of fifty feet to drayage is a beat generation.

Can you describe beat?

Sure, it's said about the rig and a gusher. Down it goes, and up it comes. There's twenty-five lights on the east coast and almost forty on the west. Oil makes your life; it alone produces household heat.

So how do we get John Fortune?

In Congress social circles he is known as the hammer jack on the ruby that turns the stone prior to a gusher shooting skyward by upward of three hundred feet for cubic controllable plankton space.

What do you suppose became a consternation?

Well, it could have been a driver.

This being a mechanical part?

Yes. The driver controls the amount of chemical laid in shale.

Why does Jack become obsessed with a warehouse accountant? We are led to believe it is over an evil drug called ragweed.

The facts may be similar. The chemical when used on crazy quill in miniscule drops make an extremely potent wreckage.

In other words, we are looking at a costly commodity?

The clubs will say so. An ounce of wink is worth a junk of spray.

So, he continued, confidant he had the collective ear of the entire courtroom, might we agree the attempted murder of a dinner church priest was to relieve a warehouse group of bangles?

I don't know I would go that far. Ohio has often been at war with New Jersey and New York over their commodity stockpile. These two coastal states have consistently demonstrated an ability to combine these chemicals for industrial warehousing. Together they can produce a suffering of ocean distilleries that give each rig drill a beat to clear a complete generation on a dime.

Would you say these few acts of violence stem from the need for the automobile?

Well, that does suggest itself as the controlling association.

Where is the commodity evaluated for effective discharge?

Primarily on the Charles River that overflows regardless of nature and humankind. Its banks of knobby hills steadily give way to an encroaching waterway of winter rains.

What did you see on the night of the bus fire?

A small light ignited and then fumes of dark clouds spewed skyward filling the air hours before actual flames leapt upward.

Is that typical of the chemical in question?

No, only of a condenser. It burns on land only.

Not underwater.

No, it's not a sea anchor.

Whose vehicle?

It was a Plymouth Dodge, brown, identified as Tres Falagher, Dutch sailor recently released from Stag 5. He had done hard time for shipping light off the coast.

What is light?

Straight arrow. It is a flying rampart.

Is it a weapon?

No, it is not a dart. It acts like one though. It showers mercury like a ballistic.

Off a ship?

Yes. The ship sits at a distance of two kilometers. The effect is to fry a coastline.

Do you know what initiated this realm of terror?

It is rumored Tres was sought for dead theater at Front.

The cost of incidentals had gone way up; a bottle of booze was twenty and a box of fags ten. The costs in Manhattan had risen, each morning on the way into work there was a suicide as though a refresher course in severe anxiety how to make it combined with no space available. The times were taking a nasty turnabout. Despondency left marks in alcoholism and rag dysfunction.

James would say there was a derived benefit to the nine state hospitals and fourteen pens although so much devouring violence produced a society of roughnecks. A thorough chemical manufacture analyst of ten special licenses, among them dysplasia due to contact of ice in environmental fault shifts, reduction speed burns and scars from handling isotopes, brain wave vision loss caused by sea digression after moment, and scattered hearing provided the court with expertise on beat hoops.

Can you explain beat as it pertains to a generation?

There are typically four set off in a half day. This is done at a quarter mile to sea off a platform after which the drill lowers and the cartridge fills up with oil.

It sounds quite dangerous.

It often is. Six men work a rig. Once the clams are shot and blinking emits across the sky, the pressure that yanks the tug is serious enough to maim if not outright kill in the resulting hurl. That's why these rig men are known as the hurly gurly at the spook wheel. They usually leave the platform while the hoop blast is on a run.

How many platforms exist on the east coast?

Twenty on each coast, nine in the gulf.

An hour later by the time he made it home to Andy, the wind was up tearing over the land in a common dragnet as it pulled sand in long drifts to sea.

Andy was barefoot in the kitchen whipping a stiff parfait for a crab cake casserole. She had teased her hair to perfection. She wore a chenille with large sunflowers on a pastel blue background.

How was the old bailey, she asked turning her face for a kiss.

How is my girl, he queried.

I slept all day in the sun. You have a call.

Good. Smells delicious; what time will dinner be ready?

Seven.

I'll wash up.

Don't forget your call.

When he next came in, the table was set with a salad and meat dish. Lyle has found the theater; it's run by a janitor of all people.

Just doing his job.

Something like that. The spray is scheduled.

How are people there?

That is the mystery. They seem to enter about two for a late late show and rag.

What do you make of it?

I think it's a drug scam for youth.

Who are they, Jamie?

Tall, dark haired, twenties, non criminal. Someone's

workforce, possibly. Crayfish.

Fish that come in with the oil.

Oh, big time. They come up in parts. Boat loads, so many they clog the drills.

Are they sold?

Absolutely, predominantly in Louisiana. Well, that may put a whole other dimension on it.

They ate silently for several moments eating the entire meal finally settling to an after dining port sherry and berry trifle composed of custard flan, cherry Jell, a pint of rum and lady fingers in layers.

Who wanted these men, do you suppose? She asked.

Same assailant apparently.

They sipped, each thinking over the matter.

Andy said, what country is this thug from?

New archipelago. Lyle thinks he began as a pirate on the cruel seas.

Really? A smuggler?

Did I say that? I meant a buccaneer.

Oh, inexcusable.

I agree.

She is his only love. He has not ever even wondered what another woman would be like.

He never tired of her voice; it is soft, a tat husky, invitingly allure. When she twinkled at him, a radiant smile, he brimmed in pride, glowed to his root, could feel the fresh sensation of arousal claim him, and he told himself this is sweet love, even after thirty years. Nothing else mattered, only to be consumed in his loins.

She was suddenly aware. What is it, James, she asked queerly meaning to inflame him for she had never yet failed to draw him out. Are you still pondering, dearest?

He'd be mundane if not for her. Just a man.

Where does the theater case spring from?

It's audacious, outrageous, utterly without discernment. Do you want me, And?

I'm ready, sweetheart.

How many times have they sat side by side, books on their laps in bed, daylight slanting in through the slats. Too many times, it seems continuous. Shoulders touching. He has a scent of her. Chanel No. 9. It makes him drowsy with emotion, desire and possession. He decides he will never be absent; she has a right to keep him, and he kisses her ear, her nape. Always a love dialog before sleep; he promises her that much. So he can fall to her. In her embrace he is safe, nothing can intrude, it's just them and timeless love. Love is the immortal value. In the sacred act of love, idolatry and solitude are preserved. In the act of love making, he whispers to himself, oh, Andy, I am yours for eternity. Love me, love me in every act, I am your humble affection.

And she answers in response, take all of me, my love, in every facet of my soul.

This was a social system of deep-seated emotional blackmail. Each un-favorite act was looked upon as an undesired adjudicated outcome. The terms drifting about were accuser, ajudi-sitter and smolker, all which defined the mechanics of short range target projectiles. The floods were coming in, each successive wave burrowed through tunnels and drenched sand. In the nice and cool room that overlooked the canal, where her artwork was stacked, Andy pondered the too real problem of the attack on 139th Street, Bronx. She was critical of having slid into an over-do it syndrome and felt consumed by having eaten too much food. She had left the fire on in the hearth despite the heat of day and crawled to bed too tired to think feeling life had abandoned her and the winds too strong to bear out on the deck. The one thought that struck her was a large group of ex-inmates had conspired against the sheriff and city police in a rage of impudence, left over from a crime against the mid-Atlantic which no one could prove substantially. The warehouses either contained mud or fire and although no one knew which the state dockets showed merely repeated arsons. The subject made her perpetually tired. All around James, homes were admitting any number of men whose work lent them special advantage into the throttle of nursing homes, an entirely modern phenomena.

She fell asleep in the strength of the sunlight. Today was Monday when all day the river sky burst with shooting stars on the opposite cracked mud flats. She would tell herself even James was exhausted with the shock of the type of death, a morose ingredient of treachery, affidavit clerks from the courts that governed the prisons of Cape New Jersey, each defiantly killed by inmates who bombed prisons. It were as if there were no sense of right from wrong; no ability to preserve against an ocean tide striking against the normalcy of society.

James considered the most recent reports about the stag theatre, a mild disappointment on the rehabilitation of prison ex-inmates. There were almost a hundred new heresy trial clerks from Illinois State who had lost their lives.

Soho was Madrid in September. The trees in the park shimmered in reflecting greenery, in the birch pine of forests all up and down wild meadows of new forests along the Great floodplain up through the Pennsylvania canals. A smattering of grazing trees in stands of hundred mill reached in roots into an underwater of cold and taciturn lakes as dormant as the pasture land that surrounded each naturally until the muddy earth hardened and formed hard mud cracked stultifying cliffs. Along the colder Hudson a crop of new brick warehouses were asserting their liberties. The new team of attorney offices which provided consultation were off the canal on the east side in fine stucco porticos with three rooms two which overlooked a riverside park and quiet flow of river which at night lit up by a light on any stair. An office came with a kitchen, bath and one and a half bedrooms, and James primary litigator shared his lot with Lyle's brother. Twice a week the three discussed the cases over dinner and wine in the library, a longish dining room confined by two narrow walls on the other side of which were three powder blue sofas around a fireplace opposite the kitchen.

Lyle had an office at the Spanish Gothic cathedral on 158th Street uptown, all Girona buildings along the Hudson River; a Dutch County hall church of Dominican Republic marked the police precinct located at the mid section of pope Spanish Harlem where oddly pharmacy theatre gave out the ragweed and popcorn and a late night staff took the lives of anyone from Spain. No one would forget that beautiful Girona lived by acts of suffocation the Spanish Dutch met with their deaths. James proved ten fingerprints on each head defined a particularly bad group of killers whose sole necessity was to wipe out investigative detectives who worked night shifts along the Hudson.

The prisons were filling up with the Dutch New Guinea, an older Romantic prison situated in Eastern Delaware, hostelers out of Virginia.

Canada had its own prisons, uptown New York was where all ten prisons were, the Soledad, the L'Vey, the Cormel, the Don Levy, the Harrison, the Munch Ford and Breaker, every last one hardcore, when released after seven years they each resembled a walking machine gun. No one knew where to look for papa John who torched his father on a bus. It was rumored he had gone to Illinois. Gotten a job on a newspaper. The year was 1930 and the Bronx had just been built. While it was evident a war had begun no one knew what to make about it. There were no soldiers in bunkers for example, nor ships on the coast at port. It was an oddity of sleekers living in a new city who camped out on their lawns and outdoor balconies.

Lyle might have adequately predicted in the population who solicited the mass deaths of marine officers who supplied the sweet dreams of patients at the hospitals upon discharge habituated the salons at the Cotton Club and Savoy. Brooklyn was a brook of refinery for the Antilles brown school girls whose husbands had come up to study at physician schools. Those few homeowners lived in beautiful East End apartments along the Hudson after having served on the Rhine where any sailor required treatment of Barcelona morphine. For the school of tile layers who entered upstate New York to collect a slab of rock from the Labrador peninsula, their smaller houses in Pennsylvania supported an entire industry of lime alabaster district, the most expensive tile laid in state congresses.

Over custard cup desserts and demitasses, Lyle's three lawyers meted out foundation. Each of two dead theatres turned out fifty Dominican males over the age of thirty who looked identical, each slender, tall, about six feet two inches, bluish fingernails, pink lips; slick brownish black hair; coal black eyes, a racial hatred of the island police. The three studied this new phenomena.

The dead worked as street sweepers all over

Brooklyn.

They took inventory for the warehouses.

They supplied furniture cellophane bags in preparation for shipments from the Antilles labor yards onto ships to Miami.

They attended one church, met for Sabbath weekly at a Domin.

Moon Over Giza

1.

The train clicked through the cement passage, at once extinguishing the serene snowy landscape which gave the Alps its territorial domain. Despite a dominance of lively chatter, silence packed the compartment with awareness. Reflections of women bundled up in woolen skirts and scarves lit up in the windows and then became subdued blurs as the train glided around a bend. As it passed into sunlight, the scale of darkness vanished. Long thin grey trees stood a foot in blanketed snow in a forest, their thin branches like a wintery fog obscuring a lake with three story chalets. The train glistened crossing a bridge – from the last compartment Janice took in the ravine and beyond the mountain of pine trees, their rugged coats adorned only with light. Here and there would be a sluice of wooden crates and a ski run of wood while a smaller train wound beside rock face and wedged trees, roots dangling midair. But for the absence of shadow, darker slabs of stone veiled a continual exposure to the forces of wind and lightning. The distance called in short due to a descent into the forest, if for no reason but the landscape appeared to fall in succession to a decline while rough rock came into sudden observation, each granule perfectly placed in symmetry to flat stones and damp slate. Ever further behind, the city of Grenoble receded until the forest reasserted its own sublime skyline. Another bridge gave the train a tranquil avenue, relaying a series of delayed images – thick intact snow, a peaceful drop onto a meadow, a rushing creek of dark aquamarine water, jets of spray over emerging rocks which in summer without a winter runoff would seem to crest a jumble of haphazardly positioned rocks, a gravel bed alongside a river, and then slowly into view a rising bank of frosted muddied pack, the ice melting onto the soil. There was no fear, she found herself thinking oddly; no terrifying feeling of sudden weightlessness as the sensation used to flood her the very instant she stepped out of the plane and grabbed for the release tag of her parachute and wondered whether free fall was a good idea. That sudden jolt as a wind current lifted one higher always took her breath until she secured her fingers around the drawstring and then confidence renewed its hold. The world didn't reel as one might suppose – the wind buoyed one in space as the elements of air and light seemed somehow to catch and cradle the body. It was hundreds of feet down before weight became its own preemptive and then no amount of pressure locked one in. It was in that exact moment the body was released that one had to yank hard on the cord or the body would become its own rock, its own force of gravity. Once, when she hadn't counted on the worst circumstance – the cord being deadlocked – did she have to cut her speed to prevent her death. She angled her body and shifted her weight, continuing to do so until she was over trees and then plummeted into the branches. Now when she saw downhill skiers careen off a steep rock face into empty space, she regarded them with cool apprehension noting her tendency to position them in advance as to how they should fall, drawing back to the skier's body, watching with innate horror knowing each second counted as they eyed the surface of snow for the safest landing. Coming down too close to rock would cause the body to bounce like a rag doll. Once down, nature gave the limbs a robot like posture making arms and legs mechanical, unable to move in synchronicity as though the brain were unable to connect the simplest arm movement. Only if one came down in a comforter of dense snow, the weight of the snow would take the speed of the fall. Snow reflected light and light masked density; a thin sheet of snow contained a waterfall, or ice. The trick was to sense the depth of snow and as any skier would advance an opinion, depth was conveyed by angle of light as one looked down upon it. The practice of landing on snow with both skis down kept most skiers able to return to the slopes despite the initial terror of flying.

The train seemed to stretch with a minimum of elasticity as it climbed an incline. The forward compartments including the small one that represented the dining car moved in unison without so much as a hitch. The silver panels glinted in the daylight while all around the snow lay piled high with the barest degree of perturbance. Although there were no windows open, nor a way to open them, she thought she detected a spark of pellet fire from the compartment behind the cab car. She was on her feet in a second, long legs striding to the door, hand on her belt to feel for her pistol. She slid open the door, dashed through the narrow aisle, wending her way past a woman in a brown parka and denim pants returning from the bathroom, opened the next door and barreled into a man getting out of his seat. For what felt like too long a tango, she tried to politely extricate herself until it occurred to her the man might purposely be attempting to block her. She pushed him hard by the shoulder back into his seat mumbling that she was in a hurry, taking in a red shirt with ruffles and a bolero, as she seized the moment to rush to the next door and slamming it against the opposite wall, she fought an instinct to turn around and shoot him. The train was moving over a white landscape with a creekbed, rushing water spilling over a portion of dry bank. She forged ahead taking with her an urgency. In the dining car a waiter served wine while people in parties of three and four feasted on lasagne and beef stew with vegetables. She waited a tense second for the waiter to step out of her way; when he did, she moved quickly into the next car.

She scanned for a passenger in distress but no one appeared hurt. One man, an elderly gentleman with an elegant face and handsomely dressed in a dark grey three piece business suit, sat with his hand held to his waist, while on the opposite side a young blonde with chiffon hairdo, was applying her lipstick as she eyed Janice' approach. The others – five women and six men – were reading newspapers or paperback novels and seemed so thoroughly engrossed not to have noticed a thing.

Janice went through the final door to the conductor.

"You can't come in here," said the train conductor, a pencil thin man with a bald spot at the back of his head, otherwise brunette.

"Someone shot a gun. I saw the sparks," she said, and showed him her badge that listed her as an investigator for Pinkerton. "I'd like you to call ahead to the next station and alert them to a potential crime."

"I would have heard a shot."

"Not necessarily. It's possible it went off with some type of silencer."

He gave her a reluctant glance. "Yes, I can call ahead, but it'll be another good forty-five minutes before we arrive."

"Then perhaps you could stop ten minutes from the station on the track."

"That will stick us inside a mountain tram."

"Is there any problem with that?"

"Only that when it gets very cold the windows rattle if another train goes by."

"Can you use heat?"

"I can, but it's bound to get stuffy."

"That will be good. Please, if you could, when you notify Annecy, could you tell them I am awaiting instructions."

"Certainly. What is your full name?"

"Janice Marin Sardan."

"Alright Janice Marin Sardan, I'll wire your request to Zurich."

2.

The train came to a halt on a ridge overlooking a castle on a small lake. The snow was five feet on the ground. At 3:01pm the broadcaster commented on overhead television sets that over the weekend there would be some snow, lighter rain showers, that Zurich was looking good and that it would be high pressure nose down by the start of the work week. The woman beside Janice looked to be in her early to mid sixties, a tame redhead with a coiffed hair style, black silk blouse, white pants and red boots with a rhinestone bracelet on her left wrist. Her clothes said class but her smooth skin at her age said sleep was taken on plenty of money, perhaps with a daily billfold of fresh fruit, a spa pedicure and white towel robes and hydrotherapy.

A group of white haired men who looked like train conductors and wore the traditional garb of white cotton shirt and navy blue trousers came out of nowhere to conduct routine interviews. Their questions consisted of: did you see or hear a gun fired, did you see who fired, and do you own a gun. The questioning for all passengers on the train took the better part of two hours, after which passports were duly noted and notes taken. The men disembarked and the train then wended its way through the mountains to the Annecy station.

At the crest where the tracks met the dirt road, a red-haired man sat with a bright red scarf around his neck inside a Cadillac roadster painted tan and green. His face was pasty white, his features oddly handsome, remarkable for his poise, the impression of charm replacing wit, a humor of genuineness for boniness and irony. A glance at the man's face gave Janice a clear perspective on the riders in the first compartment – all were related to him except perhaps the youngest and she was either a girlfriend or an associate.

Janice was met at the station by a shuttle which took her and six others to their destination at the Grand Duchess Hotel at Annecy. By the time she checked in and had signed for her suite, she was given a Northstar teletype from her husband at Interpol which read:

Jani,

I've taken the liberty to send this wire. The man being detected is Sir Edmund of the Opposition party. This may shed some light on your crucible.

Sir Harry Sardan had added a postscript: Sweetheart, take care not to overdo it. Your being American is the perfect foil. As one who adores the Cannes film festivals in Colorado, you will note that the night air is thinnest over Durango. Now here is the deal. Nato Pact made use of infrared in an aircraft illegal. Infrared works on wall. Your most possessive HS.

Wall had not been used since pre World War II after

it was found to have been the favorite weapon utilized in conjunction with electric wire to blow up glass buildings. Because Sir Harry was a wire expert who could take apart any scheme using wire, he was put in charge of the detection of all mechanisms that involved wire. Just as he took a bedtime potion consisting of bicarbonate and biscuit in a cup of warm milk and forbade Janice to drink it, he also used code instamatic images which he permitted no one including home office and other Interpol agents to draw upon. A business card tossed into a glassy ceramic bowl was when photographed a pier of rotting timber and was sealed onto a bookmark as a Christmas marker. An ink pen scrawled in gold with a person's name, while meant to be a friendly souvenir, was under infrared a glowing wand which in the wrong hands was an indictment if left behind at a crime scene. Sir Harry had an ombudsman gift for appreciating the absurd – stationary with barely visible decals on woven linen that resembled writing when powder blue laser was applied and a lapboard with typing keys which when plugged into a telephone or outlet worked on everything but a television.

Sir Edmund's wife would not be on the train. She would travel in style escorted about by a chauffeur driven limousine, a bar on the inside, sipping a Dubonnet as she filed and polished her nails. A party dress made of stiff crepe with an over shirt of silk and lacy nylons with high heels would take in her desired image as a jet-setter.

She removed her laptop from its cover and sent Sir Harry an e-mail. I saw a man in a roadster near Annecy who resembles the party in question. Could you send me the file? Yours, JMS. Always the possessiveness. It was like a brand. Once married, forever married. The lean muscular curve of his body, the notes he left for her around the flat, the garden in which he grew the salad stuff for meals he cooked for the two of them, the fond practiced inattentiveness meant to underscore his dependency and other emotional needs for a wife, all contributed to the persuasive armour by which he afforded her leniency of travel and time on her own. She would take up an assignment, run it to ground and in other ways entertain a handful of related files and then having sent it in for assessment be off to join him on the slopes at Aix.

The photos paraded across her computer. The family name was Delmark. Because her skepticism normally helped her think a file through by keeping her interest distant, she would take out a notepad and make notes of everything including Sir Harry's comments. Once she had the opportunity to review the file, she would return it without opening a companion copy at this end. The Delmarks traded primarily in fashion. Slave ships took prisoners to the Slave coast to till the fields for cotton and once done brought cotton back with their workers to weave silks. They were a pretty grouping, fashionable, monied, happily coupled, pleasurably suited. But for a misfit or two in the family, Sunday brunches would be set apart by tension, petty envy and continual subordination. The likelihood that one member had shot another made for the supposition that living was somehow bereft of satisfaction, and the fact that no one had paid attention suggested an ongoing drama of murderous ambushes if not outright insanity. If the tightly knit club was staying over at various hotels around the lake, then the chances for further escalation had hopefully abated, unless they had brought their problem with them.

She ran a check on the family and turned up the following information:

Saul Delmark, age 60, Caucasian, India Interpol

Nya Abbe, age 25, Indian, wife to Saul

Kara Delmark, age 48, Caucasian, shopkeeper, designs women's fashionwear

Mark Delmark, age 50, Indian, buyer, travels to Singapore and Malaysia

John Delmark, age 75, Caucasian, investments, travels worldwide

Laurta Delmark, age 75, Caucasian, wife of John

Ridalfi Delmark, age 25, part Indian, runs manufacturing industry with companies in the Mediterranean

Jarn Delmark, age 27, Swedish, design consultant

Ken Delmark, age 21, Caucasian, investments, handles sales

Ellen Frast, age 19, Caucasian, girlfriend to Ken

John Delmark Jr., age 31, son of John and Laurta

The family was a corporate family by the looks of it. Fashionwear design came in crepe gowns with chiffon arms and silk bodices and bright colors – hot pink with gold trim, silver leggings with low cut gold shimmering tees, black evening wear with low cut backs and sparkling rhinestones at the throat, stars and spears for the hair twists and coiffed doos, backless heels and open toe pumps, an array of purses, rings, necklaces and chokers. All priced too high, all inviting, all a statement about what money could buy if one required no convincing. All ads displayed elegant, bony women situated impossibly in the bright sun in Thrace or Turkey, their bodies leggy and girlish, striding down a sandy runway amidst coliseums, Parthenon, ruins and columns set against a sparkling blue ocean. A flash of tanned skin, of sensuous lips, short bronze hair like a swimming cap, long necked, toga silk, tight sashes, chartreuse, lime, cranberry, violet, smart, carefree, contained. Something every woman would want to buy, if she could.

Moon Over Giza

3.

At the other end of the line Sir Harry was adding his calculator. "Well, the likelihood of a point fix is dim," he told Janice who had awakened while it was still dark. "It's something other than another ship. The file suggests an interface with another plane. The question is whether it is airborne or stationary."

Janice was silent. She relied upon his expertise. "Are you saying it is responsible for hanging photos ---"

"And reflections, Janey. That's the trick. The best way to sink a ship is with a sub with a picture of the ship on its screen dragging it."

"Who would be so bold?"

"Usually an aircraft that isn't flying has the same image of the ship on its screen, and then the sub wouldn't be able to get it. It's when that aircraft is forced into flight, the sub could then get it. Or as the Americans have done by sinking battleships, an enemy sub is then caught by that battleship."

"Would you have to know someone who could arrange this or could you do it apart from anyone else?"

"You would require at least a sub and another ship."

"Can you leave me a message if you come up with an

answer?"

"Sure. Wear a hat."

"And don't stay in the sun too long. I know."

The houseboat was unusually crowded. Looking about Janice saw the Corners and the Delmarks minus Saul and Mark. Nya was nowhere to be seen.

Larta was in rare spirits. She had donned a comfortable white suit and was wearing the choker her husband had purchased for her. Beside her sat her daughter Ava who despite a cigarette and morning coffee and sleepy appearance was content to guard the den and was shooing everyone away from the seat she and her mother occupied. Around the table sat Ken and Ellen, Janice, John, Jarn, and Ridalfi all in various stages of casual wear from short shorts to knee highs, who but for their well mannered temperance were making small talk with the alleged traitor of the shipping industry.

"I was thinking last night," Larta said to Eleanora, "we ought to discuss mirrors. Mirrors, you know, account for the national security of the dynasties and thus these ancient civilizations are to be afforded with our respect."

Eleanora was cordial. "I was surprised to learn that many of these washed out temples were once treasuries."

It was the wrong thing to have said and while Larta offered no visible response, Jarn hastened to recover her, saying, "It's difficult to know where the lines are drawn. The temples for example could not have had so much space and the plazas must have had some other roads available to them."

"It's the attraction to the river that I find fascinating," Eleanora said, not understanding that she had said something that someone she was talking to might find hurtful. "In Spain we reside on the ocean, so one has a common sense about the nature of shipping, whereas inland one has only a sense of the roads."

"She lives on the water, I live in my office," Raul remarked.

Larta said, as the boat pulled away from the temples of Beit el Wali, "we used to dock quite regularly in Italy and northern Greece until we expanded to Spain and Portugal. Despite the ocean currents we found we had a fair degree of commerce at these places."

Raul said, quite candidly, "I remember your husband now. He's tall, strident, a naval officer."

"Air force," she replied. "I asked last night because the name Corner sounds quite familiar for some reason."

"Yes, well, I must hasten to reassure you I have no spurious intentions."

"That's very good to hear," Jarn said. "You remember that bout of bad weather we had some while ago off Tanger."

"Tunis, I thought it was," Larta put in. "Near Tripoli. We got our ships docked at the stairs and then could not disembark."

"It's very gaelic," Raul said, out of generosity then, "that portion of the northern shore. We've had many good seasons there."

Eleanora, sensing a rift, asked, "Is there something wrong? Are we talking about a problem?"

"No, no," her husband assured her. "Everything is quite fine."

"Nya Rapaur is traveling with us. She married my son Saul."

"Do I know this Nya?"

Janice said, "She knows you."

Jarn said, "I gathered she knows you from an insurance corporation."

"Jarn is intuitive," Larta said. "Tell us what you think."

"That's all I am aware of," Jarn said.

"I once had reason to know a man of your talent," Larta said; "who burned to the ground everything he had insured."

"You must have me confused with some other person. What business were you in?"

"I'm still in it. I create drawings of our line of men's wear."

"I thought you were in women's apparel."

"No. Do you recall a man named Durner?"

He stiffened. "My name is Eluti."

"We aren't speaking of you, Mr. Eluti. Durner was one of these self-stylized grandiose personages one expects to run across in an industry in which there is too much of everything. At the time, some thirty or forty years ago, he was in charge of all armed robbery, heists and murders, a very noxious man, if I don't say so myself. He thought he would streamline the movie industry first with bright splashes of color and then with ---"

"That's enough!" he cried out, catching everyone's surprise. "Who do you think you are?"

"I'm not through," Larta said. "Have another scone or piece of fruit."

He slammed his fist on the table. "Do have some courtesy!" He stood, his body trembling with anger. "Who do you think you are to talk to me in such a manner? Come," he said to his wife, "we're going down below to our cabin."

Eleanora stood, instantly apologetic to him. To their host, she said, "It's the air. Raul's not accustomed to the heat at this time of year. I'm most sorry for his outburst. Perhaps we will come up for lunch."

"Dear," Larta said, "ask your husband when he calms down who he had on the train with us who fired a shot above our heads."

"You deserve to die!" he shouted. "You placed people in mass graves. You are an insane family, a nauseating group of infuriating — "

"You're causing a scene," Larta said. "Ask your husband to sit down." When it was clear to her he was about to walk away, she said to snag him, "Our Mr. Durner had an insatiable need to injure innocent lives. He committed atrocities against any number of people – Nya's uncle, against my previous employer Farenholt, his own brother, and then had several principles insured against their own deaths and had Nya deliver these people to their own deaths."

He sputtered with upset. "I warned you back then, Rea!"

"Oh, I'm not Rea Ertin," she said glibly.

"She was my mother."

"I was the set artist for the opening bill."

He eyed her, trying to figure out what he remembered compared to what he thought she could be guessing at, and sat down. "Durner was my father," he said, lying as much to her as to himself. "I take it very poorly to have my relations accused. The disgrace follows like a dog at my heels."

Eleanora sat, now hesitant and cautious.

"We should view the situation from the nest, should we not?" she asked to no one in particular. "The waste of human life cannot be under appreciated, can it not? To have to consider there are people in the world who must seize people's lives for no reason than they cannot be corrupted is indeed a consideration. What is your thought on this?"

He continued to stand as though to unleash his instinct for pride or to restrain the ambitions which he did not readily declare. Finally he said, "How did you acquire me here?"

"I did not acquire you here. You came for some other reason. Either it was because Nya warned you or someone in her confidence warned you."

Eleanora asked him, "Shall we leave or do you wish to stay?"

He ignored her for the moment. Instead he asked Larta, "What do you plan to do with me?"

"You'll have a boating accident, after which you will be confined to a wheelchair. That's awfully liberal, don't you think, for all the misery you've wreaked over the years? Where it began for you one can only imagine. Perhaps with your own string of pearls."

"I had every right to insure against sailing, and if it made a sizeable industry I had every right to spend it as I saw fit. It's not for you to say in what manner people should have their fun nor count their blessings."

"Sailing is not the sum total, is it? To make a mast out of a bolt is one thing, to set sail on the ocean quite another, and to take shots at boats and at yachts altogether a mean spirited enterprise. Imagine your sense of certainty that must come from knowing when you will cancel some person's livelihood or worse, will send them to an under water grave by virtue of the fact that you and you alone have devised a way to make them pay for some slight or other remark. What do you suppose your preference is? A U-boat in the fog? One minute the lake is clear except for fog and the next out slips a boat very nearly the same color as the windy fog. Too bad for you that the U-boat was declared illegal. A sub while a bit cumbersome sits below its periscope trained on any shape at the water's surface. How are we to contend with rising and dipping oars, with that sulky place of our imaginations that tells us the reason sharks attack has to do with the presence of a boat at the surface, its shape surrounded by light, when we all know that sharks despite their teeth and size of jaw rarely attack anything, not even a dead fish? Are we to comprehend your instinct for blood, your desire to have a meal out of someone else's savings such that when the money in the bank is sufficiently accrued you must send someone to retrieve it from the person's own withered grasp? Where do you suppose it all leads to anyway, if it doesn't go for you or to you you nevertheless have to devote ways of jiggling it free like an errant wind on a branch? To be displaced from your profitable industry as if from your point of view you were shorn of your own flaxen locks and then turn around and become worse than a hungry shark, worse than a piranha, you became an insurance evaluator who went after anyone who stood between you and your prey, you should have been buried beneath a fourth or fifth pyramid, your eyes sealed off permanently from any light or any restoration.

"I'm certain you have not forgotten our family name. How could you? Delmark. It's a mark left on the item like a seal. You sank several of our ships and then insisted as insurant that because we could not promise delivery we therefore were a bad risk."

"You ought to be used to the idea by now that if your only merchandize is a dead body, perhaps land disposal is less risky than at sea."

She had anticipated the jibe for some time and was ready for it. "Our sole merchandize as you convey it is neither sole or soulful. It is the necessity of ridding the context of its robbers and bringing them to a place they won't be able to seduce more people to crime nor attempt to hurt yet another unsuspecting individual again. If we could walk across the ice, it would be easy, would it not?"

"There are repeat numbers," Sir Harry told Janice. "Why the party in question develops this apparatus is not understood, nor how they achieve this is unknown. It's probably the reason that when we get through, we can't understand what's going on because the numbers themselves have already been established for some other event."

"How does he obtain them?" she asked him.

"He has to have a duplicate scorecard. Maybe it's the same motor, based on an American manufacturer. Based on a Porsche."

"Do you think the Delmarks are aware of this?"

"I think they made an error, Janey."

"You think they brought in the alternate motor?"

"What I think is that they downloaded – and it's sheer guesswork – someone staffing may have gave the preferred tactic to the opposition."

"How do you get invited?"

"You have to be on active duty with the Marine Corp."

"You must have a number of friends," Janice said, taking Larta into her confidence.

"Like it? It's a pyramid." Larta showed her her design.

"Why a pyramid?"

"Well," Larta said, pencilling in the blocks beneath the letters, "when you look at the side there is a certain consistency. If you adorn the sides with paper, then you'd have a paper pyramid. I like the idea of perspective, of being able to look in as well as to look at."

"Any preference for Roman numerals?"

"We went through a cycle of Roman numbering but we set the entire line in Turkey and called it Roma. It was a very productive season for us."

"Why did you stop?"

"The computer couldn't keep tabs with it for some reason."

"I suppose there are no exact translation systems that allow for sameness," Janice said. "Perhaps the items you were producing were tagged as though they were different items."

"Art should be able to be art. That's what I think."

"Put one too many letters in there and your product becomes another item, impossible to transport let alone wrap up."

"There was no attempt to be dishonest."

"If you're trying to enter another port and you use a product in such a way it gets catalogued as a thing that is made of solid stone and the problem is that it's too costly to change your entire system because of use of language, then what do you think happens?"

"That's a stupid problem. We always used to get in just fine."

"It's probably why titles are not included in port fees."

"We don't trade in books."

"Stamps might prevent that."

"As long as one doesn't require storage."

Larta said, "Storage generated too high a fee unless one owned the buildings. It became subject to inventory laws."

"I noticed you put a compass on every page."

"That was when our first ship went down. We put

north and south on every page. Some idiot made our warehouse roofs north and the floors south. How a ship steers by its own star as north is beyond me. It's not as if the map does not contain cities that have north as part of their name."

Janice felt she was playing at tug of war with the older woman and that she knew perfectly well what was meant but out of some inner need to not be second guessed had steered clear of the crux of the issue.

They were floating into Sudan where one dynasty was alleged to have conquered the next – Macedonians all, none pharaohs or Egyptians, who had conquered, tried to assert rule and had failed. Temples were built, then bones were buried of Assyrians and Christians who set up societies and then were invaded, and with Cleopatra the Nile finally died. Thousands and thousands of miles of papyrus stymied swamps engorged miles of silt as the Blue Nile, one long arm of river, overflowed its banks in winter to join up with the White Nile. They walked onto ancient river banks at Sulb, Sesibi, Kerma, Old Dongola, Kuru and Nun, to view the ruins of famous plundered cities, now turned to dust, before they drifted past islands in the torrentially flowing river – Dirbi, Boni, Us, Sur and Shirri, forever lost, forever isolated, past civilizations chalked up to sands dredging into the water to the next dam.

While the majority took their luggage to a station to then be carted to Victoria Lake, the Delmark party prepared to accompany the boat back to Aswan in order to locate Nya or if needed, to fetch the authorities.

"Having a good time?" Jarn asked Janice.
"So so. I had hoped we could have taken more pictures of us as a group."

"It's always that way," Larta said. "It's either a fabulous time and you don't remember a thing or you wanted something more and you wind up feeling there's more to see. I suppose you wished you had seen Assyrian remains or that sort of thing."

"No, I was quite comfortable to know they only haul out the skeletons for movies."

Jarn laughed. "It was a delightful trip. I'm glad you came with us. How're you two lovers doing?"

Ken said, "Couldn't be better. Ellen's never been, you know."

Ellen said, "I enjoyed every minute. I felt it was important once I was here to see all the sites including Athens. The ruins there are very different."

"Yes, they are," Ken agreed. "Athens has a very sophisticated look."

"I agree," Ellen said. "At night the city is stunning. Ken and I had a small room that looked onto the Acropolis and I spent half the night looking at it."

"I'm glad you took the time," Larta said. "At night the Nile can be very pretty too."

"I could see that last night. The alabaster looks very royal at night."

John who had kept to himself on the way home said, "This is the one river that takes a person into the past and gives you a sense that Time cannot defeat man's efforts easily."

"That's true," said Jarn, in eagerness to include his reticent brother. "It's a real trip into antiquity. That, and you have a clear idea of the magnificence that these people built. Nothing like the puny housing developments that you see all over."

"Well, the chalk adobes in Greece are nice," Ellen said airily. "As are the stone ones and the stone walls surrounding the groves. It's very pretty against a backdrop of the sea."

"We will take you everywhere, Ellen," John said, "because you are so complimentary."

"Oh, I mean it."

"I have no doubt you do," John remarked in a tone that said he thought it was her youth. "It's nice to think you were paying attention."

"John means," Ken said, "that he does not notice these things if he can at all help it," putting an end to the perceived malice he thought John intended to get started on.

"Well, I hope Nya has had a pleasant time out," Larta said.

"Mother, do you mind?" Ken asked. "It's bad enough Saul and Mark had to miss the trip."

Ava said, "Mother is concerned Nya is not on the up and up."

"Maybe she's not. Can't we leave it alone?"

"Why did she come?" Ava asked.

"Saul brought her," Ken said. "I doubt she would have said no."

"Then she should make more of an effort to be cheerful."

"So should you. Let's not talk about everyone behind their back."

Ridalfi said, more to Ellen, "I hope we're not putting you ill at ease. We're a large family."

"And complicated," Larta said.

"No, I'm fine," said Ellen, feeling slightly self-conscious.

"Did you like my dissertation?" Larta asked her.

"Oh, about the sailboats. Who was he, that man?"

"A friend of Nya's," Larta said, as though all her

opinions were now justified. "He's a vicious, underhanded goon."

"I thought you invited him."

"I did. I wanted him where I could set my sights on him. I'm only thankful Ken's father wasn't there. He would have ripped Mr. Elut's throat out."

"How did he come to be at Aswan? Is that a coincidence?" she asked.

"Nothing is ever a coincidence where we are concerned. You'll find that out shortly enough if you stick around."

"We're going to be married, Mother."

"That's what you said, dear. I'm very happy for you both. Marriage at your age is altogether different than it is after fifty-eight years. Contentedness and companionship have long since faded and in it's place is the knowledge that if you were separated for long it'd be the end of you."

"That's a long time to have been married, Mrs. Delmark."

"It goes to show anything is possible. How's your sketch, Ridalfi?"

"I got as good a face study as anyone will ever get, Mother."

"Good, good." To Ava, she said, "Would you please put my hair up? I want to look fresh by the time we dock."

"I can do that." She stood, took the brush her mother gave her and brushed her mother's hair. The Italian sheen came through suddenly despite her all-too blond hair and pale complexion. "It's nice that your hair is so manageable."

"You always say that, Ava. Don't pull so. You'll take out too many strands."

"I'll be careful, Mother."

Janice said, "Where will we stay tonight?"

"Probably we'll fly into the Sudan to Lake Victoria if they have a late plane; otherwise we'll have to stay at Aswan again and fly out in the morning. Do you have somewhere you need to be?"

"No, I'm on my own for a week. You?"

Larta said, "We don't have to be anywhere for another week, and then he's due in Rio in Brazil. It'll be a scurry tying up loose ends but better to have everything in order."

"I was wondering whether you were planning to have Mr. Corner checked?"

"It's too much to stop one's entire life for that man."

"I thought I would ask a friend of mine to see what brought him here."

"It should be obvious. He came because his wife wanted a vacation."

Janice thought Larta suspected some other worse predicament. "His wife seemed very congenial. Was she involved in those matters of the past?"

"I don't know." Larta patted her head as Ava began to braid her hair. "We should take a look and see what information is available on her, I suppose. Ridalfi, can you check?"

"Don't see why not." To Janice: "We're either hard at getting plastered or hard at figuring out other people."

"Are the extremes necessary?" she asked.

"Mother?"

"Everything we do is necessary. It's part of the packaging." Larta said.

Janice had the impression that in addition to her being sarcastic, that the family was responding to her with some hidden understanding of the packaging with which they provided clothing but that it was neither the catalogue they would put together as a result of this particular trip nor the actual boxes they would ship to the ports they still had permission to enter. There was some faint suggestion that this was a family that lived for their influence on human life, that the colors they sought to find expression with and the styles they would conjure up were somehow intended for the benefit of bringing some sort of abstract from the world of the dead and recreating it for the living.

"Could the packaging find a more sympathetic route?" Janice asked her.

Larta said, "No, I don't think that would work. It is after all the method of the packaging that permits real understanding, real terms. It is when we fail at these understandings and try to motivate ourselves into a sense of self-righteous anger that human kind most nearly fails."

John added, without the touch of humility one would expect forthcoming, "There's no real dignity, you know, after the fact. Civilization is not meant to be conjured out of dust. It's not intended for people to run amuck. The staggering face cliffs should tell people who wander beneath them that life is meant to be dreamed about and that dreaming consists simply of accepting beauty into one's heart."

"Very touching," Ken said. "The business we're in, Janice, is of taking the human mind and showing it to itself exactly as it is for each person one must enact this for."

"I'm not certain I'd like to be shown much of my inner nature," she said.

"Well, there's not much about you that requires a harsh mirror. For some, for this buggar we encountered, the one who denied being himself — "

"I know I wouldn't want to see his interior personality. It wouldn't be nice and it might not be safe."

"It's not a metaphysical journey," Ken said. "For the packaging, it is whatever one finds. It is not based upon what you'd like to see. It's whatever is there."

"How does this relate to the clothier line you sell?"

Ridalfi said, "The trip down the river is for the most part on a very shallow body of water. The light of day is almost always revealing, clear. The tour takes you to very large statues, to temples in actuality, the interiors of which are also large, well lit and show now dead societies. The emphasis is on clarity of what happens when one comes before the Great. The fact that you can't take any dust with you, that these are only places to be in awe of, that all Time stands here and is without judgment and that the cultures were presumably black – there is no other place like it anywhere. The place holds a visage for people who believe they are without, who look upon themselves as needing something powerful to be larger than all the corruption one might be capable of and that can make them numb to their own desire for heights. That's the mirror. When we put together a new look as we will do for Cairo, we try to instill a desire to be faithful to what is Great without also having a desire to possess beyond what is reasonable, to be able to look at the world as having limitations and shoring up a consciousness that emphasizes not hogging it all through acts of deceit, greed for money or envy. The task in the packaging is to create something a person would like to have that they can be satisfied by."

"A garment can't do all that," Janice said. "That's a value system you teach a child as they grow into adulthood."

"It's what Ken meant by the term."

"Yes, I understand the intent. I'm just not convinced one could expect that by a clothing line."

"Yes, well, it's what keeps us together as an extended family," Ken said. "I suppose one could always be buried in their rags."

"I wonder what that would look like," Larta said.

"So, what's the drawing?" Janice asked her.

"Oh, the pyramid. I was fooling around with a concept in my head. The pyramid stands for an idea of perfection, it's the same on three sides and converges on a zenith, an absolute point. It also represents a point which if one could pull at it, if it could be moved, would be like a tent and would take down the entire structure."

"What is your concept?"

"I haven't developed it yet. I'm still working through it."

"Where are you looking for it to take you?"

"That's just it. I'm not sure. It's a powerful symbol, all those blocks stuck together. It reminds me every time I see them of the ultimate reality, but beyond that I'm not sure."

"Will you try to incorporate a concept for Giza into your new line?"

"I'd like to if I can get it to work."

They had arrived to the drop-off point. From here a bus would take them up the hill into the city and to the hotel.

Nya waited in the lobby with Solly and Mark. She seemed oddly out of sorts, her husband also somewhat disjointed, Mark the one who was in sole control of the manner in which his time had been spent within the last twenty hours. Solly rose to meet his mother and took her satchel off her body. The others exclaimed at Nya's recovery and conveyed she had missed a most interesting trip. After finding they could check in for the night, they moved into the tea room to a table by the windows and proceeded to unveil their drawing pads for Nya to look at, which she did both with interest and a smallness akin to envy. Larta took up residence at the head of the table and discreetly contained herself, while Ava described to Solly their excursion and the points of interest omitting the scandalous conduct of Mr. Corner.

"We scarcely have time as an entity to travel together or to place ourselves in the palm of antiquity," she said to Nya and Solly. "The sun beat down on us making us wish we had brought our own umbrellas but the chance to work together made up for that."

"Yes," Ken said, "it's a wonder Ellen didn't pass out. More of the same I expected and then was surprised to discover the grand scale proportions, even more dominant than I thought they would be. Very humbling experience."

"What happened to you?" Janice asked her politely.

Nya said, "I wandered about in my stockings on the beach until I lost my sense of direction. Although I tried to retrace my steps I couldn't find my way. I sought a motel, then discovered I did not have my purse on me. As the sun lowered into the horizon, I grew genuinely afraid I had lost my way and would not be found."

"Saul and Mark found you then?" Janice asked.

"I had lain down on the beach near a dune but was quite drenched after I was awakened."

"You could've been dragged out by an undertow," Ellen said.

"When we hailed a cab, I was shown my face in the mirror and I realized I looked frightful. My face was cut, my hair shagged and sticking out, my eyes haggard. It was quite a thing to have slept in the trees."

"We're glad you're alright now," Janice said. "Have you eaten?"

"Solly fed me hot soup and an ice cream sandwich. I feel temporarily restored. I think after a good night sleep I'll be back to new."

Mark said, "I've been asked by Mother to drive you into Malakal in Sudan to have you checked over for abrasions. The physicians here are not very experienced with fatigue to the body."

"I'll be fine," Nya said, after she realized he was serious.

"You have no choice, honey. You've kept your husband up all night, slept out on the beach and have bruises all over your arms and legs," Mark said. "We'll leave in five minutes as soon as they bring the car around."

She turned to Janice. "It was nice meeting you." To the others whom she glanced at with some aversion, she stifled whatever she was going to say. She got up stiffly and dusted herself off and was led by Mark out of the lounge to the car outside.

Once inside the sedan, Mark said to her, "You've been on a gravy train for quite a while, Nya. I understand you were intending to set my brother up."

"I married him."

"That seems to be the way you score. What's this business of taking off when Raul is in the hotel?"

"I didn't know he was here."

"No one believes that. He's traveling with a wife. Did you see her?"

"Eleanora's not a wife. She handles his accounts."

"They seem pretty tight to me. What does it mean that he showed up with her rather than some other broad?"

"I wouldn't know. That's his choice."

"Well, your operation is no longer as slick as it used to be. Did you know the Brits sent in Argyll to Annecy?"

"I don't do spas."

"I bet. What about men like Solly? A chance to get another one? That's rather banal even for you. Solly is half Indian, you know; he's not Larta's the way I am."

"Larta is no great shakes," she said. "She has her secrets buried all over the map."

"Larta? She's merely the wife of a shipping magnate. He's the one with all the power. It was his ports you tried to nickel and dime with those tangos of yours."

"I'm no dumb person, Mark. You're looking at the wrong picture."

"Am I, Nya?"

The road was dark with only the golden line in the middle visible in the headlights. If the desert contained salt pillars or stone temples, they were too far off the road to be seen. Periodically low trees moved up the road in succession and then for several miles there was nothing but chalky dust and drifting gusts of sand which caused traveling ravines to move across the road from one side to the other.

"What are you going to do with me?" she asked.

"Tie you up to a tree and leave you to wild wolves."

"Do you want me to die out here?"

"Tell me which one it is. Janice is too polite to ask."

"Why do you think I know anything about it?"

"India Interpol you're not."

"You have all the control. Why not toss me onto the road? You wouldn't have to bother with me again."

"Solly has to take you to Petra. Did you know that?"

She didn't look at him, or out the window into the glare of the headlights. "Anywhere civilized?"

"Probably not."

They rode into the silence, she more alone than she had realized it was possible to feel. She had assumed that since the Delmarks had lost the port in Portugal that they would have less opposition to contend with.

"Couldn't we do piano bar instead?" she asked him.

He continued without comment thinking her naive, that either she hadn't considered what piano bar was or that she somehow found the notion of delaying what she thought he intended to do with her a possibility.

"You took out insurance on the last poor man whose life you robbed," he said after a while.

"We don't give them anything they aren't willing to sign up for."

"There's a cool wind blowing, Nya. When you bury a man on purpose, you wind up buried. What do you think it would've taken for you to have gone to the police instead?"

"The police are as guilty as anyone else. They only want their cut."

"It's a jaded attitude to have at your age."

"I've made out fair and square. I had a home in the foothills."

"Which you lost."

"That's because even Raul got to be too much," she said, as if taking him into her confidence. "The world can be a swamp with fifty bodies bobbing like buoys. I couldn't take much of that, believe me."

"You're lying. There are no killing fields outside the Kalahari."

"None there. It's too dry, too wind swept. If the sands bury someone, ten seconds later they are exposed."

"Do you think God punishes or do you just hope we can be?"

She shifted her weight uneasily. "Morocco is no

comparison to India. You can live forever hoping to be expelled from her poverty. It's no way to live."

"You've lost your ability to touch the depth of my heart because you cannot relieve yourself of your own brutality."

"Women are not brutal in the same way men are, Mark. Men have needs. Their entire lives abound with hostilities and the need to subject others to their notion of what a life should consist of, whereas women only serve the men they must learn to put up with."

"You were free to leave Raul."

"I have left him, Mark."

"Never for long enough. Eventually you fall back to him."

"I did not invite him here. I did not ask him here. When we meet for business it has been in Algiers or Tunis or Tripoli, never here on the Nile."

"Why didn't you go to the police?"

"It didn't occur to me. Why must you make yourself god? Is it wanted?"

"Nya, let's get one thing straight. You kill them for money. It stops; it's over. If you can't be stopped, you won't be here."

"He was a young kid."

"Who did you put up to shoot my parents?"

"It wasn't me. I don't do parents," she replied. "I really wish you'd stop. Just take me where you're going to take me and throw me on the sand."

He pulled off the road and parked. He then opened her door and pushed her out. He slammed her door shut and took off.

He was somewhere over the border. He drove a few kilometers and pulled off the road. The night was absolute darkness. Not even the swathe of stars gave any light. The moon would be rising in a few hours bathing the chalky landscape. She would probably begin walking if just to stay warm, but a mile out here was a long walk with pitfalls and uneven terrain and after an hour or so without coming across trees or a shack she would probably give up.

"Where can Mark be?" Larta fretted, as she sipped coffee and took a bite of exquisite fruit bar dessert.

"He won't be along until morning," Jarn said. "Maybe not then, if he took Nya to a clinic."

Ellen said, "Will Nya be alright? She looked a little pale before he took her."

"I'm sure she's fine," John said. "We'll put a lookout for them before we have to leave."

"I'll call Mark, if you want," Ava told her mother.

"Could you, dear? Get some idea of their itinerary, if you would." Larta had completed her drawing of the pyramid. The letters had all but disappeared beneath shadings of blocks, the inner sepulcher chambers hidden from all but a long central hall that appeared about ten feet down in the soil. She showed it to the members gathered there amidst utterings of approval.

"Very nice," Ridalfi said. "Might we learn what your concept is?"

John took a swig of brandy. "It's obvious, isn't it? The only way inside is to walk in."

"It's an archeological dig," Larta said. "We could rent a dig for a week, shoot a handful of photos and put together a tour package and bring over photojournalists after the rainy season. Wouldn't that be fun?"

"The idea is a nice one," said Ellen. "I bet many people would go out for that."

4.

Sir Harry walked into the interview booth and eyed the chief command of Air One. Sir Harry glanced at his subject, Christopher Royce, a naval officer originally from Paraguay, before he turned on the tape and closed the door. The time was 11:02 am. The air inside the room was stultifying.

"How is it you brought your Invader into our base?"

"We have a contract with your air force."

"Who put this together?"

"A man named Jickson. He was asked by your A-team."

"Well, we can't approve this thing being here. You'll have to take it out."

"It's the only thing of its kind. It permits us to rewire cannisters on spec."

"The problem for us is that it flies silent. So when it is in air space no one knows it is there."

"Yes, well, that is only a piece of what it is designed to do. It can scramble transmissions, borrow on code literature, and fix focus without orders. When we fly over water and landscapes with alot of water it reprograms the map thus automatically widening the channels."

"What if people are on the ground?"

"Well, that's easy. They have to get out of the way."

"What if your bird just shows up? Does it warn people first?"

"You wouldn't want it to. It's the surprise element that counts."

"What about farmers? What do they do?"

"They shouldn't notice it. Your screens will pick it up. You can issue an air raid."

"What about its capabilities?"

"It is governed by the fact that water on land that is not on the map should flow downhill, not uphill."

"Are you trained to fly this?"

"Well, although I am trained to fly this I don't because I am too busy."

"So, who flies it when you can't."

"My son."

"How much training does your son have?"

"Same as me."

"How old is he?"

"Thirty-one."

"Don't you think that's kind of young to be given so much power?"

"No, he's very good."

"Is this him?"

"No, that's his cousin. He's irresponsible."

"In what way?"

"He drinks heavily, parties alot, sleeps in until all hours."

"Does he have a job?"

"Yes, he repairs air planes."

"Does he use a central computer for repair?"

He hesitated. "He uses a similar panel."

"How many panels do you have at large?"

"Maybe a few hundred. We use them all over the world."

Sir Harry left the room and joined his command in the observation unit. "What do you think?"

"Scary."

"Okay, here's what I'm going to advise. This panel spooks people. It can create earthquakes and if people are on the ground they can drown. It takes the land fast so people can lose their footing in an instant."

"How many degrees does it cover?"

"Fifteen degrees only to reference."

"How many Invaders does he have?"

"I'll ask." Sir Harry returned to his interview. "How many of these flying machines do you have?"

"Worldwide? Besides the one at home? Two. One here and one in Korea."

"Why Korea?"

"Because her rivers flow in the wrong direction. The Koreans don't want water coming from lakes."

Sir Harry declared a break to give himself time to review the tape and obtain Eye feedback. This being of consternation to the subject whose response indicated a desire to withhold pertinent information gave Sir Harry an idea as to how far the subject had been willing to go to attempt a continual interface with the satellite motor of choice.

"What does it look like to you?" He asked the Star room.

"He's lying. He didn't think he'd object to the Fiat until their building went in. It puts a crimp in the way ceiling charts are designated for recalibration. If the culprits can't get it with revised transparencies, there are always bridges."

"Ah, yes, a bridge tells you it's not a building. What

a disgusting man."

"Don't you find yourself asking, what time of day it is."

"Well, Big Ben sits on the London Bridge."

"The flats and gardens are withdrawn from sight whereas the warehouse district sits at the bottom of an incline. Thus you can't detect any ceiling where we are. Therefore he wanted a position from which to test time released film."

"Right, no movies."

"Why should that trouble him?"

"If he has scheduled something on a train system, then he needs a star chart that does not pick up a train because it moves too quickly."

It was an hour after Sir Harry returned to his subject.

"What do you think of the new Fiat?"

"It's alright, a bit slow."

"As a motor?"

"As a device. It lacks speed and force."

"Why do you think the French like it?"

"They like anything that doesn't work out right."

"A little sarcastic, you are."

"Well, I can't see how the size of the building will alleviate the problems of the past."

"How is that?"

"They're in love with their idea of stone. It doesn't compute."

"Can we return to the subject? It's the Fiat. Why doesn't it compete in your mind?"

"Ask any mechanic. He thinks the steering will be hard to handle."

"Why is that?"

"It doesn't test. You put the motor in your sports coupe first."

"What do you think about the Corvette as a motor?"

"It's a car. Oh I can appreciate its speed but it lacks compatibility."

"To what?"

"Well, laser for one thing. Why don't they give it to a mechanic?"

"A Fiat mechanic?"

"Any mechanic. Don't you hire in opinions? The way I hear it the motor is still too loud."

"Let's talk about lasers. What is your preference?"

"You could strip down the VW."

"And do what with it?"

"Spruce it up with an outfitter."

"Such as?"

"A Nissan for starters. It won't lag. Your Fiat doesn't come close to what we like to see in a motor."

"What would your motor do exactly, if you had one?"

"Fire on command, run a course, outdistance a golf ball, read between the lines, view everything from a distance, search and destroy and then replicate."

"You already have that. It's the Internet."

"The Internet is not a motor."

"It's in the Intrepid."

"But that's an aircraft."

"Try the Ford."

"That's an American motor."

"Yes, tell me how your garden grows."

"They all boarded boats and traveled to a distant country that is too big."

"How does that concern you?"

"They left nations to fend for themselves."

"Those nations are free to govern themselves."

"Not with a finite number of people. Eventually there's few products to sell and not enough money to even pay a military which no government can do without."

In the world of pleasures and garden delights – teas, coffee, spice and flavored herbal candies – mystery was about morality for the social order, romance about love and betrayal and espionage about military exposure – about the placement of subs worldwide, the use of motors and hologram transparencies and satellites to keep world governments safe from crimes and gangs. Power was the most conniving inducement to kill, power to control the outcome of life by governing and changing laws in order to amass sums of wealth for a single group.

Sir Harry reviewed the man's file before he met for a late lunch with Lord James. The file headings read, "Reasons for providing files to other govts since 1962; tel calls made on behalf of foreign officials and inability to post oneself." He read thoughtfully thinking Mr. Royce a mad dog, agog with a hunger for ambition, a most deceitful influence in his station. Upon closing the document, he walked through the Commons to the prudish apartment of Lord James Likeable.

"Jani asked that I solicit your opinion on a somewhat selfish matter. She was riding a train through the Alps when she witnessed sparks coming from the first compartment as the train went round a bend. The party in the first compartment are members of one family, specifically the Delmarks. A friend of the family informed Jani that the gun was on the person of the eldest son who never leaves home without it. This friend also intimated that the family while having manufacturing concerns in Spain, Switzerland and Egypt has a use for a motor which is capable when applied to satellite of hiding the tree from the forest."

Done with his explanation he tapped the glass into which the chef had poured his mint tea. The meal consisted of a small salad of greens, radish and small sliced oranges on chinaware from Limoges, a gold trim offset by a checkerboard of white and black and apricot flowers; lamb curry with white and sweet potatoes, a side of an artichoke heart and a dollop of rice pudding. Later, they would enjoy a bitter cup of Turkish coffee without sugar and a sweet Vermouth on the veranda overlooking the ocean.

Lord Likeable dabbed with a silk napkin. He was sturdy looking in his late seventies, a receding hairline of blondish matted hair, an opinionated mien having conducted one too many forays into the human experience, wearing as he was accustomed to in the privy of his home linen trousers with suspenders, a white silk Bermuda short sleeved shirt and bright black tie.

"My advice to Jani is per the usual: minimum involvement despite the fashion shows."

"They're into garments, are they?"

"The most expensive, dearly priced I'm afraid."

"Do they have a line?"

"Yes, they have stores throughout Europe and a catalogue."

"How do they advertise?"

"By the column inch. They also solicit by direct mail marketing. Why a motor, then? Certainly a hitch will take care of it. The rooms will be lavish with baroque and metal, the furniture shipped in from Tunis, the food carried by tray, the lighthouse a distant light across the strait."

"Why a motor you ask. Perhaps the motivation is not as simple as you might think. Perhaps the invitation came by someone known to the manufacturer. These crimes while frequent are not often an obsession nor necessarily a passion. In certain instances they come about due to persuasion in deriving a more extensive code list."

"Could be they want to increase what the insurance covers, or they have concerns as to the associated parties. Or," he said, thinking about a cost one might incur if the task were difficult to achieve, "the individual is overly indulgent and with means."

"If they steer clear of room management, there is no permissible association to a horse box car. Therefore they must want to eliminate the use of the moving car. This suggests a problem with the actual way the file is normally implemented."

"I see," he said, not sure he did see and hoping his friend would fill in the gaps. "Couldn't we assume that the Delmarks have contracted out with a third party to ascertain certain types of information?"

"And they don't want to be documented as they are building their file? Yes, that is the more likely possibility. It's either that or they have brought a problem with them."

"You've been very helpful. Might I offer you a second glass of Vermouth?"

"Not for me. I'm afraid I take small portions these days."

At length Sir Harry excused himself. He had considered sending an e-gram to Jani as soon as he got home but decided to postpone his summary until he had a chance to run a check on Delmarks traveling abroad.

It was a rarity when the first transmission gave him a

blurb on Saul Delmark. The item said he was residing in Morocco with a much younger woman of eastern Indian descent. He was seen within the past week at an outdoor cafe talking to a journalist in Barcelona while his attractive friend was taking a sunbath at an outdoor pool at a nearby hotel.

Sir Harry enlarged the snapshot of the female. She was pretty but had taken a hit from the sun. He wondered about her tan. It had come off rather dark, atypical for Indians while not so for a light skinned black. Shape and size had been unaffected. Her name was Nya Raupur and her statistics were as follows: age 38, height 5'0", birthplace Cairo, Egypt, UK, workplace El Kebir, Morocco, magazine color editor, marriage Raul Eluti 1962. The only match was for the marriage.

He checked the name Eluti. The man was medium height, thin, tan, with jet black hair covering his ears, a letter mail certifier who when he worked worked at a station that used laser to process mail. The file on him said he had at one time produced VCRs of mail and shipped these with VCRs to news stations. Because he was seen as a frequent traveler in those cities where the Delmarks distributed their stock, he came to be regarded as a trustworthy confidante and was given information that was not in anyone's interests to give over. However when the Delmarks were asked about him, they were unfamiliar with him in any capacity even as driver of their trucking fleet or as postal letter carrier or mail clerk distributor. When they ran a clearance on him and turned up the fact that he ran a small outfit on the docks of a handful of ports insuring mail delivery by shipping, they restricted those ports to their own staff thereby forcing him out. Despite the apparent lockout he turned up here and there like a bad penny always with any of a number of attractive women who but for modest salaries would have scarcely been able to enter the markets in which they found themselves. Could he successfully have gone into currency exchange and thus followed the fashion industry by the nose, it was believed that he would have found backers to establish fashion ports and put himself into power as a mini demagogue; but the bite of reality saw fit to remind him that he was not a man of means, rather he was a man of measure. The measure for him was in the proportions of being excluded from necessity. To ask for too much was to invite upon oneself a need to know, and thus in knowing more than one's status in life came a jealousy and rage that pinned to those who exact standards of revenge. Whatever must be paid for in ethical terms was then misappropriated to the few who would not surrender and favor was paid to those who would. He had a cat in the bag: his insurance covered the lamentable, the regrettable – parents or siblings or friends who stood in the way of the damned. He represented the damned and fed them on false presumptions that one could succeed by feeding on others, by taking what was theirs and then declining their needs for representation and eventually for friendship and security. He was deemed a monster if merely for the reason the world was too big a place to adequately patrol or to prevent the usurping of personal rights.

5.

Janice cooly regarded the Delmarks. John was a stony cut of composure and authoritarian decision-making while his wife Larta was medium height with short, wavy coiffed bronze hair swept up her nape and impeccably dressed in a red jacket with grey slacks and black backless open-toed sandals. But for her hazel eyes and a red stone at her throat she was without the exception that makes older wives their partner's ambivalent counterpart. She would rule her husband's heart, and mind, and where he left off as well. If his travels took him on long holidays, if the files he packaged consisted of new social orders, she was content to sit at a pool, read a book on the country he had gone to and create decoupage or look over new designs. She was of the belief that a wife ought to prepare for her husband's return, that were they separated for any length of time, he should know something about the interior of her dependencies upon him and that he should have further knowledge of her in a manner he knew to be true of her without having yet discovered it. Janice suspected the next trip by train would be to the lower coastal regions of northern Italy into Greece and from there to the Baltic, perhaps to Constantinople or to the Crimea or southerly, to the Caspian Sea and into Turkman eventually to arrive in Iran or India. The glimpses of the Sea would congeal the worst of human experience replacing the deadly sins of avarice, envy and jealousy with an awe of the ocean, of artifacts of antiquity, and of the barely perceptible horror at a hundred miles of ice and crusted sand on which nothing has ever grown or is likely to grow. Then she would have to answer the questions as to who fired upon the eldest Delmark, whether he sustained injury and what person in the family wanted to dispose of their own flesh and blood. For without the certainty of being victorious the gains would be like sand, forever escaping through one's fingers, dust being swirled about in a lithic landscape of gradually crumbling and wind driven stone.

"Well, I suppose I fell asleep," John said in his own defense. "I was tired when I boarded, somewhat overly preoccupied. My son was facing me, trying to talk to me about a new idea, and my thoughts were drifting."

"What was his new idea?"

"He wants to reconvene India once she comes of age in the seventh lifetime in some two hundred years. His thinking is that the elephant will be long dead and with it, the mansions that have housed it. He was speaking of creating a new culture – lilies floating on the pond but without roots. The roots you see have all the problems and whereas the water reflects and one can see in a shallow pond, it is nevertheless not a reflection."

"What did you have in mind?"

"India houses the glass eye. She is squeezed between two men who are content to betray and seduce but always behind the veil and I will tell you, it is not an article of fashion. It is meant to be a shade, pulled down as a front to a store and the store is what keeps it going. The information it amasses from its dominant counter along with its articles of shadow tell as much a story as the blades on any helicopter. She stores the threads along with the timepieces and the minute she turns white she goes back to the modern world to collect her art."

Larta complied with a helpless look. "He thinks it is the designs of the rest of the world that calls her back, although I suspect what calls to her are her pools of water, the belief that for precious months it is snow and then becomes water one must rely upon for one's survival."

"Why is this an issue? Do we not make a practice of freeing countries so they can govern themselves?"

He answered, "No, actually we don't. We are only in the business of helping people to understand themselves so they will refuse to injure other people and their property. To do that we give them fashion to help them appreciate what should go on their bodies."

Janice eyed the rose colored glasses with gold rims on the table. What had young John said to her? That Lord James was running the show? Where had his view come from, she wondered. "What is your opinion of Lord James?"

"Jim? Why he has all the pictures at once," he remarked slyly. "He stores these in a file which he shows off at private groupings."

"Is there a crime in that?"

"Not in and of itself. The friends he invites are people who should not have access to these pictures."

"Such as? Would Mr. Eluti be one?"

"No. They are his friends from polo."

"Do you require these pictures for your work?"

"No, however I require assurance that my fashion wear will not be worn by his friends who have seen them.

INQUISITION

1

THE idyllic lake in its serenity appeared in early summer to be a perfection of all that was natural inhabited by scintillating oaks, ashen twisted branches heavy with coin shaped leaves dipping to a mirrored bevelled surface below which few minds intercepted. Lilies like new hegemony emerged from an icy reflection of glaciated drapes of languid elms steeped in a darkly despondent pond over which twigs had come to rest in repressed repose. Only the resplendent shade visited by an occasional breeze wavered in its watery depth. Long roots sought nurtured replenishment in a shallow murky film, as did periodically thriving branches so still as to be an undercurrent life of barely perceived intricacies. Although the staid elms at the edge of the property had outlasted time, had placidly defended an abridgement of turf, they too weathered down to a stoicism as though time had stopped and minutes were counted by gradually shrinking somber darkness which in the breeze borrowed from a finite barometer of florid beckonings of hyacinths, violets, lavender bulbs, red pistons and blue madcaps. The shimmering green luxuriant patterns served no purpose other than to stand witness to the reflective order. The ambling expanse of meadow, cut short to fine measure, gently persuaded by columns of marble always seemed to me a distant view through dark remembrances of oak and elm for this is the very place where I met Dory and fell in love amidst a plentitude of grey black bark with etchings of a hundred lovers, come and gone. Not the least boundary to ward off dismal brooding behind which in a portal of desire, illusive figures in glittering masks and sashed elegance, velvet heels and striped stockings descended from ballrooms of light into a garden of sin. At night on a distant shore a string of lights penetrated the night with no other knowledge of deceit than what little the tutors of wisdom were capable of to disguise unwanted truth. One world held apart from the other without sign of forgiveness nor recognition of love was a burden joined by ethereal essence of silk, a grandeur of form and virtue.

I was an eleven year old boy when I came with my father, Lord Edward aux Dimes, to Edenhill, a marble showplace of some three stories of columns, broad stairs, shuttered windows and five wings, as magnificent a palace as any coach footman might on a sultry August day pull in front of in the invitation of its future prince. My father's future wife was the exactingly beautiful daughter of Edenhill, a young English woman, Lydia Declar, of presumed impeccable refinement and breeding, raised by a widower who in passing had left her all worldly possessions, a splendorous estate of some two hundred acres, a small harbor, villages and notwithstanding resorts in the mountains and on the seawall coast. Her beauty proved a fascinating effect of statuesque conveyance while maintaining an air of what I would learn to suspect was a deeply conflicted yearning to pursue educational ambition, having stopped with fluency in six languages for which she disciplined her knowledge by reading four books a year in their original text, novels, philosophy, interpretation and textbooks. A rather costly encumbrance of feigned joviality mixed with a poetic interior placed her in study halls of laborious discussion of merits, a worthy celebration which my father, being an esteemed scholar and gentleman himself, sought to encourage in her lest her knowledge became antiquated. My father by comparison was a rare sort of dash about, a handsome manifestation of height in his six foot one inch, illustrious lacy brown hair which was none altered by a comb nor a brush, deeply brown searching eyes, and the sort of mystique one comes to associate with men of a studious nature, gold shirts with bow ties, embroidered vests, linen trousers, stockings and velvet heels, often dark purple or green, sometimes black leather. I was just there, to be handed a station in life, which in time would consist of the study of the Mind to be enhanced at age twenty-one by a study of architecture, without being first expected to prove my worth or sensibility. In the fashion of my father whose chair I should at thirty sit upon, I attempted to mold life's circumstances about me such that I kept a pace with the classes of society by working in the stables a morning a week, attending a medical school program three days a week for young fellows on insect fever, setting bones and malaise, all which were often applied to the horses, and the remainder of time given to rudimentary drawing, harpsichord practice and reading music. Although busy I was often lonely. The sense of walking about a sixty room mansion looking for someone to adhere to would become embedded in my mind as the intolerance of the old for the disorder of often utilized rooms when they were not quickly returned to a neat semblance of pristine accommodation. That there were as many as twenty rooms that had only hardwood floors or impressive patterned carpets, swirls, embossed gold, stripes, roses or abstract design, waiting for seasonal events such as Christmas trees or February's winter candelabra of all sizes and shapes to fill them seemed to suggest a single minded whimsy about the owner's desire to captivate while forgetting, or that's what I imagined was going on when I grew bored with toys and lessons, that a child walked amidst the thirty adults who inhabited the rooms. When I grew inconsolable and my father found me sitting under an elm tree or on a bench at the lake, he hastened to offer to return me to my mother's who he would say frequently left us both because she was a selfish woman obsessed with an unreasonable mindset. Years later I would grasp what was at ten inconceivable, that she had fallen in love with a younger man and fled her life and obligations to live with him. My father would say, you cannot tame someone to agree to stay with you if they want to leave badly enough, you only cheat yourself to tell yourself it isn't true. In rarer moments he would say, she didn't mean to hurt you, Mariano, she is oblivious of the injury. When I turned fourteen he blurted out one angry afternoon that she had another son, and I thought – why was I not enough, why another son – and I dismissed her from my heart, shutting the door on any remaining sympathies I had, thinking her young husband a selfish creature for he had locked me out of her life and she had allowed it.

I deduced I was not meant to have a life beyond my studies. I was supposed to have no friends but to draw on my ideas to formulate the world and what it had to offer me. I had a mother who had abandoned her station, I had a father who despite keeping all meal times for me nevertheless expected me to pull out of these lively interactions with him something I had not yet developed a passion for and thought I probably never would, an insatiable hunger to learn the age old mysteries of the science of psychology. Some few years later when I had entered my adolescence I would look back on this time as relatively untroubled because he was always there, always ready to place me in the very room where he took his sustenance and composure and talk to me about his day, the funny amusements, the fair weather consistencies, the people he liked and what he thought they were made of. For me as a child though I was caught up by a perplexity I could not put a name to – a belief that a child determining himself to be worthy carved for himself a memorable life on his own. My jealousies were carefully guarded, as were my yearnings for friendship, and thus when I turned that corner when I could understand that everyone in Edenhill was suffering from a code of non interference born of a mistress' disposition that sorrow disposed of itself by quiet uninvolvements, I saw that to not become stifled by this oppressively futile atmosphere I would have to initiate my own arrangements for companionship. There were occasions when I thought to look for my father in his den and as I approached his study I overheard plaintive pleadings, cries of anguish, as if someone were entreating him not to leave, and he, caught in a complex web of having been left, succumbed rather than become a knowing instigator of someone else's pain. Another time I slipped in through a slightly opened door to find myself in a large sitting room, my father seated humbly in a chair looking beaten down, his new wife angry or upset slapping his face as though she had caught him in an act of malicious deceit and my father, pausing in a drama of distress, caught sight of me and ordered me from the parlour without explanation. After a good scolding I did not admit myself uninvited to their suites again, and although I would have enjoyed showing my consternation to my father that he may have entered into a new marriage hastily, I did not dare, disappearing from a noisy lunch when the temptation of willful behavior threatened to expose itself. His surly remarks to send me to boarding school were met with pleadings of my own at which he kneeled and grabbing me hugged me to him fiercely as though a separation from me would be unthinkable.

 That my father was in practical matters a specialist in the field of psychiatry would have predisposed him to suggest a cure for the vivid flights of hysteria to which the Lady Lydia was prone. In mastery of veiled disguises such as what the mind must by its own discretion alter to make living tolerable he was a scientist at his core, rather than a treating physician. While we resided in the walled gardens of a stone manor and its courts and gardens, he gave seminars on the gradual lifting of the spirit from its nocturnal wayward dementias, discussing with Freudians and Jungians alike the import of the mind's interior disposition. Women he perceived as vital in a manner men were taught not to be; despite this, he gravely noted that for a man to succeed in Austrian society unless he were an architect of renown he required the enlistment of a listening female to sponsor his concepts. The boldly encompassing sphere of compassion was illustrative of Freud in his notions of a suppressed subconscious terrain and of Jung in a powerfully symbolic aura of the male achievement of the feminine. Whereas Vienna herself had reasoned that the modern industrial course was far superior to humble agrarian origins, her apt structure for social moderation was borrowed from beliefs that women when positioned in esteemed roles kept them in perception from becoming estranged. Estrangement from the possession of mental faculties was the method by which newly industrialized societies were seen as becoming overly autocratic, conjuring up oppressive weights of indoctrination that invariably led to civilian unrest and apathy.

Were I younger I would have followed him everywhere, a faithful shadow, but I was approaching an age of rebellion, or so I was told by the maids who came to make up the beds and dust the ornate furniture, and I determined to bypass whatever sins of rebellion might lead me astray. I had been told before my mother left that the streets were filled with young men who because of one mistake could never return home again, nor set eyes on their family again, who were relegated to living in shelters or institutions and learned to live by another law, one not recognized by the church or decency. It was enough to scare me to live by my father's bidding even when his bidding made no sense or produced a reaction of anger in me. Thus when I made my first discovery as to how my father made his living my response was to retract from the suggestion of threat it posed; indeed I thought I might be safer if I were to live on the streets with ill reputed adolescents for at least with them, were it ever learned what I had witnessed, there could be no presumption that in the future I could do what my father appeared to be involved in. I was barely sixteen when looking out my bedroom window after dinner that evening I saw a caravan of wooden carts be drawn to the door leading to the easements and two men carry a long box along the gravel inside the mansion. I thought perhaps my father was setting about to teach anatomy to a new physician intern, but as I gave the problem ample concentration I decided what I had seen was too odd to overlook. I waited until almost bedtime when my father should have come to wish me goodnight but hadn't or in his absorption of task had overlooked it, then I crept through the halls to the stairs to the basement. At the base of the stairs I came upon a long hallway which took me beneath the length of the mansion lit by dim lights emanating from torch like devices hid behind guttered windows. There was a damp chill that permeated my skin to the bone. I passed a room with an opened door inside which were chains and metal handcuffs, a table with a grill and other barbaric instruments of torture, some pronged, others sharp with gleaming edges for an unnamed cutlery. I must have been in the process of deciding that Lydia's father had performed the ocular arts and left her an unsophisticated dungeon for her to throw herself at someone's mercy, when I encountered the locked room. It was off the hall on its own down a much shorter corridor with a sliding window such as what is written in books on sixteenth century France. I tried the lock and finding I could not get it to budge I slid open the wooden window and on tiptoes peered inside. A man my father's height lay on a table, his wrists and ankles bound by iron shackles, his face and chest steeped in sweat and blood. He bore sharp cuts on his chest of such depth I could see ribbons of tissue, bloodied like an animal for slaughter. He had been handsome once, his dark curly hair cascaded past his shoulders, his coal black eyes burned with feverish disease, his thin shoulders and thin arms gave me the impression he was little older than myself. I could feel an oppressive heat clamp against my skin from somewhere inside the room where a raging fire burned. Instantly I pulled away from the sight, fled down the damp hallway oblivious of all thought. It was a shock that there was a tortured man in the manor who could not even cry out because unbearable pain caused him to be rendered speechless. By the time I had scrambled up the stairs and was within the elegant hall of silver and gilded framed mirrors, I was skittish of everyone including the servants, with the uncomfortable knowledge that they all knew about this secret and all played a party to it. I no longer cared whether I might rebel, it now seemed a good idea, but to be a prince's son footloose in the English countryside any endeavors to escape knowledge of this man's misfortune would probably surrender me to impoverished circumstances. I was more afraid of poverty than of losing favor. Poverty, it seemed, walked a line of immorality as though the stigma of being poor would in time cancel all graces and toss one into the char house for want of a simple meal.

As I turned to go upstairs to where my bedroom was on the second floor, my father met me coming down. My face, I am certain, registered dismay. I gasped up at him trying to figure out how I assumed he had any idea as to what was going on, then recalled the men who delivered the box were his employees. I wondered also how he came to be on the stairs above me, thinking there must be other staircases in the bowels of this great house, wondering who the man was in the locked room who looked so much like my father and would not be in the house without his permission.

"You look as though you've seen a ghost," my father said; then as if I had been sleep walking, he added, "Where're you off to in your bedclothes? I expected to find you already curled up in bed."

"I went to find you. Where were you?"

"I was detained, sleepy boy." With that, he picked

me up and carried me up the stairs, down the hall, to my room. He set me on my bed, propped my pillows, and covered me up to my chest. "I was talking to men from town, there was a small rather inconvenient mishap that required my immediate attention."

"Did anyone die?"

"Mariano, who put such a tale in your head?"

"I heard someone scream in agony."

"Nonsense, you were dreaming. I'll stay with you until you fall asleep."

I had more of his attention in that moment than I had in months. I burrowed into the quilts watching his face for a sign of betrayal. He dimmed the lamplight and lay on the bed beside me, the same father I had always known, the adult I knew I would someday grow into. Yet in that moment I feared he had done a terrifying act and could not discern why he had selected to do this in a place I lived. As I traced his forehead with my eyes, memorizing the face I adored as though his act might separate us for all time, I had not the slightest hint of any need in him to have contemplated causing another man his misery, and so I lay there, cuddled up against him, listening to his breath until the constancy of it made me drowsy enough to sleep.

In dreams I knew myself to be dreaming although it was without the alert recognition I could come to at an instant. I was somewhere inside the mansion that was dilapidated, where no one went because the floorboards needed repair, the wood walls were warped, the ceiling was cracked. I floated into and out of rooms, none furnished, a ghost of an adolescent without comprehension of what the state of disrepair could mean. I came across a stunning leaded glass window in which each panel shone like rhinestones, the hint of rainbow color at the corners of each pane. Through them I looked down at a fantastic gravel garden of roses and hedges, replete with Roman statues of every sort, each with severed arms as though the acts of the beloved were long dismissed by an unknowable consequence of self destruction. The pond was similar to the one I was becoming a steadfast companion to, branches lay in the murky waters collecting dust as thick as honey, the weeping elms gently brushing the water's surface, upsidedown their reflections like thick drapes permanently hiding view of the upper wings of Lady Lydia's home. A coachman in blue velvet attire waited on a cherry wood mantel his hands clutching the reins to four horses, the windows of the coach hiding the person or people inside. A glance at the mansion showed it to be alive with light, a happy occasion filled with wonderment and fancy. Through the elms across the lake a house was being built, the yellow stone walls were being hung over a darkly slabbed stucco. In my dream I withdrew from the scene aware I was older inside a mansion of my own, no longer a helpless youngster, a grown man, cynical, and not without my own ideas for solitude.

∧ ∧ ∧

Dreams are the mind's directive to restoring the body from ailment. They house the symbolism of one's life guiding the unsuspecting creature of habit away from the depths of an anguished passive self toward a productive process of enchantment, a necessary restorative awakening which could blend into the day to day activities of a youth's essential learning as to the mysteries of life. Distortion is perhaps the best parallel for absorbing the complex conflicts that beset us, for in the dream, as in any meditative art form, distortion itself becomes a symbol to be comprehended. A youth of my age however has no strict definition of sin nor damnation. Sin is an act of committing oneself against the moral conscience of society and damnation is the hell a sinned person is subjected to in order to seek retribution and to ward off other contemplations of wrongdoing. But I lacked a firm experience as to damnation; certainly my mother sinned although I had insufficient evidence of it. She had deserted me; without question she was no longer to be found within our home. Despite the fact that for a year following her desertion I spent many a morose night trying to grapple with profound loneliness, confusion and concern for her, I knew in my heart her sin did not involve me, only my father and that it was between them, for his anger, hurt and devastation to resolve. Since I had witnessed the near dead man in the cellar I had arrived at a new perception of damnation. The damned were removed from their circumstances of living, placed in a most excruciating and debilitating confinement. They were surrendered to exquisite laments involving humiliation, disregarded as vultures to be destroyed, and in a rite of passage were destroyed by debasement and institution. My sympathies turned on a question of my mother's situation, and when I awoke the next morning to discover some hand, possibly my father's, had pulled open the drapes such that the all too bright sunshine flooded my bedroom, rays highlighting every pattern of carpet and ensconced wallpaper, I felt at last exposed in an essence I had not understood to be present in my world. Loneliness took on a dimension of awareness that my mother could become shamed, if not tormented, by her act. I considered asking my father whether he had plans to imprison her, and dismissed those thoughts. Her outcome was removed from me as much as her second son was but a rumor never to become known. I only knew that in my heart she was still my mother, that I loved her dearly, and could I arrange to visit, I would go swiftly to her.

My father fetched me at noon. He had an errand in town and wanted to show me a sight he felt would benefit me, although, he said, he would have much preferred to show me when I was several years older. I asked him as we stepped inside the horse driven coach if my mother were well. He replied he had no knowledge that she was not in fine spirits, yet as the horses clopped on the pavement I realized he could ask for retribution and expect she would surrender her life to it. The realization cost me an awareness that had he been the one who asked her to leave, by the same token he could have refused for her to leave with me. Thus her fortune was now dependent upon her new husband, for what father would pay a mischievous wife when he was raising the child himself?

The sight my father took me to was of a spired church on the outskirts of a bustling city I knew to be London. Because I had come with my mother to any number of seamstress and antique shops, I had seen the grime and clutter of older effacements and it stuck in my mind that despite wide avenues and clean flats made of alabaster, stone and iron, the city was possessed of a seamier low brow complexion made of factory soot and weathered unrepaired rows of tenement buildings. The church, however intricate its awnings had once been, had succumbed to causes beyond its aging. The stone in front of the entrance had been gutted which would render the establishment incapable of being repaired to its original architecture. A wall also had fallen and lay in bricks about a courtyard the elaborate arched glass which framed by an intricacy of greenish iron that once had resembled tiny apertures of leaves above leaded glass french doors now was incomprehensibly twisted, marred by destruction as though a mighty wind had emasculated doors, glass and iron to unwholesome rubble. The remainder of the abbey stood intact, moss laden ocher walls of Madrid-imported concrete, leaded glass french doors that opened onto an outdoor hall constructed of Spanish gold and malachite tile, the outdoor hall enshrined by marble ribbing at its ceiling, an interior square of a rudimentary courtyard containing a two tiered fountain that stood in a dark blue tiled pond with stairs leading into it. My father explained that the exterior wall fronting the interior courtyard had been destroyed by an evil act, the entrance also, along with a corner portion of ceiling and roof. The force of the explosion although it was done at night was intended to disturb the aesthetic peace of the friar whose rooms adjoined the room where the explosion had reduced the enclosure to rubble, this being a good size, taking into account not only a twenty foot foyer, but also a coat room and vestry, and holy waters of the virgin. The small church with a hundred old wood pews and scarlet velvet lining on the floor between the benches had not been touched nor had the altar. The damage was selective. After a team of auditors was finished with its assessment it would undoubtedly determine the damaged area was chosen purposefully because it would not permit the building to be restored in design. The flooring had suffered too substantial cracking, the wrought iron had been twisted to an unrecognizable bent, the ceiling had been blown through taking too much of the wall with it. Restoration aside, because the abbey edifice was a landmark, the code payout would prove enormous far exceeding any repairs and thus it stood to reason that the damage was intended for the exorbitant money that could underwrite additional salaries or enhanced programs, even though it was highly unlikely a priest had anything to do with the crime.

The systematic undoing of one of the most holy institutions of God was viewed by royal lines and their lords as one of the worst types of crimes ever committed, for this type of intent struck at fundamental precepts for the living. The criminal when he or she was caught would be made to suffer the exactitude of the intent. Thus if the intent were to imprison the society who worshipped here with intimidation and fear, the criminal would be put to the tests of ultimate fear. He would be expected to undergo an abandonment of self. He would be shackled, given any degree of pain sufficient to render his mortality and only if he chose a method that could not actually breach a person's life would he be permitted to quiver at the brink of destitution; otherwise he would be put to death. Certainly my father upon leaving my bedside had investigated my terror and had deduced after coming upon the opened wooden window that I in a moment of curiosity had stepped into the realm of the unsightly and come upon a horrific finding. Perhaps he knew nothing of my discovery but perceived I might encounter the shackled man whose mind by now must certainly be given over to a state of numb despair. The lesson however was clear – no one who stepped over this threshold lived. Once the dreaded act had been undertaken the wheels of justice operated with precise measure and the individual was cornered to obliteration.

My innocence was gone. I was not yet an age to consider myself a man nor would any member of an upstanding nature upon seeing me think me one, for I was short in stature, thin enough to be confused with an under aged youth and no greater esteemed by education nor by apparent station to be given the presumption of class or authority of opinion. In my father's protective shadow I could now not return home and throw myself on my bed and weep for my fears nor for my newfound knowledge of the brutality of those individuals who had created such utter defilement. My father was watching with the studied awareness of the parent who comprehends those experiences one has that catapult a child into sudden manhood. He had no choice to reject his station for which he was made, and he would probably say I had no choice either were we to discuss this fact of our noble inheritances. We would never discuss it, I would in less than five years be cast into the mould that was my father's responsibilities and, now I saw, I would be expected to hold to the same obligations. For all my imaginings awarded me by those things I did not understand, my wanderings through the estate, my careful studies of medicinal properties and alchemies, I was nevertheless at an age when the perceptions of youth my age were sequestered by a finite set of beliefs. I was still a son, I was still taking classes although these were not given in a classroom. I had not yet selected a group of fellow students to be around and have my opinions be shaped by, nor had I been chosen by such a group to join them, and I had not fallen in love and begun sculpting my expectations around the desires of a beloved. Having shaped my thoughts for this particular understanding, it was plain to see that my father hoped to skirt numerous problems associated with sons. I knew at that precise instant he expected to control every single aspect of my life, that nothing would be left to chance, and I asked myself whether I thought this was a good idea. The picture I saw unfolding was not a happy one. His passion for my mother was not imitated by whatever he felt toward the Lady Lydia, indeed, she seemed to possess no maternal abilities, she was aloof, detached, frequently morose. Although beautiful, her strangely silver bluish blond hair piled on her head in a perfect cascade of curls, her dress an odd mixture of tight bodice silks and buoyant gowns with a hint of lace, she lacked spontaneity, was stiffly ill at ease in my presence and because of these imperfections I grew to think of her as icy, truly incapable of ease, much less undesiring of being subjected to a son. She did not present for meals, her boudoir was always maintained for show, she did not invite friends to stay, she was in many respects like the artful fairy princess Rapunzel who did not even walk outside in the sunlight, garden or sit by the lake. On one occasion when after the tutor was through with my studies for the day I heard a strange lilting music, the strains of notes high pitched to break the heart with pity, I went in search of it, discovering in a blue carpeted room her ladyship plucking the strings of a beautiful silver harp, her eyes closed, the french windows thrown open, the wind blowing papers about such that scores of musical sheets lay scattered about. She herself was too absorbed to notice my entry but she cradled the instrument in her arms and her fingers of her right hand moved with grace, barely touching the chords, eliciting a wizardry of sound that caught me breathless. I pulled back unless I disturbed her and stood close to the door to listen. She was as free as I would ever see her, under a spell of sound, yet constrained by her fashion, an entity hoping to be fulfilled by purity. As with all people who come into our lives by some unseen ordination, so too Lady Lydia took a promise of virtue in her power which although I could not grasp this was firmly situated for my father as a signature bestowing a finite truism of convenience. While I would marvel at this soothing enchantment I would also try to attune myself to her misery, for in that way whether I could palpate the discomfiture of her life transitions, I wanted to be able to see in her my father's motivations. If she needed a kindly psychiatrist to arrange her diet according to mercurial tonics my father's service could be to my way of thinking more clearly viewed, but her periods of calm consisted strictly of music. All other pursuits gave rise to ambitions defined and in those recitals I suspected she was snagged much the way I was, that the cost of achievement lay in a stripping away of one's spontaneity, replaced instead by a carefully studied pronouncement of posture. My father lived with her, he was neither a watch guard nor a priest, his accommodations of her moods did not dominate by a course in draughts.

By my sixteenth birthday I had accepted a keen sense which I would deliberate on profoundly by error of thinking. I found the subject of the timing of my mother's abandonment which happened to coincide within a few days of my nativity a gruelling period of anxiety causing me great impatience and surly mouthed discourse. As I was learning how to quell this often openly disdained acknowledgement of my winsome behavior, I afforded myself with periodic ruminations of my mother as my father's model for circumspect posture, during which I combined sketches of various scenes of the manor with poetic scribblings. I therefore went through the manor room by room, sketching a baroque wall here, a cupid statue there, leaded glass doors that opened to the sky, a wooden balcony overlooking the secretive pond, a bench in the herb garden, a palatial amphitheater coveted by overgrown, now rambling, rose bushes whose stray leaves never ceased to remind me of a midnight blue dress my mother used to wear when I was small, the outer garment strewn with coiled satin threads of grey and tiny silver rosebuds, when I came upon an elaborate door carved in exquisite patterns resembling a church cornice of elaborate figurines; pushing it open I walked into a domed room such as where angels could they be seen or heard might speak to one from a radiant celestial ceiling of subdued lights. I discovered it was a suite of several rooms, each as exquisite as the previous one, gold wallpaper beneath intricate woodwork painted white with a thin line of peach to emphasize the woodwork around the doors, red damask walls ensconced by gold baseboards and a gleaming rich amber wood floor against a set of french doors which also looked to the sky, these without railing or balcony, as though one could step to one's death, and there in the smallest room, one designed for a young girl perhaps, amber floors, marble sculpture, the walls emerald green with soft lights jetting from the walls over glass framed prints of beautiful nude girls, each a beauty in her elasticity and moribund wealth of softness, a steel framed bed on which my father was furiously pounding Lydia, she entirely without dress except for a red and black lacy low cut brassiere and black garter belt clipped to vividly black stockings that showed a spectre of leg, her thin body itself a work of art.

"Oh, Mariano, not now," she said, when she glimpsed me, her green eyes alight with an interior wilderness I was unaccustomed to.

I tried to withdraw but my father came running, his shirt over his tender parts as he once told me they were called.

"I'm sorry," I said, running to outwit even him into the hall as behind me I heard her tell him, "I cannot abide by this, sweetheart."

I said when he was inches from me, "I thought these rooms were under construction."

He pulled me by the neck, a large cat steering a young one from a mishap. "I know you don't have enough to think about, so I will send you for a few weeks to your cousin."

"How awfully selfish of you," I said. "And all this time I thought she was crazy! Will you permit that woman to destroy my mother as you've allowed to happen to that man?"

He eyed me, himself suddenly cold, and said unkindly, "All I ask is that you don't get a girl pregnant, it will interfere with my plans for you."

"What sort of plans would those be, no friends, no sports, no interests of any social graces?"

He waited to make certain I was as resigned as he looked. "You're a spoiler," to which I smiled. "Do consider knocking next time." He left me there.

I waited for him to return but when he did not I found an intolerance arise in me. I was in the way of his new life, but he wouldn't send me to my mother, he'd let my memory of her rot first.

It was impossible for me to like Lydia. I began to perceive rather meanly that she meant to come between my father and myself in a way I could not compete.

My mother was a beautiful woman who had required no benefit of artifice. She was dark eyed, jet black hair that tumbled in curls to her waist, full breasted without imperfection, in high jump riding pants and a man's shirt she was both mannish and remarkably female, the swell of her bosom a continual refrain straining against the garb, only her legs and ankles and feet exposed as though in her capable habit of riding bareback or roping a calf she was without unbridled sex, a female able to perform a man's task. Not infrequently I thought she was without concern for my father's teachings, she spent her days pruning trees and plants, laying squares, making a waterfall, periodically preparing a dinner for guests he would invite.

Lydia on the other hand was no mystery once I deduced that she had cloyed my father by seduction. I was sure she had brought him into her house of the dead if for no reason other than the manor required another physician to school it along. She was not trained as he was, she had merely letters to keep her value appraisal worthy. Her father's passing had left alive in her a different type of abductress, and I scarcely thought from that moment on had he lived that she would have sought a husband. Fragile women retained fragility through necessity of a domineering parent who obviously relied on her intrinsic difficulties to shield from the public whatever arrangements my father was employed to take over.

That evening prior to my father sending me north Lydia came to my music lesson. She floated in dressed in an elegant gold and cream colored gown of stripes, lace and petticoats, the skirt a shimmering hoop of spectacular conveyance as though she herself were an appointed coach. Her hair, far from being put up in a bouffant style of a Cinderella ball, was loose as I had seen her earlier in the day, her arms and fingers bejeweled with glittering armor. She excused my harpsichord teacher, a man her age who in dark trousers with suspenders and a matching jacket looked after my mistakes with the eyes of a chord tuner.

"Mariano, you must know your father and I are married," she said pleasantly as though she believed I had accused her of an indiscretion.

"Yes, I know, Lady Lydia."

"You must appreciate we have done all we must to not interfere with your perception of your mother's honour."

"Thank you," I replied, inwardly upset at any reference to my upbringing. "I did not mean to spy."

"You must ask yourself if you are not being somewhat unfair, somewhat prejudicial."

"I don't expect my father to carry on so in the middle of the day."

"Truly? Because if your insolence cannot be contained we may have to restrict you to the first floor."

"You wouldn't care to be shut in a few rooms in such a large mansion."

"I will have you know that for the first eighteen years of my life I was forbidden to enter any room except where my tutors instructed me and I was confined from my bedroom until bedtime."

"Why? Didn't your parents trust you?"

"I was raised by my father. I had no mother. He felt as I do about you that a child cannot be expected to mind when they are persuaded by curiosity to look in places they ought not to be."

For the moment I was without speech. I thought, this poor waif, and then instinct, finely tuned to her psychic abnormalities, reversed my sympathy. "Do you intend to treat me with so much contempt?"

"It isn't contempt, I assure you. I have for this last year found it necessary to stay as far from you as I may. My life in this house is unusually complicated by my brother who when he spends time here brings doom to this very fine home. I cannot risk for you to encounter him, he is both cruel and severe and he would unjustly want to defile you if only because he is bored and meddlesome."

"Where does he stay?"

"In another wing in the house, one you haven't slipped into as yet. I wouldn't know what to do if you met with a nasty fall because of him, and so we have to have a series of little talks so you know not to place yourself in danger."

"Yes, I quite see the dilemma. Perhaps you could introduce me to a girl."

She eyed me with brimming hostility. "I see we are not to progress in this utmost of simple comprehensions. I am directing your aunt to structure your activities and to send me word of how you fare."

I was reminded of the reprimand she must have given my father. I sat as he had to demonstrate she would in time have two men of the same ilk to deal with who would passively acknowledge her and then be done with her.

"Your gestures are hollow, meaningless," she said. "You have much negligence, Mariano. This is my house. I have paid a dear price for it and you will submit as I require." She stood, gathered her skirts at the hips and strode from the room, no longer pristine nor elegant.

My aunt stood on her stairs to receive me. I stepped from the coach and dutifully went to embrace her. She expressed surprise that I had outgrown my boyish clothes and now stood five foot ten inches in well turned out threads, tan and green, my hair trimmed to the quick.

My father's sister, an unfashionable complement to my father with short wavy black hair and coal black eyes, was a wholesome woman who stood medium height in a black corduroy dress, a string of onyx beads and heels who but for a slightly overbearing manner possessed a jocular humor. She took my bag, held my hand and marching me into the house comprised of too many walls deposited me in my cousin's ample quarters. Her son Randolph William was soon to be eighteen, a perpetually anxious young man with bouts of alleged bulimia interspersed by periods of abstinence. Narrow in every way he was four inches taller and was beginning to resemble his father in looks, oblong skull with almost no hair, dark tan complected, budding with an iron will, yet nevertheless managed to seem as though any amount of responsibility would descend him to a further agitated nervous disorder. He was feminine as evidenced by the rouge and trace of lipstick he wore, not to be confused with a reversal of roles, his significantly older father of seventy years asserted, joining us with a tray of iced mint tea in steamer mugs.

The hours of the week apart from my cousin's voice lessons proceeded in the company of a young woman on my uncle's side. She was the baroness Karge Faust, tall, very thin, a bronze blond, delicate features who in every way stayed to the exact description of my cousin in artificial color, her selected style of clothing a plain line skirt, usually blue or grey, a long sleeved starched blouse and an over sweater of white cashmere with inlaid pearls or a grey wool with out-turned small collar, and saddle shoes, brown and white, collegiate. Both my cousin and his friend hoped to join a traveling ecclesiastic choir at eighteen, a benefit of which was to sing in Catholic churches in Europe. Together we studied our respective music call sheets, intent merely on anticipating the correct notes in the harmonious blend suggested by the sonorous pitch of preceding crescendos. Between music lessons we went by train to London where we sipped drinks in outdoor restaurants, roamed through architectural plazas, took confessions and entered boutiques to borrow ideas as to current trends. By the end of the week still having failed to elicit any utterance about my home life, Randolph launched into a rehearsed diatribe about spending my time constructively. Annoyed by the intrusive nature of his delivery I asked pointedly what my father's new wife had relayed. Randolph twittered with suggestibility, altogether infected by brainless innuendo. Lydia was my stepmother, she was the sole owner of a manor that controlled fifty acres of land, which as any respectable fellow understood gave her land rights to house twenty lords. For agrarian rights she could have produced fifteen bushels per acre. For countryside she could build five mansions and for scrupulous outfittings she could maintain up to five prisoners a year. Each acre was worth forty thousand pounds, each mansion in turn could be set to acquire fifteen hundred pounds and one prisoner a year would net no less than fifty hundred pounds per season. She was squire England, no laughing matter, my father was neither squire nor city proposed from Vienna, he was fetchingly dolorous. This being a season unto itself the pounds were worth as much as the constituents. I readily understood I was being instructed not to complain, my station as a young prince would in several years hence fetch me my own clandestine stolen armoires. I sat ears pricked with my tea and sugar unreasonably deploring my carthage, thinking the best comfort was to run afoot behind my mother to disregard, impugn or worse, but Randolph thinking my mindset as loud as a proclamation took me to stead. He blithely suggested I had no means nor a profession, in time I could gain a lowly meal ticket performing tasks for a group of physicians while I obtained a higher decree, or I might marry wealth, but those were the strictest modicum of opportunity. His pronouncement was straightforward:

when I returned home I ought to choose my career forthwith, find two or three damsels and have them over every day for several hours. This he felt would assure I was either outdoors where I could be spied upon or in the library conducting myself in a lifestyle and manner fitting for a son of my age.

The visit for my sentiments was a ruinous excursion into the self perpetuation of a social order I had no false perpetuity to hope to enter. If I had exhausted my options I would better have assessed my gratitude for an expression of baser design, although feeling trapped by the inherent negativity of the enshrouding atmosphere I deigned to merely conserve my encouragements. Lady Lydia did little to treat my re-entry to her mansion as a sign of value, and I suspected that whereas my father could entreat her to show some interest in my hastening of showmanship he had decided on his own to send me abroad and thus untangle himself from a series of indecencies which were they produced publicly would end a handsome entitlement.

2

SOPHIA stood beneath a navy parasol in the Champ d'Elysess. Even now my mother was a vibrant female with handsome chiselled modeling. My heart yearned to hold her, to keep her as close as appropriate behavior would allow, to know what aspects of myself she had quietly sought to engender. She wore a dark brown linen silk over a darker brown slip with coffee brown leather sandals strapped up her well developed calves in laces, a matching shoulder bag slung over her arm. It had been four years since I had seen her and she was more beautiful than I remembered. She had chopped off her cascading curls and wore a new style of softly underturned coif below her ears without bangs. Deep blue stones on her ears showed her off to be cosmopolitan, leather gloves, also deep blue, to her elbows added an Eiffel exaggeration as though frivolity as shown in magazine ads were now an accepted style. She took my hand on her bent arm as we strolled along the Seine waterfront toward Chaillot to an outdoor eatery chatting about her new life. She was compassionate with regard to my desire to live with my dad, she didn't want me to think that because she had not taken him to court she felt less loss, but she believed if I came to visit I would get along smoothly with her husband. She said she too had grown up the product of divorce and imagined only my desperation at feeling deserted, yet she sent me hopeful thoughts that as I grew older I would become less judgmental. She had sent boxes of goodies, flowers and toys which one by one were returned as undeliverable until they relocated to France, not wanting my father to learn their whereabouts she discontinued the practice. I instinctively felt a mixed reaction, I knew her to be the one person I could trust implicitly without fear of discerning loss but the idea I might lose track of her kept me silent. I listened as only a confidante might, my attention riveted to her sleek health, her inopportune caution. She described their flat, the walk up, rain stained stone exterior, a slate roof off which rain froze in icicles, the aged copper gutters, the oak floors, french doors separating the rooms, a den that waited for my presence to fill it overlooking the buttressed Notre Dame. Despite the small apartment of four rooms and bath, she had made an adjustment, fitting into the busy french pace was more difficult because as one walked on the street the likelihood of brushing into another person became a daily reality. She had given her new life a good deal of thought especially after her life with my father which had demanded a certain appeasement to detachment and selective withdrawals. She wouldn't go so far as to say his demands restrained her for normal residence but that once she had matched his desire for nonchalance she found it a hardship to put back into place a resilience for other people that did not require fastidiousness. I made every effort to blend in with her descriptions, every response for whatever emotion she used to draw upon that she feared was fading. When she ordered for the two of us, sardines, onion and beets on thick fresh baked bread, I was possessed by a fleeting image of her and I inside her kitchen, the doors closed to shut out the prying attentions of the gossipy servants, we as greedy of our privacy as mother and child might be, the normalcy of our lives already offset by the need of the lower elite to sponge up tidbits to get on the good side of a man who couldn't read his wife well any longer.

"I intend to come to Etoile when I complete my education to work," I said, when she was through talking.

"This is no place for a young man, better to enlist for two years if you must."

I would not permit her to persuade me. "I have friends here, I will reside with them."

"Paris is calm only in its coldest months," she remarked, inclined, I presumed, to warn me of a father's wrath I as yet lacked sight of. "Your place lives in Vienna and to her ornate mind you must remain with affection. Your life has not been so unbearable as all that, has it?"

"It's empty," I cried out, taken aback by my own startling outburst but quick to tears. "I was shut away like a maiden inside a cloister."

She stretched her ungloved hand across the table to mine. "Maria, please have patience with yourself. It won't be worth it if you leave, you will be forever in the clutches of condescension once you are acknowledged for who you are."

"Are you? Has he come after you too?"

She looked shaken. "Your father does not earn his title by that sort of work."

"He must. I've seen it with my own two eyes."

"Impossible. He won't entertain it for any reason."

"He brought a man to the cellar to be put from misery, of that I am sure. An alleged plucker."

She grew distant, a coolness that invited me to don my jacket to prevent its chill from permeating to bone. "I was born to a common man, Maria. I had no presumption as an educated female nor could I seek a post abroad as your privilege entitles you to accomplish for the merits of earning your degree. Your father gave me the education. It is no sordid education. It is a deeply compassionate ember that rules his heart."

"Then he does it for her," I responded impatiently.

"What type of baroness is she?"

"Mean, selfish, intolerant."

"What does she value, Mariano? Her gardens, music, title? What amenity can she not afford to do without?"

"I don't know. I'm not sure she permits one to see her clearly."

"For what purpose does she exhibit her mansion?"

"Love. She prances about stripped of decency in unused wings as men in dungeons are whipped with chains."

Sophia smiled. In a rare event she shed the simplicity of fashion to become the ideal of nurturance I held as a supreme truth. It was a complex selfless mirror but not martyred emotion, as one who allows themselves to be known intimately in every way, for falsehoods as well as transparencies. She said, coaxingly, "If you allow yourself to honestly love someone, Maria, female or man, you ought to give yourself an afternoon or two to slip out of your trousers. Otherwise life can worry you deplorably."

I was for once admittedly recalcitrant. I gave her the whip end of my disapproval knowing she would neither fault me for it nor find a weakness in my temper. "On one hand she broods, on the other she tromps."

"I knew a female who glided across polished ballrooms as though she were drawn by invisible reins. She was elegantly opulent, although stiff, a rapprochement of pretension, refined for the handsome blade. I used to find myself in subconscious rivalry asking myself what virtues her outward impression extolled. Men were either attracted or oblivious yet not without self control. She was just there, part of the interior display of sculptured beauty. She gave lavish parties, masked balls, theatrical masques, yet she was on the periphery, the effervescent host, the sum of her pearls and amethysts, gowns and stockings."

"You have the mirror at hand."

"You are without a consoling nature, Maria. You must train yourself to see the effect her nature has on those around her, of drawing into proximity the trains of other people's needs."

"It's too controlling for my tastes," I said.

"She must have been reared by a master. He would have taught her to project merely style without essence such that apparent lack of self was precisely what any observer would see."

It was nearing two in the pleasantly balmy afternoon. I had a class on anatomy to attend at half past and began to collect my fags, matches and notebook. "Would you like to see my sketches?" I asked. Turning the flap open to the pages of declaration, I produced a variety of male nude bodies.

She gave them a detached review, but I knew they represented a unique compilation. She turned to an empty page, picked a pencil from her shoulder bag and dabbing it on her tongue proceeded to draw. When she was completed she scribbled her name.

I took the pad from her. She had sketched my face, a roughly detailed scale of the young scholar with defensive contempt, the hard bitten suppressed annoyance in the jaw and mouth that I acquired from my father. The eyes too were narrowed with inner perception, the world had extinguished its import of commodity rendering just a trace of regret.

"Show merely that much," she instructed.

I took her hand in mine. "I won't make it without you, my dearest Sophia," to which she replied, "I'll send you my new address when I have it."

"So how is your mother, dear chap?"

I had only then entered the foyer and was removing my jacket and scarf. I walked into the sitting room, an accommodating creation of antiquated red and yellow damask sofas and loveseats, dark end tables, and ceramic lamps, set against leaded glass french windows in front of a large black marble fireplace inside which a fire burned. The man whose voice boomed with resonance resembled Lydia, although he was older, robust, a ruddy color of bluster beneath a flap of blond hair and saucy blue eyes that sought to define me as an intruder.

"How would you know about my mother?" I asked him.

"Perky lad, aren't we? The name is John Declar. I had you followed for my sister's sake."

"The Lady Lydia is your sister?" I instantly recalled Lydia's warning about him, locked in the recesses of memory, coming to the surface with an unmistakable dislike.

"Splendid introduction, if I don't say so myself. You've been away since I've arrived."

"Yes, at medical school in Paris. How's my father?"

"He's fine. He sent for your uncle's son, Randolph, an eager diva. I will say it's a full house if you're unused to large company."

I stood my ground, not to feel undermined nor outdone by his pomp. "Has Lydia given you a tour of the wings?"

"She's put me in her childhood room."

"In the green room?"

"A rather pretty suite," he said, with implication.

"It is pretty. Please, don't hesitate to make yourself at home. The rum cakes in the kitchen are quite the shortbread for afternoon tea." That said, I went off to find my father.

I looked in his den for him and not finding him nor any indication of him, I went outside onto the grounds in search of him. The air was fraught with connivance, a cloying scent of jasmine wafting about. I rather thought the erected estate across the lake was somewhat an intrusion by its size, so close to the water, a rowboat on the beach, and wondered why Lydia had not given the place to her brother but I suspected she had invited him to enact purposes of my acquiescence. The inlet where I had endured many a restless mooring seemed to have shrunk, the elms had taken a step forward, their weighted branches dropping into the dark waters, a fresh scatter of pollen having gathered on the glace. As I approached through the trees, the rolling grass absorbing my footfall, a young woman stepped into view. She was slight, five foot nine if that, a brunette beauty with long curly hair past her waist, dressed in petticoats and emerald tresses, high sleeves at the shoulders, tightly fitted to the arms, ample skirt as full as a bouncing hoop, her dark glance mystified by curiosity. Up close I saw she was cream complected, eyes widely green or made green by the clothing, a choker of see-through green stones linked by lacy gold threads. She introduced herself as Lydia's niece, Dorathine Barrough, but she preferred

Dory. She had come to spend the summer and as she was yet to receive advanced studies on the Mind she and my cousin Randolph had applied themselves to a musical composition she would put to the harpsichord. I was enchanted by her gentle feminine persuasion, her manner of sitting on the grass, her gown propping her at its center, her quietly comfortable style, like my mother, yet younger, with a minor degree of artifice. Seated beside her I told her I was on leave for the weekend from a boarding school in Paris, I described myself as brash, high strung, unclever and deceitful, in short a bore. From this she said with the wry grin of a cat she could deduce I was unaccustomed to the company of eligible females or ill at ease with my social standing. Was I any good at something normal?

I quoted Milton making light of paradise lost. Throughout, she sat as if mildly contented, yet underneath that unstressed demeanor I thought I spied Lydia's domination, a coldly inconsequential ardor that would cause a man to feel when he required his mental strength most meek and intolerably self conscious, rudely awakened to his flaws like specks of damnation. Whereas she disposed of no merciless rejections, nor gave off an air of superiority, she offered no encouragement, her placid artifice neither flirtatious nor offending. She was merely there, a fixture of time, as seamless as the water was unwavering, as though in adherence to principles of order or propriety. As I encountered the first passion of the poem, while my voice trembled, she continued in an infinite repose, a breeze ruffling her hem. Lace peeked up momentarily and I hesitated at the thought her legs were thin, flawless, as Lydia's had been, giving me the slightest invitation of an inflamed blush, and thinking I ought to know better and reveal none of my sensibility, I became as still as she, pausing merely to assume a breath taken was a fairer self reflection of oratory. At my pause however she glanced at me, her eyes wide with certainty as though if she had experience of coquetry she displayed no unusual instinct for it. I was certain as I gazed for only the briefest seconds at the reflecting elms and oaks that were I to make a gesture to her she might startle like a doe and thus I kept my voice as impassive as I would, until the spell was broken by a rather insensitive lout, I thought, as Randolph dropped all of a sudden from nowhere behind Dory and lacing an arm around her narrow waist planted a kiss on her chin.

She smiled at me then. She placed her hand over his arm pressing him to her while a glance at me was finally given in a melting expression. Randolph bent into her to reach past her shoulders to take a swipe at me. Laughing he told me he would share and in the subsequent moment he dropped his hand from her waist to her leg. It was she who suggested we take a stroll about the lake. Randolph and I stood and we helped her to her feet, she light as a feather, then he placed his arms around her waist and asked how my visit with my mother had gone.

I talked about her as if she were aged and nearly unrecognizable, telling myself I could no more be truly open in their presence than with my father. I described a nearly arthritic female who had found the restraints of marriage to be her prison, the day to day burden of maintaining a villa without many servants a life of servility. She had grown beyond me, a distant echo of her youthful self, her husband of four years having squandered her fortune leaving her destitute. I told of her fear of my father, of his implied brutality, a mix of condescension and inhospitality, a regular diet disguised as moderation under the strain of which she lost her verve. We had come to an icy blue finger in the channel where an island of reeds dominated. Randolph put his hand on my arm in recognition of the perceived hardship. Illness was her best suit, he said, and pointed to a flock of white birds flying above the tree line. He said, if the mind couldn't be fixed, the depression would set in as a physical disease. We stood there in reasonably reassuring silence, his arm about her waist, his hand locked onto my arm. He had grown to be a man in the absence between us. He was without contemporary masculinity, a posture of benign indulgence, whose friendship was honest, without complication. I glanced at him in gratitude causing him to smile at me and he drew us together until we stood in a circle, Dory with one arm around my waist and her other around him. We stood like this for a long time listening to the jagged cry of a heron lost in the thicket of trees. Randolph ended the moment by fishing a kiss from Dory, then hugged us again freeing himself from some long repressed indentured servitude which I grasped only too well. I laughed in release of my own restraints kicking at the dirt until Randolph scooped a kiss from me. I let him do it thinking at once it was harmless and knowing it wasn't. When he stopped I wasn't prepared for him to stop, my body coursing with throbbing pleasure. He let his hand run down my back to my waist holding me with a male firmness until following his example I drew them both to me, planting a leg between his feeling him like a welt against me. He put his hand in Dory's long cascade of hair as if to show me his thrill of her and took my hand and let me touch the silky softness. We laughed delirious, he spilling her hair over my hands, he kissing her, then kissing me. The day was free, breezy, and all we had he said was our mortal sin. When we left the spot we walked the long path to the mansion, he pausing to trace Dory's curve of her neck to her breast as though she had long ago agreed to do anything he wanted.

The day descended with immortal longings. Randolph and I took a liter of sweet Vermouth onto the roof to watch the sunset. After dinner he had put on the rouge and lipstick and a tinge of iridescent green eye shadow. We talked about our parents. For him living was tolerable if he could express himself without inhibition. He was his father's object of disgust. His father perused him about their home as though at any instant he might give himself over to smoldering exhibitionism. He was from hour to hour either loathed or forgiven, as his father drank into oblivion. Even his mother who openly disapproved of his use of color tried to fend against her husband's derision. While he knew he would one day marry, the trick for him was to overcome the nail that pinned him to a bulwark of deceit. It was everywhere, his father had admitted to numerous affairs, his mother had maintained a friendship with a lover from college days. The course of a man's maturity was measured by his success at seduction. What the hell did it matter to people whom one could not meet, let alone talk with?

We drank the bottle to the rouge. Randolph said he had measured his own success of love by the female's kindly tolerance. I asked, Was it tolerant of Dory to have expressed no objection to Randolph's caress, or was it a suspension of disbelief? Randolph replied that he considered Dory exceptional in her acceptance of him. He was freest with her. If she possessed Lydia's contempts, she lacked wherewithal to denounce him. The thing was he felt he could tolerate debase imposition if he had somewhere in his creative psyche to expend the anger he felt at knowing he had to take a man's life. He resented brutality, resented his fear of it also.

He was thoroughly drunk when he took me to Dory's wing – he barged into her suite without subtlety to find her dressed in her pantaloons and corset. He told her we were drunk and there was no hope for fit behavior. He placed his mouth on hers, pushed her against the wall and tore at her, a ravenous clawing act with no aim except to spend himself. She released the clip from her hair and it tumbled down her back, silky and extreme, her arms locking around his neck as he untied her corset freeing pendulous perfect rosy breasts, her pulse evident in her creamy sensual neck. He was handsome, as thin as she was, his ribcage lean and stomach tight as if the luxuries of their youth were their languid bodies, his muscle still firm, ripe from pleasure, his decadence his interior soul. Her glossy hair filled forward covering her narrow shoulders, her luscious breasts, her sleek torso, draping his head. I thought her brave to have forgotten I was in the room or perhaps she knew with a distant knowledge that I must be here. He broke into muffled sobs speaking to her in indistinct words, his hands running up each leg, telling her he had broken his promise and didn't mean to. He said he didn't mean to have her see what he knew himself to be capable of but only thought about. I was certain he spoke of infidelity, not of his private innermost thoughts which he had a right to keep. They moved as one entity, him reaching into her pants, she pressing into him, and in the moment I unlocked her door and left, thinking my hands had gone dry and my breath had stopped, he shuddered against her and fell, his mouth open to receive every inch of her exquisitely proportioned body. It was after midnight when Randolph appeared in my room and lay in my bed.

His blotchy red eyes said he had been crying. I made a move to turn on the lamplight but he refused to be seen. He had arisen in the dark feeling the clutches of claustrophobia as though he had given Dory too much of himself and had almost nothing left for himself. I asked him what he meant by his confession to her. He said he had once told her he wanted to be discovered in a liaison, but it was a lie. He was not attractive to women often enough to have a liaison.

He hadn't wanted me to leave mad at him. I said I didn't think of it that way at all. I said Dory was the most beautiful woman I knew. He asked me whether I was a virgin, I admitted I was. He wanted to know what I thought about Karge. Until that moment I hadn't given her any notion of concern. He said he would have her down. She had been his first. He touched me in a way I had not ever been touched. The feeling was overwhelming. It was a haunting, powerful jolt making me feel intrinsically alive with intense yearning. I thought I understood his sense of loathing, his need for women, his desire for me. He told me to resist him in every fiber of my being, but it was impossible, all I wanted was to submit to his hand, to cry or whimper at my helpless pleasure, to have him draw me out without end. He knew things that had not occurred to me. He said he could make me want him with such excruciating desire I would do whatever he asked. He said friendship was more important to him than love. He promised he would always love me. He had seen the way I looked at Dory, he knew my desire the way he knew his own. He said I had to learn to resist her too. As he took me, as he finally kissed me, I knew I was taken in my depth.

We took music conservatory at nine, Latin at ten. Each day was the same. At eleven we were free. Randolph and Dory wanted to spend the day at a quiet secluded area about a mile from the manor they had discovered. We set off, Dory dressed in a wool plaid of green and red; Randolph in fine beige silk, myself in a tweed grey suit with rollup sleeves. Randolph strolled with his arm around Dory as though they were longtime partners talking to me about the Victorian notion of deceit. He didn't think it could matter if there was explicit consensual contracts; I said he was being duplicitous ignoring jealousies. We batted his ideas of open marriage about, he occasionally asked Dory for her opinion. We eventually arrived at the spot they had thought to bring me and Dory dropped to the green and Randolph suggested we sit on either side of her. He placed his head in her lap and invited me to do the same. We laughed about Lydia and her brother and Randolph said he couldn't wait for him to leave. Dory didn't think he was that bad, a bit arrogant, but he wasn't around much. We counted the number of clouds in the sky. Randolph described a letter he had received from his mother. In it she said my father had invited their family to live at the new house, Randolph didn't think his father would afford the upkeep. We fell asleep in the sun using our jackets to shade our eyes. I awoke to the sound of Dory's voice. Randolph was still sleeping, his body curled up around her back. She was reading a volume of poems to herself. I took the slender book from her hand and glanced through it, then I righted myself alongside her and we both took turns reading the lines. She was enjoying my humor, and laughed when I laughed, commented on the poets' educations, from time to time ran her palm over my arm asking me if it tickled. At length I turned on my side to gaze at her. I told her I had confided in Randolph that I considered her beautiful, to which she asked whether I knew Karge would arrive by dinner. I said, no, I didn't know. Randolph awakened, took a pint of whiskey from his pocket, removed the cap and passed it to me. I took a swig. Dory read him a poem about love and he agreed with the author, that there wasn't as much time in the day as one would like. He drank another few sips, handed the bottle to Dory who took a sip, then he removed an opium cigarette and lit it. The deeply pungent perfume odor gave Randolph a queer look, Dory smoked some and I did, thinking it caused the leaves and fluttering water to appear more starkly vivid. Randolph smoked the final dregs washing it down, his gaze now brimming with distraction. He and I rolled onto our backs while Dory laughed gaily at the idea of the three of us not having a concern in the world. Randolph said out of the blue that I was a virgin. I told her I was embarrassed to speak of it. I was a mere sixteen. She said she lost her virginity at fourteen to a man she knew only the once. I told them I'd be returning to France in two days. Randolph promised they would visit.

The afternoon was breezy with a bit of spray from the lake. I wished we could stay until dark and Dory as if reading my thoughts said she hoped we could be friends forever. She said I was a man at peace with himself. I bent over her face and tasted her mouth. She told me then she knew I had to be hurting on account of my parents' divorce; separation caused a polarity for to love one parent was to deny the other and they were usually aware of it. I kissed her forehead, and Randolph slipped his hand beneath my chest and ran his palm over her breasts mesmerizing her. She gazed up sweetly at me, pulling my hand between hers, let me kiss her again. I was overcome as I distantly remembered I had been with Randolph in the early forbidden hours of the morning; this was different, if only because to my way of thinking it was not fantasy. As she permitted me to touch her breast, to feel the fullness, I perceived a sense of acceptance by her. Randolph lay his hand against mine feeling me stroke her; he slightly lowered her corset and kissed her throat on his side and instinctively I borrowed his gesture kissing her that way too. She laughed then, put her arms around our waists and we lay on her. She kissed me deeply, no longer teasing, then kissed him. He held her soft throat with his palm, explored her mouth with his tongue, until they were inseparable. My eyes flickered as I realized he was bringing Karge for me, that Dory was his female, that without his approval I would probably never hold her and he had all the possessed control, and knew it. I lay on my back then, stared toward the sky, thinking I showed too much. He went on kissing her shadowing her face with his as if to prove his ardor, to negate his other desire, until she pulled fiercely away so much so to be able to breathe. He remained positioned, a man to his future wife. I on the other retort could make no such claim of her.

You see too much, he said critically when at dark Karge had arrived. She stood in front of the fireplace in the sitting room warming her back to the fire. Her bronze blond hair was twisted covered by a sequined net at her nape, at nineteen in a glittering black high waisted dress and black high heels she gave an awareness of sinewy well developed muscles and tone. I handed her a cup of coffee in an ambrosia like green and purple teacup with saucer, a rough hewn brown cube of sugar on the plate with tiny gold spoon. We discussed her train ride, the scenic swath of manicured countryside of rolling greens, hedges, low lying trees and the novel she read, a story of a young girl who comes to love a significantly old man. She had, once she unpacked, freshened up, and studied for an examination she was to take in the next week, found John, Lydia's brother, soaking it up in the parlor, quite inebriated. He was a pest, Randolph explained, yet likely to purchase the house across the water unless my father bought a gardener and a dozen servants for it. Karge said she knew about estate houses having become bereft of her family because of her family's debt. Randolph feigned flattery of his longtime friend until Dory came down, her hair flowing without restraint, fashionably relaxed in a riding habit and thick purled long deep blue sweater with white specks of snow, and white boots. She lovingly greeted Karge, they exchanged cheeks, then Dory took Randolph's side taking from him the gold tray and serving coffee, sugar cubes, spoons and custard meringue tarts. For each of the rest of us, myself, Randolph and John, Dory poured, stirred in cream, appropriately placed the accoutrements and added a sliver of pie. Karge discussed the house on the lake and wanted to be shown it, I asked who had the key, and John said he would give it to Randolph after dinner. At length Karge, Dory and I stepped into the garden of armless statues and rose trees leaving the two men Randolph and John to argue the merits of abbey-dominated imposition.

    Karge and Dory were college friends who had met in Randolph's house. There, Karge had taught Dory to study drawings of the brain. Although nineteen, the oldest of their social group, Karge was nevertheless gifted academically and had placed with a high intelligence quota to enter college two years early. The two exchanged information about various friends, one had been accepted to Oxford to study language, another to Man to study Law. One would soon travel to Algiers on naval expedition, a male friend had been given a grant to study wind effects in the Kalahari, Karge herself had talked with an advisor as to changing her major from the Mind to architecture and was told she ought not to throw three and a half years away when in another two she could become a professor. I listened politely, bored with their inability to include me, while reviewing in my mind the earlier events of the day, occasionally gazing at Dory for recognition. She appeared oblivious of me yet after an hour or so as the sun waned and the pleasure of remembrances had satiated her, she drifted to me, put her arm around my waist, and told Karge a pretty lie that I had talked of no one but Karge, for which Karge said I had been to Randolph's a few months ago and he insisted I was there only for instruction. Dory told me then the plan was to have Karge who was traveling to see a school chum accompany me to Paris.

We skipped dinner and went straightaway to brewed wine and cheese on wheat crackers with a dollop of caviar, taken on expensive blue Spode. After a good fill we bundled in winter feather-down coats and piled into a motor outboard and boated across the choppy waters at sixty miles an hour to the new house. We spilled onto the pier and freezing looked back at Lady Lydia's expansive estate. It rose in the distance, an imposing structure of yellow and white stone, three floors lit by warm radiance, the bright rooms reflecting swimmingly at the water's edge. Night fell stapling the twilight behind a curtain of shimmering stars.

The path to the entrance was constructed of large

stones. The house appeared dormant waiting for life to resolve it. A brevity of light streaked across the windows at the second story balcony but Randolph assured us the house was quite empty, never before set foot inside. We entered into a massive room, the scale and grandeur of a ballroom, with chandeliers, bevelled glass, shutters, a wood fluted ceiling, larger to narrower frames around the doorways, a large white alabaster fireplace, a gleaming amber floor. A mezzanine with bookshelves filled with hardbound volumes over imposed onto the room, a handsome staircase carpeted in black spirals added a spirited signature, upstairs five bedrooms each had a separate bath, a walk-in closet with vanity, and a small porch with chairs to while away time with an eye to the lake and to Edenhill, downstairs a slate tiled kitchen had four sinks, an island counter and all the cupboard space one could hope for, at the other far end of the house was a comfortable den, amber floor, dark cherry walls and ceiling, a black marble fireplace. We settled in that room on scarlet velvet cushions and told ghost stories. Through the windows we watched the goings-on of Edenhill, the flood of light staining the edge of the lake, becoming deeper in breadth. In contrast a lone blue light shone at the end of the newly built pier.

Karge said she had lost a child earlier that year. Everyone knew whose it was. Dory said, without malice, she could have many others, all handsome, beautiful. I told her I felt immense compassion at her, it was hard to lose so much, I said, not getting the point of what they already knew until later that night. The charms of living seemed to evaporate all too quickly, as though in an instant of regret. Randolph said he didn't think she should have had to lose, and she accused him of trying to bind them all inexorably to him as though he alone could give more than each one of them. He said he thought she was being unfair. Her silence filled the room like a chill; at length I got up inviting Karge to come with me. We ambled through the large room into the hall, took the stairs and parked ourselves on the mezzanine. Her eyes had welled with tears giving me a reason to hold her as I had wanted to do with Dory, yet afraid to act on it with Randolph right there, thinking I didn't want Dory to come between me and him even though I would have welcomed it, although if there were a slight chance I could wedge Karge between the item they had set into play, I'd try.

Karge had put on a cheerful face at Robinhedge, she had followed Randolph rather like a chum without any of the emotion I was used to seeing Dory express. In her own right she was bluntly honest, a traverse of straightforward discussion that lent her an air of superior knowledge. Yet I held her thinking I ought to seduce her as someone like Dory or Randolph might to opine a need for just me, although I wasn't altogether certain how such a thing worked. I was after all passive in the act of love. I began. I removed the sparkling net from her hair, definitely surprise as her hair uncoiled into a long braid. I placed my hands on her shoulders and let my palms slide down her arms slipping my hands under her palms to her fingertips, she swooned slightly, her gaze swam, electric. I ran my hands along her sides, discovering every inch of her, unprepared for what I felt, almost no hips, a very narrow waist, hollowed abdomen, thin ribs, firm pendulous breasts which from her style of dress I assumed would be small. She pressed against me, I thought I would die. I pressed my lips to her skin as I lowered to my knees. I told her she was a wet dream, stunning beyond words. She was radiant as she leaned into me, her skin suffused with warm color, I lifted her dress slightly and kissed her leg. In the end I decided she was neither enough for me nor like Dory to suit me and I wished I had not gone all the way with her, but I fell asleep beneath her coat, my face to her breast as though she had life to sustain me, until Randolph appeared saying it was time to leave. I suppose I wanted little disappointment, even less reminder that she didn't have the spirit to possess me, an exhilaration that had not lasted beyond a few minutes.

Back in the hospitable warmth of Edenhill I sat in the sitting room to read a newspaper mindful of the fact that if John showed I would go to my room. Between articles I paused to reflect on my developing maturity thinking I had rather formed myself after Randolph by a hunger for being found. Stretching on the sofa I studied myself to find a miniscule of error that led me upon love of one woman to the arms of another. Caution drew me into conscious self admonishment – I did not know where I stood with Dory and until I knew, my emotions for her were infatuation, not the surrender of adoration. Lydia came through the manor to turn down the lamps and coldly asked me to sleep in my room.

I flicked on the light with a start. Randolph sat in a high backed white silk upholstered chair waiting. I told him I thought he had gone to bed. You silly fool, he said, he asked me what I would do if Karge needed an abortion. She gets pregnant just like that. He snapped his fingers. I told him I didn't know I had to ask.

I showered before bed. He joined me, an angry force of arbitration aimed at restoring whatever lay lurking in that dark pool of unforgiving desire, limbs of branches long ago given over to an underworld of watery discontent. He embraced me, put his hands all over me, said he craved me like insanity, couldn't understand what I needed, Karge was only to admire. He turned me to the wall inserting three fingers into my rectum, said if I learned to enjoy this I could live without becoming miserable, after Karge I agreed to my own destruction. He said he knew things I couldn't begin to guess at and someday he would break my stupid young heart. I asked him what was wrong, why he was angry with me. He said very humanly it wasn't me, but that he had given in again. I let the water pour over me thinking I could cry. He said he had asked Karge to come to Edenhill for me, that she had done a favor, that he had given her what she always asked for. He dried me, dressed me, held me; he said he had it in his soul to hurt me and he would. He fed me a glass of draught with a mild sedative and took me upstairs to his suite. He put me in his bed, said if I could let him do what he had done I would get used to everything else.

I reached for Dory but found Karge. She lay sleeping, her braid undone, it was so unexpected that for a minute I was unable to think at all. As my mind adjusted to the idea that Karge had me in order to have Dory, I considered leaving, but Karge somewhat awake moved against me and Dory moved with her until I could touch Dory across Karge. In a swift second I realized again that I could not have Dory to have her, Karge could, very possibly Randolph couldn't either. He would always reach for her and she might allow herself to be loved but somehow she understood he was made of something that couldn't be affected no matter what she gave of herself. I didn't care, I touched her curved hip taking myself as close to her as I could, pressing the two females together, sliding my arm beneath Karge, I grasped her by both hips. Dory slid on her friend's body, Karge wrapped her arm around her neck and whispered that she loved her and Dory kissed her on the mouth. Karge arched up to her, Dory told me this was the way she made Randolph grateful. She slipped between me and Karge and guided my hands to Karge. It was Dory I held, I felt as if I'd go on holding her the rest of my life.

The meadow awaited us. We strolled arm in arm, I with Dory, Randolph with Karge, she carried a picnic basket. I felt ecstatic. Dory tickled my neck with a feather and laughed. I didn't demand much. I kissed her every now and then. Ahead of us Randolph groped at Karge, both of them tipsy. Cottonwood blew about shedding tiny wisps of cotton. We came to the place we had been the previous day. Karge laid out the tablecloth and we sat, helping ourselves to turkey sandwiches, three bottles of wine, table cake. Now that I had a good look at Karge I discovered she was possessively inclined to Randolph handing him portions of the meal, trading what he took for what she felt he should have. Although he sat glumly allowing her to manage the affair he was removed from her, a male permitting a mistress to set a table for dole. Dory watched these exchanges through the long stemmed glass of wine, when her gaze met Randolph's she was lost to me. Whereas we feasted like languorous kings, I had the all too reluctant impression my night with Dory was almost at hand and I therefore suggested Randolph and I take a walk and leave the females to the cake. While my intent was to escape Dory's boredom and be free of Karge's obsessive conniving, because I with renewed sense of insight as to the inward compensatory nature of the man who in obscure ways rivalled our needs to be adorned came to see he was mentally trying to ward off an unseen yet prevailing common threat, I took it upon myself to take a bottle of spirits for our stroll. I asked him, when we were in a separate milieu, where he had spent the night and he said in my bed with the scent of me on the sheets. He told me he had once come upon Karge and Dory and it so angered him he had shamed Karge by taking her to bed and telling her anything Dory did he could do better. I said I didn't believe he had it in him to rape a female, he said after a bitter show of frustration, tossing a branch at the wind, that if I didn't comprehend matters now I wouldn't amount to much when it came to my intended station. I answered that while I did not possess his desire to humiliate I knew my passion was neither corrosive nor hampering. Indeed he could not not oversee every breath, he expected himself to insinuate himself into all our underpinnings thus managing our lives by unpredictable chaos. He paused then, he said not with particular disdain toward me that I was much too trusting to the effect of naive quietude. If I begrudged his love to me I would no more possess Dorathine than Karge, if only because Dory went in the depths of her soul where he wanted her to be.

"Why in God's name must you do this, use your nature as a pistol?"

He stood stock still. "Why do you not see it as fascination?"

"Probably because it's a compulsion with you."

"Dory belongs to me, Mariano, she has long before she met you."

"Then why did you show me them?"

"Because I know traitors, dangerous ones, and could they steal Karge, she wouldn't know it, Dory might protest yet would be ruined, you would fight the only person you must adore, and I would have my most cherished, indeed freest, moments thrown in my face, and not for humiliation, but for theft of my station and merits."

"Who are they? Do I know them?"

"You must see it as I do, you cannot permit them to know what you are really truly possessed by for they will have you and poison you, you must become someone who if they can learn any concern about you, you appear foolish, already branded, already unscrupulous."

"I ought not to have asked you," I said, thinking once I saw into the emotion I would no longer permit it to influence my acts.

"Your mother is not aged, she was not thrown out, defamed, she fell out of love and surrendered herself. John Declar is no more Lydia's brother than I am, he is her confidante, her spy. His interest in your mother is to bust you, thus when Lydia is ready to strike you won't get in the way. To know what I know about your mother —"

"Who tells you these things?"

"My mother, she gossips mercilessly about everyone."

"I don't care to know it."

We stood like enemies, squaring off, counting the seconds before one of us threw the first punch. He was ashen in the burning sun, his features were exacting, he had my sympathy in a vise, knowing it I became docile, intentionally feminine.

"You must always be able to know what they assume about what they learn," he said.

"What is their opinion of me?"

"That you are enamored of Dorathine, have become eclipsed by her."

"Do you think anyone is aware of you and her?"

"No, nor of her and Karge or of Karge and you."

I gave him Dory, dropping onto the grass, reserved. "What is the point of this posture?"

"It permits her to be looked at." He stretched out beside me, uncapped the bottle and took a chug. "Isn't that what attracted you, that she appeared to be caught, snagged?"

"Yes, I thought her beautiful."

He said, "I think she's beautiful too. But then I thought that about Karge when she first came for the summer two years ago. I've known her for a long time, she can't help herself."

I would return to Paris with Karge and she would look after me at Randolph's bidding. Her tasks, whatever he decided they were, would weaken her abilities to assert, would make him more all powerful than he already thought himself to have become. But I took another sip watching him remove another deadly potent opium cigarette and light it. In a way he was a monster, having no control over his greed, seemingly no concept for what he was about. His masculinity required slaves, he himself wandered afar seeking mere sedation, I wondered whether he was capable of actual love in the sense of a desire that could restore. The opium did what I knew it would, caused me to have a heightened awareness of sensation, it eliminated my self conscious awkward uncertainty, made me carelessly at ease. It would be an expensive habit, one I could not afford in any sense, monetarily or socially. Yet some small part of me liked the effect, for it gave me a degree of confidence which I rather suspected could otherwise take years to accomplish. He told me then that I must also resist taking on a feminine role lest I become jealous toward Karge and make her a competitor. I had a sense that he spoke from experience, that his initial shock at Karge stayed with him, almost that he had gravitated to Dory so as to position Karge to himself. He said Karge was the one person who had ever truly surrendered to him, that she used Dory as a pleasant diversion and that while he sublimated her instinct toward him, in his heart he knew only Karge and not Dory gave into him and accepted his abandon. He said we would return to them, find them lying side by side, that we could lie beside them, enjoy them, yet we could never become as free as they could with us. He said to comprehend this about a woman I thought I loved was everything. Society would not forgive readily, only they could. He told me to loosen my collar, roust my hair a bit, he removed his belt tossing it aside, took his shirt partway from his trousers. They would learn he said and lay partly over me. Life lacked ambition, I told him I was alone in what I felt.

We walked back, the bottle a persistent accompaniment. We talked about the house on the lake. I asked who it was meant for. He said he had tried numerous times to derive it from Lydia and finally determined it was to be the future home of someone my father knew. I wanted to know what sort of home as it was accessible only by boat. He said there were many who would enjoy the privacy, that they could be there as guests of my father's, or of Lydia's. The unnamed fear surfaced, I told myself Randolph's one failing was he wanted to point out that he knew more about me than I knew myself. I now steered clear of any discussion about the other house sensing it could be of immense importance in a fashion I might not understand until long past an awareness of the situation.

I asked him what was my father's opinion of my mother having left him. He said I was to be pitied, her husband was a traitor, not to England, but to France. The penalty was to be ferried about over a wide expanse of water, dead. He said knowledge of it would kill my mother.

3

PARIS is the best city for the instruction of life. Slanting bronze and copper rooftops, borrowed from antiquity of statuesque mouldings, its rain stained embellished stone, cornices of intricately carved angels and layers of silver and bronze thresholds, would formulate in my subconscious a world of elegance known only to lovers of art. Courtyards and palisades their facades and arches; I was held in awe of ecclesiastical breathtaking beauty. In a converted wine cellar I gave descriptions to my dreams dredging from the interiors of the mind long corridors of vaulted, ribbed ceilings and fresco ocher walls and rose colored alabaster floors with wanderings through the pulse of the city, its hum distant. A gallery morgue into which I tossed ideas, magazine cuttings, postcards and photographs contained an aestheticism of quiet elegance – trying to resurrect a constancy I knew would never be anything other than what it was.

My father purchased a flat for me within view of the Eiffel, it had been a large alabaster marble with ornate gold trimmings that had been turned into six flats, each approximately four hundred square feet, elegant shining blond hardwood, high ceilings, layers of moulding and baroque style ceilings in every room, kitchen excepted. At eighteen I was a free man who within three years had to establish a cultivation; after I stepped into my father's decorum I would have twenty years to hand select any depravity to manage by construct. My uncle thought striving to reside in the province where my mother allegedly lived a poor choice, Dory and Randolph had joined a small research group whose aim was to produce a volume about the success of Jung's precepts on expedition, my uncle said Randolph would always go his own way, inevitably he would view anyone as a poor choice for emulation and my father who was tied to high society by Lydia's purse strings would decline invitations anywhere but London.

I took to the habit of purchasing a coffee and newspaper at an outdoor cafe early every morning before I started my day in the hopes of seeing Sophie. It was a few doors down from the avenue terrace we had lunch. My thought was she lived in the area. I would watch the passersby talking or riding a bicycle and find myself thinking that the street filled up by eight, a lively quarter of males in business dress and women in pants with anklets and poufy hairstyles. The color of the scene was fresh, as the croissants vendors rolled out on wagon carts to their curb stands, soon to be joined by flower wagons, pastries and fried potato strips. The clerics knew to appear exactly at the hour hiding beneath billowy cloth, postmen like moustached police delivered mail out of a leather bag with straps, the old ones waited for their checks by their mail stoops. After an hour I ran for the tram to ride upriver to my two-hour class for the day, stepping off the stair across from a large brick building where I would listen to a lecture on research methodologies and take an autopsy before lunch. My fellow students numbered sixty, all were males, most were fourth and fifth year post-baccalaureates in white lab coats who were taking internships at nearby hospitals and sanitoriums.

In a week my aunt would come to measure me for a suit. She would bring me several Oxford newsrolls, a bottle of new convent wine, sardines in a can, brisket, trifle, peppermints, a volume of poems, a sachet of roses. We would walk the town, dine on board a riverboat, row in the lake, swim at the monastery, horseback and take in an opera and stage. She'd be full of gossip, things she couldn't possibly know, whipping in her own pleadings, her most favorite licorice about the deadly sin of failure. She'd say she didn't like Dory, Karge would make a better companion except she was so breve, my father worked until late, this, that and the other. There would be talk as to changes to the neighborhoods, new shoppes, trade, parks. Then we'd go out again.

I threw a few shillings into the man's hat as we strolled through the park, my aunt perturbed as she was by his benign stare drew me into a different direction and steered me hurriedly across the square. She herself was at an age when through a complete resignation to her husband's lack of interest in the marriage she wanted to use their fortune to set me up in business. Randolph, she said, didn't want their help, he was determined not to be bound to his father's recalcitrant ironies, as he called his father's ideas to incorporate a bipolar practice within the corporations of his friends with capital. She would rather that her son was a martyred philosopher whose circumference of their lives took utterly no one into account, often she thought he ought to have settled on Karge for at least with her there could be a relationship, but Dory was persistently distant, iconoclastic in her social realm. I could not enlighten her, although I leaned toward Randolph's tendencies, the less our families gave us, the greater we were capable of combining the arts, religion and our own pertinacious reverences.

We had arrived at a Florentine fountain piazza littered with coin. I took her hand and gestured we take off our shoes and socks, and we walked through the water which came halfway to our knees. We chatted about Randolph, his ambitions, her apparent vindictive disapproval of Dory. I told her I thought they might marry and she said absolutely not, my uncle had offered her a bribe to leave him; in time she would have to take the money, enough to buy a flat in London, because as far as she knew they were almost dead broke. I was dismayed for her impugned integrity, she said she had tried to collect Randolph several times and wasn't able to find him.

We emerged on the other side of the road. Across from where we stood on the other avenue was a female who looked remarkably like my mother. She wore a grey dress, a large brim grey hat, sandals and sported a striped bag filled with store purchases. For the instant she eyed the fountain behind us, I considered waving her signaling her to wait, but I didn't. I had the odd sensation the last of the sun's glare prevented her from seeing us, however my aunt spied her and yielded a gasp of dismay saying she had heard Sophie had gone to Antibes to stay at a friend's villa. I politely asked where her new husband was and my aunt told me he was dead. As I recovered my astonishment my gaze travelled back to the other corner only to discern she was no longer there.

"What did he die of?" I asked, as we crossed the

avenue to one of the bridges.

"Consumption, he was quite ill."

"How did you become aware of his illness?"

"He went to a sanitorium for a short stay. Of course he left your mother a good deal of money," she said, probably to allay my concern.

"I had no idea."

"We received a letter from her after. She wrote from Caen. That's why I thought she was in France."

"Might you send me the letter?"

"Yes, I'll do that when I return home."

I dropped her at her hotel and kissed her cheek.

She said carefully so as not to make a commotion. "She won't benefit by your attempts to find her, she's already in a different world, Mariano. She made her disastrous choice years ago."

"She said I did not want to go with her. I was never asked."

"It wouldn't have been appropriate to ask. All young children prefer to live with their mothers, the sad fact is she ran off with a man who did not guard his health. Without good health one cannot hope to survive."

"What did my mother's husband look like?"

"He was blond, very fair, and nine years younger than she."

I had not known her to know other males. "How did she meet him?"

"Apparently in the subway. He sat beside her and they exchanged notes."

I hadn't believed it at eleven. I was tempted to withdraw a vindictive pin myself to pierce that indomitable pride of hers, to ask about her college friendship Randolph once told me, but I didn't know the truth about it and I feared Randolph was evasive having omitted as much as he revealed.

"Good night, Auntie, don't forget to send me the letter."

"I won't, Maria, tell Randolph to write if you see him."

I would stand in the street for a good hour hoping for sight of my mother before I turned around and retraced my footsteps. The sin of shock was almost as great as my family's castigation of her, because even if I had developed my own questions I had not known of her declined circumstances. I put my hands deep in my pockets and walking past the fountain, my hand seizing on a coin and tossing it in, I asked myself why my mother had not sent me word as to where she was.

Even when Karge stepped out in the height of fashion, in a ballroom silk dress of tight tressed bodice and full skirt barely pleated at the waist, the allure of antiquity of black and gold over shiny gold, tens of petticoats to obscure her leggings, with her hair adorned high on her head, she was still herself, an innocent whose seduction primarily counted for sensuous females who might spend a night. With Karge whether in an illustrious coach with two footmen the splendor of decadence was weighted with anticipation, with her delight over a diet of rum cakes, delicious sweet wine, a miniscule order of beef bourguignon or of salted pork. I would wonder if this sometime fed elegance lent itself to anything other than mere triviality for during those times she let me bed her, I felt more than seduced, she connivingly entranced me until I was satiated far into a world of dreams. I suspected were I not so youthful, had I more of life about me, I would have seen some transparence about her, but I was indeed of seeking years, as yet not distracted by what I might come to know about adulthood, differences between the sexes, their moods, ambitions, whimsical natures. In wanton disregard for my sense of orderliness in the world, as I crammed for the first of six examinations that would take place over the next three years, she left our small flat and went in search of the family that had deserted me, upon return she negated my sensibilities with pretty journals covered all in wallpaper and lace as though to proclaim wallpaper at its best was a stripping down of pinnings of wire and ribbon, a desultory commentary of the inordinate fashions that were taken by staggeringly befallen mystery from behind whose walls would no more weather passion than privies. Upon reading these I encountered a small poem my mother had read to me as a boy, for which she became to me as one who is captivated in gardens of quiet, and I copied it and sent it to Randolph for his thoughts adding that I intended to marry Karge as soon as my exams were completed.

> The moonlight thick as sluice
> Brims in her fullness weeping
> A daneless captive crown
> Whose miserly dappled hoofs are trod,
> Then harness joints and jug
> That only stone might clasp
> Turn up the sorrow knoll
> Forget the rapturous quell,
> I alone return, my breast afell with grief,
> You my still grown son, you my meaning sown.

To this hour Randolph contained a pattern of petty jealousy, in written declaration he claimed I had maneuvered Karge far enough away from him as if maternal captivity consoled itself with no less and Dory whose lively merriment could have washed him to shore was now given into produce a cloying impatience which with Karge close by might destem. He asserted that not even Karge would want to stay long and any introduction by me of other femmes, no matter how breathtaking, would prove a waste of time, for in her heart Karge remained fixed to Dory and through her to the steadfast errantly winsome dagger that Randolph on those occasions when Dory sought her inopportune rest gave into Karge. I was merely a succulent lad imbued with their secret treasons, none to match his aching lonesome tetherings of chronic despair, when Dory could be had but unpossessed.

I lay long on my bed Randolph's letter in hand yearning to see to the bottom his scoldings, his psychology of hoisting me to him, the melodrama of what I imagined was his conceit as unclear as ever, feeling my frequent passion for Karge ebb and a hunger reassert itself to loin in Randolph's complacency. Karge busied about between sewing me another winter coat and writing a sheet of music, being as contained by study she rarely expressed a grievous emotion, despite our few words, I was at an age when if I tried to find my mother it occurred to me I may well come across her in any other way than what I was being shown, for my express consternations seemed to produce art in forms easily predicted to them.

My search began at Le Cloister du Monde, an impressive spired abbey constructed entirely of carved wood and intricate laced bronze, a tower which rose high above its own plaza overlooking the rugged domains of smallish amphitheaters and packed in structures of flats with high brow balconies of Caen. Le Cloister was hidden behind a round of monasteries whose trim cement blockings belied extravagant porches only for the celebratory nature of its clandestine monks, their quarters risen above these crevassed tireless moorings, the sides which cut ravines through the outcroppings of hills and toiled alleys they stood in. This particular ensconced architecture held a stunning view of a far off surrealistic areas of rooftops, some tiled, others sandstone congruent with their walls and awnings, gave a city its unusual degree of staid remembrances. I met with a friar monk whose dismal countenance caused me to imagine he himself may have given birth to a holy order of Danes whose near desertions were entangled with the needs of church commerce when threats to its housed in communities found themselves without sufficiency.

"Your mother," he said in a sonorous clouded tone, "has not practised orders here."

"She is Roman at her essence. Wouldn't it be natural to think this would be a doorstep on which she might by necessity alight?"

"She may have friends here, but if as you say she is English born, it is within England she probably remains. Her surname is neither posted nor retained," and he slid across the massive walnut wood desk a large volume containing names, through which I leafed, seeing with certainty no familiar names of my civility. "When a woman of your birth must leave, she most probably has been excommunicated and thus must reside beyond our walls. To learn her condition, you would have to first learn whether she has ties to any other ordinance as they record unfortunate lives who can no longer be preserved."

"She has a young son, by now he would be nine or younger. Could you look for him?"

"The fact that you think you saw her on Parisian streets does not rule out she may yet live with the husband's family. She may visit regularly, if only to see her son. We could look for him."

He invited me to stay the night and join the order for meals, which I did. Neither seeing her nor any femme resembling her, discouragement crashed in around me, causing me serious distress and inability to think clearly.

I went to bed after midnight, having anchored myself in an ecclesiastical library which was composed of much philosophy such as what my father had prescribed during my youth, Duchesne on economic, Descartes on a centralized wisdom of commodity, Kant on the brevity of life, Marchant on the useful whimsy of the upper class, and scores of autobiographies of musicians, both practical and sinister, their schooled ranks leading me to view a few hundred years of decline as the purview of need for opalescent wealth commingled with the attraction of light and mechanistic prevailings. I also walked the velvet throned halls, saw without surprise the center pavilions, both interior and exterior, contemplating the enchantment of duty without reward, wondering while knowing that riches are not afforded except by blasphemous degradation. The kitchen, earlier that evening attuned to bustle, stood quiet, severely restricted, not a stick of butter or ample strait of dessert made possible, the floors glistening, windows locked tightly against all sorts of wayward hungers.

In the morning gathering my nightshirt and brush I departed back to the avenues of population, significantly achieved of no greater than apostolic cravings, my soul calling to an unsightly universe wherein stood only empty corridors, desperate realism, monks preparing for a new day's worship and study. My sense of life and living had begun to undergo an alteration made enduring by the fact the seams of my life would not be opened, and when

I entered the hall of the disgraced I was already seeing a hundred eager faces that looked at me beseechingly as though I had arrived to take them to a work camp or some other equally unfavorable dejected farm. None held my mother's face, none made visible any likeness to myself and after hours I withdrew feeling the world of falsehood held from my revelation the manifest figure of my mother and indeed of her progeny. I was still young, I told myself, still new to the world in its mysterious complexity, it was almost void of any certainty I hoped to restore for myself. Two and a half days gone from my bed, I was desiring to place my weariness behind me, to single out the unsonorous meal halls and look afresh at my dilemma in some other, more creative vein, but had no sense of how I might go about it. My need was only the driest of compassionate beginnings, it filled me with the soulful resonance of sudden and frightful loss of belonging, and as even I might expect for a stranger, it steadied me for an as yet uncontemplated course of resolving human tragedy, wherein a voice took root, a warning that one hoping to achieve a license to heal could also not withstanding the fortitudes of time beckon unholy turnings for impure acknowledgements. Thus I returned hoping to surrender my idealism and longing to Karge, to have her renew me as she was so capable of doing and instead found Dory, the embargo of all endearments, my density of salvations waiting to chase from my yearnings the newest demons which for all I could know were teeming with destruction in wake of a childish immortality.

"Randolph sent for Karge," she said, taking my coat and gloves.

"It's been over a year, why can't you both stop interfering. I'm settled here, a few short years before I'll have my license."

"Your uncle doesn't want you to go abroad on expedition."

"I have a training post at L'Evrie that I'm content with."

"You will want an after hours position once you have your completion."

"I'm happy to be recommended for it."

"You cannot dispel to the sick and needy."

I looked hard at her then, she was blossoming into a real beauty, her dark coal eyes large and promising, her creamy complexion divined by sinewy limbs as though in her absence from me she had studied a demanding sport that had carved from her the girlish resilience, her expression still held an unintrusive accommodation I liked so well, not like Karge who had managed to transplant that adoring captivity for Randolph toward me. I suspected it was over with Karge, that Randolph had decided upon some other mischievous designation for her and when she returned she would be less capable of any true admiration for me, a shadow of the female in whose tenderness I was learned to become a man of possession. Sensing this I resented Dory's presence, yet knew too intimately that if she wanted she should have me, that I was no good at saying no to her, she was the one adoration I would not steer myself ashore from for long.

"I thought I might try abbey medicinals," I said.

"Your father won't permit it," she replied.

She took off the stove a goulash created of braised lamb, carrots, sweet potatoes and cinnamon and served it over rice. I tasted it, and finding it and a spicy mint tea with a swig of whiskey to my liking, ate two servings as though I had not eaten in a week but had through abstinence starved my palate. For dessert she served a dry upsidedown cake with minute pineapple and deep brown sugar and I ate a piece thinking to compare Karge's simple vegetable recipes and salads to cleanses that gave me inordinate energy, giving into the rich suggestion that for the briefest of hours that Dory took Karge's place my time was to become stultified by desirous laments from which I would awaken slowly.

When she stood before me in a linen dress, her bath having left tendrils of damp perfume on her skin, I saw in her a fulfilled feminine form, neither burdened nor implicit, her soft blush no less unscrupulous than reviled. I let myself be taken to my bed, be undressed, her scarcely sensual touch over my thinness nevertheless awakened my resolve, and as easily as that only time I lay with her, I succumbed, my dizzy stirrings no less fevered. With her in my bed, her long flowing hair enveloping us, I borrowed the one accommodation I knew from those days and mimicked Karge in all ways until it was she who shuddered beneath me, hanging her arms about my neck with languid desire pressing herself to me as if with urgency for no separation, her splendid ribboned texture seeking to hold me and finding me always a bit escaped. As she slipped toward sleep I awakened her, enticed her, moved her ever deliberately to that brink and subdued her, slipping into her silk for a briefest instant, holding her by her rib cage, again and again, promising only to be elusive, until she was as I had seen Randolph in her room that late afternoon, urgent, demanding, relentless. I let myself become dominated by her, and thought in a fleeting instant Karge had taught me all I needed, to be awakened and unfulfilled, to be comfortable with some passion but not have my soul driven from my body. I knew then I had crossed a bridge and there was no turning back, I had left my need for Dory and would be seeking release a long, long time, and endeavored to not have learned so much and all the while tried to return to the moment a few seconds ago that I had not yet become aware of it. If it were possible for me to want to seek out Randolph after all this time, if I went to him now, at my maturity, implored him to return me to an unwise unripened state, then what I was discovering was in error. Dory was now known to me, I was still unknown to her and I had the insecure sense that she had no realization that she ought to try to palpate my interior nature of which I knew almost nothing.

Long into the night I asked her about Randolph. She told me an unthinkable story, however which I did not doubt, that he had been accused of trying to kill his father. The entire family had grouped at Lydia's a weekend ago and in the wee hours of night muffled cries came from a room on the entry level. Randolph's father claimed Randolph had taken leave of his mind and Randolph was restricted to a wing until his father left for London the next morning, on Monday.

I turned on the lamp light, it provided a sensual light amidst the folds of drapes covering the windows. I recalled merely that Randolph thought his father was a traitor. "What would the problem have been?" I inquired of her.

She lay dreamily, her curly dark brown hair making her like a painted female in a museum painting, the silk sheets and blankets covering her just enough to make her appear indelibly feminine. "Randolph's father has a friend when your aunt is on holiday. She's a brooding type but he seems quite the man of importance with her."

"Who is she?"

"She's a Magritte."

I was disbelieving. "She's a short bronze sunny blond

widow whose husband was a pianist?"

"Yes, she's quite lovely, petite, somewhat younger than he. She used to save your uncle a seat when he stayed over in Oxford."

"I can't believe he's the sort to keep an affair."

"It's not an affair, apparently it's business."

"What sort?"

"She designs gardens for music conservatories."

"What does Randolph say is the harm?"

"He has expressed remorse to me that her designs convey time. They have sundials, nymphs, pools."

"Which constitute the danger?"

"Pools. Emptied, they become landmarks. "

"Was the argument put on hold?"

"Lydia has granted the other home to your aunt and uncle and they're in the throes of moving in, but your uncle wants a powered boat and Lydia is opposed."

"Because of the pools?"

"Randolph hasn't explained the problem to me."

For Dory to whom Randolph presumably entrusted everything to not to have any idea as to what could constitute a problem for my uncle was an oddity. "What does Randolph want?"

"For my uncle to reside in the second house without so much as a rowboat."

"He would be stranded there."

"His solution was to invite this friend in your aunt's travels. Randolph's solution was to post Karge there."

"Why?" As though the bottom had been pulled out from under. "Why must I endure this?"

"Oh, Karge will be back in a day or two, or I'll bring Randolph down. He can explain."

"It's not as if my uncle is unable to get around," I said. "What is it Lydia wants?"

"Originally she had the house built for some degree of servant, a composer or an architect, but after your father married her he determined the new quarters would be used for extended family. That way he could keep everyone together on one set of parcels."

Discomfort overcame me. Although Lydia's estate was superlative in its breadth and beauty, it would not be out of fashion if she commissioned several homes on it – at the lake, in the forest and in the dell. In time she could bring in cousins, landowners, even stable physicians, although were these son-in-laws the ready suggestion could be that at least one was present to surrender leasehold, casting question as to Lydia or her family which was not my understanding of them.

"Do you know the number of families my father intends to put there?"

"Only three, your uncle, a man of squire capability and a rank."

Not yet had I become a licensed physician with several years of service. "Will I eventually reside there?"

"No, Randolph says you will remain in Paris as a physician."

"Who will pay for the property?"

"Your father."

I invariably fell back to an unfitful sleep haunted by remembrances of statements my father had made and suggestive remarks filtered in by Randolph whose methods by now struck me as wholly unconventional. If he possessed such remarkable persuasive reasons to set me into a glimpse of a tainted upper class, he had obviously deciphered a failing which when bent to its unacknowledged outcomes surrendered a lifestyle known only to those in it. I doubted had my father known what Randolph had exposed me to he would have very simply booted him out on his ear and sent me to a paid boarding class, but parents are none the wiser when they have relinquished control of a child. I lay thinking were I capable of locating my mother's second son, I could remove him from his squalor and raise him to be a gentleman. I wrestled with an uneasiness that the friends in my life were scarcely better than I was to support the structure to which the society had become accustomed and removing false impediments set it back to a time of elegant and knowledgeable entrapments.

Morning came on the fractures of space resounding a lilting breve of fluid light in which I stretched like a satiated man of his older years, competently complete in the barely secret knowings of how one comes into life and rests with assurances that one has not overlooked an essential. Beside me Dory lay, in startling peace, as though in sleep she had acquired what I would always seek. I thought perhaps her youth had been tempered by parents who made her their center and thus she was never without their adoration, I on the other hand was a pauper, unable to shake myself from a queasy uncertainty that at some unknowable edge lay an as yet unrealized perplexity and this could take me years to uncover it. In my mind I remembered Karge and Dory grappling in sleep for one another not taking in my presence and filling a secret longing to return to the desire that I had discovered that night I reached for Dory with the same desire, she came toward me unconsciously brushing her body against me, something about her lack of awakefulness enticing me, and I ran my hand down her back until she lay snug against me, the moment not long enough, my perception that were she younger by a few years my rapture could be poignantly recalibrated. Dory took my hand and placed it on her inner leg, then drew me to her neck and put her hand at my waist urging me to her, I tumbled into her as a boy would, forgetting any need to control her, and told myself she would forever have me and forever I would deprive myself of others for her.

"Don't leave me," I said, to which she cried softly. "Honey, don't." I said, as though until she cried I was incapable of guessing her most private thoughts.

"I've been engaged to him a good long time."

"I know," I replied, but I hadn't known, nor wanted to.

She left that morning and I rewrote a paper that was due midweek. I went out once for a tonic and newspaper. I had my short dissertation of the anatomy of death for drownings nearly rewritten when Karge showed up with Randolph. She was dressed as she was usually, in a pleated red skirt with a short sleeved cashmere white top, nylons and pumps. She had cut her hair to her mid back making her seem much younger. Randolph wore tweed brown trousers, a tan shirt, and a brown over sweater with brown loafers. I convinced myself that a ponytail did him no more harm than to accentuate his boy face and long neck with Adam's apple. We went downstairs to the bakery and grabbed a few scones and tonics and went to hear a concert in the park.

We chatted during the first intermezzo about their ship passage to France, the balmy weather, the crowded disembarkment. Karge was perky, her hours of typing my papers gone from the tension of her posture, Randolph told me he had taken a beating from his father and he was leaving Edenhill for good. He had found a job at a pharmacy dispensing drugs to clinics which he was happy about and Karge had promised him a few weeks until he found a place of his own. I gave in, not as a matter of course, because we'd be crowded into my three rooms, but because I had decided I would not live independently of Karge and having decided this had also determined my life to be a mixture of thwarted needs and unconsoled graveyards. The fancy of our adolescence was a congeniality of innocence given over to Dory but she was not here and I could not imagine Randolph's sexuality without her, anymore than I could render a thought of wanting a shared promiscuity with Karge. The string quartet lasted an hour and twenty minutes with two intermissions after which I left them to complete my paper and provide an illustration; this took me the best of the afternoon and a late lunch, I tidied up, put a mattress in the dining room for Randolph and went to a local smoke shop for fags and licorice, a pint of bourbon and a container of sweet pecan torte, when I returned I found them mildly drunk supping ladled chicken soup because Randolph had a cough with baked focaccia and red sardines. They were deep in discussion about a lecture they had managed to scrap up at the hospital and I was all ears, a short course on the nature of how change occurs given by a female who was studying Freud. I helped myself to a round of dinner and divvied up the torte and liquor, topped off by a smoke and smoker's candy apiece. We chatted about my aunt, about the letter and poem I sent Randolph, about Dory's stay. Sometime after midnight I put Randolph in the dining room and fell into bed with Karge.

 We lay awake for an hour, she talking about the places Randolph took her to in lower London, I gave her a rundown on Dory. I had expected Dory to stay and expressed disappointment for Karge over the fact she hadn't, to which Karge said Randolph had told her it had to be over between herself and females. Did he explain,

I wanted to know; she shrugged saying Randolph said there was a backlash and she would in all probability lose her credential if she was discovered to have associations. There was a rumor that femmes were racking churches and he didn't want her to come under censure. She said since the idea for the *ménage à trois* had been Randolph's, it was an easier idea to get over than others, yet she said she thought Dory might be having a hard time. I told her I was glad to have her back and that I hoped it wouldn't be too long before we had our privacy again, to which she smiled and told me she was used to the intrusion.

It was Friday. I was between classes and Karge was in dissertation all day. I had returned to the flat intending to have lunch. The door to the bedroom was closed, but it was clear Randolph was using it with someone. I opened the door quietly and saw him with a young black man who was fisting him in what looked to be vigorous foreplay. I closed the door, took lunch and went to sit in the park. I felt sorry for Karge then and gave into a rush of egotism and sent Dory a postcard requesting she come for spring semester break. I dropped in on Karge at the end of the day and took her out to candlelight dinner on the Seine. I asked her about Randolph and she said he was sinking into a morass of illicit affairs, none of them champion material, one or two whom she thought might be Jesuits. After far too much champagne I took her for a walk on the Seine, I told her as young as I was or because I was younger than she would ever be to me, I wanted to take care of her for a long time to come, and she laid her head on my shoulders and said that could be all right with her, she'd happily help me understand what her crazy life consisted of but she didn't want to feel she would own me, that that was the start of unforgivable jealousy and she couldn't ever go back to that, at which she told me she had a long time ago been married to a man who cheated and she had to get far away from him to recuperate herself. I put my arms around her and told her no female was as beautiful as she and then told her I had discovered Randolph in our bed with a young black amagio. Karge laughed gaily, oh good heavens, Randolph was not so ungodly different than in the past. I held her to me intensely until she wanted to know if something were wrong, I told her nothing. Houseboats floated down the Seine with canvas lights and gawking tourists.

When we went home we encountered Randolph in the living room scourging his way through plates of food from the frigidaire. Karge flopped beside him and I dropped onto the loveseat, the upholstery scenes of lively midnight blue with bright yellow, pink and gold Parisian flats overlooking the Eiffel and Monte Saint-Clair. Shoving aside the food, he comfortably secreted Karge with her back onto his lap and put a blanket on letting it sweep to the carpet, a rich emerald, then as I lit a fag and poured three shot glasses with bourbonette he set his hand on her abdomen and asked whether I could rent him a roof window if he gave me a check. I said I didn't mind, I'd go tomorrow if he wanted and he said next week was fine. We watched a television show and Karge removed her sandals, I turned on the heat and passed out English licorice mints and dimmed the lights, then moved to the sofa and placed Karge's legs over mine. Randolph said there was a time when all he had wanted was to study art but he had taken his mother's advice to become a general practitioner and now he was aching to enter fresco design. We sipped the eighty-six percent proof and smoked and Karge chatted about her coursework on Renaissance ceiling molding and scaffolding while between commercials we chatted between us about my classes and the exams I had just finished. I raised my hand up Karge's leg as I frequently did when we were alone and Karge said something funny reminding Randolph about being up north but he didn't respond or didn't consider her idea well situated. Eventually Karge drifted to sleep, I asked him to help me get her into bed, so we lugged her into the bedroom and arranged her under the covers and then he went to turn off the box and I fell in beside her. Randolph came in at length and said apologetically he had done something and probably shouldn't have, I said it was no big deal, he lay down, kicking off his shoes, put an arm around her waist, and went on talking to me about the flat he'd found, a nice place on a third story with a view of Montparnasse, good copper rain gutters, raked cement, a small garden in the back. He was sorry to barge in like this, he didn't intend for it to be rude, he sensed Karge wanted the good old days but he had to tell her no more broads or she would wind up a broad herself, then he told me he would put inquiries out for my mother, there was an explanation as to why she didn't approach me, maybe it wasn't her, there was such a thing as look-alikes. I said I hoped he wasn't in a dangerous state, he said no, everything was more or less manageable, he had taken a dangerous assignment a year ago but it was done. We chatted into the night, a loose derangement of satirical sarcasm and amusement, a rattrap of sardonic entitlements, his periodic comments about his stepmother thinly veiled hostilities, his father, he said without chivalry, was finally succumbing to witticisms of newspaper carnivalities, he was soon to get away from estates altogether, shore up in the outdoor restaurant for train and busbaggers to bust onto an open scene.

When I awoke late in the night I saw Randolph had his arms wrapped around Karge's chest, her head was beneath his chest, and his body pressed against hers presumably to prevent falling. I was neither cramped nor had I been aware of them; I moved over on my side and attempted to take Karge with me to give him more room.

The flat Randolph had selected while small was flamboyant, art deco in its remodel, an interior made up of real bathroom tile, an entry with a hardwood floor of cherry blond wood that extended throughout the living room, hallway and bedroom, grey Formica on the kitchen floor and modern glass cabinets and a tiny washer and laundry room with storage and a door that led to a walled in balcony. Except for it being unfurnished, it was highway robbery for the twelve fifty he was asked to pay for it. What surprised me was he didn't intend to share it, he'd be residing alone, I wasn't to worry, he promised to drop by three nights a week, he hoped I would come at least weekly and bring Karge every now and then. He intended to buy some outrageously expensive art, tasteful furniture, modern stuff, he had a designer in mind. In a few days he'd be set.

Karge and I went there a few days later for an open house. He had invited half of Paris. The flat now furnished was like something out of a magazine, a beautiful blue abstract hung in the living room, the furniture was pure Mont Van, the kitchen table was clear glass with decorator white chairs, the bedroom was Grange and Thomasville trousseau on a dark blue carpet patterned with raised swirls. Guests milled about sipping champagne, there were an abundance of gay men, a few couples from Évry, some physicians who practiced in Tuileries. The gays stayed for an hour and left, their laughter like breaking glass could be heard in the street. The couples left at dark having made a meal of hors d'oeuvres of liver pate, caviar and shrimp finger sandwiches, and the remainder filed out down marble stairs shouting goodbyes as they bundled onto motorvans and pealed into the alleys. Only we remained, Karge in a see through beige dress, myself in a dark suit with a transparent white shirt. Randolph was clearly tired from the ordeal. He begged off, invited us for dinner at the end of the week and told us he'd be in touch.

Dory had arrived. She waited for us in the park waving to us as we stepped off the tram and headed toward the row of off white stone apartments where our flat was located. I could see she had cut her hair a fraction, she was dressed in a burgundy tight fitting skirt, a light blue blouse and a burgundy scarf and webbed hat, she held an average size suitcase in hand, we stopped to greet her and I suspected for my awareness she embraced Karge, slipping a hand around her waist and holding off with the other, kissed her cheek. They walked, their arms around one another, like girls and I followed, they exchanged compliments, my long awaited surprise for Karge now palpated. We crowded into the iron gated elevator and we rode to the top. Emerging into the hall Karge unlocked the door neglecting to explain Randolph's new flat and we all moved inside the living room. Karge was getting out shot glasses, bourbonette, fags, leftover cheesecake, and we sat completely at ease, lighting up and sipping eighty-six proof. Karge and Dory talked to me about medical school, who was who, who I was studying with, my plans. We talked about the weather and back home. The hour came and went and we had a late supper of grilled steak with steak sauce and hot tea. Karge brought out some of her cornice designs and pictures of gardens and statuary, I contributed to the assortment a few poems I had written since Dory left. We were at ease as we had been years ago, and we made tentative plans for Dory's stay, Karge promised to take off a few days of school. Dory talked about how London was changing, even Edenhill was different, my father had commissioned the construction of two more houses, estates everywhere were filling in with houses, it was an idea whose time had arrived. Karge said sipping her shot that the social morale were suffering setbacks and Dory, unaware of what Karge had been told or where she was taking the discussion, said she thought male homosexuality was on the rise. I changed the subject saying I had less than three years before I graduated and wanted to know if Dory wanted periodic company up north. Dory didn't know how that would work, Randolph had stuck her at Edenhill and although she had the east wing she was at Lydia's disposal, her freedoms inside the estate curtailed. My father, she said, had brought in twice the number of stable hands and moved everyone off the first floor into the other wings. Although it was a full manor, the place was run like a whiphand; any impugnment was grounds for dismissal.

 Dory designed a suit for me cutting the pattern and attaching inner seams, measuring arms and legs, waist and back. The material was black and grey damask and the inside grey silk. In its time it would serve as a winter garb, in spring it would require a casual vest, Dory planned grey and white pinstripes. Karge who had deftly measured all pieces had gone to collect her dissertation from the typist to bring to her professor leaving me with Dory and jam and butter and hot scones and Russian tea. I showed her my mother's poem and she said Randolph had let her see it, she felt my mother showed promise, the images out to be crisp, the indoctrination of a single theme, I asked, what could a condemned female want of indoctrination, to which she brushed my face with her palm and called me a fair boy. I told her I could have lived in Paris if it were at my mother's hems, I would have been content with a closet room, my mother's adroit fingers gliding over a piano. Dory took my contemplation as allure of a different sort and explained while she lived at Lydia's with Randolph she knew much about hunger, without him though there was a missed element the sum of which left her feeling tragically composed, without those favored sweets, a mere outline of herself. I took her hand then, told her I believed Karge missed her sorely and wouldn't she nightly sweeten her footbath, brush her hair, give her a refined poultice. Dory held my face softly against her breasts and I felt her beating heart, when Karge crashed in, the satchels in her hands fell to the floor. We burst apart like two guilty doves, I hastened to explain, Dory grasped her by the shoulder and said mean spiritedly it wasn't as it looked and kissed her hard on the mouth, I thought Karge might cry, but she recovered her momentary consternation and took Dory with her into the bath. It left me to wonder if Randolph cared at all about either female or if he had conjured up the entire nature of their friendship, for what a female might be willing to do for a man she loved was not to be held up to the need she coveted of that woman. At length they emerged, dressed down to their tresses, their hair tied in pretty glittering clasps, beaded finery at their necks and wrists. I sat Karge on my lap and told Dory I was going to marry Karge, and Dory said she had told Karge all and that she wasn't nearly as fearful of Randolph as she let on. I asked Karge about her dissertation and she said it was submitted and she was relieved, for the semester was over and she could sleep through the night without worry, I spoke about the end of exams, the useless worry one grew to be knifed by, when Dory said that it was Randolph who had entered her into a private college for fabric design of interior castles, to be used in conjunction with celebrated events of white stag, mistletoe, cranberry ornaments and metallic stars covered with silver powder, all show for All Saints Day. There was now an organic tension between them which were I not able to administer some degree of favoritism might dominate us for weeks to come, I caught Dory's eye and holding her gaze ran two fingers held tightly down Karge's neck round her bodice until Karge became of a heightened awareness to be unable to make light of the situation, I was no Randolph although in my lack of creative constancy I did not understand enough of their rivalry to put it to use. Dory sat then, a patient study, following with her gaze until I had realized a succumbed Karge, Karge's bitterness temporarily vanquished, my capable skill at love replaced in an instant that it was Karge who was the aggressor and Dory who was meant to be caught off guard, I wished I had more insight as to how their et duo had originated, was it my uncle who seduced Karge and my aunt who brought the enticing Dory to lure Karge away, or my uncle who married after he deceived Karge, in the flurry of emotion I felt next as Karge plucked a fan from her pantaloon and opening it to an all white scene of village and snow she relieved herself, damp flush breaking over her face, then leaned forward and fanned Dory, lifting tendrils and crimping her hair. After a while Karge went around to Dory, brushed her hair into a gracious fountain, curls descending in soft crescendo, Dory now still, permitting herself to be primed. I would forever recall that this was soothing, neither honesty or love, a sort of wizened taming without ignorance of the error in judgment. Perhaps there was a weak acknowledgement that if I could not rescue Karge from Dory and Randolph my attraction to her lessened, without Randolph though I lacked confidence I could attain what I thought I wanted from the situation. Randolph would have by this moment stolen their affection for himself, he would have declared one a wife, the other an infrequent mistress and never varied from his assignment for them, I was as yet an eager adolescent and had not the slightest knowledge as what to do to accomplish either desire nor governance over them. Karge kissed Dory's neck, Dory merely turned her head, eyes yet averted, Karge softly ran her hand over Dory's front to her leg, Dory gave utterly no indication or response; without my astonishment that females were capable of such drama, the perception of intensity must be lost, to imagine I had outgrown what once utterly fascinated struck me as lost candor. I chose to hold my breath as Karge repeated the sensual gesture, by minutes Dory smiled as though my desire had at last been produced and the two females took me to my bath, playfully disrobing me, filling water in the basin, taking turns to soap my back and chest, drying me off and putting me to bed, until at the last when they stripped and climbed in with me I confessed to my silly response to Randolph's admonition.

Karge said it was Randolph whom she had married, Dory said she met him through Karge, the object that stirred so much intolerance for Karge was a tryst who my uncle had kept whom he periodically sent to Randolph, the Magritte I supposed although the lineup seemed to suggest another, when Dory came to visit my aunt it was for my uncle she brought Karge who successfully kept my uncle from her, but the fact was they began their lives of love with Randolph and it was his desire to have them together in his bed. Karge was sweet, she clung to me as I submitted to drowsiness, Dory was merely there to further arouse my passion, when I came to Dory was kissing her gently down her belly, her skin fevered, her eyes virtually unable to comprehend my momentary awakening, Karge seemed barely to breathe and I knew in a flash of truth this was what I had wanted to invite, they were without guile, or pettiness, the repetition of the scene I'd fallen into at Edenhill remained vivid, no longer lonesome. Dory took my hand then as she kissed Karge, I felt sheer exhilaration, Karge was dreaming in entranced vigor, she was even more beautiful than Dory but Dory was where I belonged, her raven instincts flooding Karge with jolts of anticipation.

The two females set off on a much needed holiday while alone in my tiny flat I wrote a final ten page essay on anatomy of death by suffocation, as all the while I listened to cathedral choir music and watched sheets of rain sweep across my panes. My thoughts were held captive by the ever changing French landscape as rain turned to pastel skies and without warning to a deluge, a violent wind storm that battered the shutters with the driven force of desperation. My wretched essay knew no such deflection, I gathered my notes and skimmed the highlights only to derail my only bewildered self-castigation that had I been less morose of fantasy during lectures I should have a compelling focus, not a feeble nomenclature on which to position great words. Over the afternoon the sky turned dark, the melodious haunt which takes its toll during a storm I attributed to bored whimsy, by efforts I hampered for scenarios that could reach for an adequate discernment on the subject of suffocation, the item that could catapult me to raw afford rested in the lofty discussion I had immersed drowning.

At half past seven sharp the constable rang to my flat, he asked that I should surrender myself to the Central Portal of the Cathedral Notre Dame where, he explained, a loosening of flooring had resulted in a set of unfortunate circumstances, a man who had been seen at my flat was pronounced dead. I grabbed my jacket, hat and gloves and went running out with him, we piled into his upholster lined coach whereupon the two horses began their consoling trot to the colossal spired tower for which Paris is famed. My instant fear was for Karge and Dory but he assured me there was just the male. I had awful thoughts of Randolph lying with broken neck, his body an upheaval of ribs and collar, but when we dashed through the intricately fashioned entrance, hurrying down a lobby of buttressed flanks to the entrance to the Nave, the soaring ceiling manifested by thin arched pillars as delicate as green cement portals to God could be, I spied the black man who days before had been twisted in passionate forbearance with the only man I'd ever known to be handsomely endowed for love. I pulled back into a threshold of safety realizing I must warn Randolph, until it was he who stepped from the shadows, he who, his face drawn with dark downward creases, told the constable he would not expect me to have known the dead man. Upon the necessary exchange of information, I retreated with Randolph and we walked barely saying a word to his new flat, the sounds of the city lost in the rising steam from the street gutters. I put the frightening episode behind me, although I knew I ought to be full of questions, I gave my will over to him, his knowledge, his decisions.

"Your father will expect you to move in with me at the end of the month," he said, as he hung our coats and hats on various hooks in the entry.

"This has nothing to do with me," I complained, going to fetch myself a cup of tea. "That man is no physician," I added, wondering whether he knew of Dory's return.

"That man was an abbey frock who had studied architectural plaster as an instrument for remodel. He was known for his interface with abbeys."

I sat and he poured tea and a bourbonette for himself. Now that I was warm although I knew he meant to protect me, I felt the past resurface, that he was manipulating an outcome and feeling it, I was stifled by him, prepared to be bitterly resentful.

"I brought Dory down," I said.

"Yes, she said so."

We sat like enemies.

"I am fond of both," I remarked.

"I am too," he said, putting an effective end to any discussion.

"I will have to return to wait for them. They are sightseeing."

"Fine, you can leave at dawn. You'll stay here, I'm having company though."

"Boys?" I inquired.

"Yes, boys. They won't bother you."

"Do you want to tell me who that man was?"

"His name was Narsi, he was a friend."

I stayed out of his way. The males were his age, flamboyant and cheeky, dressed in colorful tweeds and silk ruffled collars, red and pink, purple and green, lavender and chartreuse, handsome with young faces, almost all were blond and brown eyed. He fed them bitters, melon and caviar, he handled them as if they were females, toward midnight I acquired his manner of restrained ease and they left me to the book I was reading. Toward two they prepared to leave, minimized by his fondlings, they kissed him and made seductive remarks, and when he shoved one to the foyer the others ran aside, until he told them to their obvious disappointment he had to put me to sleep.

"It's rather catty of you," I said, when they had left.

"They'll be back tomorrow. They'll want a full chest exposure," he said, with a laugh.

"How does Karge keep up?"

"Karge is a cat, I can't do much with her. It's not so bad as all that Mariano, I told you when we first met what I was made of."

"I thought it was just for me."

"You haven't been available much."

I was exhausted, bored, and asked for a blanket, which he tossed me. I put down on the couch, covered myself and turned off the lamp. "How's my dad?"

"He's fine, he's got his hands full."

"Has he ever talked to you?"

"Only once, before your mother left. He wanted me to make a study of music. I did to please him, but he's not like you, his interest is for marriage."

"Well, I'm young, I suppose."

"Yes, you are. Naive."

"It's not my intention. I just don't know what he'd like."

"Plenty of time for that, Maria. When this is over, I'll take you home."

"I was going to make Montmarte my home."

"No, your father wants you there once you are licensed."

"He doesn't like my friends."

"We'll cross that bridge when we get there."

"Have you located my mother or her son?"

"No, I've been busy, Maria. Do me a favor, wake me before you leave."

I slept like a baby. I awakened in the early hours before dawn, my head splitting with the agony of a hangover. I took a pepto and went into the bedroom to awaken Randolph. He slept as I remembered, a hand across his chest, the other flung across the bed. I bent to kiss him and he reached for my head. I let him pull me toward him with no thought other than to remember the way he used to need me, when he had me on the bed, he placed his hand on my hip and kissed me longingly as if we were still friends until he rolled on top of me, and began to whisper to me promising me he wouldn't hurt me, it would only be a little while, if I wanted he would let me do to him what I wanted, he buried himself against me holding me as he gasped, his kisses were soft as if I were a female, his embrace was knowing as though if he kept at me he could get me to acquiesce, but he was different, older in his passion as though it was I and not Dory who would spend my life by his side, and when I cried I surprised even myself.

"That's how they are with me," he said, as though I were curious when I wasn't.

"You've changed," I said. "I like it to be male."

He looked up at me. "I'm almost thirty. By forty I'll be washed up."

I kissed him brutally. "Come by, I'll cook for you, the girls won't be home until late."

"They'll try to arrest me if they can place me at your flat."

It was then I realized he was in trouble. "I'll stop by

later with Karge."

"Karge hates me," he answered.

I purchased dinner and left Dory to herself, hailed a coach and sped with Karge across Paris to the northeast section. We arrived almost after the party was over but evidence of it was consummate. Through the hall came a familiar sound of weeping, this time I stopped in my steps and merely listened for Randolph's voice, until I heard a spiteful, somewhat antagonistic utterance, I only thought he was in the throes of unenduring indelicacies. My initial instinct was anger, for after what I had confided how could he entertain a boy, but Karge busied herself putting food on the table leaving me to take notice. Randolph begged his initiate to be patient, told him exactly the words he once told Doranthine and then to my surprise asked for the boy's confession, the words came stumbling out, the boy had gone in as a choir boy, he had a biblical tutor on the outside, the matter had formulated in Laon at du Leclerc, the consideration enough to pay for a cellar. Once expressed he sputtered gagging in such a way I instinctively withdrew and went to join Karge. The spread consisted of sardine paste, a small cabbage salad, cold asparagus tips with lemon glace, iced tea, pudding bread. The porcelain was elite, Spode edged by silver, the deepest blue, forks reddish cool gold, one knife to share, dark blue webspun drinking glasses, white cream India napkins. In an hour Randolph joined us, his companion no more than twelve, my shock readily apparent. Karge was blase, she asked how his medical studies were proceeding, the boy ventured to say although he was a scholar at rue Chatelaine his service was as a tidy ghost in one of the towers, he was quite unable to acknowledge the pun of his words despite viewing his newly trim persuasion in the mirror, medieval Laon had done its utmost to capture his heart, Randolph said. Mentally I took in the circumstances, mentally I newly approached the meal, asking myself what I was to Karge, to Randolph, how did Dory fit in or did she, I wondered how much of my behavior my father might be aware of, and recollected vividly the church in its portal ruin outside London's squire district. The boy seemed too young to be what the sounds I had overheard suggested, and equally as poignantly I remembered the wails of the male underground and wondered for how long the notions of scarce deprivation might go on.

4

IN this year seventeen hundred and sixty-two when France's prison population was safely returned home, she was moved from the semi-northern corner of mid Canada, from York to Vermont and inland to the Great Lacs, trade having prescribed her for wood to Europa. Although the dutch trades would attempt to congress in those states and some french would move north, the families who left for France would initially enjoy tremendous relief and jobs creating sculpturous architecture to benefit further trade from all European states. The rationale was these prisoners had repeatedly lost her trades to the ocean, tea, wood, silk, and other locked room goods to plunderings. Her new low classes went into heart failure, organic brain syndrome, or sudden drop in temperature as evidenced by extreme cold, it was classified as such. Because France prevailed in farming areas of storage for any of a multitude of products to be shipped outside the country periodically entrapped a vagrant who then died. People who stayed at inns were on occasion without stable residences, the notion of a steak and glass of wine and a clean shave was in highly unusual situations the precursor to heart failure, especially where there was a system of photography capable of seeing into rooms to assure safety in those districts where shipping dominated. More often than not the victim's death fell into one of two categories: they were a victim of foul play and were dragged unconscious into a room and left for dead, they got into this situation as a result of going out walking and picking up a femme, or without realizing they stepped barefoot on a nail or were attacked by a rabid cat, thus, undergoing respiratory complications and paralysis.

A terror like a spasm shuddered through elite classes of Paris with a cry for swift redemption, and stone villages, small and isolated from large populations, were erected surrounded by walls and governed by stations. Into this, my father came down for a short visit. He took me to chess tournaments, to knobby games, to houses where very young women awaited release, and to high step tea, board, relinquishment. In coffee houses, opera, tea on Sunday and on riverboats we talked about my practice, the complaints, the complications, he wanted to know whether I desired a position at Oxford's Trevelor Street, depending upon my exams I thought I might, if a position could take me into France, as I wanted to build a practice among abbey fortresses, especially on the sea. I wanted to be a physician on board a black sail ship someday, because my mentor owned the french alabaster trade. My father said he had come across whereabouts of my mother and entrusted to me several handwritten letters, all of which were sent under pseudonymous addresses. I retained a discreet posture, cautious not to invite his ire, he seemed not to notice the brevity of my relief. He had grown much older, was finally willing to contend with my needs apart from his own, was making his fair share of overtures and not until he asked did I understand the direction toward which he was leading. A femme life, even among close friends, ought to be discouraged; were I not the son of an Oxford gentleman there would be no further than a cautionary concern with understanding of curiosity, but I would someday have an important post entrusted to me and could not afford to be undermined. We were in a newspaper house, elegant retentions of sculpted alabaster columns topped by Doric figures, the ceiling painted wood of sedate yellow ochre intermixed with green, white and sandstone, baroque style, heavy crimson drapes sashed aside leaded glass, long, narrow windows, breakfast tea in saucer cups placed on lace mats on distinguished dark wood chess tables.

By the time these five thousand prisoners had been within the country for about twenty years France began to contend with infrequent malicious occurrences, each seemingly associated with her abilities to recapture her industries, her farming, her shipping and her secure borders. The nature of the deaths however would confound French doctors of medicine, if only for the fact that these were nearly all associated with having eaten before they died, were not at home, and almost all exhibited REM. There was no evidence from the history, physical examination, or laboratory tests, of significant cerebral-vascular disease that could be etiologically related to the disturbance, amount of intoxication insufficient to cause death, no evidence of nausea or vomiting, malaise, however it was certainly a condition affecting respiratory system and eventually shut down heart function while allowing REM. There was a good deal of effort put to the consideration as to what caused a person to be asleep and unable to awaken as this was a brain function.

Whereas the condition was not known to occur in a group of people and one could not know whether a blackout had occurred, in northern France there was occurring research as to type of stimuli – did they fall, did they step on a nail, were they poked in the eye, did they take a fast acting barbiturate or drug, could they have listened to buzzes all night, were they stung by a bee. The key question was, when stimuli was received, what prevented the person from recuperating. Being required to take at least one class, preferably two, I took lessons on multi-infarct etiology of pathophysiological, focal neurological signs and symptoms, and weakness of any extremity. My professor, a male of clearly superior competence who liked to speak, proffered a series of questions: was this a virus because it spread to the heart, or a bacteria because it couldn't become airborne, if it caused paralysis, it had to be a bacteria, if it caused edema, it could be a virus but could be the result of heart attack only, a virus would be rare, if it were congestive heart attack, then the lungs shut down due to a pneumonia virus and a chest X-ray ought to show irritation. These deaths, he said as a point of humor, were called locked room deaths; if one had to say, they were due to a circumstance, possibly unknown but not unprovable, of an etiology not unlike clairvoyance or telepathy and although they might be audiovisual, possibly sensitive oratory special methodologies as real as any direct contact with an actual provoker, an example in an inn a person on the other side of the bed against the wall of the other room inside which any object inside the room was used, the explanations were to be had with common sense. Bacteria included botulism, salmonella, eschercolla; viruses were Influenza and locked room, and personality problems which might kill might be hunger, vomiting by self inducement, self infliction or suicide, but the belief about suicide was that these were all without exception homicides. Therefore until a locked room death was further categorized all of us dressed in tailored tan and white suits of high fashion, our shoes mocktoe. I was coming into my own, his fair son, now twenty, yet to be in classes another four years before I could be granted a position at a hospital, dark black curly hair, moderate shoulder width, thin as cultivation would prefer, dark black eyed intensity, the appearance of french disposition. Now that I was married, his complaint ought not to be won, I said. He wondered whether my introduction to the infrequency of despair had caused me to seek a remedy focussed on situational extravagance, to which I replied it only occurred a handful of times, certainly just once with the male. I inquired how he came to understand this, he said he had seen a figure leave my room on seven occasions, to which I instantly regretted my confession and said not a once was I in my room when a man was there. My father disclosed he was invited to attend to research on viral dispositions resulting in excruciating dementia, for which the signatory complaint by women were men leaving their husband's quarters, and he uncomfortably recalled having observed what he thought must be such a situation. I replied my marriage was suitable, that Helene was personable, tender, knowledgeable, I did not wish for a child, was this his concern; he told me all men of my upbringing eventually had children. Despite my reaction which I did not give, I was wont to be bestowed of any commands and found myself close to tears. He then said, as though he had finally discerned a consideration he had been unaware of, that he would make all necessary arrangements for me to raise a child. While it took me days to recover from this disagreement, in the course of days when he at last was ready to leave, he said he felt he knew me much better, he commented my education had gone well, that I was married young, while of concern, was no longer subject for thought, his worst preoccupation for which he would set aside funds was now to become a matter of recourse. I saw him to his ship, went with him to his suite, helped with his luggage, we hugged and I was overcome with great sorrow when he said he had been told he was not long in his life and was advised to make arrangements. When I disembarked I stood at the ready waiting until the ship set sail and saw my father at the port rail. I waved, he waved back. I would know no other parent. When he was too far away I walked home, thinking of my eventual loss as though it might become an abandonment.

Until Chloe invited the seemingly guileless Karge for violin quartet my weeks of unending contentment were unharnessed in the spellbound commonplace appreciation of wilderness and garden nature, Helene and I spent hours discussing the types of grass of the gardens, learning which were medicinal and luxuriating in lounge chairs on that narrow glade of grass. Helene was emotionally distant, as I began to hunger for a less reserved feminine presence, I received word from my family that my father had been admitted on a short stay to a sanitorium, and not to come. I discovered I could be solitary, without even companionship of associates, books, or wife, and as I naturally gravitated to long walks at night I released from Helene any serious expectation, including the raising of a child. With four years to go, every last potential hour for any contemplation taken up by coursework I did not anticipate that during these few years I could be saddled with a child. Thus, when Karge arrived, deposited by coach and Chloe sailed to Ireland, surrendering Karge in our capable study, all I could think of was to talk to Karge, who knew me intimately, about that lonely, uninsightful discussion with my father and my accompanying him to his cabin for his departure.

Karge was now erroneously thin, a foreclosed brevity of her former self, upon meeting Helene they had kissed cheek to cheek, then graciously ascended the manor alabaster stairs and fainting in the entrance hall had to be carried by the coachman to her suite at the rear past the dining hall. Perturbed by her apparent state, I found her on a poster bed with a damp cloth over her brows, whereupon I inquired whether she thought herself to be with child. She said merely that her father had also sailed on Chloe's ship with a prisoner who was to be retained at Newgate prison. I asked of what he stood accused, she described he had been referred to Lady Magritte in whose affordability she believed the prisoner was to have been disposed, wherein she recounted where Randolph and Dory lived, Karge said they put her up at an inn when she went to visit and encountered my mother. I examined her for evidence of where she was, saying my father had given me letters, she gave me the last known whereabouts citing that my mother was indeed amnesiac. I sent word to Randolph to come.

As I was in my third year, the nation's overriding concern, once villages were erected only to house people of a felonious nature, was for the safety of its free. The locked room while seemingly incidental nevertheless posed unusual problems, if only because it was not thoroughly medically known for whatever it was, Karge in her infirm state relied upon sights, discomforts, unexplained ailments, on her symptoms for which she found herself assailed with. She would on occasion be observed with mild arthritic conditions of her fingers, loss of coherence, babbling apparently inebriated talk, delirium, impairment of hearing, none of which she had ever before been given to and when they refrained did not return, lasting for brief durations under several months, known attending qualities generally absent. I stole a look at her journal while she lay dozing one afternoon, her red wavy hair sprawled over her pillows, her pulse evident in her throat, sunlight flooding over her poster bed and over the entire room. She had written, locked room – who among lords has been accosted by attempts to kill – shutdown lungs, infection with appearance of virus or infectious bacteria, immense heat suddenly, medical conditions – a fracture while in bed, not severe to require splint, head trauma while asleep, loss of cerebral functioning, heart unimposed, insect bites for no explanation, loss of taste or of hearing. Could we not deduce the rationale for a device such as that for blowing up a wall of a stone facade is chiefly done in order to derive pain? I was unaccustomed to any ideas relating to spells and hardships of such nature, I found myself reviewing, more or less as my father had done of me, the situations of human confounding which posed improbable yet nevertheless real disorders and syndromes, my primary concern was dreams, how the Mind functions, when stimuli brings about deleterious complexities, situations that must be warded off by any measures. Although I knew myself to be firmly entrenched in physical evidentiary procedure, I knew also there were inexplicable distresses for which medicine seemed unable to penetrate. The rising number of reported unusual distress caused me to consider it was not necessarily germane to females, even if females were predominantly the ones who complained, therefore I began to look at the society for plausible explanation and found but one. The justification for males to hold jobs was to thrust females to live with men, changing the complexion of the intent for society. The absorption of the families who had been imprisoned in the dutch colonies of Canada had proven an enormous risk, there seemed no satisfactory method by which to restore females from ill grace to education, no matter the incentives, nor to persuade males of ill grace to content themselves with work.

Chloe supped with me a few nights later. The black mast stood at post bale, a crescent moon shaving off half the world, the startling appearance of sparks flying from a reef window declared that on board was another man in shackles bound for the Irish peninsula. I withdrew from the sight instinctively and sat at Chloe's table dressed in white, fed by candlelight. We dined on halibut and buttered seasoned herbs, white wine and fresh berried toast. She discussed her new prisoner, a man who had been in need of shelter, a reddish brunette, medium height, walked with a cane, had fortuitously admitted himself to a friar abbey where he had taken a meal in the library, then walked out into the moonlight along the cobbled slate and to the garden where he was seen depositing an instrument of heinous terror into a reflection pool, he was seized before he returned to sleep. When dust and stone rained late that night he was already bound and gagged.

For this particular trip I accompanied her. The ship was a fine valorous vessel, mast poles a hundred feet high, black sails to every bark, two for steerage, a certain number for sighting, just one starbent for docking. Her cabins were few, below deck only the captain and several first mates were contained in tiny rooms which each had a desk, high lockers, three or four berths, several containers for supplies. My sense of her was she was constructed for rivers, not of the ocean. The prisoner although delirious was not without alacrity, although he on occasion disputed direction based upon leeward inclinings to the right he was certain he knew to where the ship was bound, he had no overt sea experience, he had learned this from having tested the sails for sturdy long hours. He was moderate height, shallow in the frame, stocky, an invective person. We were at sea some ten hours, we docked at a peculiar island with any number of abbeys, we took him to the one several hundred feet from shore, strapped him onto a bed, sponged his face and mouth, and examined him. He was cut-free, no sores, bites, welts, blisters nor any other sign of traumatic despair. When we left, Chloe was reimbursed a thousand British pound notes which she took in french coin. We supped at an inn, enjoyed a bottle of Claret between us, ate squid and lombard on pistol fire ale, thick burnt garlic bread, and for dessert had bread pudding thickened with cherry sauce. After dinner we returned to the ship, took a captain's room, and drank a fifth of bourbonette and rifled port, smoked a hashburn, gobbled up two tins of caviar and climbed in our suckers into separate berths. I suppose I must have seemed ludicrously drunk, for I told her about myself, Karge and Dory, to which she said ruefully she had kicked out a suitor when he wanted another female to join them. She said she pitied Helene, because Helene had in all likelihood surrendered a key to Chloe's company to some drifter; when I sought details, she said Randolph had hired a curtailer. I decided while I was not above reproach, I may have wed too hastily and being that my father was spending his sixties in confinement I should extract a polite visit to see him. Chloe said she would take me in a week, and I, having no other means with which to obtain transportation, agreed.

∧ ∧ ∧

Sophie greeted me at the door to her flat on the place de la madeleine. She looked ruthlessly aged, her face lined on her forehead and jowls, her hair impossibly short. She wore a stylish damask green dress to her calves, the fabric had raised paisley velvet patterns, she wore leather brown pumps. I was so unprepared for her apparent commonness that I was unable to pay close enough attention as she led me through her flat. Her home was made of expensive walnut, the walls were white, the kitchen large with deep salmon tile, it looked out to a small garden, two bedrooms faced a courtyard, the dining room was pink, a living room with three french doors and a balcony, almost no furniture, a stunning rococo couch, lamp and table and two Spanish red leather easy chairs. We sat on her couch with glasses of white wine and a lump of brown sugar in each. I inquired as to her sudden aging, and she laughed saying the females in the family aged very quickly, it was just the way god made them. Her adored husband had passed leaving her the flat. She described her passing years as quiet, without incident. I told her my father had gone into a sanitorium but was returned to his townhouse in Oxford, I said I had married and had no responsibilities. We came at last to the subject of her abandonment, whereupon she stated she and my father had observed separate indoctrinations, owing in part to her inconsistencies, and when she had blundered into an unused wing, encountered a wretched lost soul, who as it turned out was my father's brother, taking into account his demoralization, she left. She thought England was full of the near dead; having come upon so many, she moved to France. I asked why did she move to Paris, she said this was the one place a female could live out of wedlock.

I didn't have supper that evening; instead, I worked through the night. I spoke to my associate, a fully licensed physician, as to the issue of female indoctrinations. Francois said in his estimation a female's freedoms were overrated because it was doubtful she would be able to support herself, if she could her home would necessarily be in an unfavorable area, then there was the idea of illegitimacy. Males, on the other hand, were insufferable, only their freedom from becoming emotionally dependent on a female was paramount. The tug of war for romance was to be placed at odds with the desire to rear a child. I asked him, between sewing up a child's arm and dressing a stomach wound, why he didn't marry; he remarked that by the time he thought of asking, the female had married. Marriage, while installing a permanent companion, also negates, for if one was neither compatible intellectually nor enduring mentally the union would pursue non combined interests.

I would not encounter much in the way of differences, females for me were rarely necessary to my livelihood or to my comfort. Males, neither. Friendship, if it could be had, dining, always an errand, romance, out of reach. Life was just a bit past me, and I would catch up. After all I was only twenty-nine.

The buggy rolling along on the road had stopped, the driver posted the reins and unloaded a body, to my shock he dragged it by the arm to a flight of stairs which led down to a tiny enclosure with an entry, and kicked the body down the stairs. He opened the buggy door on the other side, pulling out another body, which he let fall to the street, then dragged it by an arm and coming to the stairs pushed with both hands until it rolled to where the first body lay, he drove off, the hoofs of his horse resounding on the street. I withdrew from the enclosure I hid inside, went down the stairs and attempted to examine them. The male lay on top of the female, he looked to be mid thirties, his blond hair was cut short, his cherubic face was bloodshot, I listened with a stethoscope to his chest, he had a murmur. The female, black short hair, cut almost to the scalp, while having few abrasions, was bandaged on the chest, I loosened the dressing and stared, rather stunned, icy prickles going down my spine, at large ugly black stitches that indicated her chest had been autopsied. My hands shook as I pasted down the dressing where it had been in place. Then I got the hell out of there.

I had gone two blocks when, having gotten past my fright, I absorbed the fact I had not talked to either to learn whether they were coherent, I retraced my steps hurriedly before I was aware I had walked three blocks, then I went back eyeing each stairwell and landing, until I arrived at the one where I was sure the buggy driver had put them. I walked down the stairs, knocked on the door and waited, eventually a stooped male opened it, I asked whether the drunken couple had made it alright but he didn't know what I meant, sensing I thought I should look around he took me inside and I saw his apartment was empty. Bewildered I set off, thinking perhaps I had made a mistake, I had not found the correct door, yet as I scrutinized each stairwell and landing I didn't see them, and I told myself the chill had recovered them and they had gone.

Were I older, less impressionable, better at the ways

of the world, I should have told myself the female's stitches were the result of a poor teaching hospital, that despite the driver's seemingly rough handling, perhaps the hospital had run out of carts to transport the wounded, and this was as good as it might get. But I was youthful, still learning to avoid traps, not be taken in by deceits while keeping to a minimum of vices because I thought everyone should have one or two – drinking and women, women and smokes, or plain out drinking and smokes – the strength of character to be tested by continual exposure without being felled toward crime.

The sight of them had unnerved me and I ran through Paris to put as much distance between them and my fear, until I came to my block, it was irrational to think there were a Jekyll and Hyde couple lurking about as I hurried up the stairs, let myself into my flat and threw myself inside. Helene was gone, a perfumed note said she had gone by train up to Chloe's warehouse and would return the following night. I lamented the emptiness, the precarious sense that there was too much death, more violence than seemed logical, that there was a hint of violence about, there was also a rambling material sense that France was again on the brink of war.

5

THE wail of a dove awakened me. I came to as it lit onto the porch, a grey breasted bird whose warble had quieted, comfortable in its perch in the dim morning. I watched it as it sat brooding. The sun crept over the trees, shadows receded, the forest appeared stark. The dove flew off. Branches appeared thick as if with snow, their needles grew thin in an array of minute accumulation. I sat up, sensing myself neither refreshed nor wearied, expecting my body to be exhausted, and went into the bathroom for a shave. The brush was in a bowl, the lather in a jar. The simplicity of the stand alone tub, mirror and basin and grey white tile was an elegance, a window looking onto the stand of trees caught the flash of a leaping doe. I foamed my face, took a razor and cleaned off bristles row at a time. I took a damp washcloth to rinse, took a bath, toweled, brushed my hair, dressed in trousers and shirt.

The floor was cool beneath my feet, the white austere hall without ornament. In the dining room on a long Formica salmon colored counter that separated the kitchen with steel refrigerator, basin and open shelves of food was a feast. Diced fruit salad made of ice melon, canteloupe, and honeydew, mangoes, bananas, and nuts; baked ham slices corned with cloves and finished, slices of thick homemade rye, jars of herring, juice, tea. I put on my plate a small serving of each, buttered bread, a dab of lemon jam with rinds. I stepped outside into the courtyard to a small table and chair, the fountain soothed me. Edward soon joined me, a slice, fruit, and ham on a plate, a cup with strong brewed tea and cream. We ate sparingly, I said I never felt better, I told him about the dove. The old walls of stone around the courtyard were draped with vines. I asked if he built his home, he said Sophie bought it for him.

"Did you ever wonder about me?" Edward inquired.

"Yes. I was told by my father at some point."

"Sophie said you would come eventually."

I teared. "I looked for you, you were hard to find. What is your last name?"

"It is my father's, Gabardine."

"You resemble my father. Don't you suppose we are related?"

"Ah, I am told Sophie became pregnant before she left your father. It seems odd sitting here with you. I suppose he could not claim another son. One day, I am told, you will rule France."

"I've been told that also, but you could work for me. It would be a good life for you."

"Maria, I don't work for people, even princes. Sophie said no royal ground, no monks. I can sing, write music, or work vineyards, even become a stone mason, but nothing else."

"Could you build me France?"

"I wouldn't. What I own is mine, as you see, even the house is big."

"Why can't we work together?"

"The mistake is not that we are of each parent, it is the belief that to be whole, you must have me in your governance."

"That's a limitation, to hold a belief that I might some way cause you sorrow."

"There is no limitation, in time we will only be old men."

I saw with sadness that my life was already made, that I would have neither my mother or brother near me. I wished my parents had settled for a modest living, but it would come upon me that my father, who had raised me in a strict accordance, wished me to become more like him. As I walked through the trees as far as the trees were a stand I thought if I were to shed my attributions I could then have a vineyard as well, but grapes and thorns were not my chosen calling. He could marry a Lydia and become a lord, I could love a maiden without loss of grace, but only I would be capable of producing change for France. France as a nation held me. France as a ground had long ago taken me. Whether I lived for the Queen, surrendered my treasures, I should for non hold steadfast to a french sail. Her black mast might someday call for me, but then I would answer only for France.

Toward evening Edward took me to the orchard farm in his cart. The distance was great, we talked the entire way back, he told me he had written a ballet performed by the Paris stage. It was a beautiful production, airy costumes, handsome males, exquisite ballerinas. He might write another when Sophie returned. I would not react until he pulled up to the orchard and then I asked if he could take me to the train. He did so quietly, so without comment, it was not until I boarded I realized he might have obligations, or perhaps I imagined it erringly as I knew little of him.

"Come again, won't you? Bring your medical writings, we will talk," he said, kissing me on both cheeks.

"I will," I replied. "I am so glad to have found you at last."

"She didn't come with me because you were your father's. I just happened."

I held him until I knew I must let him go. "I'll write you."

He said, "Could you have gone to London to teach?"

"I wished to return to Paris. England had become too much for me to live there."

"You will see me again, Maria." With that he shook the reins and the horse pulled into the street. I waited, my gaze on him, until the commotion of vendors and train passengers blocked my view.

DIRTY MONEY

Wednesday, December 7th

What brings you to see me?
I want to clear the air, get a fresh perspective.
Has anything happened that makes you feel this way?
I have no goals.
How long have you felt this way?
Maybe a year. A good female friend of mine passed. I have no one to talk to.
Were you close?
Yes, we talked weekly for years. Fifteen years.
Did you start feeling empty when she passed?
I'm not sure when it started, but I don't want to talk about her. I just told you as background information about myself. I want to focus on goals.
Why do you believe you should have them?
I've always had them. I've never before lived day to day.
When you last had goals what were they?
I was employed then for the county counsel. I'm newly retired.
How long?
Ten years.
Do you enjoy retirement?
Sometimes. I sleep more and feel rested.
Have you had goals for retirement?
Yes, I wrote a book on the justice system, how it works, types of standard cases, adjudication, sentencing.
Anything else?
Yes, I wrote another book on how to survive in an antagonistic job, a self help for lawyer aides. Also I put out a primer on working for a county attorney.
Did your books do well?

They have gone into sixth printing.
That must be rewarding.
It is, but the excitement is long over. I used to give seminars for college credit.
I gather the newness has worn off.
I feel I've hit a wall. Like I've run out of ideas.
Do you feel depressed?
Not really. I was looking forward to having my time and writing and doing lectures, but now that's behind me. I didn't realize it would go so fast.
They say the older one gets, the faster life goes.
I think that's true.
So how old are you?
Sixty-four.
You retired young.
In my line of work, they expect you gone by fifty-five max.
How did your co-associates deal with it?
Most traveled to other countries, China, India, Egypt, Brazil. Some got other jobs.
Did you do what you wanted?
Yes, exactly. I went to Italy and France. Traveling wears me down.
It all went by unexpectedly quickly.
No kidding, zoomed right by. I practically didn't catch it myself.
How did you perceive it while you were living it?
Well, it's odd your saying that. Often I was wound up tight, waiting for a situation to be over. Only the research was any decent. I could sit at it extendedly.
There must be a lot of pressure in preparing a prelim and arraignment.
You don't sleep. You live tied up in knots.
Did you attend trials?

A good many. I prepared witness lists, handled evidence, wrote the reports. I'm not a court steno, thank God.

On the other side?

Right, the prep work.

Do you still find yourself tied up in knots?

I can't seem to shed it. A certain dread is often present. Traveling was like that.

You must've had experiences that weren't, besides research.

Marriage wasn't; getting together with Joanie, the gal who died, wasn't.

Why do you suppose those were different?

I let down my hair with them. I trusted Mike and Joan. I could talk to them about anything. I looked forward to being around them. Mike finally kicked the bucket when I was sixty.

Was he older than you?

By twelve years. We met on the job.

Was it love at first sight?

Pretty much. We married after a year.

That's quick.

Yeah, it was fairly instantaneous. His dad was county prosecutor.

What kind of cases did you try?

Almost all 602s, mostly house deed forgeries, liquor store heists, some armed robbery of department stores, a few murders; hit and runs, vandalisms.

All teens?

Yes. Wild kids, drunk and disorderly, on the lam. Some were suicides.

How do you feel talking about it?

Relieved, actually. I've kept a lot pent up, hanging onto the insanity.

The work must have that affect.

It's very tiring. You're always waiting for the other shoe to drop.

Did talking to Joanie help?

No comparison. We worked the same circuit, different commissioners. She had worked eighteen years when I started.

So she knew the ropes?

Everything. Not a case she hadn't handled.

You must have relied on her more after your husband died.

All but move in. She propped me up for two years. Lately I've had a hard time to keep going.

People do take breaks.

Other people do.

Don't you?

I'm not sure I should.

It's just a break. Do you think you need to remain locked in?

I don't know. It's been hard to release myself. I feel like I wind up without purpose, at a dead end.

What were you raised with for a work ethic?

To apply myself, be sincere. My dad was a scientist, my mother stayed at home and took his calls and maintained his files.

Taking time out is turning your back on dad.

On myself. I have to be directed, moving toward an end.

That's not an unusual difficulty for retirement. Not all goals take as long to fulfill as anticipated.

No.

The hour is up. This is our first session. I think at the next session we can discuss ways in which goals help give you an identity and how by having them you put painful

experiences out of awareness. Will you be okay to stop?
Yes, I'm fine.
So prior to our next appointment I'd like you to start a diary. Jot down by date any strong emotion you have. Don't worry if you have none.

Wednesday, December 14th

So, I see you made it back.
Yes. I told you I'd be alright.
Yes, you did. I have to ask because the start of therapy can bring up unidentified sad feelings and we talked about the loss of your husband and close friend.
Yes.
How was your week?
It progressed.
Can you give me a picture of it?
Well, let's see. I do the same thing pretty much daily. I began my week at the law library looking up our cases that had convictions. Actually every day I awaken at five, watch the news for a half hour and drink a cup of fresh coffee, take a shower and get dressed similar to this, a skirt, blouse and cardigan, and heels; and blow dry my hair which takes about five minutes, dab on eye shadow and lipstick. Then it's two mornings at the UC Berkeley School of Law library for three hours; after which I cross campus and go to lunch with an instructor friend. I swim once a week and hang out at a pub one night a week with a group from work.
That sounds satisfying.
I've had this schedule since Mike left.
Same schedule?

Exact same, no variations.

Does your schedule give you a sense of purpose?

It used to. Now it gets me out of the house. It starts my day.

Did you make any notations in a diary?

No, nothing happened.

There was no sadness that surfaced?

Nothing, just the same blank wall.

Goals might give you a continued road.

Well, at least I would have a focus. I'd be busy, involved, making the future.

Can you define what you mean by being involved?

I would have classes, students to teach what goes on at a busy county office, cases to examine.

Why did you discontinue teaching?

I had a special state filler and you are only permitted five years in the state. I miss it.

I can feel that. Could you teach out of state?

Do you mean for another state? I never thought of that.

There may be avenues you haven't considered. What about a private practice to advise families?

I thought of that, but I kept putting the idea on hold.

Did an objection occur to you?

I didn't think I should handle cases without having a lawyer on staff and my lawyer friends work.

So is your day to day activity fulfilling?

It gives me places to be, but no, I no longer feel I have objectives. I am just existing and not really challenging myself.

Challenging.

Yes, I feel this is the essence of life. A person knows what they are made of because they can rise to the occasion.

You must know who and what you are made of.

I am a woman who worked for the county and was married.

But what were you in and of yourself?

I wasn't as independent of relationships as I thought. I was a wife, I worked for a boss in a difficult career; and I had good work friendships.

Did you have hobbies?

Not really.

What did you do fifteen, twenty years ago?

It was the two of us. Mike and I ate dinner at six, we went to the movies Friday nights, we went to the galleries once a month, and on occasion sat a class together. Twice a month we went to his family all day Saturday. Otherwise we were at home most evenings when he made dinner, we watched a movie or I worked; once a week we had sex. Tuesday.

You seem to have led a scheduled life.

We had to, or time together was the first thing we put off. We'd give it all to work. Work was a bottomless pit.

I know what that's like. Any suicides in your family?

No. Everyone was a shining star. I was the courtroom pro, my sister was a bulimic ballerina, and my younger brother swam for the Olympics.

Where are they today?

Dead, in a mountain field of daffodils. They were victims of a bus crash.

I am horribly sorry for you. When did this tragedy occur?

It's a long time ago. Years. It's over thirty years. We were shocked. My mother never recovered. She still weeps.

Oh, I can imagine. Your poor, poor mom; such a

terrifying loss.
Yes, she was a zombie for a good long time. My dad brought in an aide to help.
Oh, your poor parents.
What caused you to inquire about suicides?
Misguided instinct, I guess.
I thought maybe I have an indelible sense to me.
No, you don't. I'd say what you are going through seems very normal. A mid-life transition. I can't say why I thought it. I suppose it's the numbness of which you refer.
It's something I don't want to get too used to.
No one would. Do you think of your siblings when you experience not having goals?
No, it's nothing to do with them. I was in grief counseling for them. I accepted their deaths.
Perhaps you are enacting what you saw your mother go through.
She was in her late thirties, not sixties.
They must have died very young.
Tam was nineteen and Abe was seventeen. I was barely twenty-two. I always say Thank God I didn't major in judo sports.
Are you concerned you are losing a grip on life?
I'm not sure what to call it. I feel I am getting lost in a fog. It's obviously not rational. When I have goals I can see myself in the world, in my life, I am somewhere; life is not a void. Without the goal, I can't formulate my sense of meaning.
But what causes you to feel fear from it?
I can't say. I don't know. Is it going to kill me? Well, not likely.
Does it feel unbearable?
Unbearable is too strong a word. I can't isolate the

sense of it, but then I try not to acknowledge it.

What was the last goal you had?

To instruct. Those five years seem to have taken it out of me though.

Teaching takes a good amount of preparation. Maybe you are tired.

Exhausted.

Does this barrenness compare with what you went through over your siblings?

Not actually. Then, I felt in a state of shock, annulled. I couldn't understand how such a thing could have happened. I married that year. This is vastly different. I think of my life as having occurred; I have done what I wanted and now there's nothing more to shoot for. I can't think of anything else I'd want to begin even.

Exhaustion can negate interest. Life becomes too demanding. You may not be able to rise from the ashes so-to-speak for years. You may need to recuperate first, sleep ten hours a day for two years, shelve goals for awhile; have fun; relax.

I don't relax all that easily. As I told you, I get tied up in stress. I can't enjoy book reading or a movie. I'm waiting for it to be over, to find out how it will end.

Would you call that dread?

Yes.

Do you think you are afraid?

It's not terror.

Are you apprehensive?

That's a good definition.

And the apprehension makes you what? Unable to think clearly? There must be a rather big step between being anxious and naming a goal.

A goal takes more effort than I have energy for.

Maybe you don't mean a goal. Maybe you are talking

about evolving yourself. Maybe you are as mature and likable to yourself as you will ever be.

I'm okay with my personality.

So let's start with your exhaustion. What gave it to you?

Work most probably.

Which aspect of your job did you enjoy the best?

Drafting the petition and writing the evidence.

Who gave you the information?

Various people, the lab chemists, hospital physicians, surgeons, housing appraisers, forgery analysts, paternity clerks, coroners, sheriffs, the health department, guards at stores and schools, those sorts.

Did they each provide you with reports?

Yes. We had to write a section for each count of the crime. A teen runaway may have led police in a high speed chase. This could require photos of the chase with verifying fingerprints as to the suspect who stole the car; if there was a crash that injured another party, there might be scene photos, hospital admissions and medical narratives or autopsy reports, if they waved a gun at a liquor store manager, photos of that as well.

I gather that your fact finding could be quite complicated?

Yes, depending upon the sheriff or police report. That's what starts the process. The law enforcement officer makes a referral asking for a conviction. If a bomb occurs, there might be a hundred fifty counts to try the case depending upon number of suspects who placed each bomb, who built them, materials they had to purchase, who purchased the act. We see very tangled up situations for stupid crimes, a son-in-law steals his mother-in-law's deed on her property and tries to sell the house to a drug dealer. Usually about six reports accompany a referral.

Deals?

Many tab out in a prelim if all sides can agree to the sentence. If there's more than one suspect, consensus is less likely. It depends if prison is on the table.

Did you see many cases a week?

An average of fifteen, all different types, most involving psychiatry, often an involuntary, vehicle manslaughter detained awaiting length and type of sentencing, Oakland the worst for teen hit and run and store window vandalisms.

What about deadlines?

Everything is a deadline, two days usually, ridiculous really, the cop might not write his report for a month because he's stuck doing some deadly investigation that's going to take him a year. I'd have to locate him and go out and tape his comments and then get him pulled to testify.

You are very animated as you speak.

Well, it was my job. I loved the work.

What was the worst part of your job?

The worst is expecting a witness to prove your case when they can't. Lots of cases go by the wayside because they don't substantiate the case. The other is a witness who recants. That's why the police want cases with solid evidence so they can make a conviction stick.

Were there any scandals in your day?

Oh sure plenty like the county hall accountant who set the building on fire, and then there's the usual affair behind closed doors; lots of those.

Was that a shock?

The county hall? Totally. They say he was a long time crook from Michigan, did it once before.

Were you in the building when it happened?

No, that came later after I had left. There were all sorts of rumors.

Did you believe any of them?

Well, you know you think someone is being sarcastic. Like accounting came across a huge error anyhow, and they intended to heist the county.

It does sound facetious.

One just isn't prepared to regard it literally.

Were you concerned?

No, what for?

Do you think the county was subjected to a heist?

Who would know? I wouldn't; sitting at my desk typing reports all day.

What just happened here? You removed yourself. Is it difficult to imagine someone you may have known could have committed a serious crime?

It has nothing to do with me.

Do you think if there was something serious afoot, it might have affected how you felt about the workplace?

I wasn't aware of anything unusual; the work itself was just very demanding.

I feel we lost a connection here.

Well, the accounting office was on the fifth floor. No one ever saw these people. If they had to order money, one rarely saw an armored van arrive. Of course people were there daily paying their property taxes.

So there must have been a good deal of money.

Yes, I'm sure there was. Tens of thousands a week.

Our hour is up. I'd like you to give some thought to the idea you might have job burnout.

It's been ten years.

It may have taken the cessation of personal activities to have it surface. It certainly can be said you have had your share of losses.

Wednesday, December 21st

How was your week?

So so. I went for dinner and a concert with a friend.

Did you have an enjoyable time?

It was okay. We talked over dinner. We had Thai food.

What did you talk about?

Work; people we worked for.

Do you recall any of it?

Some. We talked mostly about his boss, county auditor, how he was so busy and many of the files were misplaced, and researching stuff was inane because it wasn't where it was supposed to be.

Did you call him?

No, he asked me out. He's the man I see weekly for lunch after I am at the law library. Randy.

So he's a good friend.

I called him after session last week and told him what you said about job burnout. He called me Sunday and said he wanted to take me out.

Like on a date?

Yes. He kissed me during the concert, and I invited him up for a nightcap afterward. He stayed for an hour for a glass of wine and then took off. He didn't stay over.

Did you ask him to?

No, I'm not sure if I like him enough. He's a nice person but he's often busy. He works late week nights.

Do you think he wouldn't take time for a relationship?

We've never talked about it.

Have you ever asked what he thought happened at your workplace?

Occasionally. He thinks someone placed a bottle of humpty dumpty inside the building. He doesn't think it's his boss, his boss is FBI.

I don't think it's wise to discuss the situation. It may endanger him if he actually knows anything. We can discuss your perceptions here, but I don't think talking about it outside is a good idea.

Okay, I won't do it again.

Does the situation alarm you?

It hasn't up to now.

I think it could be very serious. Have you ever made reports on property?

Not my department, I'm crimes only.

What about crimes involving plats?

They exist, but the state chases them down. You want to take Salton Sea where an unauthorized developer put in ninety homes without adequate plumbing and the state had to tear out the project. The state doesn't usually remove the houses, it assigns a bank to sell or rent whatever is built.

When you think back on work, what memories arise?

Oh, stupid stuff, legal aides hobnobbing in the halls, crowded alleys, double parking, clerk breaks in the sandwich shop, court running past five, the law filing office not sending up the file, lawyers crowding in the patio.

Is court a hectic place?

It is when trials are in session. The juvenile calendar makes it noisy, impossible. There can be sixty hearings a morning. That's child abuse and probation, a family, their attorneys, three or four of them, along with expert witnesses, lab chemists, a physician, an arresting officer. People sit on every stairwell, all the benches, flock outside usually conducting last minute interviews with children. I've always been dead-set against this informality. I think there should be booths but the court won't consider it.

You just gave an opinion.

Yeah, I get an idea every so often.

Did anything out of the ordinary occur?

The court opened an extension in Hayward because more families came from that end of Alameda County. Oakland put in tire claws to direct cars in parking lots and we all lost tires going in the wrong entrance by habit. Someone broke into the cashier office so they placed bars over the windows. An elevator at the back of the building broke and they had to build another elevator and lost a courtroom to do it. They moved the bad files to the security division of the building after a fire broke out in the file room.

How did this affect your work space?

Each office was eventually locked up behind one way entrances. It became very security oriented. We had to pass through metal detectors every day, have our bags checked, and sign a log to go see someone, even to go eat in the cafeteria.

Do you think this affected your way of looking at working?

It must have because every last thing required a requisition, but I can't say I took it home with me. I'd always been cautious not to take files out of the office.

But suddenly going to another office was problematic. I guess I relied on the phone more than in the past.

Do you think it caused you to become withdrawn?

I couldn't say.

Well, let's mull this over. What was your disposition prior to these problems?

I guess I was more willing to volunteer to pick up other people's route material.

Then what?

Then that became a big project. I did less. Eventually I wound up doing only my own assignments. I suppose over time I avoided other co-associate's dockets even though I was the one who received each week's schedule.

So I think this must have made you focus more on your desk.

It probably did.

Did you leave your office as often?

No, that definitely changed. I began bringing my lunch.

What about Joan?

She worked across the hall so I saw her daily.

Where did you eat?

In her judge's office. He was almost always in Hayward. Once a month on a day when nothing was on the court calendar we managed to get out and walk up to Le Cheval Restaurant for an hour.

What was her perception of these changes?

She thought it was a big hassle. They eventually removed her off court errands due to the difficulty of not having access to various departments. They reassigned her tasks to several court reporters.

This resulting problem must have created a lot of bewildering isolation.

I guess you could call it that. The staff lounge was only accessible from the plaza; the training room and basement only through the lower hall. I had no call to be at either so I didn't regard it as troublesome. A mechanic may have thought otherwise.

In what year were these changes made?

1982.

So staff was inconvenienced for several years?

About that. We became accustomed to it.

Did you have any problems filing petitions?

Some, because the filing office changed to the basement.

How did one get to it?

By taking the lowest hall. To get there required two elevators past a guard desk where you had to sign in.

So for security reasons the county decided to make certain offices contained.

Against public access, yes. That was probably the reason for it. Are you saying that awful fire was started in the basement?

It would make sense.

But by someone on staff?

Why does it have to be staff? It seems it could be anyone.

How would they get in?

Maybe a janitor service.

Then how could they pass a clearance? Maybe an ex-inmate who was convicted there. I don't know.

Maybe they entered through the patio to the lounge. Does our discussion cause you to feel alienated?

I don't know.

You'd have to think about it.

Yes. Is it time to wind down?

Yes. Same time next week?

It's Christmas.

I'll be here.

Alright, next week.

Here is my hotline should a crisis occur before we meet.

Thanks, but probably nothing will.

Wednesday, December 28

How was your holiday?

It was average. I went to Randy's for Christmas dinner.

Were other people there?

His folks and his supervisor.

That's an intimate gathering. How was that?

We talked about the problem.

The fire?

No. This is a small gold and red sequin painted helicopter that landed in the plaza a little after seven at night back in 1981 around New Year's Eve.

Any rationale as to why it landed there?

No, we couldn't agree. Maybe it was a holiday show; maybe no other craft was available for a rescue. We couldn't come up with a good explanation.

Was it in the newspapers?

Flying away. It resembled a fireworks design. We thought that was why the county remodeled the building interior so quickly.

Could the plane have gained access through the roof?

That's what brought it up. Randy's supervisor John was talking about weird situations at work. He thought the plane committed armed robbery of a school. John thought the pilot got the idea from a similar occurrence in the Southwest.

Maybe that was a very serious crime. Maybe the pilot stole a lot of county money.

John said the group left dead bodies all over the training room and lounge. We were trying to figure who worked there who stayed after six.

When does staff leave?

Everybody's gone at five.

Does it help to learn the building administration did everything it could to protect county assets?

Yes, but it's odd because no one was told at the time.

I can see where you might feel baffled. Did John say

what happened in the Southwest?

A few planes flew over the Grand Canyon in the dead of night painted in neon glow to resemble other images: one as an all red empire state building; one plane as a lake at sunrise; and one as a car winding over a mountain pass.

Your voice has a light cajole to it as though you are comfortable with yourself.

I feel that is true. I had as good a time as I could.

Yes, I catch that nagging doubt. Is this moment going to last? Do I have to lose this moment also?

There is no accounting for it. It usually persists.

Your waking state is trying to tell you something like, how much more can I take?

But what should I say it is due to?

It is loss. You are grieving. You have lost a close friend, a worshipped husband.

One has to go on.

I agree absolutely.

I just wasn't aware there were ever actual dead bodies.

You speak as though that could have been a rumor.

Well, that's sort of how it is. People come to work and a month later vanish.

Did you work Christmas Eve?

No one did. The building is closed between Christmas Eve and January 4th.

So that's why you didn't know. It was probably handled hush hush. It's a good amount to absorb in retrospect. It must have sent shock waves to those who knew.

I can't imagine it for people who thought they had a close call; who got out in the nick of time.

They probably didn't know. Did you ever see large checks?

The accounting office on the sixth floor. Once I had to ask their department to initial fifty grand for

San Leandro waterfront condos and I happened to sit at the chief county auditor's desk where he had a check for almost a million for county personnel. I remember thinking it was very lax of him to have the check on his desk.

Was there a staircase to the roof?

Yes. After a break-in, they moved accounting to the basement in exchange for training which they gave to half the top floor, the other half to the Red Cross.

So it just looked like remodeling to you?

It took over two years during which the top floor was entirely reconstructed, walls changed, draped in clear wall size construction plastic.

Lots of oddity.

We worried about there not being offices. One had to walk through this sheeting to get to an administrator.

Did you have to find one often?

Twice. I came off a central elevator, had to enter four separate doors, walk through empty space along six walls of glass before I came to the right door.

Like walking on a new floor just being built?

Yes, like that.

Were there administrative staff?

About fifteen.

Did your office talk about these changes?

No, maybe a remark.

Like what?

Mr. Smith is hiding in a closet.

That's funny.

Yes, but it wasn't said to put him down.

Is talking about all this helpful?

It might be.

But you aren't sure?

Not at the moment.

What do you want out of your life?
I don't know yet, I still draw a blank.
Have I hit a reaction?
Big time.
What is it?
Dread.
What is the fear of?
That I can't exist.
Is it having enough money to live?
No, I'm fine.
Are you afraid of aging?
No.
Of dying?
Not quite.
Have you seen anyone die?
I'm not sure whether I can call it that. I was in the training room off the lounge in the days when we had a connecting door to the lounge. The door to the hall was open one afternoon when I heard an odd sound like a large bag being dragged, thumping down the stairs from the second floor. I went into the hall but I saw no one there. I saw a sudden light of sunshine like someone opened the door into the lounge, and then it was dark again.

Did you call security?
Yes. He came by about twenty minutes later and said nothing was on camera or in the hall.
What did you think about what you heard?
I forgot it. I put it out of my mind.
Are you wondering whether you heard a body?
I'm not sure what it was. I took the officer's word.
Since the holidays when Randy's supervisor raised the item of dead bodies, have you been experiencing much in the way of fatigue?

I usually sleep through the holidays. While I was married, we spent that week in bed reading often aloud to each other, a year-end ritual.

You are evading the question.

I forgot what you asked. What was it again?

Did the discussion about dead bodies ---

Oh, right, make me tired?

Fatigued, do you think it could have caused you some resistance to wanting to be receptive to hearing ideas?

It's possible. Thinking back on it, I can't say why I didn't react, but the Red Cross sent over an instructor to give a hostage class to building maintenance staff, and I inadvertently entered when two people were sitting back to back tied up and blind folded. I retreated pretty readily.

Let's take a pulse. What are you experiencing right this minute?

I have a feeling I am drained by something pulling at my energy.

He paused a lengthy moment and she waited asking herself if she should say something additional; as though there were an implied concern that she hadn't dug deeply for the emotion that refused to surface long enough to identify.

Could we suppose it is the mind's attempt to barricade against an unwanted perception?

Oddly the question freed her, but instead of saying that, she said, I don't know if that is what is going on.

Certainly it is often confusing to palpate boredom. The mind when stressed does not permit awareness. Thought drifts and a nebulous mindlessness sets in.

I can't understand why I forgot your question; how stupid. That's never happened to me before.

There is no incorrect problem solving.

I thought I was paying attention.

Maybe you are unwilling to draw too close to the pestering emotion.

Wednesday, January 5th

I've been thinking of taking a trip out of town for a little over a week with Randy and his boss.

How nice. When would this be?

In two weeks. It would mean missing a session.

Would this be January 19?

Yes, that week. We are driving to Tahoe.

I'll make a note. Ellen Wilson on trip on January 19. Are you excited?

Slightly uneasy. This will be my first night out since Mike died.

Do you feel you are betraying your ex-husband's memory?

I guess, a bit.

You think he would object?

No, he wouldn't have minded. It's just that while we were married we did not spend our vacations with people.

Not your families?

Not at the holidays. Otherwise we were at his parents three times a month. It's not as if we didn't see them. We were there often.

So I think it's a very positive stride. Will you be camping?

No, Randy has a cabin at South shore. He gets it three times a year.

That should be fun.

Yes.
Can we talk about these short responses?
I guess so.
Are you being flip?
I don't see any reason to respond.
You came to me for help by your own choice. You are not court mandated. Perhaps we could discuss what is happening when you give a one word answer.
I can't see what you want.
I said a holiday should be fun.
And I agreed. It should be.
Are you looking forward to skiing?
I don't ski.
Get out of town maybe.
Maybe watching the snow fall while we sit by the fire and roast pine cones.
What are you feeling now?
Annoyed.
At me?
Well, we are the only two people here.
This is how therapy works. We talk about where the feelings are when I think you are ready to look at what they could be. So, what causes you to be annoyed? We are exploring a very important trigger to your sense of being lost in your personhood. We need to try to identify when you become distant what you are responding to. You may be unwittingly through no fault of your own in a dangerous situation in which you may have come across killers.
I got there.
Yes, that's rather inevitable. Could you describe the annoyance, how would you describe it?
Don't come near me. Don't say the trip will be fun.
Should I have said, maybe the two men will leave you alone and go off on a walk?

It could happen.
You are being argumentative.
I don't expect it to be fun.
Then why go?
Because I want to know what John knows.
About the bodies?
Yes, about those. You told me not to talk about it, but I did.
Alright, so this John thought he'd perk your interest. Did Randy work there?
Yes, they both did in materials management. They supplied desks, forms, Dictaphones, clocks, computers.
Possibly they encountered a part of the problem.
No, they didn't. They had to be told.
Who told them?
The police. They were interviewed.
Oh, I see.
Yes, that's the point. The police asked when John put in a new phone system. The new system did not give any of us an ability to call Mr. Smith or his staff on approvals. It's as though they moved to another planet. It also didn't connect us to other departments or to our trial lawyers or judges.

Did you have checks on the premises?

Oh, sure, thousands of dollars. These were most often for medical housing or for reimbursements for physician care.

A lot?

Yes, a fair amount; twenty-five thousand at a time, but the drawer was kept in the central cashier office.

Had it ever been stolen?

Not to my knowledge. It's closely watched by several supervisors.

Was it easy to get to?

No, it wasn't. There are several security doors to enter

to three elevators, each to a separate group of floors, two to five, six, and separately two down to the basement and underground lots, upper and lower.

Nothing very straight forward.

No. The lift plan was kept the same as for buildings past on the same square; the Montgomery Building, a light green three floor state like building on grass grounds, and prior, the Rotunda, a blue tile two floor building with a top rotunda for five offices that occupied that entire square on a strip of grass on Harrison siding the train of its era, both built by San Francisco. John said in 1870 all two of five administrators were found dead on the rotunda blue marble floor.

Eerie. Sounds to me like history repeating itself. Did you learn what these buildings served as?

The Montgomery built in 1890 was for building and garden maintenance in the county and the blue tile before it built 1704 served as the bean farm office which was a major crop in eight states then. All buildings were initially run by the same family named Children whose relatives worked for mason stone in Chaupur at the very top of India.

I would say that is an odd coincidence.

I am just saying that is what John says.

I am not doubting you – or him. I think it's an odd historical anomaly. Was there a staff physician?

None, they would refer staff to a local hospital.

I think that's illegal. Kaiser Aluminum had them.

Maybe they had to. They hired hard labor. We were court stenographers. I will say the thing that mystified me was the door leading to the underground was painted white on the other side. It bothered me when I came across it because it used to be one could look through the glass to see the pipe corridor. I came across it when

I was trying to find security and he was on the consoles in the hall.

Possibly someone thought it would be safer to mark that door if one could enter but couldn't get back.

Yes, entirely possible. I got stuck there, but someone came to take me out.

Was there ever a medical response from the hospital groups?

Once. I don't know what called them out. Twelve ambulances and two coroner vans were in the lot.

What was the year?

1985. I think it was the year we had that depraved case. A nun was found dead in the Oakland vesper at Claremont Gardens. We had to report the evidence which was scanty. She was in her late eighties and had worked donations at Christmas in front of the Seventeenth Street pharmacy on Broadway.

What did the evidence reveal?

She had managed a board and care on upper Piedmont Avenue when she died. It was a real mystery. She had gone to sleep in summer on the roof after feeding the pigeons.

What did your husband think?

Mike thought she had come across some inappropriate contact by a priest. Her hands were bound at the wrists by strong rope.

Did she report it?

She must have; otherwise who would have known?

So this situation was a big deal?

As I understand it, it was the first violent crime against the church. Otherwise these people fed the poor. They were commonplace in San Francisco and Oakland. There wasn't any major city unless you count Richmond which had plenty of free soup kitchens, money and food raised by donation.

That is a big deal. What was your impression of her death?

I think she assumed the people she had to deal with were honest. It's possible she stopped in to see how a church sponsored program was progressing and came across something peculiar.

Which building?

Oh, I don't know. How would I know? I never saw her before she died.

When you first went down to the basement what did you see?

Absolutely nothing. It was just a long hallway underground. It's a faster way to get to the training room which is on a split level off the basement.

Who would have had control of the building and hallways?

Security and building maintenance, as far as I know.

Had you met them?

I thought so. Security watched the cameras on the entry floor and there were three building crew for the roof and grounds.

Where were they in the mornings?

In their office on the grounds in a smallish house. They didn't have an office in our building.

Who did they report to?

Security. First floor.

Don't you think it's odd that you passed right by the situation as it was being responded to? There were twelve ambulances in the parking lot.

I didn't realize that was the situation.

That is when all hell broke loose. You were still there.

I wasn't aware that could be the time reference John is talking about.

Wednesday, January 12th

Nice to see you. You cut your hair.
Randy suggested it. Do you like it?
It's very becoming on you. How was your week?
Great, Randy took me to dinner.
Did you have a good time?
Yes, we ate crab cakes, wilted spinach and corn cake; for desert zabaglione and Turkish coffee. It was a delicious meal fare.
You had a good time then.
I felt alive for the first time in years.
Did you three talk about the murders?
John talked about little else all week. He said there was no wound or blood on any dead and on camera no one was killed on the stairs; or at the top in the antebellum no one was dead. He didn't get why the police didn't come out, why the twelve ambulances carted the bodies away but no one investigated.
What did you think when he said that?
It should have been investigated. How were there so many bodies? Eighteen dead.
What does John think?
He thought they were lured to parts of the building one at a time.
Maybe the man's an expert coroner.
Even were he, why does he do this? Why does a killer do this?
Maybe the others had HIV.
That's sick.
Well possibly no hospital could take them living. Was there any blood evidence?
John said a pool of blood on the ceiling in the lobby, blood outside in the garden and some in the library, but

the county had the bodies; they didn't need samples. He said where there is plague the building is burned.

What did you think?

I'm not sure I found that plausible. HIV is treated by lasik.

Maybe this was an untreatable strain. French plague which is caused by drinking gasoline. Maybe the building had a problem, was built too long ago and had insufficient sewage.

I guess.

She was drifting unfocussed unable to hold onto any thought.

Where are you?

I guess I left.

It didn't involve you. You may have to tell yourself that this was a despicable act. It's entirely possible these employees were sent to work at a place where they were not stigmatized.

Or they volunteered.

Oh, yes, a special work force. Where were they to start, do you know?

San Francisco. One was from east LA.

What agency?

I believe it was a hospital. I handled the original complaint. It was the AMA against the sewer pipe collection collective of South San Francisco on Bayshore Boulevard. Approximately a hundred medical programmers were fired after they tested for HIV. The Medical Association felt these individuals could still work and recommended a single building and forty small houses in upper estate north Oakland.

When did the fire in your building occur?

1989, it was an instantaneous raging maelstrom. I wasn't there any longer. I suppose the entire situation in retrospect causes me chilling discomfort to know many I worked with died. I thought they were each successful in their careers.

It is always horrific in retrospect. How might you have intervened? There is no way to know; you don't know the path they took to get down that road. What was your friend Joanie like?

She was an effective court stenographer. She handled all notary. She worked the mill for all commissioners, but usually her job was in evidence selection.

Did she compile the nun's death?

Thomasina Linstreet?

Was that her name?

Yes.

Who put together the last hours for her life?

That would be Noam Wagner, a legal physician from Tracy. He was a blond haired man in his forties, average stature, five foot ten, who consigned death remarks in charting after traumatic incidents. He came down from Trinity to look over the body. It was he who thought she had been robbed over a five thousand dollar check in her kettle during the holidays. She was one of the Nativity's lead money raisers.

Did you two talk about the nun's death?

For days. Joanie thought it was a homeless man's desertion act. She thought he wanted all her funds and that he'd followed her to her office in the Tribune Tower newsroom. She came across information that said the man who talked to her lived at the tower when it was the Hotel Oakland in the Forties.

Maybe he was a reporter at the newsroom.

That would make more sense although I doubt it, someone who actually knew her and knew the church she collected for.

What was Joanie doing around the time of her own death?

She was living in a small apartment over the Sea Wolf where she took a nightly dinner. She had kept copies of everything she ever filed and thought maybe her son had become involved with a bad seed. Joan didn't make much sense, she talked about a sharp knife point used in an injury during a skirmish.

What didn't make sense?

That the cops overlooked blood on the ceiling in the citadel.

Did you think that?

Me? I knew nothing about it.

Was the staff ever interviewed?

By the FBI, twice. Joan moved out of town.

You remained friends?

Yes, we talked on the phone daily. We ate out once a semester when we had classes.

What in?

Court procedure primarily.

That sounds interesting.

Yes, it was. We studied forms and law for probate, river, injunctions, and property. Joan thought she might return to work when she was older to augment her retirement.

And you?

I didn't want to. I was seeking low cost housing in Hayward when she passed.

So her death was quite a blow?

My life became very empty. I was aware of sitting for long hours. Of brooding. A few times I stopped in for bingo but for some reason it never took.

It takes a few years to form relationships.

At one year my father-in- law sent me a check.

Had your husband's family offered to take you in?

They can't. She became lethargic and forgetful. It just about did him in, he became despondent, weepy. Joan and I used to go over and make dinner.

They sat silent trying to bear an unalleviated declaration of psychological distance. Her mind emptied; she didn't even guess at his thoughts. It were as if life had caught up to the sorrowful present, a discordant and jarring brevity of life and living.

I suppose my life came to a halt.

I would agree. Did you feel up to that moment that you had a full, worthwhile life?

Yes, I was lucky. I had the world by the tail. I felt an awe of the world.

Many do in their sixties. They come out on the other side having achievements.

I don't know that I quite view work as an achievement. It's just where I was for forty-two years.

That's a long time for one career. You must have developed a good deal of expertise.

There was that. Is the hour up?

We have gone past it slightly.

Wednesday, January 26th

So how was your week?

Good, good. I entered an evening art class at Laney.

That's a great idea. Do you like it?

Yes. Randy goes also.

That's nice, a shared activity. What sort of art is it?

We are learning to draw blocks and shade in height.

Is this in color?

Black and light grey pencil.

I'd like to see your pictures if you'd like to bring them in.

Oh, sure. Randy is still talking about the burning building.

What is he saying now?

He thinks John saw it occur.

Lucky John got out in time.

Oh, they didn't work in building maintenance. They were on the other side in administration. John had to respond to a service request.

What time of day is this?

Ten in the morning. October 17th, 1989 days prior to the Loma Prieta rumble.

What does he say?

Two men were installing outside phone lines. One appeared to be imbibing from a pint of grey liquor. John says while he was inside talking to security there was a boom during which all the glass disappeared and they ran out through the court onto Harrison before the entire thing caught on fire.

That's shocking.

I thought so. He could have been killed.

Where were you when this happened?

Walking Lake Merritt at my usual time. I didn't hear a thing.

Had you met Randy yet?

Of course. I met him at the museum gallery.

Do you have any ideas about this?

No. I haven't had time to consider what it means. Importance of events takes me much longer than it used to since I stopped working. It's as if I'm in a daze. The minute my mind grabs onto an explanation it's gone. Back in '82, I thought this was over the sparkly helicopter that landed on the grass; then I thought it was about the nun's death, but it turned out to be a lot of ambulances and coroner vans. I just don't get what this was all about.

Maybe it would make more sense if you had a police logbook.

Could be.

Then you'd have actual incidents to compare against.

Well, it's a lot to ask of oneself to reframe a bunch of incidents to fit a murder ring.

What was happening at that time regarding the death of your husband?

I was acclimated to his absence by then. I had moved from our house to an apartment which was better for me because the house held so many memories, but I didn't get along with Mike's sister, not that I ever did. She blamed me for Mike's death.

Do you know why?

We argued a lot in those days over money. There was a lot of tension. He bought stereo components which were very costly and I felt we should toss the savings into IRAs. He was sort of like a big kid in that respect.

Did you have any hobby?

None really to speak of. I enjoyed reading, but I went to the public library. I felt it was the more sensible thing to do.

What did he die of?

Heart attack. He was a type A personality; held everything inside.

Are his parents the same?

No one knows where he got it from. They are laid back, no one ever complains.

So before he died, did you have any major disagreements?

Mike had just purchased ten grand worth of

equipment; it ate into our family vacation schedule. It set off our plans by two years which we never took.

That's a good deal of expenditure.

Extremely so. I didn't like to complain to him but he overspent.

Was it a problem in the marriage?

I'd say so. Everything was budgeted for the house. His expenditures put us over by too much; as a result too much piled up. It was a chronic worry. He liked to anoint the plaza with his stereo phonics.

Where you two worked?

Yes, and along the street.

Is this Harrison?

Montgomery. He claimed Randy's department had enormous difficulties with dual calls like someone was listening in.

Do you know what he recorded?

No. I kept his papers.

Have you looked at them?

No.

Maybe you can bring them in.

I can do that.

Then we can look at what he came across.

Alright.

Do you have any concerns about it?

I feel it's somewhat disrespectful to Mike's life. I think he should not have prying scrutiny.

He died.

Well, I know that. I didn't say it is logical. It probably isn't.

They sat like mortal enemies. Who was right here, she asked herself. She required assurance. Not some fatigue-able irony about discovery.

He may have died a dishonest death.

You mean he was killed.

It's possible.

Yes, I can see your point. He learned something destructive.

So I think we should attempt to learn everything we can first. Look at what was actually present. Maybe he contacted the police. Maybe he discovered the bodies.

I can't go there. He was my love.

That's a feeling.

Yes. I know that.

It will be alright, we will survive this. The truth may free you.

Well, I doubt that.

The truth may in fact make you feel further admiration for your husband.

She eyed him with scorn. It was too ridiculous for comment.

Our final years weren't spent discussing this. It was a movie, or dad's bitterness, or mom's lack of interest. We were there to make sure they ate, got to sleep, and had family to talk to. We rarely spent time together alone.

It's a hard aging to have to have confronted an unreasonable interaction over something unidentifiable, don't you suppose?

I can't say that's what caused Mike to create venturesome software. It really could be anything. Simple interest. I often thought it was an intellectual place to retreat to.

Did he ever say anything about it?

What does one say? It's just an activity, spending time on a computer, collecting curious tidbits.

I hoped perhaps he gave you a heads up; said he was examining city sounds or had come across an unusual database and brought it home to try it out.

No, nothing. He enjoyed combining sounds.

What sort of sounds?

Traffic, horns blaring, footsteps, ocean waves washing in; sometimes wind rustling trees.

What did he like about these sounds?

That they were real.

What was he wanting to identify?

I guess intrusive sounds.

Such as? Do you know?

She sat, as though struck dumb, racking through her memory. Was their hour up? She glanced at the clock to realize she had precious more than ten minutes.

Parking vans, half a dozen men entering at noon.

So Mike thought he had a bad problem.

We never discussed it. I guess we didn't think anything much.

What did the men do?

They went up to talk to the four administrators and left approximately two hours later.

What did the men want?

I have no idea.

We have to stop. Same time next week?

Wednesday, February 3rd

So how was your week?

Average, I can't complain. I was told a tidbit about the building.

Who from?

Randy. We are becoming much closer. It seems the PG&E sent over members of the carpenter union to handle various contracts, one being to manage city gardens, another to shovel out sewage crystal.

How interesting.

I thought so. Among these employees were five accountants who recorded meter readings and posted them to various categories.

And you think these are the people who worked at the building?

Well, that's who they were and where they were from in San Francisco. Randy thinks these people didn't realize there was something wrong with the lead manager.

I am listening for your hesitation to pass; often with you I have had the sense of anxious waiting as to an arousal of loosely formulated mishap.

I suppose it dates back to when the work crew first arrived in 1977. They came one afternoon and set up desks and began working.

And prior to that?

There was the records office and across the hall there were three hearing rooms to assess property tracts for schools, water and sanitation plants, post offices, pharmacies, clinics, apartments and plazas. One put their name and property on the docket and were called that day. The property was discussed as to intended utility, an appraiser was assigned, and proposed fee collected by the cashier.

What about hospitals and churches?

Those are already there, except private hospitals.

Were any of these criminal trials?

No, those trials were held at the Superior Court on 16th Street off Broadway.

Do you know the number of properties a year?

I'd guess it was about forty. Once tract constructed, the city then imposed a fee annually.

Not many.

I think it's a lot. The appraiser has to conduct soil and grade tests, plot lines, film, and assign type of neighboring business. Then take architect bids for blueprints and submit a design. This can take up to a month.

What should it take?

A week at max.

Did you submit exhibits on these?

No, I only typed submissions for trials.

Now that you have more information, do you have an idea what went amiss?

It might be the street pipes needed replacement more frequently than assumed. Or the city ran out of desirable land. Or too many competing businesses, or cars over the bridges.

What did the lead manager do?

He had to advertise new buildings in the paper, file with county and state, and arrange PG&E, sewage and cable services.

Was he good at his job?

As far as I know.

Who disseminated payroll?

He did. Checks came monthly to him.

Was there any rumor of stolen funds?

Not to my knowledge, but then I don't know.

She'd wondered about this when the cashier administrator left at the start of 1980.

The cashier left without notice and the cashier office shut down for two days. It's possible payroll funds were held up from the SF office. Ours weren't affected.

When you think over that incident, does anything stand out in your mind?

Well, of course, there are memories. Mike's family took out a cabin rental at Donner. I had applied for a higher post as evidence on estate cases for more pay.

It would have been five grand more a year. That was the winter the chief accused the maintenance division of failing to build enough parks mostly in Richmond Annex. But sometime later parks went in with city pools in Pinole, Orinda and Hercules.

Did Randy say who was found dead inside the building?

The entire building, the six cashiers in an office, four administrators in each of their offices, five appraisers in the lunch room, and their twelve staff in the training room.

What did the county coroner say they died of?

Broken necks.

Did he think they were murdered?

Yes, all. Same as the nun. He says it was a city records office crime.

Who got out?

Four accountants returned to their headquarters and the lead manager vanished into thin air.

So, what do you make of it?

It's hard to believe I wasn't aware of all this while it was going on.

Thank God you weren't or you might have been killed. What do you think Mike discovered?

Well, that's just it. I brought his tape transcriptions but they don't say anything recognizable.

Let's go through them.

The first says, package dropped on the roof in the deposit. Two grand in cash, twenties and fifties. Next line reads, who has the contract language? Next line reads, why are the checks spread out on two tables?

What is Mike's role in all this?

He doesn't tell me. He oversees some accounting and all items for process for services.

Is he hired?
Of course.
No, I mean, is he there legally?
He has a job as a process server to collect docu-proofs.
Where do the actual summons originate?
Court judges
But who controls these?
Headquarters, I imagine.

But you might not know. When you began, you worked typing for seven judges. You were in a different office than theirs because there wasn't sufficient desk space. How many secretaries did they have?

Each judge has a courtroom, a bailiff to answer phones and maintain security, and a legal secretary who transcribes.

Where do you come from?
County counsel, evidence and proven testimony.
So you are an addition.
Yes.
And your friend across the hall is?
Yes, there are four of us.
For any trial involving evidence?
Correct.
You work in a different setting than each judge.
Yes.
But you don't handle municipal court?
No, nothing to do with the lower courts.

So Mike must have said something, could it have been about the payroll?

I think he said it was odd the plat appraisers slept in the hall outside the stairs that led to the roof.

Did Mike say how often this occurred?
Maybe four times.
Could they have been worried about theft?

I guess that must be it. Nothing else makes sense. He remarked that Quinn the manager had begun locking his door at night.

Do you have an actual date for this?

Around January 25th 1980. He has here, Q's door locked tight. Need his stats. Went up to Mait's office, also locked. Beest asleep beneath window. Will obtain keys.

We have to end. I'll see you next week.

Wednesday, February 10th

I arranged the tapes.

We got to them late last week. Why don't you begin?

I'll read my notes. Pretty sure left keys in my desk drawer, asked Billo if he collected them. Then, two months later, found keys in Zanti's locker in men's bathroom. And, Billo said Beest found dead in courthouse chamber. Coroner van removed.

It must have been kept hush-hush.

I seem to recollect Joan making a remark. She said Beest got his just desserts; he authorized a private police station for gay men's clubs in East Oakland. Anyway Joan said her judge had just denied an increase in city tax to cover bar room security.

Who was Zanti?

Chief administrator. He had the clerk office moved to the second floor above the Records after an incident at the courthouse and had the cashier office on the first floor eliminated. Both he and Billo were found strangled in Billo's office.

Someone wanted them put out of the way.

Yes.

Those are very violent crimes.

There are four more tape comments. City Hall transfers maintenance funds to Telegraph and Sixteenth and assigns new industrial manager to oversee a new coliseum of sports. Oakland airport approved with sixty employees. Scandal, a million in waterfront beautification funds goes missing, and fifty thousand in assessment collected fees can't be found. Now around 1982 Joan says the divisions are going home to the city leaving just us the court staff, and Records. Even the assessor hearing rooms are closed. Nothing more happens until the day everyone is discovered. Eight dead in Quinn's office and six young petite redhead girls who worked Records, their wrists tied to the long pipes on the basement ceiling. It was hysteria, the coroners came out with a bunch of ambulances. The entire staff was sent home for a week.

What do you think about all this?

It is an insanity.

It makes one wonder who would do so much evil.

Yes. It is crazy. I don't know what to think. A lunatic did this.

We have to suppose this is the work of a gang. It must have involved a huge amount of money.

A million is a lot. Must be the carpenter's union is under fire.

Not if they built the coliseum and airport. Maybe the villains moved to San Jose. How often did you meet with Billo or Beest?

Never. They were the accountants who kept the budgets. I had no reason to meet with them. Our evidence exhibitions rarely contained budget charts.

Did you encounter them at lunch or in judge's

chambers?

No, I knew who they were because we received a memo.

What did you think about this number of new personnel?

They were just there. Another unit of process servers had preceded them. That's where Mike worked.

You met Mike on the job?

Yes. I required an address and signature for a contested review and Mike was the server.

Was it love at first sight?

Just about. We dated a month, and he swept me off my feet. We were the only romance to turn into a marriage in the office. It gave him a bit of status. The other gals teased him over me when he took me to lunch in those early days. He had a discreet dark tan Edson with the top down.

It's a satisfying picture you have described.

I was very contented. We bought a condo off the Alameda tunnel not far from the hospital and downtown which we spruced up; lots of candles, all types, beeswax, floating oil in glass, hanging gold encased candelabra. Then Mike's parents wanted us on Park Blvd so we moved clear across town into the tree hills. At that time Mike paid off their home, it was an all stone, one story, three bed, single bath with basement which dad and Mike walled in as a den with kitchen and bath which they still rent out today. We had a one bed condo a half mile away off Fruitvale and Sheffield in which we put several couches, two bureaus and deck furniture in the kitchen and beds in the bedroom and magazine room for guests. I am still living there.

A good marriage, very wholesome.

Excellent. Comfortable.

How many years was it?

Thirty-six. I was on the job forty. It's hard to believe it went by so quickly. I feel abandoned even though I still visit his family monthly.

Death abandons.

She was silent, holding in tears.

He sat silent also in respectful containment.

I trust you now. I'm sorry I gave you a hard time before.

Grief is a slow process.

She nodded. A tear fell.

Nothing can I do that will save you.

I just feel ineffective, helpless.

That's a healthy feeling.

I feel hopeless.

We should talk about that. What do you think contributes to feeling that emotion? Is it sorrow?

It must be. I feel I won't go on.

With what?

Being. I'm not sure. I have no desire to do anything.

He waited.

I didn't contribute to Mike's death.

I'm sure you didn't. What is your sister-in-law like as a person?

She and Mike were very close. For years it was just them.

Maybe she resents you. Feels fenced out.

She's a bitter person. She lost a son to the war. She says I put too much pressure on him to achieve.

Do you agree?

No. Mike wasn't a social climber. He liked his job, loved his dad.

Why do you suppose she verbally attacks you?

I don't know. She hasn't done well for herself. She

lost an investment property and had to move back in with her parents after thirty years. She owned a ranch in Milpitas near the airport.

That must've been costly.

She lost ninety thousand. She lost her house as a result.

How come you aren't more sympathetic to her?

Because I feel she should have known better. Property like that is expensive and she's no millionaire.

Was she intending to build on it?

She wanted a nightclub in her old age.

What about her husband?

She never married. She was in corporate sales of real estate in Fremont.

Quite modern.

No, nuts. Always dreaming. Out in left field.

Perhaps she feels you are too critical.

She had enough money at one time to purchase a second home outright.

So you are at it like two cats.

You can say what you like. I knew my limits. I think Mike attempted something very dangerous by filming these internal building security tapes. He learned things about dirty business.

It didn't kill him though. He just died. He was just doing his job.

For what I have learned, it feels unsafe in retrospect.

But you don't really know anything. This is second hand information. It could signify anything. It's altogether possible no one is murdered. It's possible your friend Randy has overstated the situation.

It seems like too much effort to pick up the pieces.

Is there someone you can turn to as a counselor?

Only Randy. I can't really talk to mom; it's like a risky

exposure. The family is very incestuous when it comes to personal feelings. Everybody knows the worst things about everyone else.

Wednesday, February 17th

I talked to Brenda this past week. I invited her over to my condo with Randy and John. I served wine and oysters for starters, onion soup with hard cracker and Italian salad with crumbled blue cheese and salami. We had a decent dialogue on real estate planning for the city.

How successful was dinner, do you think?

Alright. We talked about various debates over assessments of city gardens, whereupon Brenda said she dated Beest. She thought it was Beest who asked for a coliseum.

Odd.

That was John's response. He thought she handled the slate.

And did she?

Apparently so. Brenda said she convened the annulment of county land and redistricted it for the city of Oakland and wrote sixteen permits to include five parking zones, two impresario halls, a movie theatre, highway exit, three restaurants, A's stadium, and four malls, all with litigious demonstrations each having their own set of laws.

So Brenda must have seen the first fee assessments for land use. What does she say about your building?

The administrators conducted to budget controls.

What does she say about San Francisco?

Nothing, she didn't know about that county staffing for Oakland. She did agree the other county ran out of work for contract landscapers.

So these must have been state jobs.

That seems about right. These men worked all counties for parks and PG&E parks.

You had a bird's eye view. You saw up close what sort of gardens the various hospitals and city parks had. The fees must have included those costs, built Lake Merritt and maintained her, put in rose gardens at sanitariums for example, stretches of grass at malls, parkways, airports and schools. Your job as court steno may not have had direct play, but a street builder would have had some idea.

It just feels beyond my grasp.

What do you think Joanie would have thought?

She would have quoted her judge, Commissioner Cassavettes. Everything for the avenue. A new lawn each twenty-five years with picnic tables and a lake with walking trails for a thousand homes, can one afford it; paid by the day, it is four thousand dollars per lake for four men, built in a month.

Would she have viewed the tragedy that did happen as dirty money?

She said it takes three robbers to steal a year's worth of lateral funds in a well-perpetrated heist. She thought it was the state parks that paid well, the KOH's, the Marin and Napa counties with outdoor showers and stoves, and up to the Oregon boundary.

Did she think the landscapers for state parks killed their staff?

No, I doubt they could have. I think it's a small group, Mike said five, but I think he thought they were aides for the four chiefs. It was a real mess, wasn't it?

Based upon what you have uncovered, yes. Did she know where the hecklers resided?

I guess she assumed they owned a home somewhere.

Maybe a warehouse along the 880?

Oh I wouldn't know where. I think they may have lived in the building.

Killed off their counterparts for future jobs perhaps.

I can't figure it. Brenda was fairly certain the lakes they built dried up.

Was it difficult with her?

Well she likes to do all the talking like she's the only person who knows anything, but she didn't listen to either Randy or John, or myself for that matter, or do any give and take. But Randy liked her. He likes that she carries a conversation. He didn't feel oppressed.

So you didn't feel closer?

I learned more about her work. She did talk about the BART, they did roads only, road traffic wasn't affected at all, Richmond houses took invasive noise, but no more so than the train although the train predates houses.

What were her earnings?

She's never parted company with her annum, although I tend to think she worked on a contingency.

Where is the competitiveness?

You can't be hurting around her.

Or what?

Or she tells you about it.

Like what?

Like my only blessing was I was smart on the job, if Mike had not bought me a house I wouldn't have one, and it's impossible to talk to me because my mind drifts.

Do you think any of that's true?

Well, it's never been, you look sensational, Ellen, gorgeous hat, fancy gloves. Her parents say stuff like that. Dad likes my new T-bird, says I can drive him to the stores any day. He asks Brenda if her Chevie is still in the shop.

What do you enjoy about this repartee?

He likes me better.

He might. Brenda may have been a trying teen. She may have run them ragged.

My own parents wanted me on my own by nineteen, not to mention my siblings who died in the nick of time . Mike's just want a big hug.

Do you feel it's realistic to say his dad favors you?

They wound up raising Brenda's son when they expected to retire, so yes, I do. I've put a lot of effort into their life. I paid off their home. I drive dad to his appointments. I take them at New Years to Tahoe for two weeks, bring them household appliances, go over and cook and make the beds.

Why doesn't Brenda do this?

She goes on a cruise to Italy with Mom every two years for two weeks.

Are you with Dad when his wife leaves?

Yes. We play cards and watch TV and snack. He sneaks cigarettes.

Has Brenda ever invited you on a cruise?

I'd have to pay to get a separate cabin. I don't really want to do that.

Do you know why you are impatient with her?

I agree with Dad about her. He describes her as egotistical. He says he can't take all the bickering. It's as if she brings a dark cloud into the house.

What purpose does being judgmental serve?

Purpose?

Function.

You mean, like am I more disapproving when I am dissatisfied?

Are you?

She talks me down. It annoys me.

Let's step away from Mike's family for a moment. Let's rate the deaths in your life in terms of too painful to general acceptance. How would you evaluate the bus crash of your sibs?

Acceptance, with personal loss.

Mike?

Painful. The lights went out. They are still out.

Joan?

A major absence. I am cut adrift. Aimless.

So what do you do to ward off against these very powerful emotion states?

I talk to Randy. I'm just not all that close to him yet.

How do you express absence?

The tears are invisible.

Maybe they are barbs.

I am frozen.

Are they ice chills?

I guess I am angry.

Can you give that more description?

I thought Mike and I would live together into old age.

So you feel cheated?

Yes, I feel saddened.

Could you be let down? Life didn't turn out as you planned.

Defeated, overwhelmed.

Crushed.

It's humiliating to be around Brenda.

Do you know why?

I can't think right now. I'm drawing a blank.

We will just sit with this. Try to tell me any words that crouch in.

Nothing.

We will wait.

I feel degraded.
By her?
No, by Mike's departure. It's hard to grasp. Difficult to define, amorphous. My life has become vague like I've been set free.
Can you get out of bed mornings?
Yes, but I have no zest. It's just another bleak day.
You eat, dress formally in becoming pants and cashmere sweaters with earring clips, you have friends, regular activities you enjoy.
The longer this goes on the more depressed I feel.
How does being angry or sarcastic make you feel?
It's a spurt of feeling alive. It cancels feeling listless, lethargic, far away. I'm in control of my life.
I think this is a good place to stop.

Wednesday, February 24th

How was your week?
It went well. Randy wants to live with me.
That's fast.
Yes. I told him I need to talk it over with you.
Do you have concerns?
Some. He has a rental so it makes more sense that he lives in my condo, but I think we should buy our own place so we aren't tied to Mike's family. He wants to remain close to campus.
So you have a few decisions to make.
I am leaning in favor of marriage.
That would change your life. Do you love him?
I think I could. I enjoy his company. He likes me a lot.

You seem ambivalent.

That's what John commented after we saw the Ice Capades Saturday. He thought I was of two minds, that I could decide either way depending on a mood.

Do you feel you are along for the ride?

It's not that dismal. I don't do well in crowds.

How is sex?

It's tender.

Do you like his parents?

They accept me as I am.

Do you trust him?

I feel I am beginning to let go.

Getting over the death of an intimate can take over twenty-five years.

I'll have to chance it. I'd like to have a partner. I think I'd feel less uneasy.

What would your married name be?

Mrs. Ellem Normal.

That's Randy's last name?

Yes. It's funny, isn't it?

It is unusual. From Ellen Wilson to Ellen Normal.

Better than a name like Slaughter, Butcher or Creep.

Almost anything is better than those. Have you talked about where you want to live?

Only incidentally. We have walked through neighborhoods surrounding the campus and discussed houses we like.

Do you like the same type of house?

We seem to. Large first story, upstairs two dormered bedrooms.

Do you defer to him?

I try to talk out my sentiments, but as I told you I tend to space out. I am easily distracted. I can drift for hours.

Still?

Yes, I feel I do that here.

What do you think is going on?

I don't feel tuned in.

Could the interactions be different from what you are familiar with?

Well, of course, that is actual, but I think deep down Mike was just more responsive. There are differences, Randy and I aren't in the same profession although I relied on him for law references.

Many ways to cut a pie for simultaneity. It may be he doesn't hold you to a focus.

The hours are endless.

And you feel uprooted.

Yes.

Everyone who is widowed feels the same.

I find I can't decide which conversation to be in. Often people talk right over me.

But you are not helpless.

I don't feel present yet.

Have you ever described this to Randy?

I don't dare. I don't want to push him away. I am waiting until I feel differently.

Do you ever have a sense of urgency?

Yes, all the time. I think I should be doing more in my life; that I am procrastinating. I have lagged behind somewhere, but I don't know where I should be.

If I said it takes twenty-five to forty years to get over the death of a spouse, what would you say?

Too long, my life will be over. I'll be in my eighties.

Often there's no way to hurry the grieving process. It has a life of its own.

I can't wait that long. I'll be an old hag.

That's an emotion, not necessarily a reality.

There are situations I can't tolerate to be possessed by so much nothingness.
Did Randy know Mike?
Yes.
What did Randy think about him?
Mr. Happy Go Lucky; Mike had it all.
Does Randy have it all?
I think he has a lot. He certainly knows a lot. Would you like to meet him? I can bring him with me next week. I think he'd like to meet you.
Yes, I would like that.
Put us all on the same page.
It's a very good idea.
So although it's not quite four years since Mike passed, I'm of the opinion he would be a strong asset; it would be a good way to move on.
What do you hope this relationship can give you?
A better life. One with hope, meaning. She was thoughtful focused at some interior weeping regret. An end to the drifts.
Do you expect Randy to remove your loss?
I think just being in a new relationship should absorb me.
She is retreating, he feels her leave. It probably isn't that she has caught the sting of denial or even that a relationship may be premature, but she is tired and cannot combat that barrier of numbness that her mind won't release her from. She is far away from him, not only from herself, inside a cloud, unaware there is any turbulence to be concerned about; who knows what gives the mind such an ailment? She won't be able to recall any last thought, the reel is cast too far in the stream.
Where are we? He puts it to her.
I left.

He listens.
I can't understand why this occurs.

He descends in the elevator to the street where a whirlwind of desolation rushes maple leaves in flurries as he makes his way to the museum to arrive in time to watch a TV artist paint a wintery snowy landscape of ice laced trees hundreds of them in density in a plateau above stone slate cliff fronts rising to a plenary of drenched snow mountains and frozen lakes. He attempts to shed the skin of Ellen's nocturnal consent in favor of his perceptions and singularity but her wanderings have taken hold as though they were made of conjuring. He sees he might lose her prematurely before she can shake her lethargy, so alone on a landscape does she stand at the door to a stone church in the depths of a dark mist knelt in verdant grass. He has to have some appreciation for what is humanly possible when tangible security abandons, certainly he has suffered himself in fundamental angst in which was possible haphazard denials confine her in a transitory transmutation of illogical bereft bereavement. A marriage would postpone grief in the alchemy of restoration; just as in a great ocean the porpoise follows the slain to its descent for food, or in the chill arctic whales seem like actual small, floating isles.

Wednesday, March 3rd

Nice to meet you. Ellen has said much about you.
Thanks. I'm just crazy about her. We are like peas in a pod.
So you work in law research?

Yes, I've held this job for thirty-one years. I practically breathe it.

How old are you?

Sixty. Ellen has five years on me.

How long have you known each other?

Oh, some thirty years. I handled a percentage of her law review on appeals for reference, writ by citation, appeal circuit, and reversals.

You were made aware of the crimes at her office, I gather.

There were a number of trainings to new assessors which resulted in deaths due to over exertion.

Did you think they were murdered?

No one thought so originally. No fingerprints were found on the victims, so Alameda coroner chalked them up as accidental due to gas release.

It must have struck you as an unusual oddity.

To anyone familiar with the situation.

Do you know how it got resolved?

As a matter of fact, yes. Someone had reported the situation to the police and they investigated. They found eighteen bodies and they carted them off to the morgue. There, they discovered they had each died by having had their necks sliced in the aorta. Death must have come quickly within seconds. My guess is it's a gang at large.

Shocking, that such things occur in a government sector.

Every person I know talks about being alarmed.

What would you call the activity?

Dirty money. The tax assessor board got heisted. You don't see this going on often except in counties where services are stolen. There must be some cooperation by service.

So as you probably realize, Ellen wasn't aware

murders had occurred in the building.

Well, my boss is the one who brought her up to speed.

I heard.

So I feel it gives us a basis of commonality.

It answers a lot of questions.

Exactly. We are each learning things at the same time.

Dr. Madder couldn't help but squelch a feeling that this basis of which he referred was threatening. He said, you are under a guidance you are giving solace. The problem is grief.

Oh yes, I am well aware of what an unanticipated shock Mike's death was. It came suddenly. I'm an easy going guy, not the hard hitter Mike was.

There's probably a great deal of comfort in that for Ellen.

Ellen said, I feel I can be myself. Anything is okay. There's been no pressure to act on any idea; we are all just thinking bubs.

Well, that's what I call it, the tendency to ruminate over non-exacting material, not truly necessary to living.

Yes, yes, to over think for the control it seems to erect. To want desperately to keep the stray pieces in one place.

Research is a lot like that.

So when will you both confirm your vows?

We're intending to tie the knot in May.

Will you have a ceremony?

A small gathering of friends.

Who will you have?

My parents, Mike's family. There's no one else I'd like to wish me well.

No judge you ever worked for?

There's Commissioner Dann but I haven't stayed in touch with him since I retired. It might seem to him like a flash from the past.

Nothing wrong with that.

Well, I think it should include people I've been close to.

So, your parents, Mike's family, Randy's family and supervisor.

So that's nine if Brenda comes with her son.

Right. Just wisher-wells. You, would you like to attend?

Yes, I would, I'd be pleased.

Good, great; I can't see why we didn't tell you right off; we placed you on the list.

How much time have you spent together?

About ten weeks, four to five days at a time. Isn't that right, honey?

About that. We get along perfectly.

What do you do while Randy is at work?

Well, let's see, I meet him for lunch and then read in the library usually until he is done.

Does that work for you?

Oh, yes, I want Ellen close to me every second.

Sometimes we take a break to play tennis. After work we see a movie or go visit one of our families.

Ellen, since Joan died, your interests in writing seem to have died. Did you, Randy, know she wrote three books?

We purchased them.

I imagine you two have talked about her desire to write about work.

Oh, big time, and I encourage her all the time. My dad likes to hear all about Ellen's ideas.

She left the writing about a year ago when her work

friend passed.

I bring her books I think she'd enjoy and Ellen indexes them. In a few years she will have enough to put out another book. Lots of these are Dad's interests when he taught law at UC Berkeley School of Law.

How do you feel about this?

I just love his dad. I could talk to him for hours.

What did you think about in the past when you sat down to compose?

I relied on Joan to tell me her opinion.

What about yours?

I like to walk through what someone else thinks. It's more clarifying that way. There's no conflict.

I'm not a believer in conflict. Joan had lots of thoughtful ideas. Randy has lots of good ideas.

What will you do with Ellen's condo?

Ellen wants us to reside there, but it's on Park, not as close to Berkeley as I would prefer.

Two exits off the highway?

Two. It's alright if we can't find a place nearer the college. It just means a bit of travel for him.

It's a significant lifestyle change for both of you. Have you ever married, Randy?

I'm twice divorced. I was young.

What ages?

Eighteen and again at twenty-six.

Children?

One. She and her fourth husband raised our son in Charleston. Emmon's thirty-eight.

All grown up.

Yes, the damage is done.

What caused the marriages to break up?

I left Steph after she had an affair at four years. My second wife Bonnie and I were each thirty when the baby was two. Bonnie complained I was too tied to my mother's apron strings.

What did she mean by that?

Well, we spent every evening with my folks after the baby came. I liked my mother to know everything.

She must have wanted more independence.

Well, she and my mother didn't agree on child rearing. Bonnie put the baby in the pen or stroller; my mother was adamant a baby should be held as much of the time as possible.

So you have some experience of married life.

Enough, I think, to give it a go. We won't be jumping into the frying pan.

I wish you both a successful enjoyable marriage. It takes a good deal communication and attentiveness.

Wednesday, March 10th

He strikes me as a very empathic man.

We're doing fine. He took me to a ballet in Walnut Creek. All the ballerinas wore magnolias in their hair.

I haven't been to a ballet in years. What did you enjoy most about it?

The modern dances, very expressive and rhythmic love scenes, mirrored movements, arms entwined, passionate embraces.

Sounds riveting, very visual.

It was. There was also a dance about birds flying silver bodied on the wind. Lots of shadow, silver and pale blue in the contorted twists and bends.

How did Randy like it?

He and John talked for an hour afterward. It was

John's treat.

Just the three of you?

John brought a date, younger girl he met at the museum. She talked up quite a storm; Megan, she's studying archeology and is in her sixth year of graduate school.

Was that stressful?

A bit. She's in her forties. Thinks differently, detail-oriented, overdoes it, all elation.

Otherwise how are your plans shaping up?

Randy wants to live at my condo.

How do you feel about that?

I'm actually of a mind that is the best idea. We decided we would give it a try.

When will he move in?

He will move in next month.

Are you excited?

I'm getting there. I have to clear out a room so he can have his own study.

The glow of sunlight penetrated the winter sky like a series of orbs. He remembered he left day-old coffee on the table with a half-eaten bowl of berries mixed with granola. There were no postmarks from the mail service and that absence had caused him uncertainty, so he called them and the clerk conveyed the same answer.

Has it been four years since you lived with a person?

Since Mike was there.

Did he have a den?

No, I did. It's that Randy still works, so I wanted to be sure he has a private area.

Where will yours be?

In the bedroom. It's large with a full bed at one end and a sofa set by the fireplace and a desk in an L-shaped hall off a porch. The study is small, almost ninety square feet, it has a long desk, day bed, and three filing cabinets and a door that opens onto the same porch.

Is there a garden?

A small patio and enclosed English flower strip off the kitchen. I have a glass table with blue umbrella and four wooden chairs.

Very pretty.

I feel I've done well.

I agree. Is it paid off?

Almost; I owe about fifty. Payments are four, nothing to worry over. We will make out on his twenty-nine a year.

It is in retrospect a life made in heaven.

Yes. Mike looked out for me. Before I met him I rented a one bedroom on the lake.

Do you think it takes a man to look out for you?

It just worked out that way. My parents rent. Mike's owned. I guess it depends on how one is raised. You seem to emphasize doing it for yourself on your own. I'm not sure that is always best.

There's all sorts of ways to enjoy life.

Certainly by this age sixty-four, that's true. You don't see disappointment coming at thirty. You have no idea what to insist on.

How would you identify yourself at thirty?

Compliant, agreeable.

Is that different at sixty-four?

Well, I feel as though I have missed out.

On what?

I had the one job, few friends, I wasn't motivated to seek more.

Did you have hobbies?

Needle crafting; it's what all us girls did on breaks. I made the usual comforters, baby suits for other girls' babies.

There's nothing like no motivation.

No, I guess I would say it never occurred to me. Mike was my world.

No golf, cruises, conventions, cabins in the mountains?

No, not for any of us gals. We had husbands, two had families, or parents-in-law to contend with.

No trips to Rome?

That was in retirement. We just didn't get there. Mike had a close friend from college he got together with monthly when Jack was free from rearing five children and his wife Debi could part with him. Mike and Jack went to the bowl for drinks.

It's all over.

Went by in a whiz.

That's hard.

It feels hard. Nothing to do for it now.

Could you have predicted this, what might you have done?

I don't know.

She might honestly not. Without practical life experience, with nothing to compare to.

He climbed in his twenties to fortify himself; in the mountain's Mantra he learned self.

Steep smooth stone face with narrow foot trail into the clouds between spires of rock slab, men dressed in provocative colors, bright yellow, loud red, lake blue, pink, lilac, vibrant rust, chained to the waist, foot careful, braving the wind. A train track looming in space miles high, nothing but shadows of precipices, sharp hung over ledges; scattered lakes peered in through an infinity of mist and fog, each step calculated for visible caution, bodies bent, passive breath came slow; behind the summit yet more mountain tables arose, a fortress of avalanche perpendicular stone, no one pessimistic, time passed gradually.

Did you ever dream of traveling?

Once. I joined a rock collection club, and I thought it could be fun to spend a month in China studying jades.

What prevented you?

Mike's mother got ill.

Illnesses are often interpreted as signs. Maybe it was a beneficial omen.

Speaking from an afterlife?

It kept you at home.

Yes, it did.

He was silent thinking as he often did that she spoke from behind a mask.

I feel I should talk about my siblings.

Why now?

Randy feels it would be good for me.

I think we should wait; the hour is nearly up.

That's fine.

I think we should first explore this sense that life has escaped from you. My intuition says we should spend some time looking at why you check out. Are you bored; angry; aware of having a feeling; thinking about a chore you have to do.

I remembered Randy asked me to talk about their deaths.

The bus crash?

Yes, and my reaction.

What was it?

I cried for days.

That's unusual for you.

It was normal then. I had reactions.

Maybe you suppressed Mike's death.

No, I cried for weeks. I got numb.

About?

I guess Joan was too much.

Does that make sense? Joan was your friend, not your spouse.

I got numb after I realized I was on my own.

Didn't Mike leave you well provided for?

Wednesday, March 17th

You coiffed your hair.

Yes, Randy's idea for a bob. Do you like it?

Very attractive. Color is becoming.

Thanks. It is called a shine. The silver blonde's supposed to make one look younger.

It's very nice.

Thanks.

So where are we?

Randy moved in, I gave him Mike's shower and closet.

I can feel the reminisce as you speak.

I can too. It catches me up. I didn't expect it to.

Do you think Mike will pop out at you?

I hope not – in any sense. I gave Randy his own room because he stays up so late. He puts on coffee before he goes to sleep; I'm on a fourth cup by the time he awakens. We stayed in all weekend due to the rainstorm; drank coffee and read books. Once he went out for a newspaper, but other than that we put books away in the basement on the shelves near the stairs off the den.

Do you feel at all displaced?

No, I'm okay with all this.

Good. How are his in-laws?

Very inclusive. It's Mike's I worry about. They are getting old, and I can't leave them. They seem to like Randy, but he's not their son.

It'll be a lot to juggle three families.

Yes, I thought we might try bridge night once a month.

That's a nice idea.

Randy had a friend over for dinner on Sunday. Dale works for the Maritime Museum in the city as a landscaper for city gardens.

How did that go?

Well, apparently he knew some of the crew who worked for the Hyde Street pier who transferred to the Oakland office of garden maintenance in the late seventies.

What was his opinion as to what transpired?

He thinks the killers arrived by van in the middle of the night. He thought maybe they were young offenders who picked up the mail and took it to the post office weekly for a service fee.

Do you think that's likely?

I never came across them. I think it was the US Mail that picked up every afternoon. I doubt we would have entrusted our mail to teenagers.

I'd be surprised also.

Dale thought the Maritime sent the staff to Oakland as building and construction for new stores. He thought they assigned security. He also said his office received confirmation of a police report that read two dead bodies were retrieved from an office. There were other similar reports sent in over the duration of three years. Apparently fingerprints matched for thefts of coin-operated meters in San Francisco. Many dead had long rap sheets.

So some of these people came up for illegal transaction codes.

Apparently; under jobs listed for actuarial reports, market planning and transaction service. Nothing was ever called that in my day.

Or in mine. Maybe they found places to hide in these buildings and they were caught eventually.

Ridiculous.

Well, you never saw them.

But who would have besides the security?

Who worked basement?

Garden maintenance and actuarial. They had desks in the training room before the lounge was built.

So the police carted off the dead staff.

That's what he said. Shozciatz building was the original building. Dale said a fire destroyed the entire place in 1992.

Were you aware that happened?

I don't read the news so I didn't realize it was no longer there.

The building is gone?

It's been replaced by an all glass convention center for lectures and ballet.

Sort of puts history in an entirely different cast.

I asked myself, why would some group want to burn a garden contract building in the year of the Oakland arson?

It causes one to wonder.

Maybe they put in illegal gardens all over the arson area.

There were a lot of parks there. Near the wedding center and tennis courts, across the street, in upper Piedmont, near the old Lake Temescal, at the Claremont Hotel.

None of those lawns burned.

It raises questions, your building.

Yes, like a war got fought there for each and every generation of building.

I wonder what the issue has been.

Must be some tug of war over property. I can't imagine what else.

What government jurisdiction owns the arson area?

As far as I know, it's still the property of the water district. It's not technically Oakland or Alameda County.

I'm asking myself why the maritime assigned most staff. That would seem to make the men astronauts having two hundred combined hours of sky diving, advanced underwater, and mission shuttle physical training. Were they trained for ocean car crashes?

I wasn't aware the maritime trained astronauts. Would this be for Apollo, Challenger and Endeavor missions into space?

Yes, it is done I think to have photos as to where a crash might be occurring; at what height, speed of landfall, is it in an airplane, over a cliff in a car or truck, in an earthquake?

What would have brought them to Oakland?

Possibly plans to build another airport. Maybe they had to design it.

That makes lots of sense.

So then that could explain the number of electricians for burial ground cables for very large airport buildings, laying roads, establishing incandescence, mechanical engineers for runway flight and solid waste turf and guard tower.

I'm surprised we had so many kinds of crew working our building. What brought them there?

Maybe the 1975 major highway crisis determined

the necessity for another airport. After all, that bomb shut down access to fifteen highways.

It's a much bigger issue that eighteen men died in the building.

Yes, indeed, a frightening proposition. Does Randy have thoughts on this?

If he does, he's never said.

So, let's take a few minutes to discuss you. Where are you in terms of life?

I feel I could be getting back on track. I don't have as many fade-outs.

Good, good. Did you still want to discuss Randy's list?

No, I don't feel I need to please Randy. He was just concerned for me. My sibs died in a crash; that was years ago. My husband passed, nothing much to be said for it; I just feel cheated by his death. My best friend – I suppose this has been more about me, how will I pick up the pieces.

Yes, that is realistic. Who have you become in the past year?

Well, it's not always easy to know how one is changing. Sometimes you can't view yourself clearly.

Often one can't grasp onto significant personal change. Kubla-Ross talks about grief over the sudden death of a loved one and poses the issue of having faced a life interruption with what was left for the relationship that you both might have wanted to try that has been stymied.

I would have to think about that, but off the top of my head I'm less bummed about my life. I feel I can go on. I'm hanging onto more of what I think. I'm just not sure it will keep.

That uncertainty is normal. We aren't adequately

trained for what to do with ourselves in retirement. Life seems endless. There is nothing to do. Getting to a special project is over more quickly than expected. Sometimes living is unpredictable. A disaster sets us back, and we are unprepared for how to respond.

When my clients reach this point of the self-revelation of uncertainty, it indicates the core issue has begun to tussle its way out of the subconscious. We should take awhile to see how you are handling the resolution and what modifications might prove helpful.

Wednesday, March 24th

I asked Randy's friend Dale about missions flown by any of the staff. He said one chief administrator flew Moon landing to the farthest eastern island. He trained at Pendleton for sky diving and sub surface recovery.

What happened to this man?

He was hung by rope and band in his office located at the top in the colloquium.

Any other trained deck crew?

Besides four fully trained fire fighters, there were six men, all with rope measure training, each over the age of forty-eight years old, with calling expertise at, let me look up my notes, oh here we are; rotation in lunar capsule at fourteen days in space; shock mill for penetration to hull of flying plane in icy atmosphere; windfall at speed of falling body, and cool air recognition, enough expertise to build an airport for any eventuality.

Don't you find these circumstances rather bizarre?

Yes, yes, I do. I wouldn't be able to explain it. Who could have wanted so much death?

Well, just for the record I verified against the labs. They died having black bile. The central administration of the hospital took the bodies to a hospital and made a finding of bio fax varicular, an unknown disease.

You did that for me?

Yes, I believed it was important. The only known evidence was a splat of blood on the ceiling which when scraped killed the technician in the same way. It was neither a virus nor a bacteria.

I wouldn't be able to account for any of it. It seems to me maybe fatigue of some sort brought on by too many plots constructed too quickly. What did they do, did you learn?

They filed for land annexation, plotted, built improvements in the ground, water, waste, electric, approved windows and egress, roof adjournments, doors, and assured no duplication. Physicians listed accommodations.

Maybe they built too fast. It could have been overwork.

I think Oakland and Richmond were thought good growth cities for twelve hundred stores, public parks and road access.

I just can't take it in; you know, digest it.

Yes, it's a good deal of information.

You'd think there was someone who knew.

Maybe there were. It's not on public record.

It leaves one so uncertain.

It is hard not to know.

Yes.

The fact of death plummeted into her. She couldn't think.

So much death.

They sat in silence through what seemed an endless waiting, over a half hour as if thought was dormant.

Any ideas?

None. Can we stop early?
We can. Is something the matter?
I am too tired to stay awake. I need to sleep.

Wednesday, March 31st

What happened last week?
I collapsed.
Did you sleep?
Two days straight.
What did you think about when you awoke?
All the construction of that era.
Which in particular?
The refinery in Richmond.
Which car did you drive?
Pontiac.
What company owns it?
General Motors Electric.
What do they own in the car?
Great Lakes lumber for the frame, the Timex clock, Rockefeller speedometer, GMC radio, Ashby window glass, Detroit Co. automatic transmission, roughly fifteen Michigan carpet companies; and Aladdin heat and air which produced Alameda station island's first lumber for the car.

So there you have the significance of life.

What do you think goes wrong?

The tail pipe catches on fire? Of course that would be the problem right there.

Do you think those engineers came across the problem?

One doesn't know. Did you ever see a court case?

Yes, for Fomher Engineering in 1988; he controlled the emission. He is God.

Alright, so where are we?

Well, I guess it helps to know. I'd like to have my life back.

No way to do that.

But did these situations take Mike's life?

We're back to the same idea.

He took photos of the building.

You brought a description in, none of it fatal as far as I can see. Any of dead bodies?

No, not in those.

So how does all this look to you now that you know some of what transpired?

Frightening. Who knew?

I don't know.

Someone must have known.

Why? Would that make you feel better? Your building was the Office of Deeds, not just of inventions and city landscaping. Perhaps after that fire that took houses in Piedmont, someone wanted there to be no record of any property.

That makes some sense.

Might be a market for foreign interests, a quick insurance glut which created a fairly instantaneous increase in housing.

Where would they have come from? Industry? Lumber? The university?

Well, let's see. Oakland became a ghost town after Kaiser Aluminum shut down. For over forty years Oakland was a vacated ghost town. Those miners were sent to Appalachia to mine coal and no one was left. Or prisoners of world prisons decided to destroy the city where their guards resided. I think it was a response to imprisonment.

You do?
Yes. Bums who wanted to study to be nurses.
It's an awful lot of plunder.
I agree. A real imposition on life.
So where am I with all this?
Yes.
I don't know where I can meet a new friend. It can't be Brenda, Mike's sister. She fights me every step of the way.
What about one of the other girls in your typing group?

Wednesday, April 7th

I took your suggestion. I called Shana and we went out for girl's night Monday evening for a movie and dinner.
Did you enjoy yourself?
It was comfortable, we talked about our reports, the security who knocked on the door after five when we stayed late, the mail we received for other departments that we took down the hall to the tax commissioner's desk; our lives.
What has Shana been doing in the last four years?
She went to work as a secretary for the new courthouse since her building burned to the ground in 1989. I have my life – gardening, preparing meals, talking to Randy after work; she has her life – running the lake with her husband of 45 years, driving to Goleta to visit her daughter at UCSC; and volunteering for meals to seniors. She's as busy as she was when she oversaw the court calendar as lead steno and assigned.
That's a healthy act.

Yes, I feel good about having contacted her.

So where are you in life?

I'm alright.

Just alright?

Well, I've remembered things I had forgotten.

I didn't mean that. I meant, how do you see yourself?

One or two words come to mind, but I have to imagine the rest.

What do you suppose that is about?

That I don't have much energy to give.

Are you cognizant of what that is about?

I am very tired.

How could you expound on the realization?

I feel cut short of oxygen. My life with Mike restored me. We had a harmony which I don't have even with Randy.

You haven't known Randy long. Intimacy takes time.

I realize that. I just thought I'd have made a better adjustment by now instead of feeling I am floating about in space.

Recuperation from being widowed often takes thirty or more years. We could spend some time talking about your life with Mike.

I can't see what good that would do. It won't bring him back.

Nothing does that, but we can hone in on what gave you enjoyment and a sense of containment in that marriage.

I used to have to rummage through the evidence warehouse on the third floor for complaints over inadequate sufficiency. From time to time, a trial was conducted as to building code. Mike knew at a glance what was on a blueprint and easily predicted loss. He had that sixth sense about him. I suppose he developed it in traveling Europe's high places; I lived through his look at life.

In what ways do you differ from Randy?

Well, I write from time to time. Of course he sees to journal articles.

Anything else? Activity of any kind?

I like to remodel. I like to create open living spaces. I think it would be nice to create a more open kitchen.

What would that consist of?

Knocking down a wall. Mike's dad is willing to do a trade. I offered to move their patio across the yard closer to the back deck.

That sounds like a lot of work.

I think I could do it in a weekend.

I'm impressed.

Yes, it's hard work but no less than removing a wall.

That really is a man's work.

It might be. I expend a lot of thinking that way. It does separate me from the men.

So in all, this could be a good way to set you back on your feet.

Yes.

So what does that say to you?

Well, this transition has been a difficult and trying period. It wouldn't have occurred to me just to talk about it that I could escape the doldrums with physical activity.

It's time. I'd like you to consider we are almost to the end of a journey. When you first came to see me you felt lost, forsaken. You have adapted to another lifestyle which seems to be progressing well. Perhaps we can discuss that next session.

I could do that.

Good.

Then I'll see you.

Wednesday, April 14th

Did you give any thought to my suggestion of ending?
Yes. It feels rather sudden. I'm not sure I am ready.
I think you are. You have come a good distance, resolved your essential complaint.
I'm just not sure I know why I entered this quandary.
You don't want to cancel your gains.
I suppose it's my nature.
Your nature is to be ambivalent. Maybe it was the job. More likely it's the way you have defended your choices. A self message that says, If it doesn't turn out alright, I wasn't sure anyhow. It's possibly how you have dealt with the number of tragedies.
I like to have options.
Most people do. Self doubt at the start of a major transition is normal.
Is losing track of what you think?
Is it also normal? It can be the way the mind handles unbearable stress.
And all that confusion? I still have to fight against it.
Confusion as you call it is what I call nebulous detachment combined with withdrawal. It can become severe. Disassociation to the environment is a call for help. You'd want to ask, Would this be due to Joan's death? She was your coping mechanism for losing Mike.
I guess I would say life got too difficult.
Exactly; your aids stopped being affective.
I wanted to crawl into a hole.
And did. You are no different than any other person facing midlife crisis. The crisis is passing. Your mind has returned in the establishing of a new support system. Randy is a caring man. Your instincts did not let you

down. Mike's family is still there for you. You do have your own identity. You might not feel giddy in love, but it is a close friendship. He knows you.

There have been so many changes.

Lots of people resist change. There's no real way to hang onto your life of the past in the face of a death. You can of course find other people to share your life with. So how is the new patio?

Good. I spent all Saturday putting down sand and dirt and laying flat large slate pavers, and putting in grass and a small vegetable garden of onions, potatoes, cucumbers and eggplants along the fence. On Sunday dad came and knocked out the wall between the kitchen and dining room. He put in a nice trim. We ordered a new marble counter and back splash.

You must feel you accomplished a lot.

Completely. Dad and I are very close.

I can see that. I think the real trick here comes down to what you can do to see yourself more clearly when you need to give yourself feedback.

I've kept a journal for three years. It's how I remember Joanie. Are you mad at me for having left session last week?

No, is that how it feels?

Suddenly I was overwhelmed. I couldn't take it all in. Those eighteen accountant deaths. Why would anyone want something so heinous? What would they have been working on besides a state audit? So, yes, I feel you are punishing me by asking me to stop coming.

No, my sense of you is that eight sessions would have done it.

Really?

Yes. At that point you had turned the corner. You demonstrated self insight in the sixth session. You defined boredom as a psychological release from uncertainty of the future.

We had Shauna and her husband over for dinner. We uncorked a few bottles of Champagne Brut on the patio; it was a breezy, pleasant evening. Hubby Margo talked about his work tracking steeps to combine rolls which see into halls, there were as many as seven bare trauma locked in a room off the garden entrance.

What just happened here? You changed the subject.

I thought you were done.

No. I was looking back at your therapy work.

When will we stop?

Next week will be closure.

I feel I should have that say.

I think it's possible you never reach this point.

You think that I try to hang onto situations despite obvious outcomes?

I think it's helpful if we will look at the course the presenting problem has taken.

Well, I came to you because I was experiencing difficulties. I couldn't stay focused in conversations. I didn't know what to do with my life. I felt I lost interest in having friends.

You went through a process of identifying feeling states.

It went by fast.

We examined who you were as a person in your marriage.

Yes.

We gave time to the significance of fear in your life. We have also looked at your indecision, your readiness to accommodate a new start, your tolerance to inevitability. You don't really lack flexibility or new ideas. We discussed how well you know yourself. Other things

– despite a demanding on-the-job schedule, you kept up with the deadlines. You have enjoyed achievements in your books. You are cautious, you weigh a decision long before you make it. You have longtime friends; that rules out serious depression.

Yes, I can see all that.

So what is left?

I don't know.

So by next week you will have had time to process this.

Alright.

Alright.

CPSIA information can be obtained
at www.ICGtesting.com
Printed in the USA
FSHW021925270820
73248FS